Matilda of Flanders

=   Edith of Scotland   Stephen = Adela
of Blois

STEPHEN d. 1154   Henry of Blois
Bishop of Winchester

Eustace   William
d. 1153   d. 1159

Matilda = (2) Geoffrey of Anjou
the Empress   (Plantagenet) d. 1151

e = (2) HENRY II   Geoffrey d. 1158

Geoffrey (Hikenai's son)

ung Henry   Matilda   RICHARD I   Geoffrey

H ERE IS a novel that splendidly evokes life in England in the mid-twelfth century, an England only just emerging from the grip of the old pagan gods. It tells of the love of the first Plantagenet, Henry II, for his Saxon mistress—half witch, half wanton—the love that alienated Henry's proud queen, Eleanor of Aquitaine, and sowed the seeds of his tragic conflict with his brilliant chancellor and archbishop, Thomas Becket.

As the novel opens, the anarchy of King Stephen's reign is over; the gifted young monarch has restored a measure of order. But throughout Henry's realm, deep in the forests in the sacred oak groves, the ancient pagan rituals, though outlawed, are still celebrated— the horned god still demands his sacrificial due.

Dominating this sweeping novel is King Henry himself. A man of colossal energy, and overriding ambition, capable of terrifying rages, Henry is surprised into tenderness by his passion for his lovely pagan mistress, Hikenai. Hikenai is a "faery woman," dedicated early by her mother to the Old Gods, the powerful and savage deities dear to the Saxons long before the Normans and their civilizing clerics arrived. It is their affair and its impact on Henry's tangled relationships with Eleanor and Thomas that lie at the heart of THE LION OF ENGLAND, brilliantly reinvigorating this famous triangle. Becket is given new dimension—an outward piety masking not just love of display and the iron will that would ultimately bring him into confrontation with his king, but also a driving bloodlust that stood surrogate for a natural desire for women. And Eleanor, more than the

(Continued on back flap)

7308

THE
LION
OF
ENGLAND

Where be they that biforen us weren,
Houndes ladden and havekes beren,
And hadden feld and wode?

       Anon.

THE LION OF ENGLAND

Margaret Butler

Coward, McCann & Geoghegan

New York

F
Bu

For Tina, who died too soon

First American Edition 1973

Copyright © 1973 by Margaret Butler

SBN : 698-10555-9
Library of Congress Catalog Card Number : 73-78741

Printed in the United States of America

25557

Author's Note

Nearly all of the characters in this book are historical figures. With King Henry II and Thomas Becket we are on firm ground for the lives of royalty and the hierarchy are well documented, and the action is as authentic as my knowledge would allow. The conversations between them are, however, imaginary and I have put my own interpretation on their personalities, as indeed on that of Eleanor of Aquitaine. At one time a great deal of scandal attached itself to that glamorous lady's name; then the pendulum swung the other way and she was considered to be more sinned against than sinning. Since we shall never know the truth I hope that this portrayal of her character and motives is as valid as any.

When we come to the lesser folk who revolved about the Court, the footing becomes more uncertain. They are all historical personages with the exceptions of Cicely Fitzurse and Dame Hermengild but I have woven a wholly fictitious tale about a few circumstantial facts.

It is generally accepted that Hikenai was the mother of Henry II's illegitimate son Geoffrey. Nothing is known of her beyond that but it seemed to me reasonable to suppose that the King had some feeling for her as her child was the only one of his bastards brought up among the royal children. She is referred to in one record as 'an English whore who scorned no filthiness', but I have got around this by attributing it to the gossip of the Court. Geoffrey did have a brother named Peter who was not Henry's son. He became a cleric, and eventually an Archdeacon.

I have tampered with history in placing Geoffrey's birth in 1156 – in fact, he was born in 1153 before Henry came to the throne. All of the other times and places are accurate to the best of my knowledge.

I think that the references to the old pagan religion of Europe (which was the source from which both witches and fairies derived; they were interchangeable in the mediaeval mind) are somewhere near the true facts but most of our knowledge of it is little more than legend. It certainly died hard and a good deal of it was assimilated into the Christian festivals.

I must thank Mr Ralph Arnold for the tale of Lithulf and Hugh de Morville's mother; she did warn her husband in the English tongue, her actual words being 'Huge de Morvile, ware, ware, ware, Lithulf heth his swerd adrage.'

My thanks are also due to the Chief Librarian of Bridgwater, Somerset, without whose local knowledge I should never have unearthed the paper by Sir Henry C. Maxwell Lyte on the ramifications of the Fitzurse family; and to the staff of Enfield Central Public Library whose help in procuring reference books from other libraries was invaluable.

Finally I must pay tribute to the authors of the works of history listed in the bibliography whose brains I have shamelessly picked. They did all the real work. Needless to say, this list comprises only a small proportion of the works of reference to which I am indebted.

Margaret Butler

I

September 1152

ON A GOLDEN DAY in early September, a company of
horsemen was following the course of the Loir through the
gently rolling country that lies between Le Mans and
Orleans. They travelled at a comfortable pace, unarmed
and without hauberks, for a truce had been declared with
France, and Geoffrey the Fair, Count of Anjou, and his son,
Henry FitzEmpress, along with their escort, were riding
home from Paris.

Father and son were quite unlike. Geoffrey's patrician
good looks were renowned far beyond the borders of Anjou
and his handsome face was matched by his popularity. He
wore his curling coppery hair rather longer than was fashion-
able and had it washed and combed so frequently that he
was rarely infested with lice. Some men said that most of his
success with women was due to this but others, more experienced if equally lousy, pointed to their own conquests in
refutation. Most thought it harmless vanity. But in an age
when cleanliness came a very long way behind godliness,
Geoffrey was unusual. Only yesterday he had immersed
himself in the river in order to wash off the dust of travel.

His son, Henry, had not inherited the fabled beauty of the
House of Anjou although he was not, in any sense, an ill-
looking lad. He had not his father's height, either, being but

middle statured; still, he might add two more inches before his growth was done. But he would never have the Count's noble bearing, his gait was too hurried and jerky, his whole appearance too untidy. Henry had no time to spare for niceties of dress or manner.

He rode a pace or two behind his father as they passed under a clump of heavy, rusty lime trees that hung motionless in the noonday heat except when a handful of dry, yellow leaves fluttered down with the breath of their passing. There had been drought all summer; the earth lay dry and cracked and the little grass left was burnt and brown but on the horizon hazy heaps of cumulus were piled, creeping up into a sky of pale and dazzling blue. Only the amber of the sunshine hinted at the approach of autumn and the chance of cooler weather.

Henry was happy. A small part of his good cheer was due to being with his father whom he admired and hoped to emulate, but most of it stemmed from the memory of the dark eyes of Queen Eleanor of France. She was not the first lady of high birth to look kindly on him, by any means, but she was the first who had not made him shy away like a nervous horse, for in truth, Henry at eighteen felt more at ease with low born doxies where his own natural coarseness passed unnoticed. She had smiled upon him while her husband had risen from his sickbed to accept Henry's homage for Normandy, and the memory titillated him so that he jogged in the saddle and whistled between his teeth. He savoured once again the look on Louis's face when he had taken Henry's clasped hands in his own. He had looked like a man who had drunk verjuice.

It was Count Geoffrey, though, who had won back the dukedom of Normandy for his son, and Henry shot a warm glance at his father. He, for his part, appeared pensive and rather gloomy; his thoughts, too, were upon Queen Eleanor but he was worried and his conscience was pricking him belatedly. He had noted with disquiet how she and Henry had laid their heads together and laughed and whispered on more than one occasion, and now he chewed the inside of his cheek considering how best to warn his son against her.

Suddenly a hand touched his arm. 'What think you of the Queen of France?' asked Henry.

Geoffrey was startled; his tone was sharper than he intended. 'She is a light woman. You would do well to tread warily.'

Henry looked surprised. 'You are hard on her,' he said at length, 'her life is not an easy one with our dear brother of France.'

'Did she tell you so?' said Geoffrey, his face unreadable.

'She told me a thing in confidence. She and Louis are agreed on an annulment of their marriage if such can be obtained. Did you know they are related within the forbidden degrees?'

'So is every other royal couple. And I know they had a dispensation from the Pope.'

Henry frowned. His news was not being received in the way he had hoped. He tried again.

'Why do you suppose she told this tale to me alone?'

'I think she is already setting her snares to catch another husband,' said his father harshly. 'Do not be caught by her, my son. She is too old for you; she must have all of thirty years.'

'She does not look so old. And whoever takes her, takes Aquitaine, her duchy.'

Geoffrey smiled grimly. He should have guessed Henry's mind was more on the lands than the lady. The unpalatable fact remained that the long ago moment of madness between this Queen of France and himself had forged a link of a kind between them – and the Church stated without equivocation that it was incestuous for a man to lie with a woman his father had known carnally. Evidently Henry had never heard a whisper of that old tale; apart from the obstinate set of his lips, his face was untroubled, and as

3

Geoffrey cast about in his mind for some means to acquaint him with the position, he thought it a shame that a man might not take his pleasure where he would without endangering his son's soul should his eyes stray in the same direction.

By now they had reached the river bank and Geoffrey shouted to his men to rein in and rest awhile for by the water was sweet grass for the horses. So they dismounted and a couple of the young squires put off their shoes and rolled up the loose legs of their braies to dabble their feet in the river, but Henry and his father sat a little apart and took turns with a leather bottle of rather sour wine and ate some of the food from their pouches. It was quiet and peaceful; over the water myriads of ephemerals danced in the shimmering air and all around them shrill pipings and small rustlings mingled with the soft champing of the horses.

'Do you think, then, that I should not marry her if I get the chance?' said Henry through a mouthful of cheese. 'With her duchy of Aquitaine and mine of Normandy, we should be more powerful by far than Louis.'

'A virtuous wife is to be prized above rubies,' returned his father, 'and she is no pliant female. Faith, it is no pleasure for a man to be ruled by a woman – or to be fast wed to one who tries to.'

Henry grinned behind his hand. All knew that the Count had once banished his wife, Matilda the Empress, from Anjou for two full years because of her high-handed ways, and she had enjoyed a decade's superiority over her unwilling husband. But what he did, I can do; I shall master Eleanor as he mastered my mother. My mother was an Empress through her first marriage; Eleanor is not so high, nor do I think she is so proud. Best of all, she desires me and a man may do much with a woman who loves him. So he said no more but finished his meal with a raw onion, eating it like an apple, and then went down to the river to splash water on his face, for the midday sun had brought up a red flush of sunburn on his nose.

4

When he came back Count Geoffrey had fallen heavily asleep; so the young Duke went down again and joined the younger men. He was popular with them although they walked warily in his presence for they had all seen his sudden terrible rages – those famous rages to which all of the House of Anjou were subject, an inheritance from that faery ancestress who had vanished one day in a puff of smoke during the Elevation at Mass, but not before she had borne several children who possessed both the beauty and the temperament of Lucifer himself.

'My father will sleep awhile,' he greeted them, and they fell to discussing the merits of their hawks, for since Henry had acquired a great gerfalcon from Norway, he had thought of little else. Even this palled after a time, however, and Henry began to cast impatient looks over his shoulder. At length he went up the bank again and stood beside his father.

Count Geoffrey's face was very red and he made a soft, grunting sound with every breath. Henry frowned and stirred him with his toe, and the Count groaned and stretched himself. He sat up and looked about him.

'Have I slept so long?' His voice was slurred and he put his hand to his forehead. 'By the Cross, my head hurts – I'm all fordone with sleeping in the sun. Come, let's to horse.' But he staggered as he arose and had to lean upon his squire.

'We'll to the Abbey hard by Château-du-Loir,' he said. 'It's a new foundation and I know it not but we'll lie there till I find myself again.'

By the time they reached the Abbey, which even from a distance looked small and poor, it was clear that Count Geoffrey had a raging fever, and Henry hammered on the gate with a violence that brooked no delay. It was a Cistercian house and still being built – there were heaps of ashlar in the Great Court – but the church was completed with the cloisters along its southern wall and the long frater

5

opposite. Henry cursed under his breath when he realised that the Infirmary stood half finished and that the sick man was being carried to a hut which seemed little better than a stable. He shouted at the monks just as the Abbot came hurrying out, then overheard someone mutter 'Plague!' and turned furiously on him instead. Through the raised voices the Abbot calmly bade him come within and sup while the Infirmarian applied his remedies.

He was a big man, grossly fat and unhealthy-looking. 'Great bladder of lard!' thought Henry whose ire was still seeking an objective, 'these White Monks are no better than the Benedictines'; but he did the Abbot an injustice for it was a sickness in him that caused hands and face to swell and gave him a piggy-eyed look.

By the time Henry had finished his meal his good humour had returned and he recounted in detail to the Abbot all the skirmishes and minor battles they had fought to regain Normandy. The Abbot listened without much comment; at the back of his mind thinking that he must drink no more today but further urge Brother Gregory the Infirmarian to find a physic that would dry up his excessive humours. Henry was speaking with pride of his father, and the Abbot was troubled with a sudden sense of shame to be thinking thus of himself and said a hasty prayer for the sick man – '*quod fideliter petimus, efficaciter consequamur*,' he muttered, lowering his eyes.

'—that I do not wax so fat;' Henry's voice cut suddenly across his musings. 'God keep it from me! I would I never drag around so gross a body.'

'God forfend,' agreed the Abbot in as even a voice as he was able to command. He forced himself to smile, and as the bell began to ring for Vespers, said, 'We have time to see the Count before sunset. Is that your desire?'

'Aye.' Henry sprang up. 'And see they keep the cauterising irons from my father.'

So they went down and crossed the courtyard towards the

6

makeshift Infirmary which was silhouetted black against a gently glowing sky of gold. When they passed within Henry was dazzled by the flood of molten light which poured through the shutterless window; blinded by after-images, he almost tripped over the pallet where the Count lay. When his sight came back he felt his first pang of real fear; he was still young enough to feel it inconceivable that his father should die but reality was before him in Count Geoffrey's dusky, crimson face and low, delirious mutterings. He knelt beside him, anger replacing panic, and said fiercely, 'What have you done? He is worse. Bring water, at least, and a cloth.'

Brother Gregory was a small man and mouselike in his swift, scuttling motion; he looked frightened because he thought that nothing would save the Count, and whatever was wrong with him might be contagious. Even if it were not, the Count's death would cast doubt on his skill.

When the water came Henry dipped the cloth in it and gently sponged his father's forehead. The Abbot knelt heavily on the other side of the pallet, wincing at the pain in his legs, his hands folded. '*Miserere Domine*,' he murmured, but Henry glared him into silence. He turned his ear towards the Infirmarian, who was whispering eagerly to him: 'The Count confessed himself when he was first brought hither. He said, "Tell my son the lady is forbidden under Canon Law".'

Henry raised his head and stared at him. He said harshly, 'To whom did he say that?'

'To me, lord. Just after he had made Confession.'

Henry's eyes glinted. 'Under the Seal?'

'Nay, lord.' The Infirmarian was a man of courage despite appearances. 'Nay, indeed. The stole was off—' The Abbot gave him a warning look and he fell silent.

'Christ's Passion!' Henry ground out, his expression furious. He went back to wiping the Count's face, automatically, wondering what the message, so impertinently delivered, could have meant. Then he remembered that he and Eleanor, too, were related, being both descended from Duke Robert of Normandy, and he felt a faint surprise that his father should have been troubled by so trifling a matter. All the same, he was annoyed that he had mentioned it to this interfering monk and he resolved to take the Count away to Château-du-Loir as soon as he could be moved. He would send a party ahead when the bell sounded for Prime.

Henry sat up the better part of the night watching his father. At least, he seemed no worse next morning, and when the messengers returned from the Château with a litter and an escort, Henry bade the Abbot a curt farewell and had his father carried there.

It was scarcely an hour's journey on horseback but it took them nearly the whole forenoon to get there with the litter, and they arrived to find that the only physician presently in the area was the one they had just left. Henry was beside himself with vexation. He blamed the messengers for not ascertaining that fact before they came back, he blamed Count Geoffrey for being so foolish as to bathe himself in the river and, worse of all, he blamed himself for allowing his pettish irritation with the monks to cloud his judgment.

All through the afternoon, Geoffrey's breathing grew worse. Henry knelt beside him and prayed more and more frantically as his father's struggles for air became progressively weaker. When it was obvious that God would not hear his pleas Henry made a sign to the seneschal, and the knights came in and knelt at the head of the dying man and the squire and pages at his feet; they all prayed, but two hours later, with a great rattling in the throat, Geoffrey the Fair of Anjou died.

They crossed his arms upon his breast and put the pommel of his sword between his hands, and over him they laid his banner with the three golden lions of Anjou upon it.

Henry wept bitterly. He must ride to Rouen and tell his mother, and well he knew he would grieve alone.

And alone he must try to win back England, that fat little island across a narrow strip of sea – England, that was his mother's birthright and therefore his. He had fought for it before in his boyhood and been driven ignominiously away by King Stephen, but it would be different next time with the strength of Normandy, Maine and Anjou behind him – aye, and the strength of Aquitaine, too. Kneeling by his father's deathbed, Henry made up his mind to marry Eleanor, Queen of France, if God and the Pope allowed.

May 1152
Henry and Eleanor were married quietly at Poitiers the following May Day, since God had guided the Archbishop of Rheims to decide in council that the marriage of the King and Queen of France was invalid. No one mentioned the Pope's unfortunate dispensation; it was plain enough to all that God had withheld His blessing from the union, for Eleanor had borne no son in fifteen years of matrimony.

When they were fast wed, he had turned his head and looked at her. Her face was on a level with his own but demurely lowered; still, he could see her well enough, her jaw a little overshot and her front teeth a mite prominent so that her lips were always slightly parted above the round, full chin. He could not look at her mouth without desiring her, and instinctively clasped her hand more tightly; her long, hazel eyes slid sideways and met his.

He thought then that he should have had her if she had been a kitchen wench; it would have been simpler so without all this fuss in the Cathedral, and he sensed that her desire ran as strong as his own. Their palms sweated together as the bells clashed overhead and the people huzzaed by the doors, but in the depths of his mind lurked the idea that it was no wife's part to have such feelings.

9

Eleanor herself knew that women may have desires as strong and as swiftly passing as may men. Through her veins ran the warm blood of the passionate South where the Courts of Love had developed with the new idea of Woman as a perfect creature, akin to a goddess, to be worshipped from afar, and if the actuality fell short of the ideal and carnal lust obtruded – well, man was but a fallen being after all, and under the blue skies and warm sun of the South, no one was disposed to harsh judgments. So Eleanor had had a happy girlhood with her sister, Petronilla, at the free and easy Court of Aquitaine; both were spoilt but Eleanor knew how to dissemble when necessary so she was better liked than her sister, and the old Duke, her grandfather, was glad she was the elder and therefore the heiress since his eldest son, her father, had died. When the old Duke knew that his time was drawing near, he arranged a marriage between Eleanor and Louis Capet, the heir to France. Soon afterwards, her father-in-law died, and she became queen of France.

She was not so happy in the Île de France as she had been in Aquitaine. Here, it seemed, everything that a young girl might enjoy was forbidden or frowned upon and Louis himself was not what she had hoped for in a husband. He had been intended for the Church until his elder brother died, and Eleanor sometimes thought he would have been a great deal more contented in a cloister.

She had been married for three years when, in the summer of 1140, she met Ebrard. He was the younger son of one of Louis' barons, a gay, carefree youth. At first, it was only smiles and secret touches of the hand between them, and Ebrard had written poems for her, praising her virtue and beauty. For the first time Eleanor was content to be at the French Court. Yet if she thought that Ebrard would continue to worship from afar as the troubadours had done in Aquitaine, she reckoned without his nature and her own. Like many another young couple it was through their in-

10

nocence they fell, for neither of them realised how quickly soft and gentle kisses may fire the blood.

On a glorious day of blue skies and brilliant sunshine the whole Court went hunting. Autumn clothed the woods in bronze and gold and scarlet; the exhilaration of the chase and the knowledge of Ebrard riding near made the day perfect for Eleanor. Pretty soon they brought down a deer and though she sighed to see the gentle creature die, nothing could affect her happiness. It had not been difficult in the excitement for Ebrard to edge her horse into a quiet glade and they had galloped joyfully until they were thoroughly lost. And then they had dismounted and Eleanor had wrung her hands so prettily and said, 'Certainly it could not be long before they were found' and Ebrard had wished a murrain on any that did so, and they had laughed and kissed and rolled about in the bracken because they were both eighteen, and the sun shone and life and love stretched before them, illimitable.

Afterwards they slept, lying like two babes in the wood among the glory of the autumn leaves.

Eleanor awakened with a sense of astonished wonder. She still lay on Ebrard's cloak and he beside her sleeping, but the sun was lower in the sky, sending shimmering shafts of light around them. She stretched luxuriously, and her body remembered so that she pressed hands to cheeks suddenly grown warm and blushing. How strange, she thought, that with Ebrard it is so right and perfect. Then she remembered Louis with a dreadful pang and knew herself for an avoutress, and she stared up through the foliage above her head as though she thought that bright patch of light was the eye of God glaring vengefully down at her. Resentfully, she wondered why He had allowed her to marry Louis at all since she and Ebrard had been made for each other.

She looked down and saw the curve of Ebrard's ruddy cheek and the golden down on it like a bloom, and was filled with such a rush of love and rapture that she forgot God and His vengeance and her own bitterness completely.

11

They got back to the gates just before sunset and entered with a handful of other stragglers. Louis had not noticed her absence, being too wrapped up in a discussion of certain odious heresies which were gaining hold in southern Europe, and before another opportunity for dalliance presented itself, Ebrard's father carried him off home.

Two months later, through the idle gossip of the women, she heard that he was dead. She dared not ask the cause, but a long while afterwards she discovered that he had been struck down by one of those mysterious fevers straight from the hand of Lachesis. She was a mother by that time but the child – a daughter – was too like Louis for Eleanor to feel much affection for her. Still, life had gone on, and slowly she emerged from the black shroud of misery and despair. If any sharp eyes about the Court had intercepted their tender glances, the affair was too soon over to cause comment, and Eleanor never spoke his name again. She closed a door in her mind upon his memory and never knew that with it she shut away all future hope of love.

She grew harder and more impatient with Louis and his incessant wrestlings with his conscience, and when, swayed by the fiery preaching of Bernard of Clairvaux, he decided to take the Cross and go to the relief of Jerusalem, Eleanor made up her mind to accompany him. Not, indeed, that her soul was troubled by the plight of the Holy Places; she simply thought it would be exciting to go on Crusade and see exotic Eastern lands. But in order to get her way she pretended to an enthusiasm she did not feel, even going so far as to recruit a band of feminine Crusaders from the women at Court. Above all, she had enjoyed their stay in Antioch where her Uncle Raymond ruled. The luxury of the place had taken her breath away.

Louis had talked to Raymond in his sumptuous Presence Chamber and she had sat quietly, saying nothing, while her husband had laid bare his dreams of freeing the Holy Sepulchre from the grasp of the paynims. Afterwards, when

12

they were alone, Raymond had turned his eloquent, cynical, sensual gaze upon her and smiled, 'Why does he call upon the uncaring sky?' he murmured. 'With all the pleasures to be gained in this life, why does he think of naught but the next?'

She had shrugged, a little shocked at such plain speaking and unwilling to recognise the response his hedonistic philosophy called forth in her. 'Louis loves God,' she said lamely.

He had fondled her hand, his dark, hooded eyes amused.

'And Eleanor? Does she, too, love God, passing the love of men?'

She shot him a swift glance and he laughed outright. 'Know yourself, my child,' he said. 'All that you will find worth caring for is on the earth.'

A reluctant loyalty to Louis made her shake her head.

'*You* do not know me.'

'Yes, Eleanor,' he said, 'I know you. I know your blood. If you may, find another husband.'

In the end, a delightful relationship developed between them, half friendly, half flirtatious, but Louis misunderstood it and dragged her off to Jerusalem, then on to the siege of Damascus which was a fiasco. Soon she discovered she was pregnant again, and had thought how ironical it was that her husband could get a child on her only when she was interested in another man. However, the babe which was born after they returned to France was only another girl, and so it came about that Louis began to listen to her pleas for an annulment.

When Eleanor met Henry FitzEmpress and felt the first stirring of interest in him, she did not at once realise whose son he was. By this time, she would not in any case have cared. Her affair with Geoffrey of Anjou had been so casual, accidental almost, no more than a sudden urgent demand of the flesh, swiftly allayed and swiftly forgotten.

And Henry was fully as pleased with his wife as with her

13

dowry. He found her as full of ardour as any maid, and for more than a week they remained on their couch far past the dawn behind drawn curtains, sometimes giggling and sometimes with long-drawn sighs and gasps so that the waiting-men and women eyed one another knowingly and whispered behind their hands. But the thought of England still gnawed like a maggot at Henry's mind, and too soon for Eleanor, his natural restlessness asserted itself, and they must take the road for Normandy with all their meinie, to ride and see the Empress.

At this time the Empress was about fifty years old, a good age by any reckoning, with a thick, coarse nose and a long upper lip which protruded beak-like when she spoke. Age had not treated her with kindness. She dressed in very full shapeless gowns in the old style, or perhaps it was the German fashion, for to her everything from that land was admirable. She had gone there from England when she was eight years old to become the Emperor's wife, and there she had been much esteemed, both for her ruddy English looks (which she had from her mother) and for her haughty ways which appealed to the Germans.

Even when the Emperor died the Germans had wished to keep her but by then her brother William was dead, drowned in the White Ship, and old King Henry had ordered her home. Since her father was the only person Empress Matilda feared, home to England she had come and had been summarily married off again – to a boy of fifteen and a mere Count at that – because King Henry desired an heir for England from her body. And long enough he had to wait for she and Geoffrey of Anjou had disliked each other on sight.

Old Henry had forced all the great magnates of the realm to acknowledge his daughter heiress, and she had been given the title 'Lady of the English'; not without a good deal of cavilling on the part of the barons who did not like the idea of owing fealty to a woman. But while King Henry lived they did no more than grumble for he ruled them with a rod of iron. At last her first son had been born and named Henry for his grandfather; unfortunately, he was no more than two years old when the old King died from gorging upon lampreys, and from across the Channel, from Blois, Matilda's cousin Stephen had come and seized the English crown.

Matilda had never forgiven her husband for allowing it to happen. Not only did he refuse to take up arms in defence of her inheritance, he gave her no help when she finally sailed for England herself. She never really recovered from the terrible blow to her vanity when she returned defeated to Anjou after years of campaigning to find that Count Geoffrey had subdued Normandy alone and installed their son in the ducal seat of his ancestors.

However, Matilda and Eleanor came soon enough to terms with each other after a short period of wary circling like two strange dogs. Matilda's ferocious pride was assuaged by the size of her son's matrimonial catch, and also by the deference with which she was treated by the erstwhile Queen of France, while Eleanor was prepared to overlook the arrogance of the Empress if it would please her husband. Indeed, Eleanor was prepared to go far to please Henry; she was not over-conscious of the difference in their ages, but she examined her face carefully each morning in her polished silver mirror and had her women rub sheep's grease on her smooth olive skin that she might not wrinkle. Sometimes she darkened her eyelids as women do in Eastern lands, and scented the palms of her hands; these things she had learnt in Antioch when she was on Crusade with Louis.

She was thinking of those days and smiling a little to herself as she looked down at the book of her own poems open on her knees. Her mother-in-law was busy with her embroidery, for being English by birth, she was an expert needlewoman. The beautiful work, sewn with brilliant silks of scarlet, emerald and blue, was stretched on a frame

15

before her; little scenes of knights in battle and huntsmen with hounds were interspersed with curlicues and, along the edge, a running curve of vine leaves.

They sat at the end of the long solar, in a small alcove in the thickness of the wall beside the unshuttered window, in that pool of silence which always surrounded the Empress, and which in her solipsistic pride she accepted as a tribute. Further down the room ladies and pages were laughing and talking but rather more subdued than when she was absent, and one lad with a sweet, high voice was singing one of the new love songs which Eleanor had imported.

The Empress raised her eyes from her needlework and saw the sweet curve of Eleanor's lovely mouth.

'You smile, daughter?' she enquired, in a manner that implied that any expression except her own of controlled hauteur was fit only for scullions.

'I was but admiring the beauty of your work,' returned Eleanor with the hypocrisy at which she was becoming adept, 'and thinking of bygone days'.

'You will do well to think on that King who was your husband. He is even now in arms against your present husband and with him he has my younger son, Geoffrey, and also Eustace, the son of my kinsman Stephen who styles himself King of the English. That King who was your husband has some jealousy, it seems, towards my son Henry, and will put him out of his possessions if he can.'

Eleanor's dark eyes were upon her hands, neatly folded in her lap, and her smile was bland. 'Louis did not like to give up Aquitaine along with me. Yet why should Geoffrey help him?'

'Geoffrey, too, is jealous. He is not content with only three castles. He is fool enough to believe that Louis will give him Maine and Anjou if they can dispossess Henry.' And Matilda pinched her lips together and looked hardly at Eleanor's bowed head, for in her heart of hearts she blamed her, both for her forwardness in throwing herself

16

so soon into Henry's arms and for leaving her two small daughters in the Île de France without a backward look. She foresaw trouble from the spurned Louis.

Eleanor only laughed. 'Henry will hold what is his,' she said and dropping her book, picked up a lute and ran her fingers over the strings.

There was a sudden stir and flurry at the end of the room as Henry and a handful of gentlemen entered, noisy with talk and laughter, and Eleanor felt her heart lift a little as it always did when he was near.

'And do I suit you better now?' he asked when he stood before her and showed his clean and shining chin, a little scraped in places and still pink from the shaving. She exclaimed on the grandness of his scarlet tunic now that he had changed and turned him round the better to admire.

'You did not carry out your threat, my lord, and I am glad of it,' she laughed, patting his smooth cheek and looking at him in such a way that the Empress sniffed and settled her lean haunches a little deeper into the feather hassock.

'Threat – what threat?' said she.

'Madam, this wife of mine has a shrewish tongue. Last night she would have me out of her bed because of the bristles on my chin for all I told her not a week had passed since my last shaving. And I said that if she would see a hairless chin, so also should she see a naked poll for I would shave the back of my head in the old Norman manner.'

'But you did not,' murmured Eleanor, stroking the back of his neck where the thick, reddish hair began to curl.

'It was not a pretty fashion,' said the Empress, 'but cleanly. For why did you not, then?' and her humourless face was perplexed.

Eleanor cast up her eyes and said hastily, 'What news is this of your brother and Eustace of Blois joining Louis to make war on you, my lord?'

'It is true, lady. We ride out at dawn tomorrow so all the scraping I have endured for your sake goes for naught.'

His face darkened. 'And if I unhorse young Geoffrey, he'll get the flat of my blade across his arse, the treacherous knave.'

'And I?'

'You remain here with my mother who will guard you well for me.'

'No, that I will not,' and Eleanor shot a look at the Empress that expressed her feelings all too clearly; Matilda's eyes were on her embroidery though her pose was stiff and listening. When she raised them and looked at the younger woman, they were as noncommittal as ever as she said, 'A dutiful wife obeys her husband in all things.'

Henry's smile was fond but there was a spark in his grey eyes that told Eleanor she should not have her way with him as easily as she had with Louis. But time was young yet. This time she would surrender gracefully to his wishes; he would be all the readier to listen to her later.

'As you say, then, my lord,' she said, all outward submission.

'Come then, sweeting, we'll down to the mews and I'll show you the eyas that's come from the Count de Vermandois,' and he slid his arm about her waist as they moved away together.

The Empress watched them go and wondered.

It took Henry the rest of that year of 1152 to beat off Geoffrey and his allies. The chief participants emerged unscathed; the only sufferers were the peasants over whose fields they fought and the foot soldiers, mostly mercenaries, for whose deaths none could grieve. A few knights were captured but were too valuable to be harmed; they were ransomed to fight again.

When Henry finally caught up with Geoffrey in a castle he had taken, it was already autumn and time to be thinking of the winter truce. He was good humoured in victory and conveniently forgot his threat; instead, they spent a few pleasant days together drinking and gambling, and Geoffrey mimicked Louis and Eustace so accurately that Henry's heart warmed towards him and they parted the best of friends.

So in the new year Henry turned his attention towards England and crossed the Channel, happy in the knowledge that he had left Eleanor pregnant. 'No daughter this time,' he had adjured her, 'it is sons we need'.

She had been confident. 'Have no fear, my lord. There is a wise woman in your mother's service who has foretold a string of sons for you and me – a race of eagles we shall breed, she said.'

She did not tell him the rest of the prophecy, that the least of the eagles should destroy its father; it was characteristic of her to shrug aside what she found unacceptable; indeed, she had forgotten it already.

August 1153

The army of Henry, Duke of Normandy, was encamped at Wallingford under a sky as black as a plum, and in the gloom of a pavilion which drummed and reverberated under a fierce summer rainstorm three great English earls drank and laughed among their followers and talked of the events of the day. Robert de Beaumont, Earl of Leicester, was quieter than the other two, being but lately come to Henry's aid, but the Earls of Cornwall and Gloucester, Henry's own kinsmen, were noisy in their cups. Leicester watched them, putting in a remark now and then to show that he felt himself among friends. He was a man who preferred to watch and wait, for making up his mind was a lengthy process with him; once it was made up he was immovable. A boyhood spent in the shadow of his impetuous, elder twin brother Waleran had done that to him. Waleran, the heir, had had all their father's lands in France; the poorer English fiefs had come to Robert.

Cornwall he had met before and thought a bag of wind;

he saw no reason now to change his mind for all that he was a natural son of old King Henry and half brother to the Empress. At that very moment, Reginald of Cornwall was thinking of his sister. He had been with her that night at Oxford Castle – more than ten years ago, it was – when the bright moon had cast blue shadows on the snow, the night she had fled from Stephen's conquering army and had been lowered down the tower wall muffled in a white cloak, for she would not be taken, she said; better die in escaping than be a prisoner. He thought of it now, and of their despair at that time and of how much he admired his sister and her high-stomached pride. That admiration had spoilt him for his wife, a meek woman whom he had married for her wide lands and the title she had brought him. Her revenues he used in his sister's and her son's cause, and thought them well spent now that they scented victory.

The knights were bandying coarse jests; he caught the tail end of one and gave a great shout of laughter, slapping his thigh. He was a heavy, cheerful, stupid man of about forty, with thick eyebrows thatched above small, twinkling eyes. He turned his head as William of Gloucester spoke.

'It's as good as victory, the fact that Stephen has withdrawn,' said William, speaking low under cover of the knights' shouting. 'We may be sure the terms were of advantage to Henry – his own desire was to do battle with Stephen. And did you mark those emissaries of the King? – how they quaked and shivered in their shoes?'

'All the omens were against them,' said Leicester. 'Three times was King Stephen thrown from his horse. Marry! I'd not care to fight myself after such a sign!'

'Young though he be, Henry keeps his own counsel,' Cornwall said. 'Though I strained my ears I could not make out what they hollered to each other across the ford. I am become a little deaf,' he added regretfully. 'Did you hear anything, William?'

'I was not near enough' said Gloucester. 'It was like the

20

bawling of bulls. They say that young Eustace has gone off to Suffolk, swearing vengeance. But the heart is gone out of the King since his wife died.'

William was the heir of that Earl Robert of Gloucester, dead now these six years, who had been the eldest son and favourite bastard of King Henry, and the leader of the Empress' rights against Stephen. There had been occasions when she had actually taken his advice but Earl Robert had not liked her and had shown it, so these were not many. Nonetheless, he had fought for her valiantly, spurning the tentative suggestions that he himself might be acceptable as King in spite of his illegitimacy. William, like many sons overshadowed by a greater father, was lukewarm in the cause dear to that father's heart, but he was a man who did always what was expected of him.

King Henry's lecherous proclivities had brought about a tangled skein of relationships to the throne, for he had at least a score of natural children, born of many different mothers. Yet even the clergy of his realm had looked upon grim old Henry Beauclerk with an indulgent eye; he had seemed to enjoy nothing, not even venery, so that one cleric had been emboldened to proclaim that it was no vice in him but a natural desire to spread his glorious seed for the benefit of the kingdom as a whole. At all events, he had placed his offspring in high positions, and none had betrayed his trust but had fought on defiantly against Stephen for his one remaining legitimate child.

Cornwall stretched his legs and winced as his knee cracked. 'I have more rust in my knees than my mail,' he said. 'God send the fighting may soon be over and we'll have a King Henry again. Does he not put you in mind of your grandsire, William? He has the same look in the eye – and he'll be as great a whoremonger if all I hear be true.' He laughed, showing all his blackened teeth. 'Bring more wine, then,' he roared, but Leicester went to the tent flap and looked out.

21

'It's stopped raining,' he said, 'and they are striking the tents. I'll see what's to do.' He went down into the steamy puddles of the water meadows and looked about him, but nowhere could he see Duke Henry who, with his usual impatience, had already gone without a word.

So the Earl of Leicester stood among the tussocky grass clumps and sucked his teeth, gazing down the river at the ford, and wondered if he had done the best thing in casting in his lot with him. In the west the clouds were dazzling white in a lake of blue sky and a rock by his feet steamed in the sunshine, dry patches spreading and coalescing before his eyes. A little group of mallards came out of shelter in the reeds and swam away down river, leaving a wake like arrowheads on the shining golden water, and a great heron flapped slowly away above them.

He turned, putting up his hand to shade his eyes from the glare of direct sunlight, and stiffened abruptly as he realised that another man stood not half a dozen yards away from him, watching him as intently as he had watched the birds. He was tall and thin, bare headed but wearing a fine hauberk; all the little metal rings of which it was composed caught the light so that he glittered like a many faceted jewel and the divided skirt which protected his thighs clinked musically as it swung with his movement.

'I know you, both by sight and by repute,' the man said.

The Earl nodded slowly. He did not recognise the man though it was hardly to be expected that he should know every knight in the Duke's retinue. But there was something about the fellow's tone — a hint of amusement, of challenge, almost. Leicester looked at him sharply, noting the heavy sword with the hilt picked out in gold and enamel and the mettlesome stallion cropping the grass nearby. The horse's legs were wet to the hocks. He had come across the ford, then, from the other side.

'There is a truce declared,' said Leicester.

22

'Aye,' said the other, and laughed. 'Or I should not have ventured here. You know me not, my lord?'

'I do not. Who sent you hither?'

'No-one sent me. I wandered here as you did. I am Fitzurse, lord of Williton, Worspring, Bulwick and Upminster, among others. I hold with King Stephen – as I believe you did once.'

Leicester shrugged. 'It is easier to decide whom one is against in this quarrel than whom one is for. For my part, I hold with England and my English, and I will place my sword at the disposal of the one who has the strength to end this strife.'

Fitzurse moved nearer. 'And you think this young Duke can do so? Before God, I think as you do. I was against the Empress – who would be ruled by a woman? – but my lands have been laid waste by both sides. King Stephen lacks strength of purpose and every baron with a following is as much king as he. Yet I know not. . . .'

'In truth, nor I,' said Leicester, 'But there is this to think upon – the Duke is nothing like his mother and there is that about him will make men follow him. And he is young.' He smiled wryly at Fitzurse. 'I think that Stephen is too old and tired to fight much longer. His son, Eustace, is a waster and despoiler. There is none else but Henry FitzEmpress if this realm is ever to be again as once it was. You are of an age to remember that, as I am.'

The two men now stood side by side, and Fitzurse sat down upon a large flat stone, carefully disposing his sword across a clump of grass. Leicester waved his arms to disperse the whining cloud of gnats that hovered over them, and in the short silence that ensued, seated himself close by. At last, Fitzurse spoke. 'I thank you for your kind advice, my lord,' and with a smile as wry as Leicester's own, 'It is well to be on that side that emerges victorious. Yet I will tell you this – there are those barons who fight for Stephen who prefer the *status quo*. It leaves them mighty in their own lands and free to pursue their own ends. So they hope that neither side will gain a victory. There is the reason why they voted for a truce.'

Leicester shot him a wary glance. 'Did you?'

'I did not.'

'A moment ago you said you thought as I do.'

'I will be frank with you. I have been fighting at intervals for fifteen years. I have been captured and I have been wounded, and to what end? My substance has been wasted, my villeins go hungry, and I am poorer now in goods than I have ever been. I too am tired of it. But I shall not be traitor to Stephen for anything less than a complete end to this war.'

'I wish that I could guarantee it,' said Leicester with a sigh. And then, 'I cannot recall ever having seen you before.'

'At Glastonbury once you were a guest of the Abbot. I had business with him concerning a fee I hold of him in Wiltshire. I have a long memory.'

'You have, indeed. So you owe fealty to the Abbot? – and to whom else?'

'Rest yourself easy, my lord. I am my own man for I hold direct of the Crown for my principal lands and I am a man who will stand by my word.' He grinned suddenly. 'And if I were not, I am in good company. Did not King Stephen himself swear homage to the Empress while yet King Henry lived? And how many – lay and ecclesiastical barons alike – have changed sides, not once but twice and thrice and more? In England now, each must care for his own.'

'You are bold of speech,' returned Leicester, somewhat grimly, but that very boldness touched a chord in him and the sentiment agreed with his own conclusion that in these latter days expediency was all and the old ideas of liege homage and unswerving loyalty from vassals were dying.

It was true that Stephen had sworn homage to the Lady of the English, had placed his hands between hers and

24

sworn to be her man, 'touching life, limb and earthly honour'; Leicester himself remembered it, the more clearly because Stephen had insisted upon taking precedence of the bastard Earl of Gloucester. They had all sworn – and then when old King Henry lay dead they had gone back upon their word, out of fear of a woman on the throne or a long regency while her baby son grew to manhood. And it had led to the very thing they feared – anarchy. But now that babe was a man, surely safety lay with him. Among so many broken vows, what did one more matter? So Leicester had argued with himself many times.

He looked into Fitzurse's face and liked what he saw there. It was a thin face with deep lines scored from nose to mouth, the lips tightly compressed so that at first glance you thought it hard and even cruel, but the eyes gave the lie to that grim mouth; dark Norman blue, they were the eyes of a dreamer and an idealist. When they met Leicester's, he looked quickly away as though he feared he might betray something. Here is a man who has tried to armour himself against the world, thought Leicester, and has still not entirely succeeded. If such a one puts expediency before principle he will destroy himself. So he pressed the Duke's cause no farther and they sat awhile in a curiously companionable silence.

At last Fitzurse stood up. 'I must away or my men will be seeking me,' he said. 'Fare you well, my lord of Leicester. We shall meet again, make no doubt of it. And when we do, perchance we shall be comrades in arms.'

Leicester put out his hand and their fingers touched briefly, then Fitzurse swung up upon his horse and splashed away across the ford. He looked back once from the opposite bank but Leicester could not make out his expression. He remained where he was for a little while until the sun hid himself behind a cloud, rimming it with fiery gold, then he got up and made his way back to the camp.

*

Eustace, the son of Stephen, had gone some hours before, burning with rage. 'What ails my father?' he shouted. 'Will he give up my inheritance without putting hand to sword? God's Wounds, it's well I did not meet him or I'd have fleshed my blade on him in default of Henry! He's become an old woman to fear the wrath of God because he took a tumble from his nag. On! On!' And still mailed as he was, he pricked his horse unmercifully and the other knights had much ado to keep up with him.

All the way they rode Eustace cursed his father and swore by God and all the saints he'd have what was his, until his followers looked askance at one another at such unfilial behaviour and fell to silence.

August 1153
Hikenai, the English girl, walked to St Edmundsbury on the Feast of St Lawrence to sell or barter two score of eggs in the market. She did not go too early in the day for she could not pay the market tolls; her only hope was to mingle with the crowds and pass unnoticed. She did not really expect to get coin for her produce. In her state of dire poverty, anything was acceptable and she was well pleased with the length of cheap cloth for which she exchanged them. She only got that because the day was drawing on towards evening and a pedlar had felt sorry for the skinny, ragged child silently offering her basket of eggs to impatient goodwives who waved her aside and hurried on.

'Hey, moppet!' he had shouted, 'I fancy a mess of eggs to my supper. How would this suit you?' He had shaken out the piece of rough cloth before her – the end of the bolt and a short length, to be sure, but enough to make a skimpy gown for a small twelve-year-old, and of a very gay russet colour. Hikenai examined it eagerly. The dye was patchy but as the pedlar assured her, it would never show when the gown was made up; in any case, it was a bargain for a few eggs.

'You're in luck because I like eggs and there's none to be

26

had,' he said, which was quite untrue; the real reason was that behind his unprepossessing looks lurked a kind heart which had led him into foolishness before.

'Put the eggs down, then,' he said and thrust the cloth upon her.

'The – the basket?' she whispered.

'What, can you talk? I thought the devil had run off with your tongue. You want the basket back?' He stared at it for it looked ready to fall to pieces. 'Then how can I carry them? No, I must have it; you can make another.' He laughed at her dismayed expression. 'Come, lass, I'll buy thee a pie to make up. May as well be a great fool as a small one, eh?'

The pie was succulent and he gave her a drink out of his mug of ale as well, so Hikenai was happy with her day's work. When she finally passed through the gate and started home it was nearly sunset so she would not reach the heath before dark. Her father would not worry; she had been late before when she went to market. He rarely ventured off the assart on the heath for he lived in fear of the bailiff. They had lived there, Hikenai and her father and her three little brothers, ever since her mother died. That was not long after her grandfather's death.

When the old man had died her father had to pay the heriot to the lord who sat in the manor and he had raved for days after the bailiff came and took the best cow, and a good pot for the priest. A few months later her mother gave birth to another boy who died within the week; she had wept for days, then died herself. Hikenai could never see why that child was so special that her mother would abandon them all for its sake. Slowly she forgot it, though, and her mother too. The fact that there was no safety in the world came to be accepted; but sometimes she thought that in her breast now lay a cold, hard stone.

All this ill luck frightened her father into believing someone in the village was laying spells against him so that he refused to go to the weekly meetings in the churchyard, nor would he allow his family to take part in the monthly feasts at which his dead wife had taken a leading part. In the end, he fled to the heath to escape the evil eye.

The lord had not bothered about the loss of one of his villeins. He was an old man himself, and Ulf, Hikenai's father, had been an awkward and unwilling worker. Another serf had moved into his tumbledown hut and worked his strips and done his boon work, and he did not mutter and glare as Ulf had done. In any case, the bailiff could keep his eye on the assart and when it gave more than a bare living Ulf should pay his due rents for the land.

Hikenai was about halfway home when she heard distant hoofbeats. She stood near the side of the road, ankle-deep in white dust, and strained her ears to listen. Overhead, the first stars were coming out and all around her was silent except when a faint breeze rustled the undergrowth which grew closer to the roadside than the old Saxon laws would have allowed. She was glad of it for it was a place to hide.

So she crouched among the bushes and watched the troop of mailed knights ride past towards St Edmundsbury with Lord Eustace at their head, and though she did not know who they were, she shivered, for knights boded no good to the common people. She did not even think of them as men; they were a race apart with their fine horses and clothes and their almost incomprehensible language. Nor did she harbour hatred for Normans as such; that they ruled England was a fact and the best thing to do was to hide and watch unseen.

She did not mention them to her father and did not think of them again, until a few days later she saw a heavy pall of smoke in the sky in the direction of their old home. She was milking the cow and sprang up in such agitation that she knocked over the leather bucket and so lost the few miserable drops she had spent so much effort in obtaining.

'Father!' she screamed, 'The vill is burning! Look!'

Ulf dropped his hoe and swung round. 'God's Blood! Is it war again? If noble blood toiled like us poor commons, they'd have no more taste for it than we do.'

Hikenai stared at him. 'The day I went to market – I saw a troop of knights, mailed.'

'What device?'

'I did not see. It was dark. I hid in a bush—'

But Ulf had gone, running with the easy lope of a man who can run down a deer. Straight across the well-known paths he ran with no thought of concealment – his sisters and their husbands were in the village and, for once, Ulf's mind was not fixed upon his own woes. Caution reasserted itself when he neared the cultivated land; here, wriggling through the thinning undergrowth, he stared down the slight slope across the large open fields.

From this distance the long strips, separated only by a double furrow, made a neat pattern. Four, or perhaps five, belonged to each family on the manor but they were far apart which made for hard work, as Ulf remembered. At the other end of the fields the cottars' hovels had stood but all Ulf could see now were smoking ruins. He made a noise, deep in his throat, clenching his fists and tearing at the grass. Then he saw the people running madly and helplessly as the mounted knights boiled through a gap and into the field. They were laying about them with their swords and some were firing the ripe wheat.

'Whoreson swine!' yelled Ulf – they would not hear him anyway, with all the noise they were making. Most of the villagers seemed to be making for the shelter of the woods about half a mile from where he watched. The knights had burnt the lord's demesne field and Ulf saw the bailiff knocked flat and left amidst the smouldering mess. He did not mind that, though.

Presently, the knights tired of their fun and rode off in groups; soon a fresh gush of smoke announced that they had burnt the church. Ulf wept for helpless rage.

29

For two days afterwards, he lay low upon the assart, but finally curiosity overcame fear and he took the long walk to the Convent of Blessed St Edmund in search of news. In the great Court among a milling crowd of vagrants and refugees he saw his sisters but went by them silently; they would talk too much and he would not get the news he wanted from them. So he spoke quietly with the Cellarer, who was known to be a close-mouthed man, instead.

'Aye, the Lord Eustace, the King's son,' said the Cellarer. 'We feasted him well but this has come about because we would not give him silver to pay his troops. All of St Edmund's harvests are burned. But his wickedness has been well rewarded –' and he leaned close to Ulf and whispered in his ear.

'Truly so?' said Ulf. 'May all these warring nobles come to a like end! We have suffered long enough from their greed.'

The Cellarer did not know Ulf and took him for a free man but he and Ulf both knew that in that parish it was the greed of the monks about which the tenants grumbled.

Ulf moved uncomfortably. 'Nay, but it is hard for a poor man to live without having his crops burnt.'

The Cellarer sniffed. 'It's not those crops that matter. It was the burning of St Edmund's crops that called down the wrath of God upon him,' and with that he retired within and slammed the shutter.

Ulf spat upon the ground. 'Aye, thy God's not a poor man's God,' he muttered, 'for all they say he was but a simple carpenter,' and he forced his way through the press very fiercely; but by the time he got back to the assart, he was whistling through the gap in his front teeth and, hearing him, Hikenai knew he was in a good humour.

'Have you news of my aunts?' she asked.

'Aye, good news.' He pursed his lips and swayed a little on his toes, watching her.

30

'Ah, tell then.' She clung eagerly on his arm as she used to do when she was a small girl before her mother died and his temper became uncertain.

'I had the news from the monks at St Edmund's. It was Eustace, the King's son, who led those knights.' He stopped, grinning at her. 'And now he lies dead,' he concluded, triumphantly.

'And my aunts?'

'Your aunts? What of them? They are alive, I saw them.' He glared at her in sudden irritation. 'Why talk of aunts? I bring news to rejoice at and all you can think of is your aunts! What cared they for thee, or for me, either?' and he stamped away into the hut, all his pleasure evaporated.

Hikenai hurried after him. 'What manner of death did he die?'

'He fell into a miserable madness, said the Cellarer, when he began to eat. And the same night he died.' Ulf gave a snort. 'He said too that it was the vengeance of Blessed St Edmund.'

Hikenai smiled. Their small crop still stood upon the assart and that was not under the protection of St Edmund but of those older Northern gods that her mother had worshipped. Perhaps they are stronger than St Edmund, she thought.

On that same August day that Eustace died, Eleanor gave birth to her first son. Even the Empress smiled and patted her hand as Eleanor lay in contented lassitude and gazed at the crumpled dark red face of Henry's heir.

'He shall be called William,' Eleanor said, 'for that is the name of the Dukes of Aquitaine as well as those of Normandy.'

The Empress was taken aback. 'This boy may one day be King of the English. Shall not his name be Henry?'

'My next son will be Henry,' said Eleanor with assurance.

The Empress sighed. More than a year of living with Eleanor, who agreed sweetly with her and went her own way regardless, had tired her.

'Sleep now, daughter,' she said. 'You have done well for my son.'

November 1153

In Westminster Hall on a dark November day, the candles on the long table were steady, but round the hall they flickered as brocade, samite and miniver brushed past. At the top of the board sat King Stephen, looking old and ill; his hair, more grey than fair, swung on his cheeks as he leaned forward to look at the parchment before him.

Duke Henry was beside him, his freckled face complacent with scarcely repressed satisfaction. The Earls of Cornwall and Gloucester, along with Leicester looking very well pleased with himself, sat on Henry's left and further down the table Fitzurse's face was turned their way; but most of Stephen's men kept their glances to themselves as though each feared his neighbour might read his thoughts.

At length Stephen took up the quill and carefully signed his name and then offered it to Henry who smilingly declined, and standing up, began to read slowly and clearly that all might hear.

'Stephen, King of England, to the Archbishops, Bishops, Abbots, Earls, Justiciars, Sheriffs, Barons and all his faithful men of England: greetings.

'Be it known to you that I, the King of England, Stephen, have made Henry, Duke of Normandy, the successor to the kingdom of England after me, and my heir by hereditary right, and thus I have given and confirmed to him and his heirs the kingdom of England.

'The Duke, therefore, because of this honour and the grant and confirmation made to him by me, has done homage to me and given security by oath that he will be faithful to me and that he will guard my life and honour

32

to the best of his ability, through the provisions discussed between us beforehand which are contained in this charter.

'I also have given security by oath to the Duke that I will guard his life and honour to the best of my ability, and I will uphold him as my son and heir in everything I can and I will guard him against all men as far as I am able.

'My son, William, has made liege homage and security to the Duke of Normandy and the Duke has granted to him to hold from him all the lands that I held before I obtained the kingdom of England, whether in England, whether in Normandy, whether in other places, and whatever he received with the daughter of the Earl Warenne.

'The Duke's mother and wife, and the brothers of this same Duke, and all to whom this treaty might apply are hereby given assurance of security. In the affairs of the kingdom I will act with the advice of the Duke. I, however, in the whole realm of England, both in the Duke's part and in mine, will exercise royal justice.'

When he had finished a great shout went up; even Stephen's barons must make the best of it and cheer too. Their years of pillage under a soft, good King were over, as one look at the young Duke standing beside the old King told them. Theobald, Archbishop of Canterbury, had tears of relief in his eyes as he held out his hands to Henry. 'At last!' he said. 'At last.'

No one looked at King Stephen. Amid the general rejoicing he shifted about uncomfortably on his chair; his piles were troubling him again. His thoughts dwelt with sorrowful resignation upon the blows that Fate had dealt him; first the death of his wife, Matilda, whom he had dearly loved, then the loss of Eustace in the midst of his sins, and now, that he must drink of the cup of bitterness to the dregs, the vehement refusal of his younger son to continue the fight for the English crown. He sighed and thought that if all were to do again, he should never set

33

foot in England which had brought him little but grief. Let young Henry have it, whose birthright it was, and he, for his part, would spend his remaining days in prayer and contrition.

II

April–July 1154

THE BARONS OF the West country returned home to their manors in the spring. It was a great procession that crawled slowly across the face of southern England, mules, pack horses and wagons all heavy laden and clopping and grinding along with a great noise and dust, for the season had been dry. After the long streams of bowmen and foot soldiers rode the knights and squires with their brightly coloured banners, and behind them, very grand on their fine horses, the mighty lords themselves.

Lifting their heads from their unending tasks in the fields, the villeins watched them riding by but no one knew what went on behind those dull, expressionless faces. Perhaps they wondered a little at such an array, but when the nobles go abroad their cups and plates of silver and pewter, their beds and stools and tents go with them; de Mohun had taken his own priest, too, with cope and chasuble, and his chalice and paten of red gold, sewn up safe now in strong hide with other sacred vessels and riding along in its own wagon.

He was the most powerful baron of them all, who had never wavered in his allegiance to the Lady of the English and her son, and who had held Dunster Castle through six weary months of siege while Stephen's men howled at the gates and catapulted huge stones at his impregnable keep.

35

He had capitulated in the end, rather than see his people die of starvation, but he had won his enemies' respect. Now, enemies and friends together, they were going home.

On and on they travelled, across the Mendips where the new lambs rejoiced their eyes, and across the flat Somerset plain, and here Richard Fitzurse and his Williton men parted company with the others for they would ride across the Quantock Hills while the heavy wagons must go round by Taunton. Through smiling April weather, almost as hot as June they rode, up gently rolling hills and down through sheltered wooded valleys noisy with birdsong, until they reached the summit and gazed across the fair valley to the folds of Exmoor in the dim, blue distance. Away to their right the land fell away, down to St Audrey's and the Severn Sea, a band of milky, opalescent light, and beyond that, very faint, like dark clouds on the horizon the Welsh hills.

Here they dismounted and Richard sat upon a rock alone and let the sweet, soft air of home breathe gently in his face. His men disposed themselves on the heathery ground and drank from their leather bottles; one or two talked quietly but for the most part they sat in silence for they, too, were glad to be home. The bell heather would soon be in bloom, and after that the ling, but the only colour now was in a clump of gorse, showing its first yellow flowers and the red threads of dodder already beginning to twine about the base of the stems. As they sat, a cloud came across the sun, the air grew chill at once and the view towards Severn darkened and grew gloomy.

They started the long descent to the Vale of Taunton, twenty-three mounted men riding home where twenty-four had left. The one who did not return was young John Ide and he had not died in battle but in his father's arms of a harsh and suffocating cough. It had distressed Baron Fitzurse that it should be the youngest of his Williton men, and above all the only son of Adam Ide, his captain, whom they

36

had lost. Now, as they drew near to his manor, he wondered how Adam's wife would take it. No one had wanted the boy to go, but twelve-year-old John had been eager to see the world and when he finally persuaded his father, Richard had reluctantly consented. If that poor, puny lad had been a villein's child, he thought, he would never have survived his childhood anyway. Still, it was a pity for Adam's wife was beyond childbearing and he feared she would take it badly.

His thoughts turned to his own sons and he speculated on how greatly Reynold might have changed in the years since he had seen him. He had gone away into Devon to de Tracy's to be educated with his half brother, Robert, when he was eight years old – and a hard task they must have had, he thought sourly. In the last ten years they had not met more than half a dozen times and nothing he had seen on those fleeting visits had caused him to revise his opinion of his heir. He was fonder of his natural son, sensing in him perhaps a greater likeness to himself, though to look at, Robert resembled his mother, that passionate, self-willed girl whose headlong determination had encompassed her own ruin.

Emma had been a Norman heiress whose blood out-ranked his own, but she had relentlessly pursued him, not caring anything for his wife and two little girls and the babe soon to be born. In the end, Richard had given way to her importunings because his wife was distasteful to him, his life boring, and he deceived himself into believing he could love her. This happened soon after Stephen had seized the throne, and in the trouble and chaos of that time he had installed her on one of his smaller Midland manors while he had gone to fulfil his knight service.

When he returned she was dead, the manor laid waste, and the only living creatures on it two servants and a new-born child. He had rewarded the servants for their faithful-ness and had taken the child to be brought up in his Household. Since Maud Fitzurse's own son, Reynold, had not yet attained his first birthday, his wife's fury knew no bounds.

Yet, to be fair, Richard admitted that there had been no overt ill treatment of the boy; her own son filled Maud's world, and if Robert suffered for Reynold's childish misdeeds as well as his own, he did so without complaint. The two boys got on well enough, they quarrelled no more than full brothers might, and if Reynold were a grievous disappointment to his father – he looked too much like his mother – he counted himself luckier in Emma's son.

It was Maud Fitzurse's tragedy that after more than twenty years of dogged devotion, she could not accept that her husband would never love her. She was a lumpy, stupid woman, irritatingly vague about the running of the Household, yet with enough simple cunning and feminine guile to procure her own way most of the time. In this one thing, though, she could not have her way but she never ceased trying to gain it. It would never occur to her that there was little true justice in life nor did she notice how rarely virtue was rewarded. This hopeless love of hers filled him with guilt so that he sometimes deceived her in the smallest matters in case he should hurt her further. Then, if she uncovered his well meant deceits, loud and ugly quarrels would develop between them for Maud could not suffer silently. He dreaded these outbursts of hers, knowing that a kindly word from him thereafter would bring floods of tears and self-recriminations and a coy, dumb expectancy that appalled him.

For the past several years he had treated her with cool kindness and kept his woman in his house under a pretence of waiting upon her. He did not think she even suspected their relationship. He was wrong there; Maud Fitzurse knew very well that she shared her husband with her tiring woman and by now she was becoming bitter from hope too long deferred. Beta received many a sharp box on the ears as punishment for his kind looks or half glimpsed caresses.

38

Richard's blood quickened a little at the thought of Beta; he thrust away the unpleasant memory of his wife and son, and looked about him as they came lower down the grassy ride.

Here were sessile oaks still naked as winter but the beeches were fat-budded and one or two already showing damp and crumpled leaves of brilliant green. Under the oaks were sheets of bluebells, not yet in flower but displaying their first purplish blush, and yellow archangel and violets hiding in their leaves. Then, as they went a little farther down, he saw a huge clump of primroses and one of the younger men slid off his horse and gathered some so that everyone had a small posy to tuck in his breast. Richard pressed his chin into them; they were cool and velvety to the touch and smelt faintly and sweetly of the earth. He caught Adam's eye and smiled, and said 'twere pity they would be dead ere they were home', and could have bitten out his tongue for the thoughtlessness of the remark.

Adam, though, did not appear to notice anything amiss, and Richard wondered how it came about that he had met so few men who noticed the feelings of others. It seemed to him a thing hard to bear that he should feel for others; if he had loved them, it would not be a burden but to have been cursed with such perception and to be unable to love. . . . In a gregarious world he was by nature solitary and so he built a wall of vague, indifferent benevolence about himself and kept his heart secure within. Once, in his early youth, he had loved and it had brought him nothing but pain; he would not risk his heart again for man or woman.

When they passed around his own great fields and across the common land the afternoon was well advanced and the geese were being driven in. The girl who drove them shouted and the villagers came running out. They ran beside the horses and yelled news at them; they had a good harvest last autumn and all was well with the demesne. There had been four new babes and only one had died, and old

Osbert who was so old that no one could remember his youth had died a month ago. The priest was running alongside the baron's horse, trying to tell him something but he was too impatient to listen; he urged the horse on, the puffing priest dropped back and Richard galloped gladly through his own gates.

His house was built in stone which was why it had escaped destruction when the surrounding countryside was burnt; it had a moat around it and within a stout fence of stakes, still new looking. New, too, were the cruck huts and stables built inside the yard on the northern side. The house itself was long, and appeared narrower than it was. At one end was a tower containing the armoury, and another small chamber with a strong door, empty now and dusty, where prisoners were kept. This tower was reached by a wooden outside stair, removable in case of need; there was another lower one leading up to the door of the hall, for the house itself was built upon a vaulted undercroft where stores were kept.

It had been built by Maud's great-grandfather, Baron de Falaise, who had come over with William the Bastard in search of plunder and ended as lord of numerous English estates. In course of time, it had come to Maud's mother, Sibyl de Falaise, and then to Sir Richard Fitzurse as part of his wife's dowry. They had come here, Sir Richard and Lady Maud, soon after the birth of their first child, Margaret, and from the beginning Richard had loved it. Here he felt at home as he had never done on any of his other manors, not even Bulwick where he was born. Now, he thought, I shall never leave again unless I am forced; surely I can bring my Somerset lands into bearing enough to support me and mine. I am tired of travelling.

Once they were within the hall – for he would have them all in who had ridden away with him – he could smell the good, mouth-watering smells of a feast in preparation. Lady Maud ran to him, all ungainly, and hung upon him so that

40

he was reminded of a mongrel bitch he had once owned who fawned and went upon her belly, but he placed a kindly arm about her shoulders as she pushed her face against his breast, and looked about the hall for Beta.

She was not there but his eye fell gladly on the familiar, unchanged surroundings, the rush-strewn floor, the carved screen within the door, the lime washed walls and the high beamed ceiling. The hall, which was in fact the whole house apart from the tower, was about forty feet long; halfway down it was a great semi-circular arch across the width. All round the arch the plaster was painted with scenes, each surrounded by a scroll pattern of leaves, flowers and fishes, faded now because they were as old as the house, but still beautiful. The red, which was the main colour, had turned to russet and the blue and green were almost grey but the traces of yellow were still bright.

Gently, he led his wife to her seat at the long trestle, noticing that she had attired herself in her best for his home-coming; over the yellowed linen under tunic she wore a bliaut of heavy, crimson Lincoln cloth, laced at the sides and full at the hem, and with the jewelled girdle which had been his mother's around her thick waist. It was unfortunate and typical of her, he thought, that there was a large, fresh, greasy stain upon her skirt. Having adorned herself in all her finery, she had doubtless gone straight to the kitchens.

He sighed, as she gabbled on, casting about in his mind for a way to ask for her tiring woman that would not sound too obvious and wound her. He had no need. Lady Maud herself mentioned Beta's name.

'What was that?' he said. 'Take time to draw breath, wife. Did you say that Beta has – a babe?'

'Aye, a bonny six-month girl. She hid it from us all as long as might be but there's no hiding swellings of that size, and so I told her. I knew not what to do for she'd name no one,' and she looked at him very sly from the corner of her eye.

He sat stiffly in his seat, all appetite gone. 'When was it born?' he said at length.

'Why, ten month after you had left. October, I believe it was – aye, it was, for it was the night we had the gale—oh, such a wind, sir, you could hear the sea roaring from here, I swear – and that was St Luke's Eve. Sir Priest pressed her to tell who was the father but she would not. She is naught but a wanton. I was too merciful to have her whipped but I do not have her round me now.'

'October–' Sir Richard said it with relief and some amusement. She cannot even calculate the time to be in pod, he thought, but I shall know whether it is my flesh when I see it, and it was certainly January when we rode away. Strange, though, that Beta should bear a child now; she was no young girl and they had been coming together for all of six – nay, seven years. But where was she?

His voice was suddenly dangerous. 'What have you done with her?'

He saw her look of fear mixed with satisfaction and thought, she knew all the time. He stood up abruptly. 'Where is she?'

His wife said sulkily, 'In the kitchens. Would you have a strumpet serve me?'

He thought with unbelief, She is daring me to admit to it. Can she really think that I will tolerate her interference?

Aloud, he said, 'Send for her. We'll soon be at the bottom of it.'

She gaped at him. 'Not here – not now, I beg you. It will not be seemly. I have prepared a bath for you – all is in readiness. Come first and wash—'

He gave her a long look and saw her bite her lip.

'Aye,' he said, still watching her narrowly. 'Aye, I'll wash first.' He decided to see Beta alone later, and so he went through to the big wash house across the yard. It was open on one side to the weather for here all the washing and scouring was done. In the centre of the floor stood a large

42

tub of water, steaming gently. He sat down upon a stool and began slowly to unwind the crossgartering from his cloth hosen, and saw the primroses on his breast all withered and drooping on their thin stems like hanged men. He threw them down under the scullions' feet as they ran hither and yon fetching screens and lengths of linen and soft cloths to wash him with. One of the pages was set to help him undress for Sir Richard, with his customary thought, had sent his man to rest. My lady fetched down jars of herbs from the outside pantry and strewed them on the water, and last of all, she poured in liquid from a little pot for – 'It will take away your aches,' she said. 'Hollyhock and mallow and St John's wort I've boiled with green oats,' and she looked at at him placatingly but he only turned away his face and spoke sharply to the boy, telling him to have a care of his leg, for the wound he got years ago had never healed properly.

So they put the stool upon a large stone flag and spread a cloth on it and sat him there, and then washed him carefully, first his face and chest and back and then his legs and belly, and when all was done he was rubbed down with coarse linen. Lady Maud had brought his best gown of fine, dark green wool, worn thin in places but still handsome, and when he put on his girdle of plaited gold with its hanging purse, she thought he was surely the most comely man in the neighbourhood, with his thin, hawk nose and the dark hair just beginning to be threaded with silver.

'Come then, my lord,' she said. 'The feast of welcome awaits you.'

And so at last they ate, all at the one board, and Sir Richard brought out the bag of salt he had kept and guarded for many a long month, and a silken veil that he had got for Lady Maud; but Beta's gift he left in the purse that hung at his girdle. These things he had had from a Jew at a great price (all but the salt – that was plunder).

After the meal his men went off in twos and threes to their

43

own hearths, except Adam who sat on by the fire with his wife, very quiet. Her name was Mold and she was a dumpy little woman with no teeth, though she was not so old. She kept pressing her knuckles to her lips and making a soft hiccuping sound and the baron was moved with pity for her; then he felt uncomfortable because it occurred to him that she might blame him for the loss of her son. He sat and watched them for a while; at last he rose and announced in a voice that was much too hearty that he was tired and would go now to his couch.

'Order Beta to my chamber,' he said in a low tone to his wife and she stared at him, surprised and silently resentful as he went past her to the small, screened-off space at the far end of the hall. Here was his marriage bed, the only private place in his whole house.

This is a fine homecoming, he thought, as he opened the great coffer at the end of the bed and rooted about within. Things are never as we expect. If she is feeding a babe – and his thought trailed away into bad humour. All the promise of the day seemed spoiled. It was unthinkable that Beta should remain unwed upon his own manor and yet he would not – could not – marry her to one who would not accept his prior rights. Unless – appalling thought – the child were not his own. But if it were not Beta would even now be married to the father.

There was a sound behind him and he turned to see her standing there. She was fatter, he thought, and her clothes soiled with kitchen work, but she was the same Beta with her warm blue eyes and thick fair brows, now drawn together in a frowning, worried look. In her arms she held a bundle. Wordlessly, she offered it to him and the gesture told him all he wished to know. He smiled and drew her forward and together they bent over the sleeping child, and so they stood when Lady Maud panted over the threshold. They neither heard her come nor go, so lost were they in each other and the child.

44

'What is her name?' said Sir Richard, very soft. He thought that he had never seen such perfect little hands, plumply clenched, nor such a beautifully shaped skull. He stroked it with his hard, dark forefinger and gently took the babe and held it in his arms.

'I call her Cicely. In very truth, I knew not what to do. But my lady was not at all unkind to me—'

Not unkind! he thought, to let her slave in the hot kitchens with the naked scullions around. He sucked in a hard breath. 'Speak not of her!' he said harshly, and then, 'I must find you a husband, Beta. Who shall it be?'

Her lower lip dropped down and she looked at him in such a way that, forgetting the child upon his knees, he half rose. Carefully, he laid it on the bed and took her in his arms.

'Marry you must,' he urged, 'if only to silence Sir Priest and my lady wife. Nothing will be changed between us – that is why we must consider carefully whom you can marry.'

She pressed her face against his shoulder. At last she said in a muffled voice, 'Warin is lately widowed.'

'Yes,' he said, slowly, 'Warin the miller. He is not young, is he?'

She shook her head while he stood thinking. Warin had a grown son of his dead wife and he would likely be amenable, especially if that son were given his freedom from villeinage.

'I will tell him tomorrow, then,' he said, and suddenly stopped short. 'I'd near forgot, love. I have a gift for you.' He smiled at her. 'I will exchange it for this gift of yours, though there is nothing in the world I could give of the same value.' He felt in his purse and laid in her hands a little bag of silken stuff tied at the neck with a cord. 'They came from London, and before that from across the sea, from Eastern lands.'

She looked at him, soft-eyed, and untied the cord. On her

hand lay a pair of earrings, very beautiful in gold, each with a shining blue stone half the size of her thumb nail, and the setting around them like a tiny gold frill.

'Oh,' she whispered, 'they are too fine for me. So fair and fine! They are jewels that a queen might wear.'

'They are the colour of your eyes. Ah, but I've missed you —' and he began kissing her and nuzzling her neck until the babe awoke with a long wail which startled them so that they sprang apart and stared at each other.

'Go then, and take the babe,' he said reluctantly, 'but not to the kitchens! Go without and sleep behind the screen where you used to. I shall have to spend tonight in my lady's bed' – and he made a grimace of distaste.

Later, when he was undressed and lying in the goose-feather bed he suddenly thought, I have a girl again, and smiled a long slow smile.

Lady Maud sat brushing her own hair and watching him.

'Did she tell you the name of the father?' she enquired coldly.

'I know the name.' In spite of himself he could not sound other than cheerful. 'I shall marry her off pretty soon.'

After she had got into bed Lady Maud lay awake waiting a long time but he turned and twisted about, and at length heaved himself over with his back to her and she could tell by his even breathing that he slept. He uses me very ill, she thought. It was not for him to use me thus that my father married me to him. Though she thought about it for what seemed hours, she could not conceive where she was at fault.

Only Beta lay awake until the horned moon rose towards dawn and the birds began to sing.

While the baron was breaking the morning fast in the hall the following day Adam Ide came to him to beg leave

46

for his wife to be excused from waiting upon Lady Maud.

'She's overdone with grief,' he said, shuffling his feet in the rushes which sent up a tired and mouldy smell, and would not look at his lord.

Sir Richard shrugged mentally. Doubtless, they all know the tale by now, he thought. Well, I am master here and shall outface them all. Underneath, he still felt the curious content that had come to him when he first saw the child.

'Think on it no more, Adam. My lady will understand.'

'It's not that she does not wish to serve my lady—'

'She will understand,' said the baron gently, hoping it was the truth; Maud was unaccountable at times.

Adam twisted his Phrygian cap between his hands. 'Will we look over the armoury today? There's a mort of rubbish in there—'

Sir Richard nodded; he understood Adam's need to escape from his wife for a time. 'But I must see the bailiff first. Fifteen months away is a long time and I know not how we stand with foodstocks.'

He stood up and laid a hand on Adam's shoulder. 'You did explain about John's death? That no one was at fault?'

'She's not reproached me – almost I'd be happier if she did. She's too quiet.' And Adam sighed and looked down at his calloused hands still twisting his cap, as though he saw them for the first time. He blinked a little and then said, 'She's gone to arrange for his obit.'

'Ah yes. I will give a mark of silver to pay for oil and candles for his Masses.'

He thought, perhaps later when Duke Henry is King in truth, I will ask the Bishop to confirm the status of my chapel here in Williton and perhaps get a younger priest, one with some education. Certainly he will not approve the hereditary succession of the parsons here. All this one thinks of is his glebe and who can wonder with three children to feed. A young priest who will abide by the rule that the clergy should be celibate – these English cling to their old

47

ways – and he gazed vaguely across the hall to the great fire-place where the smoke was billowing back in gusts. The chimney was too short; it was an innovation when the old baron built, and it ran out sideways through the wall.

Adam watched him for a moment and then went away; Sir Richard noticed that he suddenly looked quite old. When he had finished his eggs and collops he sat awhile and picked his teeth with a small silver prong which he carried in his purse, then he went to the door and looked across the yard to the bailiff's office where the lists of stores were kept.

Spring seemed to have retreated again; the sky was white but a line of little dark clouds was drifting out of the west like puffs of dirty smoke. In the dusty office the bailiff was waiting, a tall, thin, vulpine man called Herluin. He was the son of a villein on the manor and his early promise had been rewarded by an education from the monks. He was not nearly so clever as he fancied, but he was a good enough scribe and accountant for the baron's purposes.

He had spread out the rolls, pinning down their corners with a rubbing stone, and was eager to show Sir Richard how many of his villeins had paid their tallage and done their day labour, but all his lord was interested in at the moment was the state of his stores.

'It was a good harvest last year, was it not? How many sacks of flour are in the granary? How many salted beeves are left? Come, man, these are the things I wish to know, not how old Bartholomew still owes me labour because he played truant to go poaching on my rights of warren.'

Herluin removed the stones and the rolls wound up like springs. Silently, but with an injured air, he delved about in the chest and came up with a sheepskin, much scraped and rewritten. He began to list the numbers of sacks of wheat, barley and oats, running his finger down the column, and Sir Richard listened carefully, for he could read only slowly and with difficulty.

'We have plenty, then, and to spare. You sold some of the

48

harvest after Christmas? Well, we'll have an accounting of the silver later.'

He rose to his feet; now that his mind was easy regarding the stores, he was impatient to be off to see Warin the miller. Since the mill was his property and all his people bound to pay a fee for the milling of their grain, it would not look odd for him to call there so soon after his homecoming. Even the miller himself would think he had come to check on who among the villeins was slyly milling with a hand quern and evading the dues, and he could lead around to the subject of matrimony as they talked.

As the groom helped him up into the saddle a few spits of rain began to fall, and by the time he reached the millstream it was coming down in torrents. Warin heard the horse on the stony path and came out to greet him, his son Turbert peering over his shoulder.

'Come, lad, get my horse in the dry and rub him down,' called the baron, and shoving back his hood, ducked through the low door. Within, the noise of the rushing water blended with the clanking of the wheel so that he made signs to the miller that he wished to go aloft, and Warin went before him backwards up the spiral stair, surprisingly nimble for a man his age and weight.

When they reached the upper room and could hear each other speak the baron flung off his cloak, black patched with wet upon the shoulders, spraying raindrops everywhere.

'You'll not be sorry to see the rain,' he remarked. 'It will turn the wheel more merrily.' He spoke, as always to his people, in their own tongue which he had learnt at his nurse's knee.

'Aye, it will, my lord – not that I'm busy with milling. They don't bring much this time of year and it will get less, come next harvest time. There's one or two I've suspicioned don't bring me half the grain they should but I've took note of their names and have it all up here.' He tapped his fore-head and started to list the offenders, watching his lord with

49

small, bright eyes that darted here and there and missed very little.

After a time, Sir Richard began to tell him of his own doings, and of the new kind of mill he had heard about that had huge vanes which were driven by the wind, but Warin thought this newfangled and swore that it would never take the place of an honest water mill. 'Water will be there all the time but wind come and go with no explaining,' he said, 'and what if the air be still just after harvest which do be so oftener than not.'

Then the baron asked him if he were not lonely since his wife's death, with only his boy about the place; but the miller grinned and tapped his nose saying that he was not short of a female to pleasure him did he feel like it. Afterwards he could come home to peace and quiet and no nagging woman's tongue to bother him, though he did agree that Turbert was no cook. Lest he should refuse the offer of a wife, Sir Richard baldly told him that he had decided (as he had a perfect right to do) that he should marry Beta.

The miller's beady eyes flickered a little but he did not try to argue. He knew that Williton was lucky in having a lord who did not force his will upon his people in minor matters. He knew, too, that he had allowed his tongue to run away with him in admitting to fornication; it would be the death of him yet. He decided to make the best of it.

Certainly he'd marry anywhere to please his lord, he said.

There was a child to go along with her, his lord said, and no villein's child, neither. The miller said he took his meaning and then continued delicately, 'And will your lordship be visiting the mill regular?'

'I shall,' said Sir Richard, seeing it was useless to equivocate. 'The child will pass as yours, miller, but see you do not work her nor her mother beyond the lightest tasks. When the time comes for her to marry, I will see to it. I will call on the priest on my way home and arrange for you to marry after

Easter. Say no word of this to any man and you shall not lose by it.'

Because he was still feeling a faint distaste about the interview when he got home, he did not seek out Beta nor his wife but went up into the armoury with Adam and told him that Beta was to wed with Warin the miller. Adam said nothing except, 'Those goose wings we had for fletching is all rot to nothing', and the baron was glad enough to turn his attention to the state of his weapons and forget the imagined reproaches of his womenfolk.

'This old targe o' boiled leather's no use at all,' muttered Adam. 'There's a week's work in here for any man – look here, my lord, at the blade of this sword, thick with rust – and this crossbow, there's two nuts missing off it.' He scrabbled about on the dirty floor, and then peered up at Sir Richard through the grey thickets of his eyebrows. 'So it was Warin Miller, was it?' he said.

To Adam Ide, Sir Richard was as close as he could be to any man; they had been boys together, and Adam had dragged his master out of the swollen Willow Brook at Bulwick when he was ten years old. Since then, there had been an unbreakable bond between them, so now he said, 'Nay, Adam, miller's to marry her for a convenience. The child's mine own but I'll not have my lady know if I can help it. I'll not give her a stick to beat me with again.' His face darkened.

'Women's tongues,' said Adam, and they looked at each other. 'She'll guess, though,' he added.

'Guessing's one thing, knowledge another,' returned the baron, 'and I'm tired of hearing how her brothers would avenge her had they lived. Ever since we married – and all the saints bear witness that it was no choice of mine – she's said that I neglect her.'

'Aye, freemen are luckier than nobles that way – we marry where we please. My old Mold was the prettiest girl in this place.'

'Certainly,' said the baron, 'that she was,' But when he tried to recall Mold in her youth, he could not remember her at all.

The end of April and all of May were wet. Beta married Warin in the church porch at Watchet while the rain hissed down and bubbled and gurgled among the pinkish stones of the road outside. But when June came in hot and sunny, anxious faces cleared; the weather would be kind for the haysel. The villeins, who had crept about their tasks under dripping bits of sackcloth, turned sunbrowned and cheerful overnight.

The baron sent off Simon Rutele, his other captain, and a handful of archers to escort his sons home from Devon. Not that he had any real desire to see them but Lady Maud was becoming importunate. According to de Tracy, their knightly training was completed but they must wait their turn for the full ceremony of knighthood. In these latter days, when the saints slept in England, it had gone often enough by default and there were many knights, dubbed on the field of battle, who had never kept their vigil.

Reynold's mother, at least, looked forward to his return, and her anticipation had diverted her mind from the baron's coldness towards her; of late they hardly spoke at all and Sir Richard was content with the situation for it left him free to ride to the mill as often as he pleased. Since he had seen the child his feelings for Beta had undergone a change; he did not love her less but his love was quieter, less demanding; in short, Cicely had pushed Beta from the place she had always held in his heart. She grew more bewitching by the day in her father's eyes, and could already creep on all-fours, thus proving Beta's contention that swaddling bands were unnecessary. The lack of them had worried the baron at first, but Beta had been firm that no villein's child wore them, and those who got enough to eat always grew strong.

'Her legs will not grow straight,' he had objected and Beta, who was beginning to be irritated by his preoccupation with her daughter, had said tartly that that would not matter anyway, for no one but a husband would ever see them.

After his visit to the mill on a day towards Lammastide he decided to go down to his own fields and overlook the haymaking. It was gloriously hot; the sky of deepest blue was without a cloud and the big willow cast a perfect reflection in the still water of the mill pool.

When he came into the manor field, he saw that it was already half rough stubble and a crowd of women were forking up hay into a wain. Only three men were scything, swaying with the fast, rhythmic strokes, and he smiled wryly as he realised that most of the villeins had sent their wives and daughters to do the boon work while they and their able-bodied sons worked on their own strips. The women worked with their skirts looped up over their girdles, showing knotted, stringy legs, and he vowed to himself that his own daughter should never work so when she was grown. Perhaps, by then he could openly acknowledge her before the world; perhaps, by then Maud would – He pushed the thought away before it rose fully into his consciousness.

He had left his wife that morning in one of her rare, energetic moods; she had been up before dawn, chivvying the maids and men to light up the fires under the great cauldrons and make all preparations for washing day. By the time he left the house it had all been well under way; the ropes strung across the yard in readiness, the sheets steeped in lye and the cauldrons boiling and bubbling with the faint, unpleasant stench of nettle soap. It would be pleasant to sleep in a fresh smelling bed; sometimes he wished it happened more often than once a year. He had ventured to say so on one occasion, and Maud had taken great offence and informed him that her own father had never slept between sheets in his life, and to her knowledge

53

none of his coverlets had ever been washed. 'Belike,' she had concluded with a sarcasm that silenced him, 'you would also have me wash and boil your gowns?'

He went slowly along the length of the hayfield, walking on the narrow, grassy baulk that separated it from the acre or two of pulses, and came to his fields of wintersown corn, mostly wheat growing tall and healthy, but with a stand of rye at the end where the ground began to rise and the soil was poor and acid. He could not feel the faintest breeze but a tremulous line of darker green wavered across the cornfield like the last, dying ripple in a pool. He stood awhile, filled with a vast contentment compounded of the beauty of the day, the vigour of the crops, and something else that now lurked always below the threshold of his mind – a feeling of destiny fulfilled, as though his unexpected child had made of him a man complete. Then he heaved a deep sigh as though recollecting himself, and so came back to the hayfield and sat in the shade at the edge where a hawthorn bush grew, and a clump of dog roses spattered with pale, evanescent flowers.

After a time the bailiff, who was checking which of the villeins had put in an appearance, came and sat beside him; they drank ale together from his bottle.

'It's Manor Court next week,' he said, wiping his mouth with the back of his hand. 'That lass there, with her skirts hitched up to her arse will be haled up afore you, my lord. She's been fornicating again and we'll be lucky to get the leyrwite out of her father for he's a shiftless clod.'

'Who is she?' said the baron, screwing up his eyes for the hayfield shimmered in the heat.

'It's that Agnes, the eldest of Durand the carter's brood. Married she should be; she's full fourteen and hot for a man. The priest railed at her once and she laughed in his face and asked whose children those were in his garden. 'I have no child, Sir Priest,' she said, and then the priest's

54

wife came out and they fell to tearing each other's hair. She's a saucy wench,' he concluded dourly.

'Is not Durand my serf? We'll find a husband for her. That kind of wench causes trouble among the married men.'

'I have a list of offences as long as your arm,' said Herluin with a kind of grim satisfaction, 'and it will take all day to hear them. They've had it too easy of late, what with all the lords and barons being off to the wars.'

'Things will settle now that the Duke is Stephen's heir. These last months have been peaceful enough.'

'Oh aye, so far,' said the bailiff and sniffed loudly. He was by nature not so much pessimistic as hopeful of things going amiss.

He looked up then, his eyes narrowed against the sun. 'Who comes?' he said, for he had seen the glint and flash of steel in the company of men who rode across the shoulder of the hill against the sky.

The baron gazed a moment, then sprang up. 'It's Simon Rutele back with the boys,' he exclaimed, and then they heard a horn blow back at the house, for the lookout too had seen the band approaching.

Sir Richard hurried across the common with long steady strides. He watched them coming, Simon at the head grinning all over his face, and behind him those two young men with shoulders wider than his own. They slid off their horses and louted down to him but he raised them up, one on each arm, and kissed them with a rush of pride that astonished him. From the courtyard came shouts of excitement and then a whole crowd of serving men and wenches poured out towards the wooden bridge that spanned the moat, only to drop back respectfully as they saw the baron with the new arrivals.

Last of all, Lady Maud came panting, her sleeves pushed up and her head veil all askew. She alone crossed the bridge, weeping with joy, and crying incoherently upon the saints clasped her son in her arms. Robert stood to one side and watched her; the baron watched him but could detect nothing in his face beyond happiness in the moment. When Reynold finally disengaged himself from his mother's fervent embraces, Robert stepped forward to salute her with an alacrity that turned her cheeks pink with pleasure. As she kissed him, Richard thought, God be praised! She will accept him fully at last, but with his relief came a pang as he realised that now he could never acknowledge his new child without re-opening those old sores.

Next day, Reynold and Robert Fitzurse awoke early. Robert, in fact, had lain awake for some time while the milky pre-dawn light filtered into the hall through an unshuttered window and when he heard the rustling of the straw pallet next to his own as his brother turned and grunted, he whispered. 'Are you awake, Reynold?'

Reynold gave a jaw-cracking yawn and heaved over. 'Is it morning?'

'Aye. Come, let's creep out into the yard.'

'Give me a hand to tie my points,' and Reynold groped around in the rushes for his chausses, dropped where he had discarded them the night before. 'Faugh, this place is not very sweet! There's dogs' turds in the rushes. My mother does not stand over the house servants like de Tracy's lady. They need changing.'

'Come on!' hissed Robert who was already at the door.

'Rogue! You've not helped me!' Reynold thrust his feet anyhow into his boots while he dragged his tunic over his head and, holding up his chausses, staggered into the yard. The sky glowed in the east and dew lay thick on everything. Once his brother had poured a bucket of water over his head, he began to wake up and look about him.

'This is a small place after de Tracy's,' he said at length.

'It's home,' said Robert. 'I am glad to be back – at least,' he added with some diffidence, 'for a time'. Like other landless younger sons, Robert was unsure of his place and it would not do to upset the unpredictable Reynold. 'Your mother was pleased to see you,' he continued quickly. 'Did you notice, Reynold, that our father scarce spake with her?'

'And what man would speak with a woman when there are men to speak with?'

'Nay, but – Baron de Tracy always spoke with his lady. Do you not remember how at supper they would have their heads together at the high table? He even used to ask her sometimes what he should do.'

'He was petticoat-ridden,' said Reynold, and laughed his braying laugh.

'No, he was not. He was a proper man. I used to think it was as if his lady were his friend' – and Robert stopped short, feeling foolish at voicing a thought so palpably absurd.

Reynold laughed louder than ever. 'You are a fool, sure enough, brother, if you think that. A man does not marry to gain a friend – unless it be his wife's brother or father. Women are not capable of friendship, they are for one purpose only . . .' His laugh turned into a titter. 'How you could think—'

'Aye, well, that's enough,' snapped Robert, rather red about the ears, but Reynold thought the joke too good to finish there and kept leaping about, making feinting passes at his brother and explaining to him with a wealth of detail the precise difference in the functions of wives and friends.

Robert endured it for a time but at last he became angry and being possessed of a great deal more intelligence than his tormentor, told him in specific terms the difference between Baron de Tracy and Reynold himself. After this, the altercation became ugly and pretty soon they began to scuffle and then to fight in grim and deadly earnest. Since they were much of a size they were well matched and managed to inflict an appreciable amount of damage on each other.

57

Suddenly there was a violent wrench at Robert's hair and his father's walking-staff came down with shattering effect upon his rump. Robert did not make a sound except a grunt as the breath left him for it was evident that the baron was in a towering rage. When he had finished with his younger son, he turned his attention to Reynold and stirred him none too gently in the ribs with the toe of his boot. Reynold gave a wavering moan and tried to sit up; it was obvious he had got the worst of the encounter but that did not save him a thrashing too.

The handful of men who were with the baron had withdrawn a little to the well. One of them was winding up buckets of water; Robert could hear the windlass creaking. Just the same, he was surprised when he was drenched with the contents of one of the buckets and sat up, gasping and spluttering, wiping blood and water from his face.

'This is a fine start to your first day home! Or perhaps you begin every day thus!' The baron's voice was the more terrifying for its quietness. 'Understand me, my sons. What you did at de Tracy's, I care not, but here you will not brawl together like two unruly dogs! Nay, but you shall try your bellicosity against the young squires under the direction of my master-at-arms – with swords, not fists – and it will go ill with you if you do not conduct yourselves as candidates for knighthood should! And as for you' – he turned directly to Robert, pitching his voice even lower – 'if you lay hands again upon my lady's son, you shall suffer for it. What kind of fool are you?'

Robert looked straight back at him, his crest of black hair wet and ruffled so that it sprang into tight little curls, and his eyes, patched with blue and grey and gold, wide and half defiant, and greenish now as the sea is green from the mixture of colours therein. Reynold kept his eyes upon the ground after he had shot his father one venomous look, his usually loose, full lips drawn into a tight line.

Sir Richard was struck afresh by the likeness each of his

58

sons bore his own mother as though nothing of himself had passed to either, and he wondered if the reason for it lay in his unwillingness to give wholly of himself to either woman. Always with him there had been a reluctance, a withholding of something he sensed to be important, and he knew with bitterness that there had been more of lust than love in the making of his children. He also knew that the thought would never have occurred to any other man of his acquaintance. He dismissed the notion as fanciful, thinking of Robert, I must watch him, closely semblable as he is to his mother. In his blood runs a defiance of all authority.

He did not notice that he had not spared Reynold so much as a thought but he, ever jealous of the prerogatives of the heir, had seen the way his father's eyes had drifted indifferently past him. He thought, Old fool! He cares no more for me now than he ever did. Oddly enough, he felt no rancour towards Robert, and after the baron had gone about his business the two young men proceeded to brush each other down with all their former careless comradeship. Only Robert was left to wonder a little at the form of the baron's remark about 'my lady's son'.

That night at dinner Lady Maud questioned Robert about his eye which during the day had swelled and darkened until it was almost closed.

'It was I, mother. I hit him,' said Reynold with a triumph he could not quite hide.

His mother frowned. 'It is not seemly to fight like louts,' she said reprovingly. 'And why?'

'He said that a man could be friends with a woman and I said he was wrong. Then we fought,' returned Reynold simply, forgetting both the beginning and the end of the dispute.

Sir Richard looked up sharply from his wine cup.

'It's true that Baron de Tracy's lady is his friend,' said Robert obstinately.

'How so?' asked the baron.

'They talked as friends. I heard them often.'

'That is no reason to fight,' said Lady Maud. 'Not that I ever heard of such a thing. It is an unusual man who will listen to his wife,' and she pressed her lips so hard together that she had difficulty in sipping her wine.

'A lucky man who has a wife worth listening to,' said the baron under his breath to Adam.

His lady's colour rose. She addressed herself to Adam, too. 'All of us do know,' she said, 'that there are men who prefer the prating of harlots—' She turned her head and looked directly at the baron. 'Did you visit the mill today, husband?'

There was a deathly silence, and Reynold stared at Robert blankly.

'No, why should I?' His voice was loud in the hush.

Lady Maud ducked her head and muttered in her dish but the fierce whisper was audible to all. 'To see your whore and your child,' she hissed.

Sir Richard stood up, white with rage, and the denial was out before he realised it. 'She is none of mine!' he shouted.

Lady Maud lifted her head. Her face was very red but she gazed at her husband without a tremor. 'We shall remember your words, my lord,' she said.

The baron stood straight and stiff as stone. He had remembered a fisherman called Peter.

The Fitzurse boys puzzled over that scene for days, until Reynold, who lacked his father's sensitivity, began asking questions around the kitchens and the stables. From Adam he received the curtest of refusals to discuss the baron's affairs, at which he mentally marked the captain of archers as his father's man at all costs, but one or two others were more forthcoming on the principle that it is always well to be on the right side of the heir. Neither was the bailiff any help to him for he thought him an arrogant young whelp, and a fine quarrel developed in the office after Herluin denied him a sight of the tenants' rolls.

The baron heard the shouting as he rode into the court and he fetched Reynold a buffet to the head before he knew he was there. 'You're not master here, you knave,' he said, 'you have yet to attain manhood. Not yet knighted! Why did not de Tracy knight you before ever you came home? There's a tale there, I warrant – aye, and lay not the blame at your brother's door!' This with another thump to the head, for Reynold had begun to mutter Robert's name. 'Out with you!' – and he thrust him out of the door; but Reynold had seen the triumphing look on Herluin's face, and he made a vow to get even with the bailiff – aye, and with his father, too, before the year had rolled round.

He was sitting in the stables, nursing a sore ear and a sorer pride when Robert found him.

'Here you are, then! What's to do? There's our father stamping round with a face like thunder and talk of having you off again, and your mother weeping and saying he's but thought of it to spite her. . . . What's amiss?'

'That swinish villein the bailiff would not give me a sight of the rolls. For why should I not see? It will all be mine one day. He misliked it because I spoke of miller's wife. Down his long nose he looked and said that was the baron's business and none of mine. His business! Aye, she's his whore right enough and so he shames my mother in her own house. I'll shorten that nose for him when I'm lord here!'

Robert realised the nose-cropping threat was directed at Herluin and murmured pacifically, 'It will do no good to mell in it. You'll have to plead pardon for interfering.'

'That can wait! I'm for a ride now. Will you come with me?' He grabbed one of the shaggy-coated work horses by its long mane and led it to the door, peering out to see if the coast were clear.

'Jesu, you're a hog for trouble. Still, I'll come, but you may take your punishment alone, I'll know nothing of it.'

Once they were past the look-out and through the gate, they galloped the horses down the stony track and past the

61

wooden hut that served as a chapel, out of Williton and towards the sea. The weather still held fair and the afternoon sun was warm on their backs. Doniford stream was still full, leaping and sparkling over its pebbled bed and swaying the cresses and water forget-me-nots with the force of its passage, but they did not stay with it until it reached the sea; they bore off to the left, towards Watchet, making for the low cliffs.

They dismounted in a hollow where the short turf was spattered with pink clumps of thrift, and Reynold hobbled his horse with his girdle and went near the cliff edge and there lay down, pulling at the flowers and throwing the little cushiony heads towards the sea. Down below, the sea lay calm, all striped with blue and grey and melting away into a bar of darker blue at the Welsh coast. Robert watched him for a while for he did not seem disposed to talk and at length went and sat beside him and gazed alone to where Watchet harbour hid itself behind the swelling ground.

'It was here,' he said, 'that St Decuman came floating across from Wales on his cloak.'

'Aye,' said Reynold and rolled over and turned his face up to the blue sky.

'And here came the marauding Danes and burnt the port.'

'Old tales,' said Reynold, 'past and done.'

'Did you ever hear of how a heathen Dane struck off the head of St Decuman, and he – the saint – picked up his head and washed it decently and then composed himself for his eternal rest with it beside him?'

Reynold raised himself and stared at his brother. 'Why tell me tales of long-dead saints? Rather tell me of that Princess Nesta who lived in Wales and her many lovers. Would I could meet one like her!' He wet his lips and grinned, and when Robert did not answer, turned on him with some truculence. 'You're not so pure as you would have us all believe!'

Robert shrugged, but now Reynold was set upon goading him. He knew that Robert was unostentatiously devout and it irritated him profoundly. He could not find words scathing enough to express his sudden furious contempt so he fell back on his usual method of heavy jeering.

'Washed his head!' he said. 'You would believe anything.'

'It was a miracle.'

'Pah!' said Reynold, and made a snatching motion, then opened his hand and showed Robert the shattered remains of a butterfly, like a smear of gold dust across his palm. 'That for your miracles!'

'I know not why I came with you,' said Robert. 'When you are angry, all God's creation must suffer for it.' And under his brother's lowering gaze, he mounted his horse again and rode away without a backward look.

When he had gone, Reynold rubbed his palm clean on his jerkin. Resentment against his brother burned in him now, the more bitter because he could not fathom the reason. He untied the girdle from the horse's legs and when he mounted, he whacked it viciously across the neck. Then he rode off in the opposite direction.

III

August 1154

In faraway Suffolk it was raining. It had rained for three weeks; hard, determined rain that flattened the corn and filled the ditches. The roads were ankle deep in mud and the pot holes, brimming with soupy, yellow water, were traps for the unwary. In the woods, all was silence except for the steady dripping of the trees.

Ulf and his children sheltered from the downpour as best they could though even in the hut the floor was thick mud. They had no fire for no one had expected weeks of rain in summer and the dry tinder had been left outside uncovered. Hikenai and the boys cowered away from their father on the side of the hut where the roof leaked, for his temper grew worse as one drenching day succeeded another.

Hikenai was his latest victim and the beating she had just received had left her both sore and angry; she could not see how she was at fault because they had no dinner. The harvest would be ruined unless the sun shone and all her little spells and incantations would not mend it. They had only scraped through last winter by the grace of God, for Count Eustace's last fling had ensured that there was no surplus to be sold in the surrounding countryside and those who had lost their crops had starved when the monks' supplies ran out. In spite of the lack of food, Hikenai had grown a full two inches in the last year and her womanhood had come upon her.

She had seen the kindly pedlar several times; in fact, she took good care to do so for he always shared his meal with her. He had told her his name was Benjamin for 'he was the youngest and best favoured of all his mother's brood', he said, grinning, and she had stared at him in wonderment for she took him to be a very ugly little man. But it was evident he did not think so and so she had smiled upon him with kindness and a little pity which emboldened him to pat her hand and move up closer to her. Another time he suggested that she travel with him and help to sell his wares, mainly cheap little pins and ribbons, but that had made her nervous and he said no more. Now, though, because she was angry with her father and very hungry, she thought of him again and of the fact that tomorrow was market day at St Edmundsbury.

Very early next morning she heard Ulf go out to look at his snares. He let the pigs out, too, and she thought it must have stopped raining. Soon after she rose quietly while the boys still slept and wrapped herself in a rough, hairy cloak; the old cow tethered at the foot of her pallet gazed at her with sad, gentle eyes and lowed mournfully. She pushed past and looked into the stew-pot on the dead fire; in the bottom was a spoonful or two of liquid with flakes of congealed grease floating on top. Her empty stomach heaved. She went to the door and looked out.

It had stopped raining but the sky was dark and leaden and a chilly wind shook cold drops from the trees. She stared across the assart at the ruined wheat, and a spasm of anger shook her. She went back into the hut and reaching into the low roof, took down some bunches of dried herbs; also a rough clay figure shaped to the likeness of a man, and with this in her hand, she scattered some of the herbs around the sleeping boys and some around the hearthstone and the doorsill. Then she spoke a few phrases in a

65

heathenish tongue and signed the door with a sign that no Christian would have recognised. Having done all she could to protect those she was leaving, she put the clay figurine in a basket and went. She had never paused to wonder what the words meant, or whether they were words at all – her mother had taught her the sounds long ago, and to her they were no more mysterious than the foreign words that the priest spoke at Mass.

It was still early when she reached St Edmundsbury and the rain had begun again. She avoided the monastery and found herself a comparatively dry corner against the inn, from where she could watch the stalls and hucksters. As the morning wore on and there was no sign of Benjy, she had a moment of doubt which deepened into a fear that he would not come at all. So when at last she did see him, bowed down under his wet pack, she ran to meet him with a look of such joy and relief that he was flattered beyond measure.

They sat together in the dirty inn and steamed gently by the fire while she told her tale of woe. He watched her narrowly and she was seized by a fear that he would after all refuse to take her with him. But she misinterpreted his look; he was only thinking how pretty she was with the fair tendrils of hair escaping from her hood and her eyes ablaze with eagerness.

'And do you belong to no man?' he asked her.

'To no man but my father, and he beats me.'

'Not to no lord?'

She hesitated, uncertain.

'Is not your father a serf?'

She was silent. He grinned at her. 'No need to worry.' His voice was triumphant. 'You are a bastard.'

'That I am not,' she said indignantly.

'Then you're a fool. See here, lass, no bastard is a serf. All bastards are born free. How could it be other when none can know the sire's degree? Sure, you are a bastard like myself, and free like me. No man can order my coming or going. What say you?'

She raised her head and stared at him; then she looked anxiously round the inn. 'We must not stay in these parts,' she whispered.

'We'll not. I'm away into Essex where it never rains.'

'Does it not?' she said wonderingly, and he laughed and squeezed her hand and kissed her for he was rather above himself, this being his first real success with a woman, though he was nearer to thirty years old than twenty. As for Hikenai, she thought that his breath stank but that she could endure for the sake of a full belly.

That afternoon they left St Edmundsbury, along with a group of other travellers; Hikenai rode on the little grey donkey with the laden panniers and Benjy trudged alongside in the mud. As they went, the clouds began to clear and they passed southwards in a watery golden glow that touched the world with magic. When they came to the church where the saint's bones lay, she saw him bow his head and cross himself; her hand crept into her basket and covered her talisman but she made no other move. Every now and again, he would cast a covert glance at her but she stared straight ahead so that all he could see was her pure, clear profile, like a cameo against the dark stuff of her hood.

After a bit, a fat, middle-aged matron on a very small palfrey came up alongside and began to talk to Hikenai; she was going to her married daughter's, she said, for the girl would soon be lying-in and this was her first child. It were well they should all keep together for fear of robbers when they reached the forest. She looked at Benjy searchingly and tried to push her fingers down the pannier nearest her, but Benjy dragged at the donkey so that he kicked and fell out of step; the fat matron was not a whit put out but brought her palfrey up alongside again and continued her monologue.

67

Nor would she leave them when they came to the poor inn where they would lie that night. 'It will be better for your young wife to share my bed than to go into the stables with you and the men,' she said firmly, and bore away Hikenai, who went unresisting.

Benjy wondered if Hikenai would tell her they were not man and wife; he doubted it for the good matron's own flow of conversation would have borne down all but the most determined gossip. In any case, he had every intention of marrying her as soon as they had put enough distance between them and her people and could find a priest who would not ask too many questions. He lay in the straw and scratched, and thought jealously of that fat old woman lying next to Hikenai. He consoled himself, though, with the knowledge that tomorrow sometime they must branch off the road at Haverhill and take the winding track to the Benedictine Convent at Castle Hedingham where he, with his wares, had long been welcomed as a diversion in the dull lives of the good Ladies. He made up his mind to keep Hikenai out of sight; she would rouse too much interest, and if word came later of a hue and cry for her. . . . He fell asleep.

The next morning the sun came out, full and strong. A little breeze was blowing, and though the ways were foul with mud underfoot, the trees had ceased to drip and tossed their branches joyously.

Hikenai had pushed back her hood and her hair, the colour of pale, clear honey, hung on her shoulders except when the wind pulled at it, teasing and flinging it about. Benjy watched and longed to run his fingers through it. Silently he delved into his pack and brought out a piece of silken ribbon and held it out to her.

Her face lit up and she tied a careful knot; then she held the tress before her to admire it, turning her head from side to side with a delighted smile. She sat in the sunshine and he saw that her arm was all gilded with fine, gold hairs,

68

her long lashes, too, when she looked down were golden, and when she glanced up at him, he noticed that her curiously slanting eyes were a darker shade of the same colour. She had the waxen skin and broad cheekbones of the true Saxon, but there was something else in her face – a strange alluring quality; a passive gentleness, as though she would accept whatever life might offer. Perhaps it lay in the tender droop of her lips when her face was in repose; whatever it was, it gave to her an air of mystery that enchanted Benjy.

'It's a love knot you have tied,' he said at length for her long silences disconcerted him.

She said nothing but only went on admiring her ribbon. They sat alone upon a grassy bank, that being higher than the rest was comparatively dry; the others of the party had gone on an hour before. Her woven basket lay beside her and idly he probed within it, curious to see what she possessed. Her face changed as she saw him.

'Do not touch!' she said, and her voice was so sharp that he jumped but it was too late, his fingers had already closed on the talisman, and he slowly drew it out and looked at it. His face changed too, and he dropped the thing as though it were hot and stared at her. All the sweet gentleness had gone from her expression; she glared at him as if he were her enemy.

'I have seen that before,' he said, 'or something like it. It is no Christian thing.'

She turned away her head and would not look at him. Uneasiness filled him.

'Tell me!' he said. 'Is it to do with the old religion? There are great figures like that, cut in the chalk hills, far to the west.' He became indignant, thinking of his intention to marry her. 'Are you no Christian, then?' he exclaimed, and taking her by the shoulder, turned her round so that she must face him. 'Tell me! I'll not marry you if you're no Christian.'

69

'I am as truly baptised as you are,' she cried, 'As for my talisman – I know only what my mother taught me long ago. He must stand guard over the crops—' She broke off, thinking of the ruined harvest she had left. 'Perhaps it was her belief,' she continued more quietly, 'but I know none others who hold to it. It does no harm, though.'

He moved a little closer to her, staring down at the thing that lay on the ground at their feet; a crude image of a naked man with huge genitals out of all proportion to the rest of the figure. She is not so innocent, he thought, if she carries that thing along with her. A little tremor of excitement went through his loins. He gave her an ingratiating smile and slid his arm about her waist.

'Nay,' he murmured. 'No harm,' and his breath came fast. He began to mutter soft words of endearment, pressing against her. She drew back and aversion was plain upon her face. He did not see it, so blinded was he by desire, and when she tried to fight him off he exerted all his strength to hold her. But pure instinct was at work in her and her rejection of him came from a deeper source than she knew. She was as tall as he and years of unremitting toil had made her strong. In his surprise at her resistance, he stepped back a pace and she raised her arm and fetched him such a clout to the side of the head that he staggered and sat down. She stood and watched him, breathing hard. There was a long silence, broken only by the sweet singing of a blackbird in a bush.

At last he got up and tried to laugh away his humiliation.

'You are strong enough to fight off all the robbers in the forest', he told her. He rubbed his ear and went across to the donkey. With his back to her, he said, 'Is your mother then – a faery woman?'

She shrugged. 'She is long dead but some did say so.' And because she heard the nervous tremble in his voice and wished to frighten him, she added, 'They said the same of me.'

70

He was fiddling with the straps on his pack and cursed with sudden violence when the buckle prong sank into the fleshy part of his thumb. A faery! A witch! And he alone with her on the edge of the forest! He had heard talk of the old religion and its followers – it did not pay to antagonise them, people said. Hastily, he crossed himself; he was almost beginning to wish he had never laid eyes on her. Who knew but she might bespell him! And when he glanced at her across his shoulder, she was watching him with such a dark, cold look. . . .

He saw her talisman lying on the ground and a sudden spurt of anger rose in him. He put his foot upon it, grinding it down, back into the clay from which it was made. He would have snatched back the green ribbon from her hair if he had dared.

'Well, come up, then,' he said in a harsher voice than any he had yet used to her, and she got up on the donkey again.

I shall be safe from her with the Ladies in the Convent, he was thinking. And she thought with a kind of triumph, I believe he is afraid of me. She looked down at him with distaste, still chewing at his cut thumb. He was too thin and puny and the idea of wedding with him had not occurred to her. He was too old; she had thought him of her father's generation, not her own.

So they went on through the quiet greenwood, dappled with sunlight and shade. The breeze was tempered there though they could hear it still in the tops of the trees. Benjy walked in silence, swinging the cudgel he carried for fear of robbers, swiping at the bushes with it now and then. He was wondering what good this maid was to him; she would not help to sell his wares, she was too silent and did not smile enough.Why should he feed her if there were to be no commerce between them? Anyway, desire for her had left him, washed away by the new knowledge he had of her. He was sure she was no Christian, and what did he truly know of her? Only what she herself had told him – the thought struck him that she was an enchantress, sent from Old Nick himself. Sudden terror filled him and he began to hurry the donkey along but that creature would not be hurried. Benjy thumped him on the flank and the donkey, unaccustomed to such treatment, immediately sat down so that Hikenai slid off his back into the squelching ooze where he had trod. Down went one of the panniers, too, into the mud.

Furious at this further proof of the ill luck she was bringing him, Benjy started to shout; and at the sight of him, leaping and gesticulating on the muddy track like an enraged gnome, she laughed aloud, peal upon peal of delighted laughter. For Benjy, it was the last straw. He was beside himself with anger and disappointment so that he aimed blows at her and the donkey with a fine impartiality. Most of them missed but she screamed in sudden fright and the donkey kicked up his hind legs, dislodging the remaining pannier, which strewed its contents in the mud as he bolted. Hikenai curled into a ball to avoid the blows.

They ceased suddenly and she peered up to see that a big, ragged fellow had appeared from nowhere and had Benjy by the arm. In his other hand he had a great, two-handed axe. He was quite young, not much more than a boy, but there was an air of latent menace about him. He was extremely dirty. Her heart came up in her throat as she looked at him. An outlaw!

'What does here?' he said.

Neither of them said a word.

'Is she your wife?' he demanded of Benjy.

'Nay, by Blessed Saint Edmund, she's no wife of mine,' cried Benjy, finding his voice again. 'A witch she is! Sir, I am but a poor pedlar who owns nothing of value and she has brought me the most cursed ill luck! My donkey has run off. Hodden! Come back, Hodden!'

The outlaw never took his eyes off Hikenai who sat in the

mire and trembled. 'Be not deceived by her, Sir!' burst out Benjy. 'She is from the foul fiend himself.'

'I think not,' he said, and stretching out his hand, he raised her up, still looking into her eyes. 'You do not want her, then?'

'Nay, marry, I do not! Take her with my blessing.'

'That I will!' said the outlaw, and laughed. 'Stop, you!' he said to Benjy who was on all-fours gathering up his scattered gew-gaws. 'Give me those!'

'Aye, Sir, most willingly.'

'Come, then,' he said to Hikenai, stuffing Benjy's belongings into his pouch. 'My horse is near. Tell me of yourself. My name is Aelward.'

'Are you – an outlaw?'

He bowed mockingly to her. 'That am I. And you're a witch, according to our friend. I have never met a witch before but if they are all as fair as you. . . .' He laughed again. He was a most engaging rascal and his teeth were white as milk. 'How came you in his company?'

She began to tell him, and then began to cry. He put her up on the horse in front of him and comforted her, and took great pleasure in the doing of it.

'There are other women with us,' he assured her. 'We are a strong band. None shall hurt you. You shall belong to me.' He lifted her chin and looked into her face. 'I have wanted a woman a long time,' he said.

She did not answer but she felt her heart knock with fear. As they rode away she heard Benjy's forlorn calling, 'Hodden! Hodden! Come back, Hodden!' growing fainter and fainter until it died away.

November 1154–February 1155
Robert Fitzurse awoke to the pallid dawn of a November morning with the feeling that something pleasant and unaccustomed was to happen this day. Reynold was not on his pallet and there were shouts and clattering noises

from the yard. Now he remembered, today was the day they were to set off for his father's manor of Worle. Provisions were plentiful there after the harvest, they would go there to eat them up and return to Williton in time for Christmas.

Worle lay some distance off up the Severn where the great river narrowed and Wales was uncomfortably close across the water; it was too far away to reach in one day at a pace the ladies liked so they would break the journey at Stoke Courcy and spend a day or two hunting, hawking and exchanging news and gossip with their neighbour, Sir William. Robert was looking forward to seeing new faces but for some reason Lady Maud had been in a bad temper ever since the move was projected. Robert avoided her when possible; since he and Reynold had come home things had fallen out that he kept his father's company a great deal more than his brother did and he was happy to have it so in spite of Reynold's barely concealed chagrin.

Last night Shepherd, who was weather-wise, had predicted a fair day for the morrow, but when Robert looked out the court was filled with a wet, white mist through which the figures of men and horses loomed like ghosts. He flung on his cloak and hurried across to the kitchens to carve himself a slice or two of meat, feeling some slight annoyance that Reynold had not awakened him earlier.

His father and Lady Maud were there, for breakfast was a snatched meal with this early start and Robert, seeing his foster-mother's flushed, averted face thought they had been quarrelling again. He heard her say, 'So be it, then,' and then she saw him enter and fell silent. The baron's face was grim as he drank a cup of ale and he cursed aloud as he tripped on one of the dogs who shared the general excitement and dashed about under everyone's feet. Robert felt a pang of pity for Lady Maud, so fat and plain with the black eyebrows that met across her nose and gave her a dis-

74

agreeable look. Yet he was sorry for his father, too, for he knew there was no communion between them.

Also, Robert had given reign to his natural curiosity and had ridden to the mill to steal a look at his father's leman; he had watched her for a long time from his hiding place in a thicket of hazel while she went about her household tasks, and he had come back unwontedly silent and thoughtful. He was, at eighteen, of an age to begin to understand (or to think he understood) the problems of an uncongenial marriage, and his budding manhood had quickly recognised the difference between Beta and Lady Maud. Yet, somehow, the fact that his father could place a serf in the same position as his own long dead mother had outraged his deepest feelings; if anything, his sense of insult was deeper than Reynold's own. And secretly, he wondered a little at the need for such dealings in a man of his father's great age.

Now, beyond a salutation to his elders, he said nothing, but ate his fill and went out into the yard again. Slipping on the wet cobbles, he made his way to the stables and after saddling his horse, stopped to look at his new hawk. Though she was only half trained he had determined to take her in spite of Reynold's assurances that he would lose her. She was a handsome bird, and he felt a thrill of pride as he tied the jesses and clucked to her. The other horses were becoming restive but the ostlers were leading them out, and shouting to one of the lads to hand him up the hawk, Robert mounted.

And so at last they all rode out into a morning of milk-white mist, so thick that no man could see farther than the horse in front of him and little drops of moisture condensed onto the hairy cloth of their cloaks. Reynold rode beside him; he was cheerful and voluble today, quite unlike his usual surly self. That was because he had found a kitchen wench who would go willingly with him into the dark corner where the dairy adjoined the wash house, and though

75

he was sorry to leave her, he felt he might likely find another at Worle, or even at de Courcy's.

'This mist will burn off when the sun is up,' he said, full of good cheer and confidence. And then – 'You have not brought that half trained hawk—?'

'Aye,' said Robert, 'I know. I'll lose her. So you have said a dozen times.'

Reynold hummed tunelessly and gently slapped his horse's neck with the reins in rhythm.

'Marry, but you're cheerful today!' said Robert, 'Are you so pleased to be on progress?'

'No, it's not that. In a way, I'm sorry to be leaving Williton. I'll tell you for why' – and he brought his horse close alongside Robert's and spoke softly to him, leaning near and grinning.

'And did she so?' Robert laughed. 'It would be well if you were wed! And lucky it is that your betrothed is far away, my lusty fellow.' Secretly he thought that for his part, he could not fancy to tickle a greasy kitchen slut but Reynold's lewd reminiscences were preferable to his black moods, and he listened with all the fascinated interest of the uninitiated.

Pretty soon they came to the foothills, and as they climbed higher, the mist thinned and swirled away. Gauzy grey veils of cobweb hung on every bush; as the sun came through, they were transformed into glittering diadems. Riding now in mellow sunshine under a pale blue sky, Robert looked back; the mist was like a white sea below them, lit to opalescence in the clear morning light.

They reached de Courcy's about mid-afternoon, in time for dinner. Robert saw the timber keep with its stone base, high upon the motte, and the lonely marshes stretching away into the distance, as they came out of the woods.

When they clattered into the bailey Robert was pleasantly surprised by the large numbers of retainers and his spirits rose further as they entered the hall. It was very grand and very crowded. Robert had not seen such a host of people in one place since they left de Tracy's.

He and Reynold were placed well down the board on one of the lesser tables but their father was up there on the High Table with de Courcy himself as he had every right to be for he, too, in spite of the meanness of his manor of Williton, was one of the *Barones Maiores* of the realm who held direct of the Crown itself. Reynold was already looking around at the maids and ladies and his bold stare made Robert uncomfortable. He bent his eyes upon the thick slice of rough rye bread in front of him on which the meats would be placed, and fiddled with the knife at his girdle. Afterwards, those thick slices, well soaked by then with the juices of the repast, would be distributed to the beggars at the gates.

By now, Reynold was in conversation with his neighbour, a large, round-looking girl with a fine, high colour, and Robert stole a glance around him. His eye was caught by the steady gaze of a young maid opposite; she had a pale face, thin cheeked, and a pointed chin. When she lowered her eyes he saw that her lashes were so long and thick they lay like little fans upon her cheeks. She looked at him again with the barest hint of a smile and Robert blushed furiously and took so large a mouthful that he nearly choked. Her smile grew wider and he saw that her teeth were charmingly crooked. He did not dare speak to her and indeed, the noise was so great that they would have had to shout across the table. Since Reynold never turned away from the girl on his other side, Robert passed the meal in grim concentration upon the food and all he got out of it was a bout of severe indigestion; he seemed unable to chew properly under the gaze of the maiden with the eye-lashes.

Afterwards, when the ladies were gone (he knew not where) and the men settled to serious drinking by torch-light, he asked Reynold if he knew who she was.

77

'Nay,' said Reynold, 'I know not. You did not like her, surely? She had no bosom.'

He did not see her the next day, but on the following morning he came across her in the bailey. She was standing near the well, wearing a green gown and a veil upon her hair, which was of a bright brown colour. She spoke to him at once, not at all shy, asking who he was, which was fortunate for Robert for he had completely lost his tongue at sight of her and would have cravenly passed on. As it was, his heart went out to her in gratitude for her obvious interest in him and he gazed at her with such intensity that she faltered somewhat. After a slight pause, she told him she was the daughter of one of de Courcy's knights and that her name was Ysabel. When they began to walk together, he saw that she limped very badly and he stopped at once and asked if she had hurt herself.

'Nay,' she said, 'It is an old thing, that. My leg was broke when I was a child and now it is shorter than the other. That is why I shall be a nun. I am to go next year.'

Robert was silent. He saw her cheeks were pink. At length, he said doubtfully, 'Is that your desire?'

She smiled faintly. 'It is no matter what I desire. My father says no man will ever marry me and so I must be a nun. I should have gone before but they are still arguing over my dowry.' Her smile grew wider and Robert was ravished by it. 'I shall be an Abbess when I am old. That will be felicitous. No one shall tell me what I must do, then.'

He managed to tear his eyes away from her mouth, and looked at his feet.

'What is it?' she said.

'Do you hunt with us today?' was all he said.

'Ah, yes! I love to ride – it's easier than walking,' and she began to tell him of her horse and a dog she owned.

He interrupted suddenly. 'May I ride with you?'

She fell silent and looked at him so steadily that he was covered in confusion and started kicking along a stone at his feet.

'I would like that,' she said softly.

So for the next three days Robert and Ysabel rode and hawked together until Robert lost his merlin, just as Reynold had said he would. The other ladies would not let her help him in the search but dragged her off perforce along with them. He rode around the coverts but never a sign of the lost bird did he see, until at last, in a very bad humour, he dismounted by a little pool and seated himself on a tussock of grass.

There, taking stock, he realised that he was not concerned about the hawk, but only Ysabel. It was true she did not walk at all well, having a curious lolloping gait, but on a horse she was the equal of any. And still, crippled as she was, she was incomparable.

Robert had fallen deeply and devastatingly in love for the first time and he was overwhelmed by it. He sat and watched the filigree reflection of the naked trees in the still brown water and dwelt upon her infinite perfections. A week ago he had never seen her and now she was all he wanted in the world. If he could have her for his wife. . . . The thought of such unbearable joy almost stopped his heart. If he could only persuade his father! He was not betrothed; no difficulty there. Maybe her crippled leg was a blessing in disguise; but for that she might have been already plighted. Surely her father would rather she were wed than a nun. It would be a positive advantage to him if the dowry could be set lower, and it was very sure her dowry would be small – her father had no more than half a hide of land. He would take her with none but he could not see the baron agreeing to that. And then again, would they let him marry before Reynold?

He sat and tapped his teeth with his finger nail and worried. After all, he did not know her feelings, though she

79

seemed to like him. She had never mentioned the convent after that first time. He would speak to his father before they left. He must – because if he waited, the arrangements with the nuns might be completed. Now the resolve was made, he whistled to his horse; it had grown darker and was beginning to rain, the spell of St Martin's summer was over. He had forgotten the hawk entirely.

That evening when it was growing late and some of the knights had drunk themselves insensible, Robert approached his father. He knew he would not be the worse for wine for Sir Richard was an abstemious man. De Courcy had gone to his chamber, the servants were dismantling the tables and dragging out pallets for the guests, and the baron and a couple of other knights stood before the dying fire. Robert came and knelt in front of him.

'May I speak with you, sire?' he whispered, for his throat had gone dry. The baron nodded and rocked slowly up and down on his heels; the others moved a few paces away but not out of earshot. Robert swallowed for his voice seemed in danger of leaving him altogether; then he said with a rush – 'Sire, I have found the lady I would wed.'

He heard one of the strange knights snort, though whether in scorn or amusement he could not tell, and burned with embarrassment. Sir Richard turned his head and looked at them; there was a little pause and then they moved off down the hall.

'Who is she? – this lucky maid.'

'She is the daughter of one of Baron de Courcy's knights – her name is Ysabel de Montsorel.'

Ysabel – to Sir Richard the name was like a faint drift of perfume from the past. He himself had been little more than the age of this lad when he had known his Ysabel. The year in which the Empress had married Geoffrey Plantagenet it was – while yet Henry Beauclerk sat upon the throne.

He stood so still and blank of face that Robert stared at him in perturbation, but he did not notice. The only face he saw was hers; gentle, mysterious, aloof. No other woman had ever touched his heart as she had, and the rush of memories called up by her dear name transported him back to his own green youth and the day he had spoken of her to his father. That hard, grim-faced old man had hardly heard him out, had laughed at his love-sickness and told him that betrothals were not so lightly broken and that he should wed with her to whom he had been promised these many years, the daughter of his old friend, Baldwin de Boullers. In any case, he had said, Ysabel was a poor thing, weakly and no breeder if he knew anything of women, and an heir was the thing, strong sons were everything!

When he saw Maud de Boullers again, short, square and solid, with the heavy chin, his boy's heart shrank within him. Bitterly he had resolved that he would never lie with her, marriage or no, but eventually time and propinquity, and indeed, a little pity, too, had done their work.

So now Sir Richard looked on Robert with unexpected sympathy.

'You love each other, I dare swear,' he said in a voice so gentle that Robert was quite confounded.

'I love her,' said Robert, 'She – I know not. . . Her father says that she must be a nun – because of her leg – he says no man will want her. But I want her.'

'Her leg? It is not that crippled one I've noted creeping about the place? Surely you cannot –?'

His son stared at him dumbly. Sir Richard turned away abruptly. Could history repeat itself? The same name – and the one too delicate, the other deformed. Yet how could he refuse the boy after his own experience? He wondered – her father might honestly wish the maid to enter religion. It was common practice to offer a child to God in this way in order to assuage a guilty conscience, though that bespoke an attitude of mind he could neither fathom nor approve.

He turned back to Robert, and at the look on the boy's face knew that he was lost. 'I'll ask him for her,' he said in a grumbling voice. 'I promise nothing – I'll ask, no more.'

And with that, Robert had to be content.

Early next morning, in pouring rain, there was a disturbance at the gate and a weary messenger on a blown horse rode in. He was closeted long with de Courcy, and about the fourth hour after dawn, word ran round the castle like fire through stubble that King Stephen was dead – of a flux of emerods, it was said.

After that, all was uproar, and the rest of the wet, dripping day passed in preparation for leaving, and gossip about the uncertainties of the future. De Courcy's lady kept wringing her hands and foretelling civil war again. Since she was a great pessimist, she had the whole kingdom under interdict at the end of her peroration – 'It is not two years agone since we were threatened with it,' she lamented, 'and only the good Archbishop's pleadings with the Lord Pope saved us. This is what comes about when a King leaves no true heir.'

When someone asked drily whether she refused to accept the late King's acknowledged heir she became flurried, and losing the thread of her discourse altogether, prepared to begin her jeremiads again, until her husband, who could never long stand the sound of her voice, started roaring like an angry bull and she scuttled hastily away to harry the servants.

Sir Richard was thinking with something near dismay of the long journey to London again and reflecting on the Council in Westminster Hall just a year ago when Duke Henry had been proclaimed Stephen's heir – he had not had too long to wait for his inheritance, after all. He felt an odd relief at the news and suddenly bethought himself of Leicester – he, at all events, would be rejoicing, late-comer as he was to Henry's aid. Ever a fence-sitter, he!

He wondered why he felt such confidence in the Empress' eldest son. Boy he might be – not much older than his own sons – but he was a hardened warrior. As he should be with such a dam! – his lip twitched. Twice he had seen the Empress, and hoped he never would again. God save them all from women of that stamp! She was the true get of ferocious old Henry. He was sure that no usurper would succeed in wresting the throne from any son of hers – had she not lacked that vital inch or two of flesh she never would have lost it.

Reynold, watching him, hoped he could persuade his father to grant him leave to go to London, too. It would be a great thing to go to Court. Robert only wondered and wondered if his father would remember to ask de Montsorel for Ysabel.

Oddly enough, it was Lady Maud who turned the scales in Robert's favour and persuaded the baron to accept de Montsorel's daughter almost dowerless. She did this by agreeing to the grant of a parcel of her own land to her foster-son and thereby earned herself the title of a virtuous and forgiving wife – quite without foundation, for her real reasons reflected little credit upon her. With the advent of a new reign she was eager for Reynold's marriage to take place. Beatrice de Limesi, his betrothed, would bring him rich lands, and the difference between her own son and Robert would be nicely pointed up if he, at the same time, should marry the daughter of a poor knight. So the arrangements were hurried on, Baron de Courcy knighted several candidates, among them the young Fitzurses, and within the month, both were married.

Unfortunately for Lady Maud, she had overlooked the salient point in her campaign – that Reynold's marriage meant his inevitable loss to her. A week after the wedding her husband and her son rode away in the bitter winter weather, en route for London to see the new King crowned, while she remained at Williton with the boy who was none of hers and two strange young women.

When Ysabel's father told her he had granted the request Baron Fitzurse had made for her, she was too much at a loss to say anything. This was as well, for her father, in his turn, would have been equally astounded that she should have any comments to make; he expected no more than the deep curtsey he got. He thought her a good, obedient child and told her he was sure she would make a good wife.

Nonetheless, had he been a man of more perspicuity, he should have wondered at her silence because she had been wont to talk to him a great deal more than most girls to their fathers. This was partly because she was favoured by him on account of her disability and partly because his house and holdings were so small that they were thrown into each other's company more than was usual in the knightly class.

Her astonishment had been so great that it numbed her understanding and so it was not until she was sitting with her mother in her bower later on that day that she discovered who, among the Fitzurse kin, her prospective bridegroom was. Even then she did not know how she felt. So accustomed had she grown to the idea that she should be a nun that it came close to sacrilege to imagine herself a wife. What would those holy women think of her, she wondered, forgetting that they, too, must know she owed her first obedience to her father. Now, all her girlish dreams of the future were changed – instead of being veiled and garbed in black, she would wear fine bliauts of rich cloth, instead of walking slowly with bowed head, she would bustle and hurry (as much as she was able), red cheeked and important like her mother, with keys jangling at her girdle in place of a pair of beads.

Before, she had been used to congratulate herself that she would not have to share the bed of an old man like her sister who had married a widower – well, she could still do so, for

84

she would share a young man's bed. At that, she blushed and her needle stopped moving in the undershift she was sewing for her father until she caught the quizzical look her mother gave her. Yet for all her oft-times dreamy appearance, Ysabel was well versed in practical matters, the nuns would never have considered her else, and she half knew, half guessed that bedlore came naturally. Still, it was strange to think of such things concerning herself – but not unwelcome . . . no, not unwelcome.

The wedding came and went and in the event Ysabel found that she was more occupied with her young husband's feelings than her own; when it became apparent that he was, in truth, as kind and gentle as he had appeared to her before, she settled into married life with ease.

She and Robert had been promised the raising of a new house at Orchard but no one was in any hurry, and with Reynold and the baron gone off to London, they remained at Williton with Lady Maud and Reynold's new wife, Beatrice. If Robert minded being left behind, he never showed it – not so, Beatrice. She carped and criticized until even Lady Maud, who at first agreed with her in all things, being determined, it appeared, to love her, became annoyed. The first real quarrel blew up at Christmas.

Beatrice complained bitterly that here there were no mummers, no jongleurs, nothing to break the monotony. How different things would have been in London. Robert pointed out that she would have been far more uncomfortable upon the journey in midwinter than she was here and that it was little use to rail at them when the decision had been the baron's and her husband's.

'Hold your tongue!' she snapped, 'It's no bastard's place to bandy words with me, who am not only true-born but shall be mistress here some day!'

Robert turned a dark, ugly red and Ysabel looked in distress at Lady Maud. 'Do not let her say such things,' she whispered.

But once started, Beatrice would not stop. She spoke of her disappointment at the miserable size and scope of her husband's home, she wailed of her own homesickness and the infinitely superior way of life she was homesick for, she screamed and stamped her feet like the spoiled child she was and finally she shouted that the husband she had come prepared to love was nothing but a clod and a dolt and she would get her father to have the marriage annulled if this neglect continued.

At this unwarranted attack on her beloved son, Lady Maud rounded like an enraged bull upon the daughter-in-law she had envisaged as an ally. Insults to Robert she could stomach in silence (even with an inward commendation) but where her own flesh and blood was concerned, her maternal instincts rose up with outraged vehemence. If one of her own daughters had spoken so to the mother of her husband, she should have expected her to be whipped, she declared, and went on to tell Beatrice that she should not stay in her house a day longer than was necessary, she should be packed off to her husband directly the roads were clear. He would know how to deal with her as her own parents had evidently not done.

And, concluded Lady Maud, with the triumphant air of one who delivers the *coup-de-grâce*, she was sadly mistook if she thought that the house of Fitzurse – or indeed of de Boullers – had any admiration for the ways of the Franks in Outremer!

Since this last remark completely baffled Ysabel and Robert, they eyed each other in silence, but Beatrice, who had caught the reference to the travels of her parents in Syria at the time of the last Crusade, tossed her head and remarked acidly that she, at any rate, had never expected any appreciation of civilised living from the folk she now found herself among, and that she was not surprised that such had sat safe at home while their betters had travelled far to save Jerusalem from the infidel.

86

And, turning upon Ysabel, to find herself related by marriage, even upon the wrong side of the blanket, to a hideous cripple—

This uncalled-for shaft was the last straw; Robert and Lady Maud both began to shout at once and Ysabel burst into a storm of tears and cried that she wished – oh, how she wished that the convent had been her portion. There, at least, she would have met with kindness in her affliction.

Beatrice fell silent for a moment, perhaps feeling that she had gone too far, until my lady, unable to leave well alone, said that Ysabel could well have been equally unhappy there – of a certainty she would if it resembled in any way the nunnery in Normandy where Beatrice's aunt was Prioress – 'and as loose living and carnal a lady as ever disgraced a religious habit!'

So the wordy battle waxed fiercer, going on to take in every aspect of the relationships in both families, legitimate and irregular, and thence to the characters of individual members. Beatrice possessed a gift for invective that might have aroused admiration had it been directed otherwhere and an insight into people's motives positively uncanny in one so young.

Robert, who had before felt sorry for her, found himself in the position of one who carries home an orphaned fawn only to find it overnight develop the habits and disposition of a wild boar. Thereafter, he avoided her as much as he could, as did the women, until Beatrice, while scarcely repenting her evil behaviour, at least regretted it.

So she set her mind to work, and being of that temperament which has little pride but an enormous determination to have its own way at all times, she lighted on a plan to bring herself back into Lady Maud's favour. Every morning she would go into that little coign off the hall which had an outlet down into the moat, and there, after relieving herself, she would make retching sounds and groan softly at intervals. The stench that always hung around the place made the performance easier and since there were invariably one or two others waiting about outside, she knew it would not be long before it was brought to the notice of my lady.

Thus it soon happened that Beatrice was questioned upon feminine intimacies and she played the part of the ignorant young bride so well that Lady Maud was quite deceived. As Beatrice had suspected, this was the one excuse she could find acceptable for her daughter-in-law's ugly moods; everyone knew that women in the early stages of pregnancy turn against those they love best. Even Ysabel was prepared to forgive and forget in spite of the pangs of envy that she felt, for to her the phases of the moon still brought the proof of an empty womb.

On the Eve of the Purification it turned bitter cold so that all were glad to huddle within doors, blowing upon their fingers and screwing up their toes inside their shoes in an effort to keep warm. Beatrice had claimed the best place at the fireside and sat there all day, petting her little dog and drinking spiced ale. The others had accepted now that she should not be called upon for household tasks lest it should upset her temper and, in turn, influence the expected heir.

It grew hourly colder and that night, a hard frost set in. This was unusual in the West Country so long after Christmas where spring normally came early. Cold or not, Lady Maud was adamant that all members of the household should hear Mass next day at Watchet and receive the Candlemas blessing. The risk of sore throats was greatest at this time of year and it would be the uttermost of foolishness not to take advantage of the protection of the Saints.

When they had pushed and scuffled their way out of the little church, the sky from being a clear and frosty blue had grown dark and heavy with cloud and a great stillness hung in the air. Today there would be snow, said Herluin with the air of one who, if he had not arranged it, had certainly been consulted, and most of the men agreed with him. Only

Helias Attewelle differed and that was because whatever Herluin said, he must oppose him. Nonetheless, the day passed without event, only the clouds hung lower and more yellow so that night came long before the time of sunset and torches were lit in the hall for dinner.

Robert was late after checking the seed corn in the garner near the wash house; as he crossed the court he trod through a film of dry white powder, and – 'Oh!' they cried as he came in, 'It's snowing, then!' for the hood and shoulders of his cloak were thickly besprinkled with a coating like wheaten flour.

By morning it lay so thick that all was strange, the banks and small bushes mere undulating mounds, quite hidden and disguised. The sun rose, red as a ripe apple, bringing colour to the frozen world – as Christ lights and warms our frozen hearts, thought Ysabel when she looked upon the transformed scene. Certainly, the snow had translated even the muck heap into a thing of beauty and the usual strong smell of dung was notably absent. So does He to us, she thought, and was comforted. But Beatrice did not even see the beauty, nor did she have poetic fancies: she only felt the cold and grumbled more than ever.

Robert had gone off with Herluin and several of the men to help Shepherd, for the ewes were dropping their lambs and in this weather half the flock could be lost. No one else did much work apart from clearing snow in the courtyard. The cooks were the most fortunate among the servants; it was a good deal warmer in the kitchens than in the hall and gradually everyone who could find an excuse to do so gravitated there.

With so many other willing hands around, Lady Maud set some of the scullions to clear a way to the wash house and to sweep up the snow which had drifted in the open side. As soon as a path had been opened up she went along to make sure they were still working and not idling about wasting time. 'As if,' said Beatrice with a sniff, 'any would stand idle in this cold! Only a fool could think it –' and she looked sharply at Ysabel to see if her face would show whether or not she might repeat the remark back to my lady. But Ysabel appeared not to have heard, so Beatrice helped herself to one more of the little wheaten cakes the cook had just drawn from the oven in a heavenly tide of heat.

When Lady Maud saw that the knaves were working well, brushing and shovelling the snow and piling it up along the outer wall (they had seen her coming in time to stop the furious game of snowballing which was in progress) she went on into the wash house. The snow cast a pallid glare into the darkest corners; objects whose existence she had forgotten showed up now: old paddles for washing sheets, the tub which leaked and had never been mended, and here, thrust down into the angle of the wall, was the cadge so long lost and grieved for by Reynold! It had never any business to be in here; she clucked to herself in annoyance, reaching down to get it and covering her hand in dust and cobweb.

As she pulled it out, something else caught her eye; a little cask full of some anonymous liquid with a thin crust of ice on top. She stared at it suspiciously and then, still with the cadge in the other hand, picked up one of the old paddles and prodded at the ice with it. It cracked immediately, the contents evidently water which swirled darkly around, and something rose sluggishly to the surface. Lady Maud made a face indicative of disgust, nonetheless she persisted in her poking and at length drew up whatever it was upon the paddle. It was a heap of stained cloth – or cloths, as she saw when one fell back into the water, splashing freezing, reddish drops on her hand. She stared at it in puzzlement. The vessel was full of bloody clouts.

Who in Christendom—? she thought. Why were they not put in the soaking vat? and then, Can one of the household have been wounded in a brawl and they have kept it from me?

She stood for a moment considering the matter, and then dismissed it. All of her household were hale, none pale and wan from loss of blood. She bent forward and examined the cloths more carefully – without doubt these were the clouts in use by women for the monthly flux. But what need to hide them here? She was thoroughly confounded but it was icily cold in the wash house, too cold to linger any longer. She let the cloth drop back off the paddle and left the cadge forgotten once again in its corner. She would leave all alone until she came upon the explanation.

When she was back in the house she called Mold to her and questioned her about the women. Mold was as bemused as she.

'If any hath been unlawfully pregnant and then miscarried—'

'What need to hide what should have been seen long before? It makes nonsense.'

'All know they must soak their clouts in the vat before washing them,' maintained Mold. 'All – down to the wenches too young to have such need.'

'What of Lady Beatrice's tiring woman?'

Mold's voice brooked no gainsaying. 'I showed her the vat myself.'

They stood and deliberated awhile, and then my lady moved to sit upon the stone seat in the fireplace, lifting the skirts of her bliaut that the blaze might warm her ankles. They were alone in the hall except for a handful of servants doing something with the trestles at the other end.

A thought was trying to surface in Lady Maud's mind; it had to do with pregnancy and she mentally ran over the argument again, and again concluded that no serving wench would wish to hide the proof of luck or virtue. Still, something nagged at her but she could not quite come at it. There was guilt of some kind here, she was certain, and she could not rest easy until the culprit was found.

'Well, Mold,' she said at last, 'I shall tell you what we

shall do. Your husband shall set a man to keep watch, and soon or late, one will come, either to wash those clouts or to bring more. Then we shall know who it is and I will know the reason why.'

'Also,' she continued, 'the jade shall smart for it! It is very filthiness to hide them thus!' Lady Maud was a poor and shiftless housewife and because of it, she punished the same shortcomings in others most rigorously.

But Beatrice had always her wits about her, and when she crept along the next day to hide the disproof of her condition she spotted the man lurking behind the stable door; being a simple fellow he was following the instructions to watch the wash house quite literally. It did not take her more than five seconds to add two and two and come up with four. Yesterday my lady had gone to the wash house, had spent an unconscionable time there and had passed the rest of the day lost in thought. That in itself was enough to make Beatrice wonder; her own guilty knowledge supplied the rest. Well, she had hoped to keep it up another month but it did not really matter.

So as she came up in front of the stable, she gave a little shriek and slid down in a heap upon the snow. Out sprang the watcher and – 'Oh' she cried, 'How you startled me! Why do you skulk so in dark corners, knave!'

Hearing her raised voice, several other men appeared and, between them, they lifted her to her feet. She doubled over, holding her belly and crying that this villain who had frightened her and caused her to fall should be straitly punished. The fellow, stricken into dumb terror by what had happened, could not find words to explain his presence and was cuffed aside by the ostler who was first upon the scene.

So it was that Lady Maud was never sure just where the accident took place for Beatrice was already carried within the hall by the time she was fetched. Beatrice had demanded to be alone while they found the women to attend her, and those few moments' privacy were all she needed.

When Ysabel and my lady were brought to her side by her alarmed tiring woman she was rolling and groaning and weeping with her under tunic already stained with tell-tale smears.

As for my lady, she entertained some half formed suspicions concerning Beatrice; that they never crystallised into anything concrete was a consequence of her habit of mind for her slow, drifting thoughts were strangers to any kind of logic. Nevertheless, the vague misgivings remained with her, formless and inchoate, until by a slow chain of intuitive feeling, she came to the belief that Beatrice was not to be trusted and would bear watching closely lest she bring dishonour to their house. She tried to discuss her with Ysabel but she, unable to make any sense out of my lady's rambling discourse and still full of pity for Beatrice's supposed loss, thought only that Lady Maud was as unfeeling as she was lack-brained.

Beatrice, believing she had outwitted them all, became more than ever convinced of her own cleverness, and decided that when the time came to rejoin her husband, she would be more than a match for him, too, and in that she was incontestably right.

Now that the worst of her homesickness was over she began to look forward to meeting Reynold again. She had seen him on only a few occasions in her childhood, a heavyset, thickbrowed, disagreeable looking boy who would never exchange more than two words with her. She had disliked him then, but she had accepted that he would one day be her master – she could not hope for better, being the youngest of a large family. She would have preferred the younger Fitzurse son, and said so (she was young enough, then, to demand what she wanted outright) but this called down such a storm of wrath upon her head from her mother, who begged loudly to know whether she would disparage them all by marrying with a bastard and then beat her handsomely for her impertinence, that she never mentioned any of the Fitzurse family again. However, she filed away that interesting fact about young Robert.

She did not see Reynold again until the day before they were married and she was quite unprepared for the change in him. He had been ugly before, and he was still ugly with his thick lips and coarse nose, but she found him curiously exciting; the way he looked at her from time to time under his heavy lids made her tremble with a delicious excitement which she took for love. Her body's innocence disguised an emotion that a more experienced woman would have recognised immediately, and her mother, watching her reactions, thought that it were well to have her safely wed at last.

She had done her duty and guarded her well, now her son-in-law might take on the task. For her part, she would not be sorry to have her daughter out of the house, sly, saucy jade that she was, and it seemed that the pity she had felt for the girl, to be marrying such an ill favoured fellow, had all gone for naught. She liked him well enough, and more than liked him, judging by the way she was fluttering and tittering for his benefit. Still, he might manage to keep her in order if that big, brutal jaw were anything to go by.

She caught the eye of Lady Maud, and hoping that her thoughts were not apparent in her face, leaned across the board and complimented her upon her brewing. 'And how do you flavour your ale, madame? she enquired, not because she cared but rather to draw the other's attention from her daughter who was behaving, she felt, much like a bitch on heat.

But the wedding passed off without a hitch, and when all the women who could squeeze into the tower chamber had undressed the bride and put her, naked as the day she was born, between the linen sheets, Beatrice's mother had no reason to feel shame for her daughter. She was well formed, her breasts obviously virginal, and she did not huddle herself together weeping, as some brides did.

94

And then Reynold was led in by the gentlemen with only a nightgown to cover his own nudity, and all the men cheered and shouted Hola! and Hue, hue! and the ladies laughed and cried, Be merry! and Do thy duty! when it was taken off and he was pushed (without too much urging, to be sure) into the bed with his bride.

After they had lain an hour or two together alone, all the company trooped back to ask if she were now his true wife, and since everyone had drunk deeply of wine and ale both, the quips and jests were more notable for crudity than wit but nobody cared, least of all the new-wed pair. Reynold called out with pride that his achievements numbered three and dared Robert to better that if he could when his turn came next day, and Beatrice produced the blood-spotted cloth for her mother-in-law's inspection with such a look of smug self-satisfaction that a fresh outburst of cheering and congratulation rang out.

Only the baron stood at the back, a little apart and withdrawn into his own thoughts. Lady Maud believed that was because his son had proved himself a better man then he had been, and he, divining her thought, would not disabuse her. He smiled at her gently instead, thankful only that he would soon ride away from her.

But for Beatrice, the consummation of her dreams brought inevitable disappointment. She was not innocent in mind, only in body, and Reynold had learnt no finesse from his kitchen maids so that all his efforts did nothing to slake her adolescent concupiscence. She was left deflated and eventually angry, and what was worse, uncertain whether she had played her part correctly. Her mother, cold and sharp tongued, had offered no advice beyond instant obedience to her husband; her sisters, all older than she, were long since married and gone, and Beatrice's only conversations on that most entrancing of all subjects had been with other giggling tits who knew no more than she did. She was too much aware of her own dignity to consult her tiring

95

woman and so she endured the perplexing doubts of puberty, and visited her frustrations upon those around her, and principally upon Robert because he was there and Reynold was not.

However, she was sure that when they met again she could arrange matters more to her liking; at fourteen she had yet to learn that the race is not always to the swift nor the highest guerdon to be gained by determination alone.

IV

December 1154–May 1155

THOMAS OF LONDON, Archdeacon of Canterbury these two months, crouched lower over his parchments and tried to concentrate in spite of the vicious draught that whirled around his ankles and filtered up under his thick gown. He wound the heavy cloth more firmly round his legs but it was no use; as soon as he sat up to write the gown disarranged itself and he was back in the same predicament. He sighed and stroked the end of the quill back and forth across his chin. Today he could not give his mind to his work.

Perhaps that was because this day was his birthday. Thomas was always quite definite about the date because his anniversary fell on the feast of St Thomas the Apostle, four days before Christmas. Today he was thirty-six years old and when he looked back upon his life he felt oddly dissatisfied in spite of Archbishop Theobald's favour and kindness towards him. Well, he had often thought a knight's life would have suited him better than that of a clerk, but that was not open to a merchant's son. The only road to preferment for him was through the Church.

And with the Archbishop's help, he had done well in the last ten years, had travelled widely and learned much, for Theobald had sent him first to Bologna and then to Auxerre to study Canon Law. He held the livings of St Mary-le-Strand and of Otford in Kent, and during this last year he had become a prebendary of St Paul's in London and of Lincoln, too, and finally Archdeacon of Canterbury. So he was successful in his field, and yet. . . .

The words of his old friend, John of Salisbury, came back to him, half mocking, half in earnest. 'Is it possible for an Archdeacon to be saved?' That was a gibe at the worldly attitude of Archdeacons, but how could it be otherwise when theirs was the financial responsibility of a diocese? Thomas had not found it very amusing and had been disconcerted at the laughter it evoked. It still made him feel uncomfortable and at a disadvantage.

Sudden nostalgia filled him for the happy, long ago days of his youth when he had been a protégé of that glorious knight, Richer de l'Aigle. Merry weeks of hawking and hunting in the forests around London thronged his memory. That had been the life for him, and to be plucked from it and set to clerking for his kinsman, Osbern de Witdeniers, was hardly to be borne. His father's financial reverses had altered the tenor of his life and his mother's death, soon afterwards, had set the seal upon the change. He had loved his mother dearly and still had fifteen Masses a year said for her soul and prayed for her every night before he slept, but now as he sat and recalled other birthdays in his childhood when she had carefully weighed him and then given the same weight in food and clothing to the poor, he realised he hardly remembered her at all.

Maybe it was a good omen that he should be presented to the King on his birthday, if indeed that happy occasion took place today as old Theobald had promised. Thomas had seen King Henry on his Coronation Day but he had not expected a formal presentation so soon. Pleasure filled him at the prospect. Possibly some of the taunts of Roger de Pont l'Evêque were true, and Thomas was a snob, but at least his snobbery had the saving grace of looking upward to admire and never down to sneer. To be truthful, Thomas was hardly aware that he had any inferiors except in the field of intellect and he knew well enough that his quick and clever brain was God's gift. He had occasionally been tempted to point out that fact to Roger who had been Archdeacon before him, and an ordained priest, to boot, which Thomas was not, but discretion had prevailed, and now that Roger had been translated to York and taken his petty persecutions with him, Thomas was not sorry.

He smiled faintly, though, at the thought of Roger's fury if the King should favour him. Sweet Jesu, grant it may be so, he found himself thinking. For he had taken a fancy to the young King on sight when he had seen him crowned and anointed; his self-assurance had excited Thomas' admiration and such sudden attractions are usually mutual. He drifted into a fantasy in which the King raised him to high position and enjoyed himself thoroughly until cold common sense returned. But he was loth to relinquish his dreams of glory, knowing that such marvels do occur – had not the Archbishop taken such a liking to him that he had rescued him from Osbern's accounts and taken him into his Household? – into a far more congenial intellectual climate; and stood by him through all of Roger's petty tale-bearing. Beset by inner uncertainties as he often was, Thomas yet felt himself destined for great things.

So when the King and the Archbishop finally did come in (for Henry stood on ceremony not at all) Thomas, still in the grip of his flight of fancy, greeted him with such eagerness and charm that Henry, who had expected another dry-as-dust clerk, was quite won over. Thomas' eyes shone with warmth and after his height, his eyes were his most noticeable feature, pale grey-blue they were, the colour of shadows on snow. He was a goodly man, this Thomas, tall and slender with a high domed forehead and long white hands which he used in graceful gestures.

Henry found him fascinating, drawn perhaps by his

physical antithesis, for he himself was no more than middle height and his sturdy build made him appear shorter, his hands were rough and red with bitten nails and his movements swift and jumpy. Like many another, though, he esteemed in others what he could not bother with himself, and he marked the fine, white skin and extreme cleanliness of the man before him with approval. They talked a long while, finding so many common points of interest that Theobald felt quite pushed out and even a little annoyed with Thomas, much as he loved him. But at last he prised the King away, clucking and muttering along behind him, so like a fussy old hen that Thomas had to smile.

Henry, who was looking around for men to fill some high positions, thought that here he might have found one. 'Tell me somewhat of his background,' he requested Theobald. 'Is he truly nothing but a humble clerk?'

'Truly so, my lord King. Yet his blood is Norman and he is well educated, both here and oversea. I knew his father in my youth; we were born in the same place, in Thierceville near Rouen. This Thomas, though, was born in London for his father came here and prospered as a merchant—'

'He is well versed in legal matters?'

'He should be so. I myself had him trained in Roman law and he was an apt pupil. I should not have given the legal affairs of the diocese into his hands had I been unsure of him.'

'He is clever, then. I have need of clever men about me.' Henry stopped a moment, rubbing at his eyebrow. 'I will speak with him again,' he said.

Theobald made as if to say something but checked himself. It may not come to anything, he thought, and if I speak against him now, perhaps it will serve only to stiffen the King's resolve. Yet he was left with a feeling of dubiety he could not explain. It had been with him ever since he first put forward Thomas' name to the King. For in all the years he had known him, he had never really fathomed

100

Thomas. Thomas showed different faces to different men; not that that in itself was a bad thing, it enabled him to deal happily with all kinds but it puzzled Theobald's own simplicity. And he knew by now that a man of such depths will always hide the wellsprings of his heart. It was the mystery of what he hid that worried Theobald.

Thomas had no doubts. He was delighted but not at all surprised when the King sent for him to come to him at Bermondsey where he was holding Christmas Court. By Twelfth Night they were firm friends. Thomas had never before found a mind that ran so sweetly in tune with his own. Young as Henry was, he was well read, even learned, and Thomas was quick to see that the boyish impetuosity and ready wit that bubbled forth in company cloaked an astute and prudent mind. The relationship developed swiftly, each finding in the other a fascination which every new meeting strengthened so that on the last day of the Christmas Feast it was Thomas who sat next to Henry and shared his dish, for the Queen was absent, being great in pregnancy.

In the centre of the High Table which was covered with a white linen cloth, the boar's head was resplendent, glazed and apple choked. Flat cakes of wheaten bread decorated with a cross lay at each place and pages ran up and down the hall, carrying dishes of spiced meats and crisply golden spitted fowls to lay before the guests. The wall cressets smoked and flared, and heat and noise rolled in waves to the rafters. In the open space before the High Table tumblers leaped and sprang, turning somersaults and twisting themselves into attitudes which defied nature while the band of musicians in the gallery twanged and blew at their instruments with more enthusiasm than melody.

Henry was a little flown with wine and sat with his arm resting on Thomas' shoulders; he was not sorry that his wife was detained in her bower so that he might give all his attention to his wonderful new friend and the great news he was about to impart to him. He sat and savoured the

moments of anticipation and caught the eye of Richard de
Luci, who had been Stephen's faithful follower, and the way
he murmured into the ear of his companion, the Earl of
Leicester. Leicester looked his way and somewhat askance
at Thomas, and Henry frowned. He had decided to share
the post of Chief Justiciar between these two; Richard de
Luci was too able a man to be wasted and besides, might
plot against him if he were not given high office. He thought
it might be advisable to announce their elevation before
Thomas'.

Thomas could see Roger de Pont l'Evêque near Theobald; he had returned from Rome where he had gone to
receive his pallium for the Archbishopric of York in time
for the Coronation. He, too, was watching Thomas and
the King with a cold-eyed look and Thomas would not meet
his eyes lest triumph show too plain. 'Bailhache' Roger had
called him, 'wood-cutter', because Thomas had been carrying the woodman's axe when first they met at the Archbishop of Canterbury's manor at Harrow. Thomas had
lost his way in the maze of paths through the woods and
the woodcutter had accompanied him. Thomas had carried
the axe out of kindness because the man was loaded down
with wood for the fires. The nickname had stuck because
Roger always wore a joke to death.

Thomas 'Becket' Roger called him too, though the
sobriquet did not belong to him but to his father. Gilbert
'Becket' had been so called because he lived near the stream
in Thierceville, but there had been no reason to apply it to
his son who had always lived in London. Spiteful pinpricks
of this kind had been part of Roger's stock in trade. Thomas
was sorry he had shown his irritation, the nicknames might
otherwise have died a natural death. They were used only
to differentiate between the many men who bore the same
Christian name, and the name Thomas was unusual enough
not to need one. And for those who thought it did, Thomas
of London was differentiation enough.

The tumblers had somersaulted themselves out of sight and the musicians fallen silent, and a solitary harpist came and sat cross-legged in the space they had left. With the first notes of his soft, plaintive voice, the hall quieted. He sang of the old heroes and the great days of the past, and the lays he sang were in the English tongue and manner, full of curious half notes and the sorrow of what is lost for ever.

'Who is he?' asked Henry, for either the music or the wine had filled him with an inexplicable sadness.

'Ethelwig,' answered Theobald from his other side. 'A Saxon.'

'Oh – Saxon. . . .' said Henry, 'It is a pleasing voice.' He leaned across the table and called to a group of young knights of his Household. 'Do you catch him as he goes and tell him he may sing for the Queen if he wills. And now. . . .' He hammered on the board and shouted the names of those he would see privily later. Among them were Leicester, de Luci and Thomas of London.

After the noblemen had heard of their elevation and kissed the King's hand in the small chamber to which they had withdrawn, Thomas knelt before him. Henry's eyes shone as he raised him up and whispered to him, 'Henceforth, sweet Thomas, you shall sit at my side and many shall kneel before you – Chancellor of England.'

Thomas drew in his breath sharply. Hopes he had had, but this. . . . He fixed his brilliant gaze on the old Archbishop, his friend and mentor, who stood behind the King. Theobald smiled at him but it was a wry and peculiar smile, and Thomas wondered. He need not have done so; the Archbishop had overcome his reservations and was merely worrying at a bit of gristle trapped between his teeth. Passionately Thomas kissed Henry's hand but the King shook him off and paced up and down for he could never sit still long. He began to tell them his plans for the future of his realm. He had given a lot of thought to this and meant to start as he would continue, with a firm hand.

Theobald sighed inwardly. It was difficult for old men with stiff knees to spend much time with a King who was up and down like a spring lamb, but even an Archbishop could not remain seated when the King was on his feet.

'The premier thing,' said Henry, passing right round the chamber and abruptly sitting down again, 'is to bring down those barons who were glutted with power under my kinsman – those who have built and fortified castles without licence and thence have ridden out to terrorise the countryside. We shall bring them to heel that all may see justice in this land.'

'Aye, Roman law,' said Theobald, watching Henry closely in case a sudden movement should betoken his intention of rising. When none came, he gingerly seated himself on the edge of the bench and continued. 'Too long has this land been lawless.'

'There is Bigod of Norfolk for one,' said Leicester. 'But Roman law. . . . Why not the old customs of this realm – King Henry's laws?'

'Aye, and the Flemings – the mercenaries,' added Richard de Luci. 'They are hated above all. They must be dealt with.'

Henry nodded. 'They shall be banished,' he said, 'and the law shall be that of young King Henry. Together we shall make that law – but first I will show who is master. I will tear down the castles, stone by stone if need be, of those who stand against me.'

'None will stand against you, lord King,' murmured Theobald pacifically for Henry's eyes were beginning to glare and his voice to grow loud.

The King turned to him and taking his thin, veined hand, kissed the archiepiscopal ring. 'No, good old man, not with God and you behind me,' he said, for he was remembering how this Archbishop of Canterbury had sent for him immediately on Stephen's death and held the fort until he had come from Normandy. Always Theobald had supported the

Angevins and his firm refusal to crown Count Eustace in his father's lifetime had contributed not a little to their success.

Now with the chrism still fresh upon his forehead, Henry felt safe and strong. England was his but he must keep his wits about him, be firm but just. Most of his mother's old supporters were dead but so were many of Stephen's. He would enlist the best from both sides of those who were left, but the rebellious barons must disband their private armies and cease their constant warfare or he would put them down like the wild dogs they were.

Long they talked into the night while the candles guttered and the great fire died down into a heap of flaky ash, until the Archbishop withdrew with the excuse of his office and Leicester, de Luci and the others fell to yawning so that Henry sent them on their way. When they were alone, Henry said to Thomas, 'The new Archbishop of York — Roger de Pont l'Evêque — he was the one of whom you told me?' Thomas nodded.

Henry's eyes danced. 'His head!' he cried with glee.

Thomas' lips twitched. Truth to tell, he had hardly before noticed the curious shape of Roger's head but the King's boyish delight in oddities of any kind was infectious.

'God's Teeth!' Henry went into a soundless explosion of merriment. 'I scarce could keep from laughing in his face — when he knelt before me — and his tonsure rising out of his fringe of hair like Silbury Hill —' He wiped his watering eyes on his sleeve and peered at Thomas.

Thomas laughed too, and louder when he remembered how truly very peculiar was the shape of his old enemy's head. Now it seemed that many of the things which Roger had said and done to annoy him had their funny side and he began to recount them to the King. When he had stopped for lack of breath and in near-hysteria, they lay back exhausted, gazing at each other in love and admiration. Out of such absurdities are the deepest bonds of friendship forged

105

and from this first moment of rapport grew an intimacy by which each could convey his opinion to the other with one swift, gleaming look across a crowded Council Chamber.

Afterwards they talked on, unwearied, on every subject under the sun. Only when Henry spoke of a bawdy house he knew, Thomas became quiet and his expression cool and withdrawn. Henry's look was questioning and Thomas held out his hands and sighed and shrugged.

'Why, then, good Thomas, I do but think the more of you. A mere deacon who will obey the laws of chastity! You are a prodigy, I swear!' and Henry clapped him on the shoulder, then let his hand linger a moment.

'You do not think ill of me?' he said with a curious, half uneasy look.

For the first time Thomas was conscious of his fifteen years seniority and of the influence he might have on his young King. 'That were an impertinence, my lord,' he said. 'You are my King and, I hope, my friend. As for myself, I have a devotion to Our Lady but I must not judge you. That is God's part. I ask only that you will remember it – for your own dear sake.'

'Never fear, sweet Tom. I will remember in good time – but not yet,' and Henry laughed. 'Come, it is past time we retired.'

He opened the door and stopped short. 'Look you here!' Outside, the two young pages and the elderly knight waiting upon the King were sleeping with their heads beside their forbidden wine cups. 'They must be taught a lesson,' said the King, and taking a cup in each hand he upended them over the slumbering heads, and dissolved into mirth at the trepidation on Thomas' face.

'God's Teeth!' he roared as the lads came spluttering awake, 'Drunken pigs! Swillbowls! You reek of wine and neglect my service! Up! Up, I say' – but laughter overcame him once more, and Thomas smiled sickly in relief.

'Come, Chancellor,' he said, 'you shall escort me,' and

leaving the young gentlemen staring petrified after them, he and Thomas walked slowly away, Henry's arm still resting familiarly on Thomas' shoulder.

Leicester and de Luci were standing at the side of the Exchequer Room in Westminster watching Thomas and one of his clerks. The clerk was softening beeswax in a little pot over a brazier and Thomas was talking to him and fiddling with the counter seal which lay ready to receive the hot wax. In the centre of the huge room more clerks were busily pushing counters back and forth on the great table which was marked out in black and white squares like a chessboard to aid their accounting. The counters clicked faintly as they slid on the board and a fine dust rose above it and hung like a gossamer veil in the bright shaft of February sunshine that cut across the room from the high window. It was not a day to be within doors, thought Leicester, but now there would be many days he would be within doors when he had rather be without on horseback. That was the price one paid for high office.

De Luci put his lips close to Leicester's large and prominent ear. 'Our friend has a way with men,' he murmured, 'it is not only the King who is enamoured of him. Do you note how his lowliest clerk hangs upon his words?'

'Aye,' whispered Leicester. 'Yet he seems a goodly fellow enough – and well favoured.'

'Better favoured and better clad than the King himself,' said de Luci coldly, 'and without a drop of noble blood.'

Leicester looked at him sharply. 'He has a noble look,' he said.

De Luci laughed softly. 'Men will take him for the blood royal and the King for his Chancellor if he dress so fine. But the King will only think it a great jest. Have you heard their latest exploit?' De Luci glanced over his shoulder at Thomas but he was watching the pouring of the wax intently and did not look up. 'Last night they were out again together in the City after curfew. It is said they fought the watch. I cannot see it so amusing that the King should deceive those honest fellows as to his identity. But word is spreading round. In the end, they'll fear to attack footpads with their cudgels in case it be their King out larking with his Chancellor.'

Leicester shrugged. 'Some think it damaging to the King's dignity. But he is young. Better this than the bawdy houses – there was talk enough of that in some circles before he gained the kingdom. And Thomas of London is chaste, for all I have heard to the contrary.'

'Aye, he's a cold-blooded fish. It would seem more natural –'

There was a dull thud as seal thumped down on counter seal and both men jumped.

'There was that business of the beggar's cloak,' said Leicester, loth to end the conversation.

De Luci pulled his lip and grinned. 'At least our good Chancellor was short his finest cloak thereafter. He found it was one thing to pity the shivering poor and quite another to lose a costly garment.'

'Maybe the King thought to teach him a lesson not to be so fine,' observed Leicester, 'but I should have liked to see his face when Henry said his own cloak was not good enough and the beggar should have Thomas' –'

'And to try to prevent it that the King must forcibly tear it from him – and not without a struggle!'

'It is not meet for the King to wrestle with a subject in the City in full view of the escort,' said Leicester slowly.

There was a sudden crash as the door burst open and the other subject of their discussion entered the room like a gale of wind.

'Ho! Thomas, Robert, Richard!' cried Henry. 'The Queen has presented me with another fine son this very hour. Come, man, wine for all! We shall drink to my princeling, the new Henry.'

108

But it was at Thomas' side he stopped and waited for the others to come up and to Thomas he described the babe, with his shoulder turned to the Justiciars. De Luci drank with hooded eyes in a grim silence that caused Leicester some embarrassment until he realised that Henry was unaware of it; unaware, indeed, of their very presence.

Thomas, though, was well aware of them, just as he had been when he marked their secret glances and whispered gossip while he had appeared intent upon the sealing of the document with his new seal. '*Ecce Sigillam Thomae de Lond*' it proudly said, 'Behold the Seal of Thomas of London'. Even now, when he seemed to be giving all his attention to the King, he was considering ways and means of winning over these two noblemen. Factions among Henry's closest advisers would not do. And so he drew them into the conversation, skilfully exerting all his charm until, in the end, they stood in a compact group and the new prince was toasted in amity, but Leicester, behind the friendly smiles, was thinking, You are clever, my friend, and amiable. What else, time will show.

He thought of another character who baffled him, Baron Fitzurse, whom he had met at Wallingford when the present King was in arms against Stephen. He recalled their conversation down by the river and wondered if Fitzurse had given his wholehearted allegiance to the new young King. He had wondered before if they would ever meet again, and here at Westminster, over the Coronation Feast, they had done so. But beyond recommending his son to him, Fitzurse had had very little to say.

Leicester had thought the son of a different mettle from the father but he had promised to try to find him a place in the retinue of some great man here at Court. He was struck by an idea – why not try to place him in the Household of the Chancellor? Doubtless it would please Thomas of London to be in the position to do my lord of Leicester a favour; not much likelihood that he would refuse. He smiled and put his hand across his lips lest any see that unguarded look. He had not fancied to have that young gentleman in his own following; nothing of the father in that face.

When the King left, he addressed himself to Thomas, noting afresh the splendour of his garb, in contrast with his own dark gown. Thomas' tunic was parti-coloured, blue and green, with bands of rich embroidery on the cuffs and around the upper arm. His girdle, too, was embroidered and its long tongue hung nearly to the ground. Leicester's eyes ran down it, past the dagged hem and thence to the say stockings, one blue, one green, and the short, soft leather boots with pointed toes. Their rolled tops were lined with green cloth.

'I have been asking myself, my lord Chancellor, 'he began, 'whether you would consider adding yet another knight to your Household? A friend of mine – a baron from the West Country – desires to place his son in a Household about the Court. He is young – not yet twenty – and but recently knighted. His father has granted him the manor of Barham in Kent – perhaps it is known to you? It lies between Canterbury and Dover.'

'I have passed that village many times,' said Thomas pleasantly, 'and certainly I can find him a place – the more willingly since it will accommodate you, my lord.'

'Then I may send him to you?'

'Do so. Should I know the father?'

The faintest smile touched Leicester's lips. Thomas of London was learning condescension early. He hastened to reply in kind.

'I think not, though you may have seen him about the Court these last weeks. A lean man, and beardless. He is eager to return to Somerset, once his son is settled.'

'I shall hope to meet him, too,' smiled Thomas. 'And now, my lord, may I beg a word of advice. . . .' and they moved away together down the long room.

De Luci watched them go. Without doubt, the Earl of

Leicester had his reasons for asking favours of Thomas of London but he, for his part, reserved judgment on the man. His black eyes were hard as he drained his wine cup. It seemed to him that the whole Court was fawning on the new Chancellor – let them, Richard de Luci was eminent enough to do without the friendship of the King's favourite.

Henry was very well pleased with himself. He had attained his boyhood's ambition and now, at twenty-one, he sat in the seat of his grandfather and great-grandfather, the re-doubtable Bastard of Falaise. England was his, this fair green land of foaming rivers and rolling hills, with its huge forests, its desolate moorland, its thriving little towns and that jewel in its crown, London, the richest city in the realm.

Even Stephen's weakness in the face of the barons' depre-dations had not harmed London; she went on growing and trading and becoming richer year by year. Into the great port came foreign ships with timber from the Baltic and spices from Araby, and now that he was King, he would encourage more trade. Wine should come from his lands in France to take the place of the sour thin stuff that was the best that England could produce, and out of England would go fine ales in barrels, wool in bales, hides, corn and honey, and examples of the goldsmiths' work in which Londoners excelled.

Aye, London was the fairest city in the world, nestled in her fields and orchards, fairer than Rouen, fairer even than his own dear Le Mans. So huge a town that within her walls lived more than ten thousand souls! Three castles she had, one in the east and two in the west, three great schools and well over a hundred churches whose bells all pealed the canonical hours led by St Martin-le-Grand off Cheapside, so that men should be reminded of God at regular intervals throughout the day.

Henry gloated over his possessions and enjoyed his weeks

of glory as a crowned and anointed King, but latterly the adulation and flattery were beginning to pall, to cloy like too much sweetness on the tongue. Only with Thomas, it seemed to him, was the flavour of sycophancy absent.

More and more frequently, those who sought his favour with over-honied words found to their dismay that the old Viking blood of the Normans still ran strong in the first Plantagenet. More and more often his demoniac temper flared so that even hardened old warriors shuffled their feet and bowed their heads so as not to catch his eye and the younger gentlemen frankly cowered under his bellowed threats. His oaths, aways lurid, would become hair-raising so that the Bishops trembled and covered their ears in horror. Thomas of London alone was safe from this violence that verged on the murderous, and he sat silent until the storm had passed. Henry never saw his tight-lipped con-trolled angers which were directed at foolishness rather than fools.

For Thomas was discovering that high office caused some to show a different face to him. Letters of congratulation from old and dear friends brought him a warm pleasure that he could now return past kindnesses, but there were eager fawning letters, too, from men he neither liked nor trusted and his nature was too direct for him to feel com-fortable about them.

This very day he had received a letter from Arnulf, Bishop of Lisieux, which began 'I have received your highness' epistle, every word of which seemed to me to drop honey and to be redolent with the sweetness of affection. . . .' He went on to warn Thomas against flatterers and to dis-course upon envy in a manner which Thomas found faintly suspicious in one of his cunning and servile temperament. 'It is an old feature in the character of the envious' he wrote, 'that they look on others' success as their own ruin, and whatever others gain, they think has been subtracted from themselves.' The truth of the words was self-evident but there was a sting in the following sentence when Arnulf took care to point out that the favour of princes is easily lost. Thomas tried to forget it but the letter nettled him with its mixture of obsequiousness and scarcely concealed jealousy.

He indulged himself for a moment by devising a number of cutting retorts to Arnulf and dismissed the idea with some regret for inbred caution had still the upper hand. He would make no enemies powerful enough to harm him if he could help it. Yet the curb he had kept upon a naturally caustic tongue for so many years was weakening. There were occasions now when he allowed himself the pleasure of speaking his mind but because above all he was just, it was a very small minority which looked with disapprobation upon Thomas the Chancellor.

Somehow though, insidious whispers percolated through the Court. He was haughty, some said, jumped up. He set himself above the greatest in the land. Henry did not hear them; Thomas did. He fumed inwardly but kept a tight rein upon himself.

By those lowly souls who worked with him and knew him well, he was beloved. They knew his unfailing kindness and consideration when the pressure of work became exhausting, and since he worked harder than any of them, they did not find it difficult to forgive his occasional bouts of impatience. If Thomas sometimes felt that the youthful admiration of a few, chief among them William Fitzstephen, outran their good sense, he nonetheless basked in the pleasant glow and accepted it in the certainty that familiarity would soon enough breed contempt.

So he and the whole Court heaved a concerted sigh of relief when orders were sent out for a progress to the North. Once Henry had decided on a course of action, no delay was brooked, and since only two days' notice was given, a mad scramble ensued. Wheelwrights and carpenters worked throughout the night by the light of torches, checking and repairing last minute defects in the great baggage wagons, household furniture and utensils were sewn up in stout hides at breakneck speed, horses who had inconsiderately cast shoes were swiftly re-shod, and through all the excitement Henry strolled with Thomas beside him, occasionally criticising botched work but cheerful once more now that he had set everyone by the ears.

Eleanor was not sorry to see him go, and his new Chancellor with him. She was weary of the sound of Thomas' name, and the fact that Henry would listen to his advice in preference to her own rankled bitterly. This newcomer was usurping the attention which should have been paid to her latest born and herself. The babe was a beautiful child with his father's fair skin and so thick a coat of golden down all over his small body that Eleanor secretly thought of him as Esau. But true to the promise she had given the Empress, he was baptised Henry – Young Henry they called him and the name stuck.

She and Henry quarrelled furiously from time to time for Eleanor was not a woman to bear marital faithlessness in silence, the more so because she had at first mistaken his determination to have her for love. It was not so much the fact of his infidelity as his openness about it that galled her, and the plain terms in which it was bandied about the Court. Though she was unaware of it, much of her resentment stemmed from the fact that in bygone days she had been obliged to hide her own indiscretions beneath a veil of subterfuge while men could blatantly parade theirs. Since the advent of Thomas she had seen very little of Henry and when he came to her bower to bid her goodbye, her displeasure was apparent in the very atmosphere of the room.

He sent away the waiting-women and leaned down across the bed but she turned aside with an abrupt movement that presented his lips with the back of her head. He straightened up and stared at her with narrowed eyes.

'I had come in good faith to you, my lady, to tell you

farewell,' he said, 'but it seems you will show me no kindness. For why, I know not.'

'Well enough you know,' she returned bitterly. 'I thought myself forsworn – I, who am the mother of your sons! Little enough time you have had for me since we came into this land. It is all Thomas this and Thomas that –'

'Marry – you are jealous, then? He can take nothing that is yours —'

'Nay, but your bawds take what is mine! Think you I do not know of them? The very servants do not bother to lower their voices in my hearing!'

'Ah, now, sweet Eleanor.' He knelt beside the couch and tried to take her in his arms and his voice was soft and eager. 'It was no lack of desire for you. But you were great with child and then in childbed.'

She turned towards him, frowning still but a little mollified at his evident longing for her.

'It is cruelty in you to lie there and tempt me before the proscribed days are past,' he whispered, knowing well how to appeal to her vanity. 'There is no other woman I had liefer lie beside – yet I am but a man.'

He stroked the fur that edged the neckline of her bedgown and then began to stroke her neck. She sighed and leaned towards him. 'Look, then, upon your little son, your namesake,' she urged. 'Is he not made in your image?'

'As he should be. Yet, next time, give me a daughter made in yours.'

Reluctantly he tore himself away from her luscious, milk-swollen breasts and gazed upon the sleeping child in the crib. 'Aye, it's a pretty child,' he said, and without a second look turned back to her. 'Give me as much of wifely comfort as you may.'

She saw his eyes upon her bosom and kissed him gently, fearing to arouse his ardour. As he rose she said, unable to restrain the words, 'Come not back to me reeking of strange women, Henry.'

His head jerked up. 'Order me not!' he snapped. 'None but I shall issue orders. Much as you dislike it, you must bear the woman's part. And watch your tongue! I am no Louis!'

They glared at each other, each recognising that they were caught fast in the trap of physical allure, neither capable of tolerance or tenderness. Eleanor's eyes dropped first but she thought that one day, somehow, he should pay for his mastery, his wantoning and his indifference to her feelings. She turned to her other side and heard him stamp across the room without another word and bang the door.

Her eyes, hot with angry unshed tears, fell upon the cradle. Much he cares for you, she thought, my little son – and then she smiled, for an idea, soothing in its simplicity, had struck her. Children's attitudes are implanted by their mother at an early age – it would be easy for a clever woman to turn them against their father. And no more than he deserved. Let him go, then. Time would bring her her revenge. Yet, as she sank to sleep again, she knew she did not hate him enough for that. And vengeance was a two-edged sword. . . .

When Henry rode away into Essex, en route for the North, he left orders for the Flemish mercenaries whom Stephen had brought in to be expelled from the realm. His Justiciars stayed behind but the other officers of government, including the Chancellor and his clerks, went with him, and most of London turned out to see them go.

It was a sight to remember, the long streams of pack horses with chests and panniers slung over their backs in pairs containing everything the King might require in his journeyings, from kitchen pots and pans to relics of the Saints, and barrels of silver pennies. There went the Steward and the Butler with their staffs of butchers and bakers, slaughterers and scullions, and the Chamberlain with the

King's bedding and clothing, the Ewer who prepared his bath and the laundresses who washed his clothes.

It was a bright March day of sharp sunshine and sudden stinging showers. The rain came drenching down just as the King's fewterers went through the City gate and the greyhounds and braches shivered and sidled reluctantly along like drowned rats. But it soon passed over and the sun came out again, illumining the bright reds and greens of the huntsmen's cloaks with unearthly purity. The twenty-four great wolfhounds went by and then came the Constable and the Marshal along with the tent keepers, and behind them the watchmen and stokers who would see there were fires for the King until Easter, at least.

Thomas rode beside the King. He was at his side throughout the long progress and many times he was exhausted, but Henry never seemed to tire. There were moments when Thomas' tidy mind revolted at the never ending muddle, for nothing was ever in the place where it was needed. Too often, when they settled for the night, the food and kitchen utensils would be miles behind them and the palliasses and coverlets miles behind that, for Henry had a habit of riding like the wind when the fancy took him and it never seemed to irk him to lose the rest of the company completely, just so long as Thomas was there. Neither did food badly cooked and served worry him but Thomas had a delicate stomach and on many occasions he went hungry to his uncomfortable rest rather than eat at the King's table. Henry chided Thomas and told him he had the bowels of a woman and Thomas smiled weakly in return and silently prayed for a good lodging and edible food that night.

How the King could endure to live like a common man-at-arms Thomas did not know but he was gradually becoming aware that the difference in their ages was showing its effect, and as much in their mental as in their physical habits. Henry talked unceasingly of women which bored Thomas, or he talked of war which was more interesting, and very occasionally he talked of books and learning but not often enough. Thomas would have liked to discuss the legal reform of England, at length and in detail, but somehow Henry's attention would wander when they reached some delightfully knotty point and he would veer back to the fascinations of womanhood again.

They passed up through Suffolk where Henry received the submission of Hugh Bigod with surprisingly little trouble. They had encamped at Framlingham, and there they had been almost comfortable with the great tents and pavilions set up. Why Hugh capitulated so suddenly Thomas did not know for he had been one of Stephen's adherents and had stayed away from Henry's Coronation, but perhaps the sight of Henry's army disinclined him for more fighting. At all events, he issued forth from his castle and knelt before Henry and promised to be his man and in return Henry gave him a charter making him Earl of Norfolk, as though Stephen's having done so once already counted for nothing. Afterwards, they all feasted together, and then they went away leaving Hugh in possession of his fiefs.

Thence they proceeded slowly into the Midlands, meandering through great stretches of forest where Henry hunted and idled the days away until another fit of impatience took him and he galloped hotfoot all through one long dusty day, leaving the baggage train to follow as best it might.

It was to a small hunting lodge they came in the cool of the April evening, not far from a thorpe called Stafford. Thin razor-backed hogs rooted in the yard, unpenned, and there was a gigantic manure heap by the gate. No look-out was in evidence. Henry swung stiffly from the saddle and held out his hand to help the slower Thomas dismount. Two archers who had kept up with them clattered into the yard and looked about with curious eyes.

Henry grinned. 'Come, Thomas, and you shall meet a friend of mine – a right good friend, recently widowed.'

Somewhere in the house dogs were barking and a rough

voice bade them be quiet, and then a woman stood by the door, a buxom woman, not young. She gave a cry of pleasure and ran forward, holding out her hands to Henry. Thomas stared as Henry laughed and grabbed her, planting smacking kisses on her face and neck. The archers grinned and nudged each other and whispered. At length, Henry turned back to him and brought him up to face the woman who stared at him with bold interest.

'Here is my good friend, Lady Hawis of Stafford,' he said, 'and this, my Chancellor, Thomas of London.'

Thomas' first thought was that the woman wore a mask, then he saw her face was white with fard. It gave him an unpleasant shock and to hide his confusion, he bent low over her hand, which she grasped and would not free until they were seated either side of the King at the long board. Under the candles' gentler light she looked more comely but the paint upon her face still chilled him, and the sidelong glances she cast upon him while all the time her hand caressed the King's.

Throughout the meal, Thomas' discomfort grew as Henry chaffed and tickled the lady of the house. Suspicion was turning into certainty that Henry had brought him, all unwitting, into the house of one of his bawds. And there was nothing he could do but smile and pretend ignorance.

At any rate, the food here was good and Thomas thanked God for this small mercy and spooned up the thick, highly spiced mush of ground meat and barley with his eyes cast down upon the dish. After he had partaken of an apple pastry well sweetened with honey which Fulk, who served him, caused to drip its contents on his sleeve, he asked that he might have well water to drink. The boy stared at him, his unformed face quite blank until Thomas repeated his request and explained in a low voice that he rarely drank wine for the sake of his delicate stomach.

Still the boy stared until Lady Hawis leaned across and cuffed his ear, saying sharply, 'Get you gone, knave, and do as the Chancellor bids' and turning to Thomas, 'My lord, is there none other drink we can procure you? Ale there is in plenty in the kitchens – or even milk from the goats.'

Henry smiled indulgently. 'The drink our Chancellor best prefers is a strange brew for which he acquired a taste in Paris when he studied there.'

'It is called a tisane, my lady, and is made by infusing lime flowers. It is a pleasant drink and very beneficial to the health.'

'Marry, it's much the same as the drink my English maidens brew from raspberry leaves!' She raised her voice. 'Berenger! Go to the kitchens and fetch for the Chancellor some raspberry leaf tisane.'

Everyone in the hall raised their heads and stared; even Thomas' own knights, who had come in later, were grinning. He especially marked the quick-witted Hugh de Morville muttering behind his hand to his companions and the scarcely repressed laughter that followed his sallies. A man like Hugh could hardly go unnoticed; he stood out among the others of Thomas' Household like a swan in a gaggle of geese, so exceptionally blessed with personal beauty was he. But Thomas had heard dark tales about Hugh, and felt that there was something degenerate in the perfection of those chiselled features, a touch of malignity about the mouth and in the shadowed eyes.

A sudden furious impatience at the trivialities that aroused their wit rose in him. He glared at them, and then Henry was upon his feet, bellowing with a rage that caused cheeks to blanch and the maidens to huddle together. He was down the hall in a few long strides and had Hugh by the front of his fine tunic, shaking him to and fro while spittle gathered at the corners of his mouth and the veins stood out upon his temples.

'Dog!' he ground out. 'Cursed insolent dog so to disdain your master! Laugh, will you? Then you shall laugh at this!'

and he forced Hugh's face down into the dish before him. His companions tried their best to laugh at the picture Hugh presented but there was a forced note in their mirth which quickly died away as the King swung round on them.

'Out!' he roared. 'Out, I say! Mannerless knaves all!'

The speed with which they went bore witness to the awe which Henry's furies inspired, only at the door Hugh looked back and shot one long, malevolent glance, not at the King but at Thomas. Thomas laid his hand on Henry's arm and felt it tremble still, rigid with hard muscle.

'Your hand must be firmer above these gentlemen,' said Henry abruptly. 'A dog must know who is his master. Be not too gentle, good Thomas.'

Thomas nodded. Henry would not allow his Chancellor to be mocked in his presence, yet there were times when he, too, could be as course and empty-headed as they. He begged leave to retire in a low voice and Fulk conducted him to a small chamber off the main hall.

It was not much more than an alcove with a curtain across for some measure of privacy and smelt stale and unaired; when Thomas kicked the rushes on the floor he saw they were a full foot thick and mouldy and rotten underneath. He slid gingerly into the squalid bed, wondering what Henry was about and fearing that he knew. Not that it was his concern – he was no priest. Yet should he not concern himself with the welfare of his dear friend's soul? But as he drifted off to sleep, he knew he would say nothing. Henry was young with all the lechery of youth but he would outgrow it – other interests would take its place. Yes, of a surety they would, for he had an excellent mind. Thomas remembered how often he had been surprised by the penetration of his comments. All would be well. . . .

The gentle April days passed in hunting and the nights in feasting and drinking and other pursuits, to which Thomas turned a blind eye. There came a night when Henry spent more time in conversation with Thomas than with the lady, and on the ensuing days he rode again at his Chancellor's side. It seemed to Thomas that Lady Hawis laughed and talked a trifle too loudly behind them, and at length Henry turned and with little courtesy bade her be quieter or else fall back. She paled with rage and they saw little more of her that day.

From that time, a constant stream of gifts from Lady Hawis kept arriving for Thomas, until he became embarrassed, thinking that her hope was to win back Henry's favour through him. He kept his silence though, merely nodding to her distantly when they chanced to meet.

One morning he awoke very early and because he could not sleep again, knelt to pray. He prayed a little for himself but more for the King, with a small bone crucifix that had been his mother's in his hand. He heard the curtain rattle on its rings but did not move, hoping the intruder, whom he took to be a servant, would go away when he saw him at his devotions. A strong smell of perfume assailed him and he jerked back as Lady Hawis crept around the end of the couch and stood before him, smiling. He saw with unbelief that she wore only a fur-lined robe which gaped at the front and showed her nakedness beneath. In her hand, she held a hanap from which a gentle steam arose. She proffered it to him, whispering, 'I had thought you might be wakeful, my lord.'

Such a storm of outrage rose in Thomas' breast that he could not speak. Did she imagine that he would care to have that which the King had spurned? At his expression she fell back a pace and Thomas found his tongue.

'Get you hence, strumpet!' he thundered. 'You limb of Satan – Beelzebub's handmaiden! Begone!'

She dropped the cup in panic, right upon the bed, and Thomas saw the liquid lying in a little pool, slowly spreading and sinking in. She scuttled across the small chamber, slipping on the foul rushes, not even staying to gather her robe about her. Straight across the hall she went, tripping over sleeping men and those stirring awake.

The breath went out of Thomas abruptly and he drew back behind the curtain to find he was holding out his mother's crucifix as though she were in truth a demon from the Pit. And so she is, he thought – a loose woman, a – and then he stopped in sudden horror. Judge not lest ye be judged!

Men were appearing at the curtain now, anxious, questioning. The King will hear of it, he thought. So much the better! We can get away from here; he is tired of her already so he will not be displeased. But as he became cooler and remembered her face as it had looked without the paint he was now accustomed to seeing on it, frightened and empty, he felt a pang of pity. She is no more than a fool, he mused, driven along by her instincts as are all women. Yet underneath he blamed her still. She had caused him to fall into his besetting sin again. All his life he had fought against his harsh condemnation of weakness in others, remembering that as he wished for mercy from God at the last, he must in his turn be merciful. But he did not find it easy and sins of the flesh particularly repelled him.

Henry, far from being displeased, treated the whole affair as a huge joke and purposely misunderstanding, said that Thomas might have the lady with his blessing. These playful moods of his were a sore trial to Thomas, and his violent rebuttals of the suggestion made Henry laugh more merrily than ever.

'Why will you never tell me aught of that most private side of your affairs? Or is there naught to tell?' urged Henry, to all of which Thomas returned only silence and an uncompromising stare.

Henry giggled. 'I think the fair sex frighten you!'

Thomas looked at him at last. 'Have you truly understood so little of me?' he hissed.

Henry shrugged, tired of baiting the older man for so

little reward. 'You're still a virgin,' he said with all the careless contempt of lusty youth, 'but I suppose it is from choice. Even so, I cannot see where insult lies in the offer of a handful of sprats.'

Henry, in spite of his teasing, was more than satisfied that his beloved friend should take no interest in women; the certainty that he would always hold first place in Thomas' heart had become the rock on which he leaned. It was this, though he did not know it, which made him feel himself invulnerable.

Reynold Fitzurse slipped easily enough into the life of one of the Chancellor's knights; it was not so different from life at de Tracy's for young men bred up to warfare are the same the world over, noisy, quarrelsome, often drunk and invariably obscene. Since there were no foes to fight at present, they fought one another, and some became friends thereby and others deadly enemies. A sprinkling of older men had found places, landless knights mostly with their way to make in the world, but the majority were young for it was a new Household, and with a new reign just begun the opportunities for advancement were good.

Reynold cared little for advancement. He had the revenues from the land his father had granted him and also from those his wife had brought. Even his vexation at being torn so untimely from her bed did not depress him too much; there were many women in the world and he meant to have his share of them. All the same, he liked her very well and intended that she should come to Barham when the fairer weather came for it was a convenient distance from London. He spent a good deal of his time thinking about her, and talking about her to his more intimate cronies. Reynold was not given to reserve and pretty soon they knew as much about Beatrice as he did, which was not so much. He knew that she was fair and uncommon pretty for all her lips were small and a mite firmly pressed together; he did not yet know that beneath her deceptively gentle exterior she had a will of iron.

In any event, he was as far from London as she was when the fair weather did come, galloping the long, empty English miles in the King's wake. Through the months of spring and summer, in the train of the Chancellor, he came to know the men who would be his companions throughout life; the de Broc brothers from Kent, William de Tracy, son of his old patron, and last but never least, Hugh de Morville from the North Country, whom he watched with covert jealousy until the not inconsiderable spell Hugh cast over most of the younger knights encompassed him, too, upon its fringe.

Hugh was older than the rest of them and had been a justice in Cumberland where his father was lord of vast lands. It did not escape the notice of Will de Tracy and a few others that he never willingly spoke of his home; they surmised that he was in some sense in exile yet there was something about him that defied the direct question.

Handsome to the point of decadence, the classic curves of his beautifully modelled lips were marred at times by a look both cruel and discontented, and it was not until the on-looker had sated his gaze upon a face startling in the per-fection of its mortal beauty that the cold watchfulness of the opaque black eyes became apparent. Sensuality and a towering pride were in that face, infinite arrogance, and something else that men half recognised so that they must look and look again. Too much of everything too young, too easily, had bred in him a cynicism that was the more terrify-ing in that it took no account of moral standards; all was one to Hugh, the whole world a pageant for his gratifica-tion. Yet it had begun to bore him even in his boyhood until he had discovered the ease with which he could manipulate his fellows.

Soon he would be married to the heiress of the de

Stutevilles, a fifteen-year-old who would bring him Knaresborough Castle to make him richer still. He had never
seen her, but of an evening when they had settled to rest
in hall or barn, he would regale his followers with tales
of the things he should do to her after he had made her
love him.

At first Reynold, whose own tastes were as normal and
straightforward as those of a stallion, was thunderstruck;
later he became fascinated and admiring at the wealth of
imagination Hugh showed. Who knew what he might be
missing?

One night he said incautiously, 'An she will not, what
then?'

The rest of the group stared at him and then laughed.
Hugh did not laugh; his dark face remained impassive.
Reynold shifted his feet about in the hay and sawdust on the
floor; they were spending the night in an old, half ruined
Saxon hall which had evidently been used to pen sheep in
the not too distant past. The night was warm but dark, the
air very still so that the flames of the candle ends stuck on a
block of wood burnt straight and clear, casting their gentle
light up under the chins of the men and turning their faces
into mummers' masks. All round the little pool of brightness
the aisled hall stretched away, dim and shadowy, and now
and then faint squeaks and rustles betrayed the presence of
rats.

'An she will not?' he repeated doggedly.

'Are you a married man, Fitzurse?' said Hugh, softly.

'Aye.'

'Does not your wife obey you?'

Reynold was torn; infinitely flattered as he was by
Hugh's knowledge of his name amongst so many, he did
not know whether to admit that he would never have
expected such blind obedience or whether to agree with the
older man's views on wifely submission and thus, he felt,
cement an intimacy he had not known he desired until that

126

moment. He could not quite work it out and so, in the end, he merely shrugged and grinned sheepishly, and then one cried, 'She'll do as she's bid if she knows what's good for her. Seigneur de Morville is not a man to be crossed!', and another, 'Aye, he'll get his mother to teach her a thing or two!'

There was a wave of laughter at this sally, and Reynold looked uncomprehending at de Morville. Hugh smiled at him, his dark eyes malicious. 'That I shall,' he said. 'My mother is a woman of rare talents.'

'What kind of talents?' said Reynold blankly, and then the rest of them set to buffeting him about the head and the conversation ended in horseplay, rather to his disappointment. Afterwards, though, a thought did occur to him but he dismissed it as impossible.

Still, the intimacy he had wished for did gradually deepen though the main reason was that Hugh's talk alienated a good many of his fellows. His high-handed attitude galled Reynold often but he slowly learned how far he could go. He must never ask Hugh for reasons nor question his judgment. And Reynold did take a great deal of pleasure in being recognised as his boon companion, even though in private he must endure what he thought of as Hugh's airs and graces.

He thought those airs and graces had taken a tumble that day at Stafford when the King pushed Hugh's face into his dinner and would never have dared mention it but that Hugh turned the whole thing into a jest, swearing that to be handled by the King was a mark of favour.

'It was because you jeered at our lord, the Chancellor,' said Reynold unguardedly one night when they were playing chess.

'Aye,' said Hugh. 'What think you, Reynold, of such a circumstance wherein a King shall strike a knight in defence of the feelings of a burgess?'

Reynold gave him that well-known vacant look and Hugh

tapped him on the breast and spoke again, enunciating each word clearly. 'Our beloved Chancellor is a burgess.'

'Nay, he was Archdeacon of Canterbury before he was Chancellor—'

'His father was a merchant. He lived by trading. How did such a one come to be highest in the realm next the King?'

'I know not.'

'Nor I. But it must have been by trickery – or witch-craft.'

'Yet he was chosen by the King.'

'I doubt not his abilities. But I cannot see why the King is so tender of him. Soon or late, the King will come to his senses, and then what will happen, think you?'

'You do not like him,' said Reynold as one who makes a great discovery.

'I cannot like a man who likes not women, nay, nor trust him.'

Reynold's eyes gleamed. 'Nor I!' he cried with fervour. 'I had thought – well, not that, perhaps – but that he was different in some way – but that's the way of it, eh?' He chewed mentally for a moment on the exciting tit-bit of information, then a puzzled look spread over his face. 'The King – ?' he said doubtfully.

'You have mistaken me,' said Hugh with a note of malice that only faintly ruffled the edges of Reynold's awareness. 'So far as I know, you are the only one who will accuse him of sodomy. That he traffics not with women – it may be virtue – even holiness.' He spread his hands and smiled as though in deprecation of so absurd an idea.

Reynold moved restively. He had no difficulty, ever, in believing the worst of anyone but that his master might truly be possessed of purity of heart he found far too much to swallow. He defended his suspicions of the Chancellor with a heat that grew greater in proportion to Hugh's cool rejection of it. When he had finally run down he sat in a sulking silence, fidgeting with the pieces on the chessboard.

Hugh said idly, 'I see you do not like him. And you have made your move and lost the game' – for in his careless toying with the pieces, Reynold had indeed moved one of them.

'Nay,' he said indignantly, 'it was not a move.'

'Leave that be a lesson to you,' said Hugh in a voice that brooked no argument. 'Consider the moves with watch and ward, my young friend – whether it be the game of chess or of life. Or, of course, in life you can follow me. . . Will you play again?'

'No,' said Reynold, for Hugh's apparently light remark had given him food for thought and he was never able to concentrate on more than one thing at a time. He knew that Hugh was offering him a deeper comradeship than any that had gone before and he was dazzled by the prospect. Then he said, 'Aye, Hugh, I'll follow you.'

'Then you shall obey me and I say we shall play again.'

'Have it your way, then,' said Reynold and began to lay the pieces out once more.

A little smile played round Hugh's perfect lips but it soon died away. It was dawning on him that there was small savour in the putting down of such a fool. He waited until Reynold had finished laying out the pieces and then said idly, 'I think I'll not play after all. Give you good night,' and went swiftly away, leaving Reynold to pick his thumbs and worry lest Hugh had withdrawn much more than the offer of another game of chess.

V

June 1155

HIKENAI WAS GATHERING ROOTS in the forest. The place to which she had penetrated through the tangled undergrowth was not so far in distance from the camp but it seemed a thousand miles away – or a thousand years ago. Here man had never left his imprint; this was virgin forest, unaltered since the beginning of time, the closely crowding trees huge, furred with moss and stained with lichen where the wreathing ivy had not yet gained a hold. Dim and mysterious it stretched before her, oak, ash and holly, and underfoot, layer upon layer of dead and rotting vegetation. Near her lay a fallen giant under whose young boughs Romans perhaps had walked; all around its children grew, feeding on it, dozens of tiny oak trees struggling for life. She moved towards it, hoping for wild honey but there was no sign of bees, no sound of any bird or insect, only a hushed silence that made her shiver. Even she, accustomed to solitude from her earliest years, felt the oppression. The forest was rampant here, the conqueror, and humanity, for all its busy striving, put into true perspective as in anterloper.

In these green depths the truth of the old religion with its belief in tree and water spirits was apparent, its fear of their malignity towards human kind magnified, nor was it hard to believe in the Sacred Trees under whose branches voices from the Other World could be heard. What had Christianity to do with this? – that religion which had originated far away in a land where there were no dark, deep woods. Here the old Gods still held sway in their silent fastnesses. She was suddenly certain she was in faery demesne; the hair prickled on the top of her head and she stared about her with eyes rolled back like a hare's when the dogs are on him. How if the great Horned God should come before her? She drew a deep, shuddering breath, falling to her knees on the spongy earth, and put her head down upon her folded arms.

The fear faded as suddenly as it had arisen but she resolved never to pass this way again. This was no place for mortals. She thought of the long miles of forest that stretched between her and her old home, with so few tiny oases of human life scattered here and there in the great wilderness. This Essex forest was too vast, too interminable, not like the woods of home. She sprang up and hastened back the way she had come, breathing more freely when she came to an open glade where she could see the sky. The roots she had collected lay forgotten by the fallen oak, to add in time, perhaps, a different growth to that wild spot.

A little sweat still stood upon her forehead and upper lip and she paused a moment, wiping it with the back of her hand. She wore the same faded yellowish gown, much too small now and strained across her breasts, but over it she had a kind of loose kirtle, dun coloured, which old Gudrid had given her. Gudrid was the mother of Harold, the chief of the outlaw band. They were from the Danelaw, farther to the North, and it was well for Hikenai that she had taken a fancy to her for she protected her from the men, her own son included. An odd bond had grown between the old woman and the young girl; they slept in the same corner of the hut and brewed simples for the many ills of the tribe of outlaws, a cut-throat crew of thieves and murderers, though there were honest men among them who had been driven into the forest by hunger and the ruin of their homes in the incessant fighting of Stephen's reign.

In this area Geoffrey de Mandeville, Earl of Essex, had ruled, that baron whose name still struck terror to the heart though he had been dead these eleven years. Dead but not buried, for his sins had been so heinous that he had suffered excommunication, and a deathbed repentance had not saved him the consequences. Murder, rape and torture were his weapons and gruesome tales were still recounted of babes torn from their mothers' breasts, brides wrenched from their husbands to serve his perverted pleasures. Only the lord Pope could absolve a dead excommunicate so Geoffrey yet lay wrapped in lead outside the churchyard of the Old Temple in Holborn, guarded by the Knights Templars until the Pope might relent.

Hikenai realised that she had lost the bundle of roots and the digging stick and fearing that Gudrid would be angry if she went back empty handed, she searched around until she found a broken branch that would serve to grub up the plants she wanted. Nearby grew a clump of pink valerian and she broke off the evil-smelling flowers and dug and prodded at the earth to get the root. Gudrid said the all-heal was a comfort to the belly and eased the wind. At last she got it up and bagging up the front of her kirtle, she carried it before her and wandered along looking for chamomile and wormwood. As soon as she found something she would go back to the camp; most of the men were away today, ranging far into the forest hunting the King's deer, and she could talk to Gudrid in peace.

Many things they talked of. Gudrid told her of bygone days in old King Henry's time when a man could pass in safety from one end of the kingdom to the other; she told her, too, of the coming of the Normans to England after a great battle between the English and the Norsemen up in the Danelaw, so that Hikenai was convinced Gudrid had seen these events with her own eyes and was, perhaps, the oldest woman in the world. Gudrid was willing to admit she might be close on a hundred. Hikenai had wondered a little how it came about that her son, Harold, was so young but he might, after all, be her grandson. The simpler explanation, that Gudrid could not count beyond her fingers' tally, did not occur to her.

They talked, too, of the spirits in the woods for Gudrid's belief in them was as firm as Hikenai's own and neither of them would set foot out of the hut after dusk when Robin Goodfellow flitted abroad and ghosts rode the night wind, in spite of the jeers of the men. Gudrid did not like men, she had been ill used by them too often in her youth; now that she was old she was afraid of no one and threatened to poison any who molested her or the girl. The rest of the women in the band were naught but trulls, she told Hikenai, they might look to themselves.

It was Aelward in particular that Hikenai feared, he who had brought her hither. He had taken her, brutally and without tenderness, beside the path in the forest a few hours after they had met. Ever since, she had trembled when she saw him and Gudrid had quickly seen her fear and beaten him off with curses. Harold had abetted her at first for he thought he would have Hikenai for himself but he got the same treatment from his mother and at last the men had given up, thinking the old woman could not live much longer.

The outlaws lived as nomads, moving from one camp to another; now it was summer they had gone deep into the forest, far from habitation. Here in their secret clearing the women even planted a few patches of corn or pulses.

When Hikenai returned with a great armful of chamomile flowers, the camp drowsed peacefully. Gudrid sat outside the hut, stirring something in a pot on the small fire and grumbling softly to herself, mumbling her lips over her toothless gums. A few of the women were moving about the small green patches, pulling up weeds and picking off caterpillars. Close by, in a sling hanging from a branch, a babe wailed. Hikenai went across to it; she had an interest in the child since she had helped Gudrid at the birth. Every time she saw it she heaved a sigh of relief that Aelward had not made her pregnant that one time.

Sometimes, when one or other of the weyves thought she was with child, she would come to Gudrid and ask her for a remedy; sometimes Gudrid gave it, sometimes not, and anyway it did not always work. It had not worked with this babe. Hikenai did not blame the women in the least; bearing babes was usually a lot of trouble for nothing, for nine out of ten died before they walked. Still, she thought that one day it would be pleasing to have a child of her own but only ' if she were wed to a strong man, like a smith or a carpenter. She did not want a child here among the outlaws.

She sat down on the grass beside Gudrid and saw at once that she was in a bad mood.

'Is yon all ye have brought?' demanded the old woman. 'Little enough for a morning's gathering!'

Hikenai began to tell her of the faery place but she would not listen. 'Go,' she said impatiently, 'and look to the patch of peas or the worms will eat them all. We have little enough unless the men bring meat.'

'What is in the pot, goodwife?' asked Hikenai humbly.

'Naught but little beets and thin little onions,' said Gudrid.

Even so, the smell made Hikenai's belly wamble with emptiness and she opened her mouth to speak again but the old woman struck at her irritably with the wooden ladle so she beat a hasty retreat. The sun struck hot upon her bare head when she stood in the plot of young peas, and she moved to the end of the row where there was a dappled shade. From here she could see right across the assart to the group of flimsy huts which were all that sheltered them in summer.

134

Winter was quite different; then the men dug shallow pits and built sod huts around the depressions, roofing them with turves on top of branches. Hikenai had hated the winter more than she usually did. She had lived in the biggest hut with Gudrid and Harold and the woman who pleased him at the moment, but in the darkest days all the rest had crowded in too, to drink home brewed ale and gamble. Fights were frequent; Harold had stabbed one churl so that he died, and broken heads were commonplace.

The personal habits of the outlaws were little better than the beasts of the field; Hikenai thought it foul shame to them when the men openly made water and squatted down into a hole dug for that purpose beside the central fire. She kept as far from that spot as she might, preferring to endure cold rather than disgustful sights and stenches. And when she whispered the reason for her strange behaviour in answer to Gudrid's kindly meant urgings back to the fire, the old woman had howled and shrieked with laughter at such fantastical niceness so that all there knew of it and their jeering was added to her misery. But Hikenai could not get used to it for her father, though nothing but a serf, was a man who observed the decencies so that when nature called he went outside the hut or at least turned his back on her.

As she moved desultorily along the row of peas she heard the falling notes of a horn from deep within the forest. She stiffened and looked up, staring into the tangled green depths. The other women heard it, too, and all stood transfixed, waiting. No outlaw used a horn. Even the birds were quiet for a space, then a fat thrush hopped along the row and began to bang a snail upon a stone. The sharp taps broke the sudden hush. At last he cracked the shell and flew up into a tree and there began to sing his lovely twice-repeated song.

Again, and nearer this time, she heard the horn. She stood rock still, her bare toes squinching at the soft, rich

135

earth, tensed and ready to run. Now other sounds became apparent to her ears, the jingle of bits nearby and farther off, the baying of hounds. Suddenly a man burst from the forest's edge and ran with the clumsy staggering gait of near exhaustion straight at her.

It was Aelward! – the fool had led his pursuers back to the camp! In that moment she could have killed him herself. Almost on his heels a mounted man bore down upon her. She dropped the hoe and fell down upon the precious peas, breaking the brittle, young stems. More horses with riders richly dressed were pouring out of the forest and she rolled aside in her efforts to avoid them.

Mouth open and eyes strained wide with fear, she lay and watched them lay violent hands upon Aelward and drag him to his knees. They were shouting to one another and at Aelward but she could not understand them. She flinched at every blow that landed on his bloody head and shoulders but at length he fell forward and lay still. They lost interest then, and more of them dismounted and wandered round the assart, kicking the limp body as they passed it. It was then she realised she was alone among the strangers – the women had gone, even old Gudrid, even the babe in its sling. She lay as still as death herself with her throat so closed by terror that no air would go down to her straining lungs and her heart beats drummed in her ears like a horse at full gallop.

It was a horse! More horses were coming out of the forest and she was in their path! In a frenzy she sprang up and ran wildly across the assart, crushing down the few peas that were left. The huntsmen shouted in astonishment at her unexpected appearance, and she saw a horse suddenly lash out and overturn Gudrid's pot into the fire with a great sizzling of steam and smoke, and the loss of their poor meal seemed to her the greatest tragedy of all. She wept aloud and stumbled towards it and blindly blundered against the flank of a horse. A huge lump came up out of her stomach

136

into her throat and she leaned on the warm, smooth coat and tried to vomit.

It seemed to Henry that she had sprung up out of the earth itself. She was Saxon, he thought, with all that wild, tow-coloured hair about her shoulders and the pale eyes fixed and staring. She looked half-witted but when she raised her head again some semblance of reason had come back into her face. She did not look at him though he had caught her by the shoulder; her eyes were fixed on Thomas.

'We have surprised a nest of wolves' heads,' he said to Henry.

'So it would appear – and the birds all flown but for that carrion – and this.'

She stared from one to the other, listening for some word she could recognise, and behind her another voice spoke harshly in Norman French and she heard it – 'Le Roy.' That meant the King! Now she was indeed terrified and would have sunk to the ground but for the gloved hand on her shoulder. The one who held her asked her a question but she could only gaze at him blankly and shiver in his grasp.

Thomas said, 'She knows naught but her own English dialect.' He spoke to her then in words which came awkwardly from his tongue but which she understood. 'Do you live here?'

She nodded.

'Where are the rest?'

She motioned towards the greenwood, her mouth working.

Thomas said to Henry, 'You will never find them. They have their hidey-holes all over the forest.'

Behind them, Aelward began to moan and struggle and a couple of archers ran across and cuffed him into silence. Hikenai, who had thought him dead, made to move towards him but the hand which still held her tightened, preventing her. Henry did not turn his head, his eyes had never left her face but now he looked her up and down. She was small and none too clean but young and comely; her shoulders and breasts were admirable, he thought, and he was startled by a sudden rush of desire so that he pressed the tip of his tongue between his teeth.

'Shall we not hang him now?' urged one of the young knights, but one who was older hushed him impatiently and watched the English maid with curious eyes. He had not missed the expression on the King's face and thought that even now this miserable lout might escape with no more than the loss of his eyes – that is, if the wench were complaisant.

Thomas had lost interest in the girl; he was staring round the outlaw encampment for it was the first time he had seen such a place. His eyes ran over the ruined vegetable plots, trampled flat by the horses, and then narrowed as they fell upon the curious clay image stuck on a stick at the end of one of the rows.

'What's that?' he said sharply in the English tongue. 'Who fashioned it?'

'It was I, lord,' she faltered, at last finding her voice, 'it is the – the god who watches over the crops.'

'What God? God died upon a cross as all of Christianity knows' – and he walked across and dragged up the image and held it in his hand. Shaped of the clay of the field, it was as long as his forearm and faceless, for the front of the head was masked by a bit of dirty cloth. Only what should have been covered was formed in detail, grotesquely hideous, and disgust was plain on Thomas' face as he held it out to Henry. The older knights craned to see, and grinned.

'It is one of the old gods,' she whispered, 'that my mother told me of.'

Henry stood with it in his hand, half frowning, half amused.

It is Priapus,' said Thomas in Norman French again, 'and as she says, one of the old gods. Cast it down, sire, it is filth and foulest heresy.'

138

Henry threw it to the ground and put his heel upon it. 'A strange god, that, and a stranger name,' he observed, but he would not look at Thomas for what he had seen had set the seal on his desire. 'Take the young pages hence, Tom,' he said. 'We'll come up with you later when we have dealt justice here.'

When Thomas and the boys had gone, and not without many a disappointed murmur and half resentful backward look, Henry turned again to Hikenai and nodded towards the hut outside which they stood. 'Come,' he said.

She did not recognise the word but the gesture was unmistakable. This was a very fair man, she thought, though he was not clad near so fine as some of the others; his cloak was too short, and now that he had dismounted she saw that he was bandy. Still, he had a manner with him; she could not put it into words but he seemed the kind that all men would obey. So she waited a moment nervously, yet with a look on her face that was almost anticipation.

Henry motioned to his men to be off and the captain murmured a query about the prisoner. 'Hang him,' said the King. 'Not here. In the forest, out of sight.'

He sat in the stinking hut and talked to her, and though she understood scarcely one word in ten of his Norman French, a little of his meaning began to filter through to her. He kept waving his arm and looking at her questioningly and she thought that he was asking whence she came. The expression on his face she recognised well enough, she had seen it on the faces of too many men since she had gone with Aelward.

She did not know when she first realised that this man was the King, not the tall, slender one who had looked at her with such terrifying coldness in his pale eyes – those startling eyes, the same colour exactly as the forget-me-not flowers that grew upon the bank nearby. This man's eyes were grey but warm and dancing and his square face was freckled

as though he spent his time in the open. Not like that other
– she shivered as she thought of him. He was the reason she
had come in here willingly with this one.

Henry saw the shiver and put his arm about her. He
watched her trembling mouth with eagerness, trying to
gauge the exact moment to begin to kiss her. He did not
want to frighten her further and there was something about
her that excited his curiosity. She did not look like a weyve
nor like a loose slut who hung around the outlaws.

Again he asked her if she was married, wondering whether
she had accompanied an outlawed husband, but her look
was as uncomprehending as ever. She seemed to be listening to the noise of the departing knights and huntsmen, and
when the last hoofbeats died away she relaxed against him.
He began to kiss her then, gently at first and then more
insistently. She tried to push him away, remembering
Aelward and fearing a repetition of the pain he had caused
her, but there was nothing fierce or brutal about this kissing,
only a warmth and persuasiveness that made her tremble for
a different reason.

She was filthy and the strong, gamy odour of her body
might have nauseated a more fastidious man but Henry,
whose sense of smell had long been blunted by unsavoury
surroundings, noticed only the essential exhalation of
womanhood. It evoked in him a response that all of
Eleanor's flower-scented unguents failed to do so that his
hands shook as he unlaced her kirtle and pulled up the
hampering skirts. He felt the stiffness of her pose and sensed
the fear in her, holding himself upon a tight rein. He wanted
her consent. Rape would bring only self-disgust and Henry
was too sensual a man to abuse any woman's body. He had
enjoyed enough women to discover there was little pleasure
to be bought from harlots beyond the relief of tension. Desire
was necessary in both partners. Eleanor was good, of course,
but her very expertise was inclined to inhibit him. And the
few real love affairs he had experienced had all been with

mature women so that he had felt himself the pupil rather than the teacher.

This would be different. He looked at her mouth and her naked bosom, and with a rush of overmastering desire, began to kiss and fondle her while with his left hand he pulled at the thongs that tied his braies to the belt beneath his tunic. When her lips softened under his he kicked off his boots, letting his braies and stockings fall about his ankles, and lay beside her feeling her naked flesh against his own. She was so warm and soft and small, no bigger than a child. In spite of his urgency, he treated her with gentleness.

And it was different. Still lying on her while his breathing quieted, he stroked her straw-coloured hair away from her face. 'Look at me,' he whispered.

She opened her eyes, so close to his.

'Who are you? But oh – I care not who you are, only so you are mine!' He rolled away from her, hugging to himself this sudden inexplicable joy, and then turned back to feel her warm breath on his cheek. 'It is very sure you cannot understand a word I say! But this you can' – and he started to kiss her again, her mouth, her shoulders, her breasts, her whole body until passion overcame him again.

Her passivity delighted him for he thought it proof that she was virgin. Yet her ardour matched his own. And to think he had avoided virgins since he first fought Stephen for England after a disastrous experience with a terrified twelve-year-old whose father had pushed her into bed with him in cognizance of his loyalty to the House of Anjou! No virgin would be safe from him hereafter!

Afterwards he talked to her again but she comprehended no more than she had before. She would not look at him at first but he held her hands so gently in his hard, calloused ones and was watching her with such kindness when she stole a glance at him that she smiled at last, and then he

laughed and lifted her up in his arms and carried her outside. The sun still shone and all the leaves were golden
green, fluttering gently in the balmy air, and suddenly
she was happy.

He put her up upon his horse as though she were a
precious thing and when he was in the saddle he tilted up
her chin and kissed her once again. Then she really smiled
and he sat quiet a moment, gazing down into her face with
a look so intent and wondering that she stopped smiling
and stared at him.

So they looked into each other's eyes for a timeless instant
amid the ruins of the outlaw camp; then Henry kicked his
heel against the horse's side and they moved off. Five
mounted archers came slowly from the place where they
had waited and rode along behind but at a respectful distance.

August 1155
At the time of the King's coronation Dame Hermengild,
the mason's widow, was past fifty years old and therefore
an old woman though her plump, pink face belied her age.
She always used the surname Mason despite the fact that
all who remembered him knew well that her husband had
never been more than a barrowman who wheeled the hods
of stone and lime. Owing to his calling he had been much
from home in his lifetime but the lusty Dame Hermengild
had had no difficulty in finding solace elsewhere. Fat, jolly,
and much given to bawdy talk, she had attracted a large
circle of friends, and when her husband died she took three
homeless young women to live with her and set up in the
most lucrative profession open to them.

At first, apprentices and the poorer sort of citizen were
her clients but Dame Hermengild had an eye for the main
chance and when, early on, she was lucky enough to make
the acquaintance of some hangers-on at Court, she strained
every nerve to encourage them, even to the lengths of

obliging her protégées to wash every day. She had thrived on the disorders of Stephen's reign and when her little house was burnt down in one of the fires that were common occurrences in that city of wooden walls and thatched roofs, she leapt at the offer of a stone-built dwelling between London and the village of Westminster.

It belonged, as did the great house it adjoined, to the Earl of Essex, that great anarchist, but since his death both had fallen into dilapidation and the gardens, running down to the Thames, were thick with weeds. It lay to one side and a little behind the great house but it had its own private gate in the thick wall, and its own triangular garden, fenced off from the rest. Still, you could see the river from the highest windows and Dame Hermengild liked the secrecy of its position.

She was mightily incensed, therefore, after she had spent good silver and put all to rights, that a new come wool merchant should build a house on her other side and place his privies next to her garden fence with an open kennel running down to the Thames. She so badgered the poor merchant that he threatened to report her to the sheriff and a feud smouldered between them for many a year until, by great good fortune, the new young King visited her establishment in the company of two or three of the more riotous of his lords. She felt her fortune was surely made.

So it was that Geoffrey de Mandeville the younger, trying to creep back into the King's favour, brought Hikenai to her house with strict instructions from the King that she was to be kept apart from the other women, to have her separate chamber and to be guarded from the lustful eyes of men.

Though why the King should think that any man would look at her, I know not, thought Hermengild. Big breasted enough but skinny in the hocks and her clothes fit only for burning, and she stared at Hikenai's legs which showed under the short gown and wondered if she were wearing hosen or whether it were truly ingrained dirt. But once

Hikenai's hair and skin were washed Hermengild marvelled at their fairness and said she should never have supposed the girl had lived so long among outlaws.

Gradually she drew from her the story of her life but Hikenai did not tell that which had happened to her beside the forest path with Aelward, an inner caution kept her silent so that in the end it seemed to her a dream like other dreams she had at times – or were they memories, too? She could not tell, but sometimes in that state midway between sleep and waking, she thought of a night while yet her mother lived and they had gone abroad together and had been in the company of a great concourse of men and women.

A moonlit place it was with trees about, and a huge fire had burnt and all the air was filled with chanting. And they had laid her down and rubbed her nude body – she remembered the feel of the hands on her, slippery and soft. And the singing had been so loud. . . . Then she was flying in sweeping, soaring arcs, high above the people round the fire. Others were flying, too, like bats at dusk, round and round, curving out and sailing back in a kind of intricate, aerial dance, but whether her mother was of their number she was not sure though she thought that it was so. Certainly, it was her mother who had led her between the trees up to – some one – who sat alone upon a grassy knoll in the bright, white moonlight. Branching antlers on his head. . . . and here the memory, if memory it were, faded as though a veil had been drawn across the windows of her mind.

She knew that behind the veil lay terror and a wild, inexplicable joy, but the terror was the greater – the same terror which had gripped her, sick and shaking, in the forest the day she met the king. Here, far from the wooded glades where They dwelt, she would be safe.

In the weeks that followed, Hikenai settled into Dame Hermengild's household easily; for such comfort and good eating she would have lived anywhere and the old woman, with her fund of stories and merry, cackling laugh, was a congenial companion.

She awakened early one August morning and ran to the window to push back the shutters and greet the day. Bright sunlight spilled in and a flood of air so unseasonably cold that she hugged her arms around her nakedness and shivered as she peered down on the pleasant little garden below with its patch of herbs and the mulberry tree overhanging the fence. She dressed quietly and came downstairs. Dame Hermengild greeted Hikenai with smiles and the news that this day they should go together to the Horse Fair at West Smithfield near the City, for today was Friday. She had all the Londoner's fierce pride in her native place and while they ate salt herring together she told Hikenai of the Priory and Hospital of St Bartholomew which had been founded around the time of her birth by Rahere, the old King's jester who had become a monk – though it was not really in the City, she said, being outside the wall between New Gate and Alders Gate. And she told her they would certainly see all the earls, barons and knights who were presently in the City, and perchance the King, also. . . this with a narrow look at Hikenai for they had had no word from Court since the girl had come to her.

And so when she had plaited a length of ribbon into each of Hikenai's long fair plaits and had wrapped her in a cloak of coarse green wool, they set off with Algot, Dame Hermengild's man, to walk behind them and carry their goods. He had the empty gaze of an idiot but he obeyed the Dame without question and followed her like a dog since she had rescued him from a stoning though, in truth, her kindness had been merely a by-product of her belligerent and interfering nature; she could never watch a street fight without somehow becoming involved.

They came into thicker traffic as they approached New Gate after crossing the Fleet. Parties of people on mules or horseback passed them and heavy wagons drawn by oxen

145

lurched by. Hikenai thought she had never seen so many folk in one place but Hermengild said she should wait until she was within the City itself, there the noise was like to deafen any honest soul.

Now they bore off to the left and so into West Smithfield which was a large space of trampled earth, full of stalls, hucksters and a noisy press of men of all sorts, from the meanest, poorly dressed kind to the fine lords and their squires. A little to one side behind a stand of ancient elms lay the Priory of St Bartholomew and beyond it towered the City wall, thick and strong, built over many generations so that it was a mixture of materials, flint and white stones, old Roman bricks and rubble all interspersed. Away to the north under a vast sky patterned all over with grey and white cloud stretched the marshes, and very clear in the distance, the wooded hills of Middlesex.

Hikenai gazed around, her heart quickening, for after Dame Hermengild's words she half expected to see the King, but though there were many who were richly garbed enough to deceive the ignorant, the face she sought was absent. She sighed when hope was gone and turned her attention to the horses. These, in which the lords were showing interest, were destriers, great war horses. All were stallions and almost twice the size of the work horses she remembered, or so she thought, and she was fascinated by the breadth of their backs, the huge muscles of their hocks and the feathery plumes and fringes which draped their hoofs. Close by, fluttering and flapping in the wind, trappings of cendal were offered for sale and she was amazed that a horse, even one as grand as these, should be clad in gaily coloured silken stuff when the King wore nothing half so fine.

Hermengild pulled at her cloak. 'We must away from here,' she said. 'See how they stare at you! They think it passing strange that a maid of low degree will watch the destriers. Come, soon the races will begin' – and she pushed Hikenai along before her and called to Algot to stay close.

146

Hikenai had never experienced anything to compare with the excitement of the races. She clapped and screamed and danced up and down until she was exhausted and Hermengild nodded patronisingly and said the racing was not as good as usual. All the same, Hikenai noticed that she tore a great rent in her veil in the suspense of one close finish and did not suggest leaving until the last race was over. Then she said they would go into the City and eat at the cookshop on the river bank and drink at the nearby Vintry; it would be like old times for her and perhaps she would meet old friends.

It was now two hours past noon and the wind that had blown all morning had died. They entered the City through New Gate and Algot went ahead to make a way for them through the crowds. He pushed and elbowed with determination and when one or another would think to complain of his shoving, they took a second look at his blank, simpleton gaze and the thickness of his great loosely swinging arms and turned their heads the other way. So they came at last abreast of St Paul's and the Dame shouted to Algot to stop and wait while she and Hikenai stood awhile to watch the builders.

'It will be the greatest church in Christendom,' boasted Dame Hermengild, 'for I tell thee a church has stood on this hill nigh to half a thousand years, and this will be the greatest of them all. See now, they build in stone! Ah, had my husband lived! He should have been employed thereon for none could shape stone to compare with him.'

'I think they will find it hard to better the Abbey Church of St Edmund,' said Hikenai; she thought sometimes that the Dame had much to say for one who had never travelled more than five miles from her birthplace, 'and I think the bones of St Paul do not rest here.'

Hermengild stared at her in much the same way she would have looked at Algot had he begun to propound Canon Law.

'Why, as to that,' she said, somewhat at a loss, 'where the bones of Paul do lie, I know not, but in this place lay the bones of St Erkenwald for many a hundred year, and when the old church burnt the flames checked at his tomb. Myself, I saw him moved, not seven years ago, to a new resting place, there to lie until a fitting shrine be prepared for him again.'

'When did the old church burn?'

'Jesu, it was long ago before my time –'

'Then they are wondrous slow rebuilding,' and Hikenai stared across to where the masons worked, hauling up the great, pale blocks of stone on a kind of hoist. All around was the banging and tapping and clinking of tools, the creaking of ropes and shouting of men, and now and then a thunderous rumble and a cloud of stone dust rising on the air.

'Nay, nay,' said Hermengild impatiently. 'It was another fire in the year of King Stephen's coming made all to do again. Jesu mercy! what a fire that was, it laid waste half of London from St Clement Danes to the Bridge. When we have eaten I will show you where the bridge did stand – it is full time we had another but perchance this young King will see to't – but the wherrymen will like it not. Wagons, though, are ever getting stuck in the river by cause that fools try to drive them over at low tide.'

A few drops of rain began to fall and they went on towards the river that they might reach the cookshop before they were soaked, and so at last to Thames Street through the noise of apprentices yelling at them to buy and the roar of iron-shod wheels on the cobbles and the whole vast humming of the City like the sound of a gigantic hive of bees. When they came to the cookshop Hikenai was glad to sit on a stool in the corner and eat eel pies among the lower class of citizen out of the bustle and the press for her head was aching from the din.

But as soon as they had eaten their fill, the Dame would

along to the Vintry and there she seemed disposed to stay, drinking and making conversation with a prosperous looking burgess while the rain pattered down outside. Hikenai did not listen for they spoke in Norman French, she drifted away into a reverie and sat with a look as vacant as Algot's own. After a time the sky began to brighten and one or two blue patches appeared in the west; soon only a few tattered remnants of cloud remained and she whispered to the Dame, asking if she might go down to the strand where the tide had receded, leaving a few charred piles of the old bridge sticking out of the water near the bank.

So long as Algot went, too, said Hermengild, loth to leave her companion but he, most ungallant, developed a sudden interest in the river too, and so they all went down to the strip of shingly beach; Dame Hermengild with many protestations that she was too old to slide about on river banks so that she must cling to the arm of her new acquaintance.

The tide had left a line of clean, ochre-coloured sand at the water's edge with black boulders imbedded therein and on the boulders thick mats of weed shone wetly. Nearby a couple of fishermen were spreading their nets to dry and laughing at the Dame as she tried to prevent her skirts from dragging in the sand. The river sparkled, running up in little lapping waves, and away to the left the Caen stone of the White Tower was brilliant against a sky so suddenly deeply blue. The cries of the wherrymen crossing perilously close to the remains of the bridge blended with the screaming of a flock of gulls, and the bright beauty of the scene affected Algot so that he began to laugh wildly and wave his arms about, and capering down to the water's edge he splashed in knee deep and pranced up and down, making a great commotion and turning his grinning moon face to the amazed onlookers in high glee.

The fishermen shouted encouragement to him, sniggering at Dame Hermengild's fury, and then began to throw stones until the burgess spoke sharply to them, bidding them tend to their own affairs.

The Dame gave vent to her annoyance by yelling scathing remarks at Algot and at last he stood still with a sullen hangdog look and then came slowly out with his say stockings wrinkled down and black with water.

'Do you think I shall nurse you with the ague?' she demanded. 'Perdy, you are a very fool!'

'Aye, so he be,' agreed the burgess reasonably. 'You should remember it, goodwife,' and he turned to see Hikenai's reaction to his good sense, but she was still gazing downriver with a faraway look and Dame Hermengild wondered which of the two members of her household were the greater fool, for the burgess was a wealthy man judging by the quality of the fine fur-trimmed robe he wore. So she forced down her vexation and asked him would he accompany them home, which invitation he accepted with alacrity.

With Algot squelching dejectedly along behind them, they went back up the wooden steps and into the City streets where the burgess bought Hikenai a bunch of ribbons and Dame Hermengild a pot of galingale for which she had angled shamelessly; this last was in the nature of a peace offering after her offence at his assumption that the unfortunate Algot was her son.

They paused to drink at several aleshops on the way so that when they arrived home Dame Hermengild, at least, was very merry and leaned heavily on the burgess when he thumped upon her oaken door with his silver-headed staff. It opened so suddenly that they would have fallen within except that old Brand, the porter, materialised in the opening, peering out with his wrinkled, sagging countenance even more doleful than usual. At sight of the Dame his face seemed to pull itself together and – 'Faith, Mistress, it's well you are home at last with the young maid!' he cried. 'Messengers from the King have we had and none too pleased that you were absent. They yet await you in the solar. . . .'

The change which took place in the Dame's demeanour was marvellous to behold. In a trice the bewildered burgess was whisked away to the other side of the house where dwelt the wenches who were the main source of her revenues and she herself donned the mantle of sobriety with an ease that astonished Hikenai. When she graciously greeted the emissaries of the King they could never have supposed that she had been anywhere but on a protracted shopping expedition with her charge. The King would visit her establishment on the morrow, they told her, now that he had returned to Westminster, and all must be in readiness for his coming.

Hikenai eavesdropped outside the partly open door of the solar. Now that he had returned to Westminster was the phrase that meant most to her. Thanks be to God she had learnt enough Norman French to follow their speech! He had not stayed away from indifference then. Her heart beat fast as she crept away and a little smile lifted the corners of her lips as she thought once more of his eager gaze and the way his red hair had curled, damp with sweat, on his forehead. Anxiously she looked into the polished metal mirror in her own small chamber, wondering if he would still find her fair. If only her face were a long, handsome oval like that of Alfled, the most popular of Dame Hermengild's wenches, instead of being as wide as the harvest moon.

She put down the mirror in disgust and then took it up again and began to comb the snarls and tangles from her hair as the Dame had taught her. After a while she heard the messengers taking their departure and flinging down the comb, she drew a long, deep breath and lay down upon the couch, stretching her limbs until a happy lassitude invaded her.

*

151

Later that evening in her upper chamber, Dame Hermengild sat smiling to herself. Her fortunes were made with this girl in her house. Even if the King tired of her quickly – as he surely would, being noted for inconstancy with women – other men would be interested. It had not escaped her that every man they had passed today had taken a second look at her companion. And not only the young men. . . . Settled-looking burgesses had looked and looked again at the face under the green hood and the knights and nobles at the Horse Fair had followed her eagerly with their lustful eyes until they were out of sight. She would play the part of a lodestone in her little house by the river, drawing men from far and wide, men with good silver jingling in their pockets and fine horses to tie to the post at her door.

She waddled to the door. 'Come hither, Hikenai child,' she called softly, 'and take a cup of wine with me.'

Henry had not stayed away from the house near Westminster from indifference. He had had every intention of making many visits there but he had found it was not as easy as he had anticipated to force his rebellious barons to give up their unlicensed castles, and his determination to impose his will on them took first place in his mind.

Earl Roger of Hereford, who had been one of his faithful supporters, had slipped away and stocked up with food and troops of Welshmen, prepared to undergo siege rather than submit, and it was only the strongly worded advice of his kinsman, the Bishop of Hereford, that at last induced him to give way. Another who took no pleasure in the thought of humbling himself was the Bishop of Winchester, King Stephen's brother, who had been one of the greatest castle builders of all. He fled to Cluny, taking the treasury of the diocese with him.

Through all these infuriating events, the face of the maid from the outlaw camp kept obtruding. Henry was unable to understand the persistence of his feeling for her. All his life he had been a stranger to tenderness and no woman, even Eleanor, had aroused in him anything deeper than passion. Yet there it was – he felt what he had never felt before, a longing to pamper and cherish another human being, an urge to give rather than to take. He could not discuss the matter with Thomas, and none of the others were any help.

'Take her again,' they urged him. 'Surfeit is the surest cure. In a month, you will never wish to see her again.'

Henry was doubtful, but decided to try the remedy. He sent off the messengers to Dame Hermengild that very day, and gossip spread rapidly around the Court. Henry cared nothing for that; he found that for the first time in weeks he was able to concentrate fully upon the business in hand at a meeting of the Great Council. Thomas, who had almost forgotten the whole abhorrent episode, was relieved to see the King giving all his attention to the framing of the articles of peace with another rebel, Hugh Mortimer, though his eyebrows rose a little at Henry's decision to allow him to keep all his lands. Such mildness was unlike him.

He tried to catch Henry's eye but Richard de Luci interposed his broad shoulder and Thomas was obliged to murmur his comments to the Earl of Leicester who had become his friend and ally. The other members were only too happy to see the King so jovial and the Council was dismissed with an arrangement to meet again at Michaelmas in Winchester.

Thomas remained behind, watching his clerk sorting and rolling the documents, while the Council members took their leave. 'Tck!' he said. 'What is that you have there? – the letter. Is it not the request from the Abbot of Battle to the King? Give it here, it must not be overlooked,' and taking it in his hand, he hurried over to where Henry still sat with a faraway look and a mind quite obviously on other than Council business.

'One more small matter for the attention of your grace,' he murmured, formal as always when underlings were within earshot. 'It is the application from Battle Abbey for confirmation of its status as a Chapel Royal.'

'Ah – Battle Abbey?' said Henry vaguely.

'The foundation of your great-grandsire,' prompted Thomas.

Henry returned to himself with a start. 'Ah yes – the great Abbey to commemorate the victory over Harold Godwinsson. What of it?'

'It appears a quarrel has developed with the Bishop of Chichester who claims jurisdiction.'

Henry scowled. 'What argument can there be? Is it not a proprietary Abbey? How, then, can this bishop push in his clerical nose? I will endure no infringements of the royal prerogatives!'

Thomas saw his cheeks begin to redden and said soothingly, 'I think the Bishop does not mean to try to infringe the royal rights; he is concerned only with hierarchical obedience. It is but a matter of squabbling prelates.'

'Well, then,' said Henry in a milder tone, 'I grant the confirmation.'

'Archbishop Theobald holds with the Bishop of Chichester.'

Henry made an impatient movement and Thomas said quickly, 'I think it would be well to postpone the decision until they have had a chance to argue out the matter and find some means of dealing with the objectionable clauses. If they cannot agree, the case must come before you, but that is for the future.'

Henry rubbed his eyebrow. 'You, dear Tom, must represent me in this dispute. In the meantime, do you affix the Royal Seal to the charter but hold it in Chancery till the matter is cleared up. I look to you to see the royal rights are vindicated. Arrange the meeting with despatch and let us have an end to it. I shall be busy with other more important things than monkish wrangling,' and he smiled with that absent look again.

154

Thomas glanced at him with sudden suspicion which Henry met with a disarming smile and – 'Come, Chancellor, I'll dine with you this night. From all I hear, you are better served and fed than your King, and on gold and silver plates which dazzle fit to blind one!'

And indeed Henry was dazzled by the magnificence of the way dinner was served to his Chancellor, and amazed at the growth of Thomas' Household. No less than a hundred knights now dined in his hall, laughing, shouting and making merry as exotic dishes followed one upon another – roast swan and peacock redolent with spices, venison in rich sauce and wild boar with the crackling scored in squares and diamond shapes, and every slit stuck full of sweet almonds from the south.

Dozens of pages ran around the hall, each with a fair white cloth upon his arm and carrying a finger bowl that the diners might dip their hands in scented water between the courses. Later there were honeyed subtleties which melted to nothing in the mouth. Only the finest wines were served, unlike the vinegary stuff so often drunk at the King's table and finally, to cap all, a great silver dish of Spanish oranges was placed before them.

Carefully, Thomas peeled one and put the tiny, plump crescents, glistening and bursting with juice, in front of Henry. Some of the King's men who had accompanied him and were watching, began to mutter among themselves saying that the Chancellor was setting himself above the King.

Earl Roger of Leicester overheard and frowned, for he had conceived a great liking for the Chancellor. 'No,' he declared, 'it is not so. Our lord King cares nothing for outward show, being frugal by nature. All that the Chancellor does shows forth the King's glory for is he not his servant?' – and he turned to de Luci for confirmation. But Richard's face showed plain enough that he agreed with the others, though the real reason for his resentment was that his office and Leicester's should rank higher than that of Chancellor and his envy was not so much on the King's behalf as on his own. He thought Leicester a fool for not seeing it and, turning his back, began to converse with the Bishop of Salisbury who also thought he had cause to dislike Thomas.

'For I am certain it is the Chancellor's doing that I am not to have back the castle of Devizes which was promised me,' he whispered to de Luci. 'He holds the King in the palm of his hand. Did not the Empress promise the Chancellorship to de Vere? This fellow has come up from nowhere and made himself great' – and he stared jealously at the dish of oranges for which he had a passion. 'Doubtless, such were bought with the revenues of vacant sees like that of Winchester,' he muttered. 'All the monies of Church and Crown lands disappear into his hands. Little wonder that he lives so fine.'

Suddenly Henry, who had seen the Bishop's eyes fixed longingly on the fruit although he could not hear his grumbling, picked up an orange, shouting, 'Here, my lord, I can no longer bear to see you drool so with desire' – hurled it down the table towards him. Thomas, too, began to throw the oranges toward the guests and all those near enough to reach joined in until the air was thick with them and half of the expensive golden globes were burst and lying in the rushes.

Dame Hermengild had all the servants up long before dawn the next day, scouring and cleaning that part of the house which the King might see. She even wielded a gigantic bunch of feathers herself, sending up clouds of dust from corners and the tops of presses where it had lain undisturbed for many a month. After all was done to her satisfaction she went to wake Hikenai but when she entered the small chamber she found her charge already risen from the couch

156

and sitting in her favourite spot in the window embrasure.

'Marry, you're awake betimes! I'll warrant you could not sleep for the itch between your legs!' she greeted her delightedly; now that she had grown so fat her pleasures were perforce vicarious.

Hikenai turned a puzzled face to her. 'A fellow walks about in the garden below, singing,' she said, 'Hark to him now' – and even as she spoke a melodious baritone was upraised under the window.

'Rats or mice, ha' ye any rats, mice, polecats or weasels
Or ha' ye any old sows sick of the measles?
I can kill them and I can kill moles
And I can kill vermin that creepeth up and creepeth
  down
And peepeth into holes.'

'Now, by the Rood, it's Ead, the ratcatcher,' cried the Dame, leaning upon her beefy arms and staring out of the window.

'Now, by Cock, it is Dame Hermengild,' shouted back Ead, very saucy; being young and comely, he was a favourite of hers and he knew it.

'We have no work for you this day, Ead,' said she, 'for I've not seen so much as the tail tip of a varmint since your last visit. Go round to the kitchens and take a sup of ale – I've no time for you, neither, there's great doings afoot here today,' and she withdrew with the utmost dispatch as she saw Ead's mouth opening for a question; she knew her own weakness for a pretty lad and she had no intention of being tempted into an hour's gossip on this most important morning.

Hikenai heard him retreating, still whistling his little tune, and then the rumble and clatter of the night soil carts as they passed, bearing their noisome burden out into the countryside, to Chelsea.

'Oh, it is pity to grow old and lose the sweetness of your

157

humours,' mourned the Dame. 'If I were but your age, that Ead should not be sent empty away from my chamber, I promise you! But who could know that hidden in the burden of my ancient flesh still dwells an ardent nymph? It's shame that the heart grows not old along with the body.' And she sighed a gusty sigh so that Hikenai must turn away her head lest the Dame read in her eyes the ludicrous picture that was forming in her mind.

So she sighed too, as though in sympathy, saying, 'You have seen much of life and love, madame.'

'Aye, that have I. Noble blood in plenty I have known – but not to compare with you. Never a King!'

A tapping sounded on the door and one of the serving wenches came in with an armful of bliauts and tunics of different stuffs which she laid upon the couch, spreading out the skirts so that the colours were all intermingled, blue and sanguine, green, silver and russet, like a great heap of flowers.

'See now,' cried Dame Hermengild. 'Shall we not make you fine for the King! Try this' – and she held up a bliaut of fine crimson wool '– or this', pulling at a skirt of stiff white samite, powdered all over with stars. Hikenai stroked them gently, she had never touched stuffs that felt like these.

'Who can weave such?' she said in wonder.

'They are woven by the heathen in other lands and come into London in the ships. Come now, see which will fit' – and the Dame impatiently pulled Hikenai's shift over her head so that she stood naked beside the pool of colour.

In the end her choice fell upon the crimson wool over a yellow silken tunic for her taste inclined to rich, bright colours and Hikenai's own murmurs went unnoticed. 'But Mass, it's big enough for two your size!' she exclaimed when it was put on. 'Your waist's no bigger than a hand-span – stand sideways and none can see you! Where be the girdles?'

She began to root about in the muddled, tangled pile, swearing to herself about the carelessness of serving wenches with the property of others, and at length came up with a twisted silver chain. 'Well, to be sure, it's a neck piece but it will serve for a waist the size of yours. What went of the head veils? I swear that girl is the most useless that ever I bred up for Christian pity – she has not even brought them' and she rounded on the wench who skipped aside with an ease born of long practice.

'They are here,' said Hikenai, pulling them out from beneath the heap and fingering them with sensuous enjoyment.

Dame Hermengild pounced upon a square of silver tissue. 'There now,' she said, and placing it upon Hikenai's head, she stood back, breathing heavily, to view the overall effect.

'It will do,' she pronounced at last. 'Aye, it will do. Stand there till I come back, and you, girl, clear up this mess.' She lumbered away down the outer stair in the hope that young Ead might still be in the kitchens, leaving Hikenai feeling much like an image of the Virgin she had once seen, stiff, gorgeous and remote.

The sun was well up now, shining into the room; where the shutters were laid back a little cool breeze blew in too, ruffling the veil on her head. The serving girl watched her with sly, curious glances as she gathered up the discarded gowns; she was young herself but exceedingly ugly because of a hare lip so that she could not attract men; in that house there was nothing for her to do but wait upon those who could. Her name was Ediva; she had a cleft palate, too, which made it hard to understand her speech, and so silence had become a habit with her.

Hikenai had often seen her about the house; now she looked straight at her, not averting her eyes from the deformity as most people did, and said, 'Will the King like me thus, think you?'

Ediva made a gobbling noise and nodded eagerly, smiling in a manner which made her poor face hideous.

Dame Hermengild came back then, having found Ead gone, and shooed her away. She took Hikenai down to the hall and set her on the bench with the skirt of the bliaut nicely spread out at her feet and a dish of early plums before her. There she left her, with many admonitions not to spot the bliaut with the juice nor to spit the stones upon the floor.

Hikenai ate the plums and while an hour crept by amused herself by arranging the stones in patterns on the dish. At last she heard the barking of the watch dogs and the sound of strange gruff voices; she sat very still with her head cocked, so that Henry was already in the hall before she looked at the door. He stood there, half smiling, yet looking at her with more surprise than recognition. For a moment, he thought it was the wrong girl, but when she turned her head and he saw the sidelong glance of her slanting golden eyes and the long curve of her neck he knew her. She was lovelier by far than he remembered.

He crossed the hall with swift, eager strides and took her hands between his own; she stood up suddenly and the dish of plum stones showered down between them. Neither of them noticed, but Dame Hermengild, who waited by the door with the King's gentleman, said, 'Tsk, tsk,' in an aggrieved manner, more for effect than from any real feeling.

'Had you forgotten me in this long time, my dove?' he said, sitting on the bench and taking her upon his knee.

She smiled at him, shy because he must feel the thumping of her heart where his arm encircled her, yet proud because now, thanks to Dame Hermengild's tuition, she could understand him.

'No, never,' she whispered, and then very slowly because she must think out the phrases, 'I have thought of you every day that I have waited here.'

'And I of you,' he said. She wondered if he would kiss her and dropped her head but he did not; he shouted for someone to bring wine for he was thirsty after the ride.

'What shall we do this day?' he said, and she blushed furiously as she remembered the Dame's outspoken remarks of what he would wish to do.

'Will you ride with me and my gentlemen into the countryside? I have brought a litter in the hope of it and you shall bring your serving wench if you will.'

She was struck dumb that he should think to treat her as a great lady – did he truly think the Dame had given her a tiring wench of her own? Then she remembered poor, ugly Ediva with sudden compassion and answered quickly that, yes, she would like it well if Ediva came too.

Hermengild was bringing in the wine and her mouth dropped open with astonishment; she gave Hikenai a long look before she went away.

Henry poured the wine himself; he had called for it because he was nervous, a feeling new to him. That was why he had brought the litter; he wanted to be alone with this girl, as alone as they had been in the outlaw camp. He cursed himself now for suggesting she bring a wench – still, she could be palmed off on one of the gentlemen. He was prepared to offer this girl anything – of gifts or courtesy that was not her due – if it would please her. He had long suspected that his success with the opposite sex owed more to his rank than his charm but he had never cared before so long as he could have his way. This was different – why, he did not know.

They drank the wine; then Ediva appeared in a neat dark gown and the Dame with face impassive behind her. Henry scowled when he saw the wench – no one would willingly take her into the woods. No matter. He smoothed his face into pleasanter lines and called the gentleman who waited by the door. A whispered order passed and wooden-faced, the gentleman led out Ediva while Henry came behind, still with his arm about Hikenai's waist. Her shoulder fitted snugly under his armpit. She was, he thought, a very proper size for a woman.

Henry rode beside the litter, but when they came through Highgate where the villeins were carting the harvest he stopped the little cavalcade beside a reed-fringed pond and said that here they would rest that the ladies might stretch their legs. Henry sat upon a tussock, his three gentlemen a little to one side, and watched Hikenai and Ediva pace sedately along by the bulrushes with sidelong glances at each other, for neither was at all sure what was expected of her.

Of the three young men, Hugh of Aumale was sulky, for the other two, quicker witted than he, had brought with them, riding pillion on their saddles, two comely young trulls from Dame Hermengild's house and he now saw that he must entertain the ugly serving wench. So he sat with his head down, pulling at handfuls of tough grass with his nether lip pushed out, listening to the giggling of the trulls behind him. They were giggling at the sight of Hikenai and Ediva acting the fine ladies, but Henry became annoyed by it and bade the gentlemen take their doxies elsewhere.

'And you, Hugh,' he said, motioning to Ediva, whose reluctance at least had the effect of spurring Hugh to a determination to overcome it; he grabbed her wrist and dragged her off through the ferns and brambles so abruptly that she gave a little shriek – it was the first sound she had uttered since they set out.

Hikenai watched her departure with some alarm. 'He – he will not – do anything to her?' she asked.

Henry gave a roar of laughter. 'Only what she will wish,' he said, 'and only that if he is brave enough. Come here, my sweeting, sit close to me.' And he lifted his arm that she might snuggle down beside him.

They sat awhile gazing out across the still pool. The sun had gone in but the air was warm now the breeze had died away and the water was a shining pale grey; now and again a fly alighted on it or a fish rose, then it was glassy smooth again. When Henry turned his head, she was gazing at his face intently. His eyebrows went up.

'So?' he said, 'you shall know me again, I think. And do you love what you see?' His voice was teasing.

She said nothing but a wave of colour rose in her cheek as she looked away. He took her chin in his hand and tried to pull her face round towards him but she resisted. He took his hand away and frowned.

'Why are you here, then?' he said after a little silence.

'Why, you are the King,' she replied simply.

He stared at her. 'So – if I were not King –?'

She was quiet a moment, trying to sort out her thoughts. Finally she said, 'I am here because you are the King and I must obey. But if you were not King – still I should be here because to be with you is all my joy.'

She kept her head bent but when he made no movement she stole a glance at him. He was gazing at the water and very slowly he put out his hand and took hers. When he turned to her, the look on his face was different from any she had ever seen. Before that eager look her own eyes fell; with a long, contented sigh, he rolled upon his back, laying his head in her lap.

'Tell me now,' he said, 'everything of yourself you can remember. For very surely, I have never met any, great lady or poor slut, who in any way resembled you.'

So she told him, very slowly and with many pauses while she sought the right words, the story of her life, first in the village belonging to the lord, then on the assart in the heath up to her flight with the pedlar. Henry laughed at Benjy's discomfiture.

'But why should he think you a witch?' he asked, for she had not mentioned a talisman. She tried to tell him then something of the old religion, and he listened with interest and no little amazement.

163

'Do the common people believe this?' he exclaimed. 'Are not the Saints enough for them that men must dress in the skins and antlers of beasts? But you are not a part of it?' – for he had remembered the pagan image in the outlaw clearing.

'No,' she assured him swiftly, 'No, not I' – and deep down a memory stirred of that far, wild night of fire and moonlight, and she was troubled.

'Tell me more,' he said, easing himself into a more comfortable position, and she told him of her life with the outlaws until they met.

'And did you truly take my good Thomas to be King?' he cried with a roar of laughter. 'I shall tell him of it – how flattered he will be! Do you not like him, sweetheart? Tell me why' – but under all his praise of Thomas lay a thrill of delight that she had so definitely preferred him to his lordly Chancellor, and that without knowing his rank.

So they talked and kissed and fondled each other while the warm, grey hours drifted by. At last, Hikenai sat up and smoothed the deep red skirt, sadly crumpled now and prickly with ripe grass seeds. She began to hum a little tune while she laced her bodice, swaying her head in time with the melody. Henry watched her with a gentle look which was oddly at variance with his usual expression, and picking up the square of silver tissue, he knelt to arrange it on her hair and then leaned his cheek against her head.

'What is that air? I have heard it somewhere before.' He frowned. 'It is a tune that Saxon minstrel plays! What is his name? The fellow who plays for my – for the Queen.'

Hikenai sat very still. Strange that until this moment she had never even thought of his wife. There was pain in the knowledge that she shared him with another.

'It is an old English tune, that,' she murmured, and remembered it was one of the songs that had been sung before the Horned God. She said abruptly, 'What is she like – the Queen? Is she fair?'

If Henry was taken aback, he gave no sign. 'She is well enough,' he said. 'I have two sons of her, and shall have more, God willing, for she is strong. She brought me wide lands in France which were her inheritance. That is why I married her.' He stopped and looked at her curiously. 'What is that to you?'

'Nothing,' she muttered, 'nothing. Only that she belongs to you while I —'

'And you are mine also!' His tone was suddenly fierce. 'Whether you will or no, none but I shall ever have you. Hear me!' and he shook her, gently at first, and then harder as she gave no sign. 'And as you are mine, you shall go where I go.'

The idea had only just occurred to him, but the more he considered, the more he liked it. 'While I lie in London or Westminster, you shall stay with Dame Hermengild. But I am soon for Winchester. . . Well, I will arrange a place for you.' His thoughts ran on ahead to the time when he should return home for to Henry, France and particularly Anjou, was home and England merely a possession, a fine one to be sure, but not one where he could settle long.

'You must have a household,' he muttered, more to himself than her. 'A cook and scullions. . . I will arrange all. Is there any you would have with you? What of the ugly wench? Will you take her?'

'Oh, yes – I will take Ediva,' she said and smiled, being certain that the girl would wish to come and glad there was to be one familiar if unprepossessing face. Also Ediva could not, except with difficulty, tell tales. She did not quite know why she wished for one who would not tell tales but it was so, and Ediva would do admirably. 'My little love,' he said, and held her close. 'Do you not worry your pretty head about the Queen. She is useful to me – at times I think there is a man's head on her shoulders. But touching upon matters of the flesh – that's but duty.'

He believed he was telling the truth.

VI

September 1155

IN THE GREAT HALL at Lambeth, Thomas the Chancellor
and Abbot Walter of Battle sat facing Bishop Hilary of
Chichester and Archbishop Theobald. Outside a thin drizzling rain fell and so the fires had been lit and candles
bloomed upon the table. It was more like November than
September, they had said, but that was while politeness was
still observed and before tempers became frayed. Lond had
the dispute over Battle Abbey raged; by now, all were tired
of it and of trotting out the same arguments again and
again.

Abbot Walter was a brother of Richard de Luci and had
the same bold, black-eyed look on a face fatter and at the
same time more furrowed and lined, and Thomas, who was
well aware of the Justiciar's lack of liking for him, was glad
that his duty to the King ran so well with his own desire
to put the de Lucis under some sort of obligation to him. So
he extended himself to the utmost on the Abbot's behalf,
which was also the King's.

William of Normandy had founded and endowed the
great Abbey in thankfulness to God for his victory over the
English and had given it a charter exempting it from the
jurisdiction of any bishop, and Henry, in his turn, had made
it plain that he would brook no alterations. Archbishop

Theobald of Canterbury felt that no layman, even a King, could grant this kind of exemption and that the Church must be immune from any secular interference. He fidgeted about while Bishop Hilary spoke, watching Thomas who sat calmly contemplating his slender white hands folded on the table before him. Thomas raised his eyes and saw the bitter, disappointed look that Theobald bent on him.

'And so,' continued Hilary in a voice grown shrill with irritation, 'it seems to me no less than a violation of Canon Law and a defiance of the holy St Peter himself through whom I hold my office' – he hesitated a moment at an abrupt movement of the Archbishop – 'and it also violates the rights of the See of Canterbury. I shall appeal to the Holy Father,' he finished in a loud and trembling voice and sat down, blinking furiously and with his heavy jowl mottled and quivering with anger.

Abbot Walter smiled coldly. 'Such heat is unbecoming, my lord,' he said smoothly. 'My Abbey stands apart and has done so for more than fifty years. I have charters to uphold me.'

Theobald said, looking straight at Thomas, 'Royal grant should uphold episcopal privilege, not conflict with it. Here is the old struggle between secular and spiritual men – look well which side you stand upon. For who is greater in the end?'

The Abbot's head swung round like an angry bull's. 'And do you place me among the ranks of laymen?' he snapped. 'I stand where I have always stood, the faithful servant of Almighty God!' He banged his fist upon the table. 'To God and the Pope I owe obedience, not to him,' and he glared at the Bishop who glared back and opened his mouth to begin again but Thomas forestalled him, and speaking quietly, recapitulated the arguments for both sides.

The Archbishop's words had caused him a qualm, though, for deep in his heart he acknowledged the truth of Theobald's remark. But he pushed the knowledge away and reassured himself that as they were all clerics there could be no real struggle here between Church and King; it was as he had told Henry, merely two groups of prelates struggling for power. And try as he might to quell it, he had taken a strong and irrational dislike to Bishop Hilary with his small eyes set too close together either side his beaky Norman nose; it was a pity he was ranged alongside the Archbishop to whom Thomas owed gratitude. But as the King's chief servant he must do the King's will and so he told them of Henry's order which he proposed to obey to the letter, to keep the disputed charter in his Chancery.

None of them looked pleased, and Hilary repeated his threat to appeal to the Pope. Theobald got up slowly, for rheumatism attacked his knees in wet weather, and another of the clerks ran forward that the Archbishop might lean upon his arm as he went out. Thomas stood up, too, and waited, but Theobald did not kiss him, only made a sign with his hand that left Thomas at a loss. He sat down again, and Bishop Hilary repeated fiercely, 'Aye, to the lord Pope! And as he is an Englishman, he will know well how to deal with it. He will not have forgot the struggle between Archbishop Anselm and King William Rufus!' and before anyone could answer, he too stamped away, making the candle flames sway and flare.

Abbot Walter raised his dark eyes to Thomas' pale ones. 'And shall I have my charter?' he said softly.

'Not yet, later. We shall consider it further. We must wait and see if he makes good his threat.'

'That one is your enemy now. Let us hope he has not the ear of the Archbishop – but the ear of a King is better far' – and smiling inscrutably, the Abbot laid his plump, beringed hand on Thomas'. 'God be with you, Chancellor,' he said.

Outside the Bishop was still rating; Theobald stood beside him waiting for his litter to come up and listening rather to the sorrowful dripping of the rain from the porch than to Hilary. It increased his gloom.

'No, no,' he muttered at last. 'It is useless to talk so. He has put off the deacon and put on the Chancellor and naught will amend it. So I shall ask him to resign the Archdeaconry of Canterbury.'

'Ha!' cried the Bishop, 'that he will not! For he thinks more of the silver pennies that flow to his purse than of Holy Church. Resign! Not he!'

And Bishop Hilary was right. Thomas ignored Theobald's plea. Most of the monies of the kingdom now flowed through his hands and he found that the more that came in, the more he needed. He made no distinction between the King's monies and his own, feeling that the great state he kept redounded to the King's credit, and indeed Henry had so heaped him with honours, including the Stewardship of the Tower of London, that perhaps there was no need. As far as Thomas was concerned, all that he spent was for Henry, and Henry himself was content with all that Thomas did. Since he had discovered Thomas of London and had won his affection a new perspective on life had opened out for him. Thomas brought out the best in Henry. Their amity was perfect, and if some of Thomas' old friends thought they detected a change in him, none saw fit to mention it to his face.

None, that is, until John of Salisbury, one of his oldest friends, travelled from Canterbury to see him. Thomas suspected that the Archbishop had sent John to urge his resignation of the Archdeaconry, for Theobald must remember how John could always best him in argument. How many happy hours they had spent in dialectics when both were members of the Archbishop's Household. John's was a mind his own could sharpen itself upon; indeed, Thomas knew that here was a man of greater mental power than himself. Yet John would never rise higher in the Church than his courtesy bishopric, he had given offence to too many, for with him truth came always before diplomacy. Furthermore, John committed the unforgivable sin of being almost always right. He was a little man with the wise, ugly face of a monkey and the sharp bright eyes under the curiously gabled lids missed nothing, either of fact or inference.

So now when he was ushered into the Presence Chamber of the Chancellor, Thomas gave a shout of joy. 'Ho, John Short!' he cried, using the old nickname. 'And are you come to tell me how to run the Chancery?'

'No, I am not,' said John, grinning in equal delight as he kissed Thomas on both cheeks. 'I am not come in any official capacity, but merely to sit by and admire you in your cometary orbit about that blessed luminary, the King.'

'Will you stay then, for a time? Can the Archbishop spare you from Canterbury? For as I heard it, you are running the diocese.'

John smiled. 'There are others who may do the donkey work without my watching over them. Truly, I am come to pay you a visit, for soon I go again to Pope Adrian and who knows then when I shall see you.'

'Well, you have ever rubbed shoulders with the great,' said Thomas, thinking not only of John's intimate friendship with the Pope but also of Peter Abelard, that tragic teacher under whom he had once studied.

Presently, wine and little cakes were brought and they sat and talked, the two of them alone together in the big room, as Thomas had not talked to anyone except Henry since he became Chancellor. Thomas sat twisting his goblet in the flood of pure golden light that poured in through the window and told John of Henry and all the good he saw in him, and the hopes he had, and how order was at last growing out of the chaos that surrounded the King's daily life.

'For he has a good mind, John, under the muddle and venery that is youth,' said Thomas. 'Between us, we shall bring law and simple justice to this realm.' Then he looked quickly at John to see if he had noticed that slip of the tongue and John twinkled back at him with his little eyes like diamonds so that Thomas smiled ruefully. 'I mean that I advise him,' he said.

'Of course,' said John. 'I knew that was what you meant.'

There was a short silence and Thomas affected not to notice John's close scrutiny.

'And the Queen? – does she, too, hold you in esteem?'

Thomas shook his head. 'I do not know. Our paths cross but infrequently – yet, from remarks the King has dropped, I think she may resent me. It matters not.'

'Never underestimate the power of a wife, dear friend – nor do you forget the unbridgeable gulf between nobleman and clerk. There is an abyss which has swallowed many ambitious men – tread warily.'

'You think she may resent me because I come of merchant stock and yet have some small influence with the King? That may be so – and doubtless those feelings are shared by many – but I cannot conceive that she would try to conspire against me.'

'She is not so light minded as many imagine. Behind that frivolous façade is a woman of wit and sagacity. I met her in Tusculum when she and King Louis returned from the Crusade and I formed my own opinions.' John laughed and stretched himself. 'I should say she is a great deal better suited to her present husband, will he have the wit to use her considerable talents. Most of the scandal that revolved around her name was caused by the boredom that drove her to clutch at any small excitement, and the evil tongues of onlookers who magnified her misbehaviour into misconduct. No – I do not think she will conspire against you – I am merely pointing out that she is a woman with strong potentialities for good or evil. It is well to have such in one's own camp, if possible.'

Thomas looked dubious. 'It appears to me that she will be fully occupied with child-bearing for many years to come

– besides' – he hesitated – 'I am not at my best in the company of ladies.'

John laughed outright. 'Oh, my dear friend, I do not suggest you seek her out to enlist her aid in any way. Try though to sway the King towards her – be sure your efforts will come to her ears through the gossip of the Court!'

'That is very well said,' Thomas grumbled. 'But though Henry is overpoweringly interested in women, I hardly think he will pay much attention to their views. Nonetheless, I shall remember what you say.'

'Never make an enemy where with a little effort you may make a friend.'

Thomas smiled faintly. 'Excepting only in the interests of truth, eh John?'

Afterwards the conversation became idle and drifted into reminiscence. John told Thomas the old tales of his youth, and of that priest who under the guise of teaching him the psalms had tried to use him in his magical experiments. The subject never ceased to fascinate Thomas who was in his turn reminded of that day in the forest of Essex when he and the King had come across clear proof of how the common folk still resorted to heathenish practices to ensure the success of their crops.

'Ah, the crops. . . That is not the worst. The most beastly and devilish rites are connected with human and animal fertility. Would it amaze you, Thomas, to know that human sacrifice is still carried out? I have spoken with people who remember it in Rouen. This god of theirs – call him Lucifer, Beelzebub, Herne or what you will – becomes incarnate in a human being and reigns a period of years. At the appointed time, he is slain for the benefit of his people.'

'It is a ghastly parody on the life of our Blessed Saviour.'

'Nay, it is older far than Christianity – the oldest heresy of all. The Church has a hard task before her, Thomas. But we shall conquer, never fear.' He leaned across and patted Thomas on the shoulder. 'How can we fail, being guided by the Holy Ghost? Come now, shake the dolour from your spirit.'

Thomas sighed. 'It disgusts me. At times I fear that man is beyond redemption – vile, depraved and vicious, corrupt and steeped in iniquity—'

'All that is true and more. Yet still God loves us.' John's voice was quiet. 'Even those of us who, like the Pharisee, separate ourselves from our fellow sinners, feeling we could not do as they do.'

Thomas walked to the window and stared out where the starlings had set up a harsh, creaking clamour. 'You are very good for me, John,' he said.

John did not mention Thomas' resignation of the Archdeaconry but he did repeat his allusion to the Chancellor's flight around the sun-like orb of majesty.

Thomas laughed at him. 'I know how closely I dare fly.'

'Take care you do not singe your wings as Icarus did.'

'I have received that advice from other sources and not as kindly meant. But I have reason to believe the King has a fondness for me.'

John said gently, 'The singeing that I spoke of, I do not fear from the King, either. But look close into your heart, Thomas, and ensure that the change come not from within.' He rose smiling. 'I will retire now, dear friend, if my chamber be prepared.' He laid a hand on Thomas' shoulder. Even standing, he was only a head taller than Thomas as he sat. 'Tomorrow we will talk again, but this evening I will spend in meditation and prayer.'

But afterwards, when he thought over their conversation, Thomas found that the memory of his own humility began to rankle so that he became indignant at what he felt was presumption on John's part. Why must they all, without exception, take it upon themselves to warn him not to fly too high? Yet it was difficult to attribute jealousy to John of Salisbury, who had moved for many years among princes

spiritual and secular and still kept both honesty and simplicity. Was it not a kind of pride in him that assumed that
Thomas could not do that same?

At any rate, Thomas began to think so, and he nourished
his own self-esteem at John's expense without realising it.

October 1155

The Court was at Winchester and the King and some of his
gentlemen had come to the Queen's apartments, but today
her mood was sour and gradually, by twos and threes, they
had drifted away to the other end of the long solar. Even the
minstrels and troubadours, even Ethelwig, the singer, could
not lighten her heavy humour; in the middle of a chanson
in praise of her beauty, she had risen and walked to the
deep, slit window, to stand staring out on the pleasaunce
below.

The two ladies who still remained by her looked at each
other with knowing glances; both were elderly and had
served her since her girlhood. The younger one, who had
been reading in a book of poems, let the thick, supple leaves
flap over one by one with a soft slapping noise; under cover
of the sound she whispered, 'She has heard this latest story,
then?'

The other frowned, pursing her lips, her eyes upon the
Queen's back, but as Eleanor made no movement, she murmured, 'One who shall be nameless – but too well known
to me and thee – did chance it out in conversation – oh,
and very sorry afterwards to be the bearer of ill tidings. But
it has hurt my lady. Not that she showed aught – she
would not, for very pride.'

'Well, the mischief is done now.'

'And it has done my lady no good. Better had she not
known the King has installed his latest minion under all our
noses.'

Their whispered talk went on and though Eleanor stood
as if lost in a dream, she was aware of it and could guess the

174

tenor of their conversation. Ever since that young lady had so artlessly let slip the spicy bit of scandal, her spirit had writhed in helpless rage. A base born wench out of a known house of ill fame towards Westminster! An English whore, they said, who scorned no filthiness!

He shall not come into my chamber, she thought, with his lips still warm from his doxy's kisses, yet underneath her jealous fury, she knew that she was powerless. He had only to smile at her with his upper lip curling slightly upon his strong white teeth and she was weak with longing for him, for the feel of his strong arms, hard with muscle, and his almost brutal kissing. Of all the men she had known, he was the most masculine, the most vital, so that she could never feel herself the stronger. She felt that as he was entirely sufficient for her, so she should be for him, and the thought of another woman in his arms was bitter as gall upon her tongue.

Yet she did not love him, though she might have done so once had his constant infidelities not nipped that flower in the bud. No, it is not love, she told herself, it is my own flesh that betrays me. Ah, sweet Jesu, I wish I were old and long, long past it all, my blood quiet and cool and my heart at peace. She did not yet know that for her, with her vast capacity for love or hate, that time would never come.

The women behind her suddenly ceased whispering and she turned her head to see the Empress approaching with her slow, dignified walk; a distant nod was the only salutation she accorded her son as she left him. Eleanor forced her face into welcoming lines, praying that her mother-in-law had not heard the gossip. They were on somewhat curious terms now on this, the Empress' first visit to England since Henry's accession. Outwardly the best of friends, there was yet a strong undercurrent of something that approached dislike between them. Each felt her way carefully in conversation, trying to discover a way through the other's guard. Mentally, Eleanor kept the score; now she felt her

175

husband had given his mother an unfair advantage over her. It was uncomfortable to remember that she had herself betrayed this same woman, therefore she did not think of it; Eleanor's memory was nothing if not convenient.

Matilda's smile was wintry as she offered her pouched cheek to her daughter-in-law to kiss. 'I am come to bear you company,' she said, waving away Eleanor's ladies. 'Too well have I known loneliness myself in the midst of great company, to watch yours without pity. Come now, daughter, sit beside me and we shall talk privately.'

Eleanor managed to smile, but it was a sorry effort.

'Not loneliness, indeed, madame, merely a disinclination for company – always excepting yours.'

'Well,' said the Empress, staring vaguely across the room, 'it is true that there are times when it is well to be alone but this, I think, should not be one of them.' She turned her head and fixed Eleanor with a penetrating stare. 'Has my son discussed his plans for Ireland with you?'

'He has mentioned it.'

'And you approved?'

Eleanor moved restively. 'I have given little thought to the matter.' Of all things, she was in no humour to talk of Henry's political ambitions, and if I were, she thought, you should not know my mind.

'I have advised against it and so, I think, should you. That is no land to waste men and arms on. It is full of bogs and savages. Already his lands stretch from Scotland to the Pyrenees, but he is insatiable. He has said that he will send John of Salisbury to the Pope to gain his approval of the plan. What think you?'

'I hardly know.' But she thought, Prying will gain you nothing. He listens to me now, not you.

'Well, I had hoped for better things from you,' observed the Empress tartly, 'but doubtless your mind runs in other channels. I see that you are truly in no mood for company.'

'Nay, madam, stay with me,' said Eleanor quickly for she

176

had seen Henry's searching, curious glances and thought she would torment him later when he wished to know the subject of their discourse. 'I have a migraine and cannot concentrate but perhaps it will leave me if we listen quietly awhile to music.' She forced the outright lie. 'Your presence is comfortable to me.'

The Empress, appeased, nodded complacently. 'I have been told before that my companionship is relaxing.'

Who by, under God's Heaven? thought Eleanor wildly. She had a strong desire to laugh aloud.

For a while, then, they listened to the musicians but after a time the Empress began to whisper vehemently again of what Henry had said to the Great Council concerning Ireland; she was much against it, she said, and felt that Eleanor should try to dissuade Henry too. Eleanor sighed inwardly and said that she thought her opinion carried little weight with her husband; the Empress disagreed with that, and then, with a sideways glance, she laid her large, cold hand on Eleanor's and murmured even lower, so that her daughter-in-law must strain her ears and lean closer in order to hear at all over the noise of the citterns and the lutes.

'If anything has come to your ears' – Matilda breathed –'of misbehaviour in my son, it is best ignored. Many in the past and more in the future will suffer likewise—'

She broke off as Eleanor abruptly withdrew her hand and sat with stony face, staring in front of her.

'Surely you feel no jealousy of such?'

Eleanor's annoyance overcame her caution. 'Not jealousy, madame, insult is what I feel,' she hissed furiously. 'That your son should frequent the stews of London is an insult to me!'

'It is an insult you may often be called upon to bear, men being what they are. As I was called upon to bear it. Treat adultresses with the contempt they deserve,' she said harshly, yet, Eleanor thought, with a hidden undertone of meaning, and, furious, she felt her cheeks begin to redden. She dropped her eyes, but not before she saw what she took to be satisfaction in the other's.

No, she could not have known that, she thought. She is pleased merely to feel that I am put down. She would be delighted to think that Henry and I are on bad terms. She shall not have that luxury, the old hypocrite! So smiling sweetly, she said, 'I thank you for your valuable advice, madam. Be sure that I shall follow it.

The Empress primmed her mouth and rose. 'Do you add your words to mine concerning Ireland,' she said. 'And for the rest, remember your degree and ignore it as beneath your notice.'

But just then Henry came up, and Eleanor's ladies, watching their meeting with interest, were taken aback by the mildness of her manner. Oddly enough, the Empress showed none of the pleasure that an outsider might have expected at Eleanor's faithful following of her counsel. Instead, she immediately took her son to task for his inordinate territorial ambitions. Henry kept his temper with a great effort for he had a wary respect for his mother, and Eleanor forgot her heartburning long enough to enjoy seeing him humbled in public.

November 1155–March 1156

As autumn turned to winter Henry found that he had been right to doubt the accuracy of his friends' prognostications concerning his passion for Hikenai; it did not in the least diminish. Much of his time now was spent at her side; in her presence was a tranquillity that soothed his restlessness; even her long silences served only to deepen the mystery surrounding her. Now he was beginning to understand how that pedlar with whom she had run off might have thought her a witch or a faery woman. Henry, though, did not fear the faery people – had not his own great-great-grandmother been one of them?

So he questioned her again about the old religion and its connection with faery folk. He had not been truthful when he pretended ignorance of the subject; even in his early boyhood at Gloucester in the care of his Uncle Robert he had heard murmurs of a religion which was older and darker than Christianity, and again he had caught hints of it in Anjou and Normandy before he gained England. Thirst for knowledge was one of his dominant traits; once his interest was aroused he would not leave a subject, and this one touched him close for he dearly wished to know the approximate numbers of those who ran counter to the accepted beliefs in his lands, not because he found it in any way offensive but rather that it might be well at some future date to have that knowledge as a weapon in his hand.

He did not pause to consider against whom such a weapon might be used, he only knew that secret knowledge was a useful asset when bargains were struck and that Henry Plantagenet must get the best of any bargain. Beneath the cheerful bonhomie and the swift, terrifying rages that most men knew lay a scheming, materialistic mind, nor did this conflict in any way with his devout belief in an omnipotent God. He knew that God ruled all and would one day judge him, but that fact would never make him deviate from any course he had decided upon. To Henry the practice of religion was in the nature of a bargain; there were obligations on both sides.

Hikenai believed his probing questions to be actuated by concern for her but even so she was very little help to him. She could speak only of her own small experience in a remote and lonely corner of his domain and when at last he felt she had told him all she knew he ceased to worry her upon the matter.

It was on a day in late November when the mats of dry yellow grass underfoot crackled crisp with rime that she told him she was pregnant. She watched him warily while she broke the news for she still had difficulty in believing in the

179

permanence of his feeling for her, yet the broad grin of delight that spread across his face and his eager shouting of the tidings to his companions told plainly of his pleasure.

'Am I not doubly blest?' he asked them, laughing. 'For the Queen, too, in the next sweet summer season will bring me another child! Am I not the luckiest of men, my sweeting?' and he seized her in his arms and danced around the chamber with her. 'Never fear, my little love,' he cried. 'Your son and mine shall hold office. He shall be as loved and cared for as my princes. No, he too shall be a prince and shall be educated along with the children of the Queen! Nothing shall be too good for him – for your child, my Hikenai.'

And so she suppressed the qualm of doubt that assailed her at the news of the Queen's expectations for she knew very well that the code for men was vastly different from that for women in consequence of the sin of Eve, and the gentlemen, well schooled by life at Court in spite of their youth, kept their faces impassive.

Henry then, at this time, was perfectly happy. His love for Hikenai in no way inhibited his relations with his wife, and if Eleanor had seemed a little silent and withdrawn of late, he put it down to the humours of early pregnancy. He was pleased with the facility with which she was producing heirs; he was glad to see his new realm settling into peace and prosperity, and most of all, he rejoiced in Hikenai's condition.

Such contentment rarely lasts. Just before Christmas he had word that his younger brother, Geoffrey, had raised the standard of rebellion once again in Northern France; having fortified his castles, he had invaded Henry's lands which he swore were rightfully his by their father's will and Henry's promise, now that he had England.

Henry's anger was roused. He swore that any promise he might have made had been exacted under duress, though he could remember none. He worked himself into greater fury than any man there had yet seen, and one by one they slunk away as he rolled screaming on the floor, clawing and biting at the rushes with the blood-flecked spittle running down his chin.

After the paroxysm had passed and he had crawled trembling to the bench, they brought him wine, edging along towards him as to a rabid dog. He glared at them with bloodshot eyes but took the cup and drank, swearing again as the wine stung his bitten lips.

When his mind cleared he decided that Geoffrey must be taught a lesson. That would take more than a month or two. And what of Hikenai? How to ensure her safety and comfort while he was oversea? She was a possession almost as precious as his inheritance in France and he would be robbed of neither. Yet to France he must go, and Thomas too; England could be left under the care of the Justiciars. Savagely he chewed his thumb nail, considering and rejecting one plan after another until at last his spirits began to rise again at the prospect of open warfare with his perfidious brother.

However, things were simply settled when he later mentioned the matter to his Chancellor for Thomas suggested leaving the Queen as Regent. That was a new thought; until then it had not occurred to Henry to leave Eleanor in England. But it was a good idea, her pregnancy could be used as the excuse and in her place he would take Hikenai. Thomas would pull a long face, that was certain, but he would take care to keep them apart. Yes, better far this way. He would keep Hikenai with him, at least until her child was safely born; he would give Eleanor a free hand under Leicester and de Luci, and both would be content.

Henry was happy once more, and to prove it he smote Thomas mightily across the shoulders and commended him for the keenness of his insight. Thomas half fell across the long oblong of the Exchequer Table (for they were in the Exchequer Room where the Chancellor was overseeing the quarterly checking of the accounts) and disarranged some of the counters on the board. Quickly he put them back again on the correct squares, smiling at Henry's boisterousness. 'Gently, my liege,' he reproved him, 'these are your monies the clerks are busy reckoning'.

'Six for the debit,' called the clerk. He muttered under his breath, counting. 'Sixteen, seventeen, eighteen for the credit.' He clicked the piles of counters deftly into position at the bottom of the columns. 'The sum is two hundred and thirty-two pounds.'

'Two three two pounds,' repeated the clerk with the roll carefully and wrote it down – CCXXXII L. – while the other picked up the next heap of tally sticks and began once more to lay out counters on the chequered cloth.

'I shall not leave the Queen as Regent, I think,' Henry said to Thomas. 'The English do not care to be ruled by a woman, but I will drop a word in season to the Justiciars. She shall have authority to draw payments direct from the Exchequer. That will sweeten her—' He thought a moment. Somehow, he could not bring himself to mention Hikenai's name to Thomas. . . There was little need as yet; later he would tell him – later.

But a propitious moment did not arise and when they crossed the Channel early in January Thomas was still unaware that in another of the ships, sick and terrified of the grey waste of water, was the girl from the outlaw camp and with her, not only Ediva but also Dame Hermengild, the most notorious procuress in London.

In the face of Hikenai's pleadings for another familiar face, Henry had at last given way. The Dame herself had leapt at the chance of what she took to be continued favour from the King, and left her lucrative house in the care of Alfled, the oldest of her girls, though not without many stern injunctions to keep the accounts scrupulously, and her sworn promise to be back within six months.

Even her bold spirit was deterred by her first sight of the

sea, and that in midwinter: she had before imagined the Channel as a wider Thames, and having come safely to land at Wissant, she began to doubt that she would ever gather courage enough to return over so vast an expanse of water. The King, though, had made it abundantly clear that her services were required only until the birth of Hikenai's child – but to superintend the birth of a King's bastard was a most signal honour. Her spirits had revived before they reached Rouen where Henry proposed to leave them while he laid siege to Geoffrey's castles.

Rouen was where the Empress lived but if she had any inkling of the identity of the three women in the little house near the walls, she gave no indication, and the English-women settled in quietly while Henry paid his homage to the King of France for Normandy, Maine and Anjou, Poitou and Aquitaine.

He came to see Hikenai once and spent most of the visit raging about a meeting with his brother, stamping up and down the chamber and swearing such horrid oaths that all the servants hid themselves and Hikenai, who had never seen him angry before, was struck dumb.

Thomas began to hear whispers about the King's leman around this time; he was quick to put two and two together and realised soon enough who she must be. Yet Henry had never mentioned her presence; he was not usually so secretive.

A constraint developed between them, each knowing of the other's knowledge and each doubting the other's reaction to any broaching of the subject. So an uncomfortable week or two passed by, but with the ceasing of the rains of early spring, Thomas's practice in swordsmanship began and both were able to forget the awkwardness.

Yet the first faint shadow on their intimacy remained, hidden because unacknowledged and in the end, unmentionable.

VII

April–July 1156

SINCE HENRY'S DEPARTURE, THE time had passed happily
for Eleanor. This was her second winter in England and
though she thought she never would become accustomed to
the bitter cold of these northern lands, she found it infinitely
preferable to the Île de France.

Henry had left her with a free hand as he had promised
and she was not slow in taking advantage. Even the frosts
and east winds of February and March had not prevented
her from travelling extensively; as soon as the best provisions in one manor were exhausted, she went on to the next,
and her hospitality was lavish, even in Lent. She used her
pregnancy as an excuse for everything she disliked doing,
whether it was eating salt herring or rising at dawn to hear
Mass – she, whose splendid health was never better than
when she was with child.

After the long, almost barren years with Louis she took
pride in her fertility, and with Henry away fighting she
could forget his whoremongering. She comforted herself
with the fact that he was under the eye of Thomas of
London whose chastity was a byword. Eleanor could not
truly like him but she had warmed towards him since Henry
had told her with artful carelessness that Thomas was so
impressed by her capabilities that he had wished her to be
left as Regent.

Now with Easter just past and she entering her eighth month, she was becoming heavy and lethargic. She would go to Woodstock, she announced, where her two little boys lived and stay there until her time was upon her. And with the departure of most of the hangers-on, life settled into a slow, pleasant rhythm.

The house at Woodstock was old and not too comfortable, but the weather had improved and Eleanor spent a great deal of the time out of doors with her children and the women. The apple orchard was a favourite spot, where the stream curved in an ox-bow around a patch of grassy sward. The ladies would chatter and embroider and exclaim with delight over Young Henry who was still swaddled most of the time although he was nearly fourteen months old, and Eleanor would recline upon cushions on the grass with her hands clasped on her distended belly, lost in the delightful, timeless lassitude of the later stage of gestation.

'Look!' she said, 'how the child within me kicks!' and indeed the ladies could see the tight stuff of her gown jerk and move as she spoke. Little William was fascinated by it; he dropped the daisy heads he had been collecting and laid his small, grass stained hand upon the bulge.

'Sing to us, William,' cried the ladies, 'Sing us a chanson!'

So William piped away in his tuneless childish treble, kneeling beside the Queen and pretending her swollen belly was a drum. He patted her gently in time with the air but the ladies began to titter and then to laugh openly as they heard the words he sang, for it was no song of gallantry but a bawdy lay that the men-at-arms roared out when they marched.

Eleanor, too, was weak with laughter when he finished. 'Who taught you that, my little bird?' she asked, wiping her eyes with the corner of her veil. 'That's scarce a song for a courtier to sing to ladies.'

William regarded her with solemn, russet-coloured eyes. 'It was Kari told me.' And at the end, she said 'shake your

185

winkie', and he pulled up his skirts and gravely waved his minute penis at the ladies who collapsed, howling with mirth, into one another's arms.

Only the oldest lady whose name was Rohesia looked faintly disapproving though she had laughed as loud as any. 'It is well he is lately weaned and that Kari sent off home,' she said to Eleanor. 'These English are full uncivilised. What else may she have taught him?'

'There's no harm,' returned the Queen, 'for the pages will teach him everything before he is five,' and she pulled the child to her, kissing him and ruffling his gingery curls until he began to nuzzle round her breasts. She pushed him off, then.

'You are too big now to suckle,' she said. 'You will soon be three years old. I have no milk for you and Kari's gone.'

The days passed, one much like another, while the apple-blossom changed from round pink buds to frail, white, pink-edged flowers and then to drifts of petals in the grass.

On a day most unseasonably warm for early May in England, William would not eat his slops. No one could persuade him nor would he be tempted with an egg which he usually liked.

'He is being obstinate because he would rather suckle,' said the Queen crossly. 'Leave him, he will eat again when he grows hungry.' But William did not eat; instead he was vilely sick and all through the day the bouts of vomiting became more frequent while his bowels ran with greenish water.

Towards evening the physician came and stood in the doorway with anxious, dubious gaze while the women tried to hold the child in his convulsions. He went away but came back at nightfall with a long parchment which he said must be tied around the patient's neck.

By next day William had ceased to vomit though every now and then he was racked with the effort to do so.

'Do not let him drink,' said the physician, 'for it will

only cause more vomiting. Be sure the parchment remains in place. It is the only cure for this affliction.'

Torn with fear, Eleanor hovered about the chamber. In the late afternoon she sent away the women and the priests, and with only old Rohesia to bear her company, sat beside the sick child. He lay quieter now, only occasionally drawing up his knees and grimacing with pain.

Rohesia spoke gently. 'Prepare yourself, my lady, for his death. See how his cheeks and temples have grown hollow. Little ones die so easily.'

Slow tears ran down Eleanor's cheeks; she leaned nearer to the child, gazing into his face as though by very will power she could drag him back from death's grasp but what she saw there only served to deepen her fear. William's eyes were open but vacant, he breathed shallowly and his little lips were dry and cracked and crusted with a whitish deposit.

A kind of numbness enveloped Eleanor; her thoughts wandered aimlessly so that she could not call to mind one prayer, one plea for help. Her eyes fell upon the parchment; she saw 'Ortamin. sigmone. beronice. irritas. venas quasi dupal. fervor.' and at the end of the scroll, just under the tiny waxen ear (like a sea shell, she thought with vast irrelevance) was lettered neatly 'AQNY Alleluiah, Alleluiah'.

Rohesia was muttering soft prayers and Eleanor found herself repeating the strange words on the parchment with dogged helplessness as though the potency that lay in them could be strengthened by incessant repetition.

William died at sunset. When she saw that he was dead, Eleanor kissed his cooling cheek and went away. She did not say a word, not even when her ladies undressed her and tried to offer words of comfort. When they asked her about the burial she said, 'Tomorrow. Tomorrow is time enough to think of that.' Nor did she weep, for old Rohesia who slept with her listened long into the night for signs of natural grief.

187

Rohesia sighed, thinking of her own little ones who had died too soon, and tried to remember how she had felt at the first loss, but it was too long ago and there had been too many losses so that all were confused in her mind. Useless to grieve, she told herself, God will send more; one child is much like another.

Eleanor had lost her first-born son and she did not find acceptance easy. Long after William was laid away in Reading Abbey at old King Henry's feet, she mourned him. She would wake in the night and see again his little face with skin like a speckled brown egg and weep into her pillow until Rohesia rose up, fumbling about in the warm darkness and whispering to her that God would assuredly send William back to her – or another such, so like as to make no matter.

Eleanor took comfort, waiting for the new child to be born, but when she was at last delivered on a fine June morning, the babe was a girl. They swaddled it up tight and laid it on the silken counterpane and the Queen raised herself and looked upon its face. The wisps of hair were ashy fair, the cheekbones wide and the nose a mere blob; it was nothing like William.

'What shall this lady be called?' they said, all standing round and beaming with pleasure as though this ugly girl were reward enough for all she had lost and suffered.

Eleanor shrugged, thinking with disgust, I care naught. Aloud she said, 'Matilda will sit well on her,' but she did not mean it kindly. The women, though, exclaimed with delight that she should choose the old Queen's name. At the back of the group Rohesia said nothing but looked at Eleanor with sad reproach; she, at least, had not missed the slighting tone and she knew that the Queen did not love the Empress.

Hikenai went slowly up the outer stair of the small house in Rouen. She had to heave herself up every step by hanging on the wooden pegs let into the wall of the house for she was huge with the child within her – too great, the mid-wife said, for so small a girl. 'All water, that be,' she had confided to Dame Hermengild, 'All water and a tiny babe, or I'm no judge. But a lad for sure, her being that shape.'

By now Hikenai did not care whether the child were lad or maid, if it would only be born. She was past the time that she and the Dame had calculated and every day that passed made the waiting harder to bear. For a week she had remained in the upper room, unable now to sit or lie in comfort although Ediva had packed hassocks round her to bear the weight of her great belly.

This day she had determined to be out in the sunshine, despite everything the women might say. She had got down the stair well enough for all she could not see the step in front of her, but once in the walled garden the sun had beat too hot upon her head, her legs had ached from unaccustomed exercise, and soon the same bored irritation that she had thought to leave behind in the upper chamber came on her again.

The women said the bench was too hard for her to sit upon in her condition and so she would sit on it and it was. The sun went in and they said it would be too chill for her; she answered with annoyance that she should be glad to be cool, but as the clouds thickened and the breeze rose her arms prickled with gooseflesh. They begged her to come within doors and so she would not; she sat there in a thoroughly bad temper until a few spits of rain began to fall and then she stood up suddenly and as she did so an abrupt wrenching pain took her right at the base of her weighted belly and she cried out.

'Ah, God be praised!' cried Dame Hermengild, who was nearly as tired of the long waiting as Hikenai herself. 'Her time is upon her at last. Come, help her up the stair.'

And so she heaved herself up the stair, clinging to each peg in turn while behind her Dame Hermengild shoved and

189

pushed, clucking and chiding her for her foolishness in descending in the first place.

All their irritation with each other had dissolved in excitement; only the midwife, being used to such occasions, remained calm and made her preparations methodically, calling upon the wenches to bank up the fire and lay a clean cloth upon the heap of straw where Hikenai would be delivered. Now, at last, she removed the strip of dried human skin which had been tied around Hikenai's middle for the last month, carefully wrapping it and putting it aside for use again on the next fortunate client who could afford such a sure safeguard.

Have you kept fresh urine?' she muttered to the Dame. 'Soon I must dose her when the pains wax stronger.'

'Aye,' said Hermengild, 'in yon little pipkin. The first she passed this morning. I have kept it in readiness as on every day this last month. Myself, I never heard of such, but then I never bore a living child.'

'It will only ease the pains, no more.' She glanced across at Hikenai who sat bowed forward, biting her lip occasionally. 'She'll not be overlong with this when the first pains come so hard. It will be this day for sure. Does the messenger stand by to take word to the Duke?'

'The King of the English lies now outside Chinon and it is to him the messenger will ride,' said Dame Hermengild with some asperity, for she found the midwife's references to Henry as Duke of Normandy singularly trying. These Normans thought the world began and ended there! And she immediately started in to speak about England, telling of London, that great city, and putting the midwife to rights about where her province stood in the scheme of things.

However, the midwife did not seem as awed as she should have been, she only sniffed and said that her husband had seen Paris once and did not think it worth an egg; for her part, Rouen was as good as any town in Christendom and why men always thought the next land was better so that they must be off fighting to gain it. . . .

At that moment Hikenai gave a gasping cry so that both turned from their half amiable bickering to see how she fared. The pains were growing stronger and closer together, the breathing space between them shortening. She set her teeth, clenching her hands as she waited for the next onslaught.

'Now it is time for the potion,' said the midwife briskly, holding the horn mug to Hikenai's lips. She wrinkled her nose, drawing back a little and then another pain seized her, making her go rigid and squeeze her eyes tight shut.

'Drink quickly, then the pain will pass.'

'No, what is it? Is it mandragora?' She writhed and groaned so that the midwife had much ado not to spill the liquid and motioned to Dame Hermengild to hold it.

'Mandragora!' she muttered. 'What next! Mandragora for childbirth!'

Desperately Hikenai gulped the foul stuff. She shut her eyes and rocked from side to side. Little beads of sweat started out on her forehead.

Outside it rained furiously but the room lightened as the clouds went over and Dame Hermengild waddled to the narrow, deep-set window, drawing aside the wet linen of the curtain to stare out.

'Please,' whispered Hikenai, 'I pray you, do not block the window. There is no air,' and she began to groan again.

The day seemed endless. The midwife and Dame Hermengild murmured together by the couch but Hikenai was hardly conscious of them, or of Ediva who came and went on errands. A long time later, it appeared to her, they made her drink again and then all was lost in mists of confusion and pain. She was conscious of noise, near or far away at intervals, but it was only when the midwife spoke firmly to her, bidding her save her strength, that she realised the sound was her own wailing moans.

191

She was lying now on a pallet of straw or bracken, she could feel it pricking her legs through the cloth that covered it. Then came a pain so dreadful that it was past bearing. She knew she could not live through pain like this and in her extremity she tried to rise as though it were possible to flee. Eyes and mouth wide open, she glared unseeingly before her. 'God, Great God!' she shrieked, and then a gabble of English that even Dame Hermengild could not understand.

Capable hands pulled her down while she screamed and screamed. A monstrous beast was upon her – within her – rending, clawing, tearing her asunder. She was aware of nothing but her body's treachery, agony too terrible to be endured, before which she thrashed and howled like an animal. Something gave way or burst and she lay still, drenched in sweat, and then, as the haziness receded – 'Is it born?' she whispered.

'Only the head. Quiet now, lie still,' said the midwife.

There was another pain, not so bad, that only made her groan, and a curious slippery, rushing feeling.

'It's a lad!' shouted Dame Hermengild with as much triumph as if she had brought him forth herself, and a moment later the helpless, gasping wails of the newborn filled the room.

Hikenai lay quietly while strength flowed back to her, then she raised her head. 'Show me the King's son,' she commanded.

With a grin that showed all her gums the midwife held up the child, her arms bloody to the elbows. He was red and black; his dusky skin hanging in great folds like an old hound's and his squashed, sly, ancient face surmounted by a cap of greasy black hair. 'Is he not a fine little knave?' she said.

Hikenai smiled. A great relief filled her. Her body was her own again and she had borne a son. A King's son!

She tried to picture Henry's face but could not, she was

192

so tired. Gradually she slipped down to slumber, and there, something in her own mind said to her, loud and clear as a sacring bell – Did the Queen, too, bear a son, think you?

She sprang awake and could not sleep for all her weariness. And all that night the child whimpered as though in sorrow at being in the world.

August 1156 – Christmas 1156
In Rouen at Lammastide a three-day fair was held to celebrate the removal of the hurdles from the meadows after the haysel; now the cattle would be driven in and allowed to graze on the stubbles and the aftermath, and since the town was not noted for the strength of its adherence to Christianity there was apt to be back-sliding into the bad old customs of the pagan revels. The priests conveniently closed their eyes to much that went on for it was known that the practice of the old religion was still rife in the area; there was little to be gained by a headlong clash with the majority of their flock and, indeed, it was generally believed that many of them joined the merrymaking and tried to pretend there was a Christian basis for the festivities.

Dame Hermengild's interest was aroused to fever pitch by these tales; being city born and bred her religious experiences were entirely conventional and the rumours she had heard from her protégées in London she had dismissed as idle superstition. Here, though, she might discover whether or not there was a kernel of truth in them; whether, in fact, there existed a different kind of worship altogether from the one she had always known, with its irritating insistence on asceticism and its condemnation of everything she had enjoyed in her self-indulgent youth. Such thoughts were at the back of her mind when she suggested to Hikenai that they should go to the fair.

Hikenai also had heard the gossip but she had recognised it immediately. He was here too, then, the Horned God.

Perhaps he was everywhere. Her first instinct, as always, was fear but it was difficult to uphold her refusal in the face of Hermengild's determination. She was bored, too, by the circumscribed round of their daily life.

It was Father Roger, the old priest whom Henry had provided to write and read letters for them, who finally tipped the balance for her. It had taken longer for the subject of the moment to filter through to his deaf ears, but when it did so it became apparent that he was not one of those complaisant clerics who turned a blind eye to what went on. He was truly horrified at the idea of wild orgies (so he pictured them, from hearsay) in the name of some pagan god. Had not the Lord of Hosts smitten the worshippers of Baal for that very thing? He waxed so vehement upon the subject in the loud, toneless voice of the very deaf that Hikenai, heiress of an older tradition and ignorant of most of his references, became resentful.

What is it to them if we hold to the old beliefs in our hearts? she wondered. What use a meek and gentle God from far away when life is hard and bitter? If the crops fail and the animals abort their young, what will their Christ do to help? But she forbore to argue, only murmuring that it could do no harm to watch while yet the sun shone, to see the jugglers and listen to the wandering trouvères, and maybe to buy a ribbon or a buckle. Father Roger agreed there could be no harm in that, so they were home by sunset.

From dawn on the first day of the fair people poured into Rouen from the surrounding countryside. Booths and stalls were set up in every available place, as many outside the walls as within. It was fiercely hot; the sun glaring down from a dazzling sky and not a breath of wind stirring.

Hermengild, Hikenai and Ediva set out early through the gates with two menservants to guard them; already the ways between the stalls were crowded with buyers and onlookers, and still latecomers were unloading their wares and

194

paying their toll for the privilege of selling at Lammas Fair. Only the commoner class of citizen had arrived as yet, but as the morning wore on little knots of young men more grandly dressed appeared, come not to buy but to watch and listen to the entertainers, and if luck were with them and fathers careless, to pick up the daughters of the town-folk. It was from these, muttered Hermengild, that her charges must be protected by the menservants; her own tongue served well enough with the meaner kind.

By now the heat and press of people had her mopping feebly at her brow with the corner of her veil and declaiming that could she not drink, she must melt or die. . . when with infinite relief, she saw before her a kind of tented tavern, complete with bunch of ivy on a pole, and elbowed her way through the throng with renewed vigour.

Here she was ensconced upon a bench with her back to the chest that formed a counter, exuding perspiration and complaints about the quality of the wine with equal facility, until at last a huge yawn silenced her, by degrees her head nodded forward upon her bosom and a soft snore proclaimed a temporary ending to her chaperonage.

'Come,' said Hikenai. 'We shall be safe enough with those two to watch over us,' and she signalled to the menservants, who downed their mugs with disgusted looks and followed the two girls out into the noisy excitement of the fair.

Hikenai thought it a splendid place. They stopped at nearly every booth to examine the trinkets or to sample honey cakes and comfits, and they laughed so loud and long at the antics and clever tricks of a tumbler that they attracted the attention of a group of very richly dressed gentlemen who followed them for some way until the menservants blocked their path and showed their cudgels. After that they behaved more circumspect, and in the noisy crowd the girls did not notice that one of the group remained always not far away.

After about an hour, though, Ediva must answer a call of nature, and warning the menservants not to move away and to see that none followed them, they pushed their way between a crumbling old wall and the backs of a line of stalls, squeezing up tight against the dusty stones and away from the flapping, brightly coloured cloth with which the backs of the booths were hung, until they came to a dark little corner in the masonry where Ediva might relieve herself.

Giggling and twisting in the confined space, each gave a shriek as the green hangings that protected them from public view suddenly billowed forward and a heavy body thumped upon them from the other side, knocking Ediva quite off her feet and startling Hikenai so much that she grabbed at it for support. Wildly they stared at each other, hands clapped to mouths to stifle their snorts of mirth. The curtain moved aside and an enquiring face, young and undoubtedly masculine for it wore a small fair beard, peered round not six inches from Hikenai's own.

A little smile quirked the full lips under the beard, and a voice speaking her own familiar tongue in accents as English as she had ever heard, said laughingly, 'God's Body, this is too much! You set your servants to threaten me with their staves and now you lurk like thieves in a corner. Am I so horrid a sight that a pretty maid should flee me as though I were a leper?'

They stood so close in the dim, greenish light that filtered through the curtain that she could feel his warm breath on her face. His eyes were that curious, slaty Saxon blue and his broad, rather flat cheeks were dusted with golden freckles.

Her voice was breathless. 'We do not hide from you, good sir. It was my maidservant who needed privacy —'

Ediva reared up suddenly from under their feet and they all laughed.

'Well, come,' he said, taking her hand, 'now that we

see we are compatriots. I am nothing to fear, though I would not say the same of those others I was in company with. I have lost them now in this mob and a fair is not a place to be alone.'

'I cannot. Dame Hermengild will be angry. We have left her sleeping in the taverner's tent.'

'Oh, come.' His eyes were curious. 'You have your maid-servant – you are English as I am and I am lonely. I will take you back to the taverner's tent later if you will send your men away.'

She still looked doubtful but she could never long sustain her will against another's, and he took her arm and drew her firmly forward, lifting up the enshrouding hangings. She saw that they had come into the back of a booth where pies, cakes and cordials were sold; the proprietor was clad all in green so she guessed he was a Green Man, that is, one who scours the countryside for its herbs and fruits. The comfortable-looking woman with him was doubtless his wife and the one who cooked and prepared his harvest.

She came forward with a smile, asking if they would not try her cowslip cordial which was famous over all this area, or possibly the conserve of rose heps? She chattered on, and Hikenai found herself ushered to a seat on a long bench before she knew she had consented. And then, while they sipped delicious cowslip cordial, the young man questioned her for he was eager to know how an English maid came to be in Normandy, and because she saw no reason to be secretive and had felt strangely attracted to him at first glance, she told him who she was and how she came there.

He was silent for a second, and then he said how singular it was that their paths had crossed for he, Ethelwig the Englishman, was in service to Queen Eleanor, than whom there was no finer lady in Christendom. When Ediva heard this, she began to mutter unintelligibly under her breath until Hikenai told her to be quiet for she was herself so overturned by the information that she could think of nothing to say. The liking she had felt for the Englishman began to evaporate.

He, however, seemed to notice nothing amiss in her silence. He talked on and on, about his music and his singing which evidently meant everything to him, about his life in the Queen's Household (he was quite inordinately proud of the fact that he was entitled to two whole candles and fourteen candle ends a week, which seemed odd to Hikenai who, in her little house, might have as many candles burning as she pleased) and about the Queen herself, for whom his admiration was boundless. She, it appeared, had been responsible for his rise in the world when she had taken him from a miserable life as a wandering minstrel and made him a favourite among her ladies.

It was soon apparent, though, that his worship of her was conducted from afar on the plane of Courtly Love. Henry himself had sometimes spoken jeeringly of this phenomenon, introduced from Provence to the rough Norman Court by the Queen. Hikenai had not understood; to her, as to Henry, love was sexual attraction. Her lack of comprehension showed on her face; he looked amused and whispered to her that carnal delights could always be found elsewhere – why else, he concluded airily, were they awaiting nightfall with such anticipation?

'I shall not stay after nightfall,' she said.

'Fie!' said he. 'Why not? There will be dancing and merrymaking – and more for those who desire it. Have you not joined the Dance before?'

'The King' – she said feebly.

'He has been long from here, has he not?'

'I have his child. And he is coming back – he is!' she cried as she saw his shrug.

'He has many women, and tires of them quickly.'

She stood up suddenly. 'That is nothing to me. He is the King – he may take where he wills! But I' –

'Sit down. I thought when I first saw you – but no matter. It was my mistake.'

Several heads turned to stare and she sat down hurriedly with a puzzled look at him. 'What did you think?'

'No matter,' he said, and then – 'It was because you were English, I think.'

'Tell me!'

He leaned towards her and whispered, 'I thought you were of the chosen – that you would take my meaning.'

She did half know, yet she must press him. 'What chosen?'

'Of the old persuasion – the faery people – those who have made the vows at the Sacred Tree. And particularly, those who have been accepted.'

She shook her head blindly.

'Well,' he said, 'I am mistook, it seems. I will not speak of it again unless you wish it' – and he began once more to talk of light matters though she did not hear a word.

Too many thoughts were jostling in her mind; old memories called up by his words and the bitter knowledge that she was not Henry's only love. Yet – love? – no, not those others; she knew that men must satisfy their appetites, it was no more than that. But what of herself? Must she wait, month after dragging month, alone and unsatisfied? Henry had promised to keep her with him and he had not done so. He had awakened her and left her. Yet she still feared the old gods, in spite of all they offered. Why? What dark memory lurked hidden in her mind?

She became aware again of Ethelwig. He had a soft and confidential manner of speaking, an easy familiarity that took the form of a constant, gentle fondling of her hands. Like everyone else, Hikenai was accustomed to the full-blooded kiss of greeting from men or women so that it was difficult to explain why these moth-like touches should seem so disturbingly intimate. She drew her hands away and clasped them in her lap.

199

'We must away,' she said abruptly, 'before the Dame wakes. Come, Ediva.'

When Ediva held up the flap over the exit of the tent, she turned and looked back at him.

'Tonight?' he said with his lips.

She breathed hard through her nose and shook her head. Then she followed the serving wench out of the tent.

On the last day of the fair Hikenai saw the Englishman again. After another day of burning heat the sun was setting in a blaze beyond the wooded rise, and the smoke of the cooking fires, deeper blue than the blue sky, rose in tall, straight columns before wavering and dissolving high in the warm air.

Dame Hermengild was tired but not so tired that she wished to return within the walls. 'Come,' she said. 'Let us sit awhile up there where we can watch,' and so they were climbing the rising ground towards the trees in company with other groups who also were loth to see the end of jollity and a return to workaday life.

From up here, when they looked back, they could see the great fields spread out, unfenced now and with cattle feeding on what remained from the harvest, and beyond that, the walls and towers of Rouen. Before them, in dense shade, the woods were dusky. Clumps of gorse and hawthorn clothed the slope so that they must take a winding, tortuous path, tripping on grass tussocks and the sprawling arms of brambles, and the stiff spikes of sorrel catching in their skirts.

Suddenly, just below the trees, they came out into a kind of natural amphitheatre, a shallow depression on the hillside ringed about with spiny, impenetrable gorse, taller than a man. In the middle, upon a slab of stone, a small fire burned, smokeless and bright.

They stared about in wonder and saw a number of people sitting quietly, as though waiting for an important event.

200

Then Hikenai saw the Englishman. He had risen at once and come forward, almost as if he had been expecting them. She turned to flee but another group was entering through the gap and before she could squeeze past he was upon them.

She stood dumb as a block of wood while he greeted the Dame, making much of her and leading her to the grassy bank while Hermengild, delighted to see a fellow-countryman, questioned him eagerly, desiring to know whether there would be dancing and feasting.

Aye, he said, indeed there would be, and the feasting was already in progress. When Hikenai looked, she saw little piles of cakes and sweetmeats laid out, and small roasted birds, still steaming from the fire. Everyone but themselves, who had come by accident as it were, had brought some contribution. It was a Love Feast, Ethelwig said, and they must share in it.

After they had eaten, they drank, and the fire was mended but not too large for fear of sparks in the gorse after the dry spell. Then someone began to play upon a lute and one after another joined in, one upon a cittern, another on a hautbois, and many upon simple pipes made from reeds; those who had no instrument to play sang loudly and joyously. Hikenai sang too, and the Dame, for they had drunk copiously of Ethelwig's wine. Hikenai began to wonder what she had feared in such innocent merrymaking.

Suddenly, beside her, Ethelwig started to sing. She faltered and stopped to listen. His glorious voice rang out powerfully, rising to a pitch of intolerable sweetness and sliding down to rich and mellow depths she had not known the human voice could compass. Others, too, fell silent, lost in the pleasure of listening, until he sang alone, wordless and strange, playing upon their emotions as easily as he played on his harp.

Now it was full dark; the only light came from the leaping flames. Gradually the character of his singing changed, and with it a soft drumming began. It was the old song he was singing, the one she remembered from long ago – 'Swete lamman dhu' – the air that called them to the dance.

Rhythmic and insistent the beat of the drums as more and more came in; hands started to clap and feet were set to tapping. Ethelwig sang on but now he stood up and slowly circled the fire, his feet stamping out the rhythm. One after another the onlookers joined him; in a long line they went, weaving and swaying, widdershins around the fire, taking the opposite direction from the sun's path. Slowly at first, but as the tempo of the drums increased, faster went the dancers whirling round. As Ethelwig went by he caught Hikenai's hand and then the Dame's, and after that all was a mad, sweating delirium.

Panting for breath, odd dancers dropped away and when they returned they had shed their garments in the bushes. The intoxication of the dance, the wine that they had drunk had done their work, and now, to add to the exhilaration, someone followed at the end of the line with a long lash, beating at those who flagged, urging them on to fresh exertions.

The moon was rising, casting its pale light into the hollow so that all was black and white, white flesh, black shadows, white faces with black holes for eyes and mouths; only now and then the dying fire limned shoulders and thighs with an orange glow.

There was release in this excitement; relief after tension, orgasm after frenzy. Nothing that Hikenai saw in this Dionysian revelry surprised or shocked her, the wonder lay in how she could have forgotten so easily – though now that she was fifteen years old and a woman, the wild dancing of the naked figures struck a chord in her that had perforce been absent in the child.

This, then, was how service should be done and homage paid; after the feast of communion, the intoxicating excitement, the furious pounding of heart and blood, the loss of self in something greater; a reminder that humanity, too, was part of the natural world of bird and fish, of plant and animal, all necessary, all interdependent.

Yet something was missing.

Her naked body ran with sweat. She leaned on Ethelwig and felt his hands upon her. 'Where is He?' she panted. 'The Great One?'

'Not yet,' he said, 'not yet', and though his gaze was on her, he seemed not to see her, so vague and wandering his look, so curious the expression on his face.

One swift glance served to dispel her suspicions – there he stood, naked and limp as a wet clout, whatever he lusted after, it was not her body. The music flooded over her, and the drums beat in time with the thudding of her heart. She stared into Ethelwig's eyes and now she saw they were quite unfocused, the pupils so enormous that the blue had disappeared.

'Come,' he said. 'Come, and you shall know joy past human loving.' His eyes rolled upwards with the effort as he pulled her away from the ring and into the shadows.

There the waiting women anointed her, rubbing the magic salve into her sweating legs and buttocks – 'it will make you dance,' they crooned, 'it will make you fly. Here's hemlock and belladonna and aconite' –

Yes – she remembered – rub till the flesh be red, rub well between the legs.

Staggering, she stood erect and Ethelwig's hand was there to guide her, to lead her back into the ring, sweating hand in sweating hand, burning flank brushing burning thigh. She did not feel the cuts upon her feet, the bruises on her legs, she believed the lie her drugged mind told her – that she floated yards above the ground. They were taking a different course this time, away from the fire, out of the secret amphitheatre and up the hill among the brambles and the stones. Into the dark wood they went for it was here, under the trees, that they would meet their God.

Hikenai was conscious of nothing but the wild dementia of the music, all was mounting in a crashing crescendo of noise and sensation. She had ceased to fear, ceased even to think. The sight of Dame Hermengild before her, gargantuan in her nudity, did not recall her to herself.

In a clearing in the wood they waited, those terrifying figures, furred and horned like beasts, and one by one the dancers approached and prostrated themselves before them. Then she lay at their feet, gasping and twitching, panting for breath, awaiting she knew not what. Was it the thing she could not remember? She jerked and moaned, trying to peer upward through the tangle of her long hair.

He was bending over her, his terrible face coming closer to look into her eyes. His hands (were they hands?) were raising her, icy cold upon her burning flesh. She looked straight into the dreadful countenance, long and snouted and surmounted by those curving horns, and then she was drawn into his embrace. Heavily she lay against his hairy chest, her legs trapped between his knees.

'And are you Mine?' he whispered.

Faint and small, yet clear, she answered, 'I am yours!'

'As you ever were,' he said. 'Long have I sought you. This night we seal the bond.'

Afterwards, long afterwards, she wept, though whether for joy or sorrow, rapture or nightmare, she could not tell. It was Ethelwig who led her back to the amphitheatre, tripping over entwined couples in the darkness, to find her clothing. Her limbs were heavy with a sweet lassitude after the abandon that had gone before so that she was glad to lie back on Ethelwig's cloak, spread on the goat-nibbled turf.

'Was I not right?' he said. 'Are you not one of us? *They* knew.'

She nodded, all docility now. 'He took me – the Great One – first of all those others. No man could, with so many.

204

He is not warm, like as a man is, but cold and hard – and there is grievous pain – aye, but paradise as well. . . .'

'Paradise. . . .' His voice was slurred.

'And you? Did you not find a partner?'

His face was strange in the leprous moonlight.

'The gods give the same pleasuring to men if they desire it. The Great One was my partner as he was yours.'

A little frown wrinkled her brow, but as the fumes rose in her head again, her eyelids drooped.

'Thus are we all one,' he murmured, and in her bemused state as she sank to sleep, his remark seemed a profundity of the deepest significance.

When Dame Hermengild told Hikenai the news – that the King of the English was in Rouen again – in the castle, that is, with the Queen, his wife – she stared at the Dame with guarded eyes. Her mind had been in turmoil since the last night of the fair. It was not precisely remorse she felt for that would imply a belief in free will which Hikenai certainly did not possess; yet if she could have undone that night's work, she would have undone it. Her worry involved her relationship with Henry, remote as that now seemed. She knew he would be angry if he discovered her participation in those rites and she feared his anger. Therefore he must not know.

She was not afraid, though, that Hermengild or Ediva would tell him. Neither of them had mentioned the events of that night to her since. Even when Ethelwig, the Queen's minstrel, had called upon her, Hermengild's garrulity had remained quenched, her looks abstracted, as if she had sufficient food for thought to last her many a month.

Hikenai was not sure she liked this unwonted silence. At first it had been a relief, now it was almost sinister. She wished that the Dame would stay with her when Ethelwig came instead of showing him in with exaggerated courtesy, then closing the door upon them. She felt, absurdly enough after her own behaviour, that her guardian was betraying Henry.

But if Hermengild were reticent, Ethelwig was not. He talked and talked, about everything, about nothing. And it seemed to her that behind the easy flow of his conversation lurked hidden meaning.

He played to her at times and spoke of music. He would show her the strings of the lyre, pointing out the different thicknesses and lengths and trying to make her see that the ratio was what mattered, that the proportions produce the notes, the pattern of the scale. She hardly listened to him but snatches of his words broke through her inattention.

'Music will purge the soul,' he said, 'as medicine the body. You know it. Is it not well to dance to frenzy, then sleep the sleep of exhaustion?'

She nodded vaguely, wondering when he would go.

'Music holds beasts and devils both under its spell,' he murmured – and so on by the hour.

Sometimes the child would wake, wailing, and she might excuse herself; oftener Ethelwig would remain till sundown, his quiet voice lulling her almost to sleep. How had he recognised her for what she was, this man whose blood was as Saxon as her own, whose origins had been in those same gloomy northern forests?

She asked him once, and he said the mark was plain upon her for those who had eyes to see. A gift was given, he said, to the chosen.

'A gift? Ah – your voice, your music. But I – I have no gift.'

'No gift? You – who have captured the heart of a King? Look well at your likeness. There is no more beauty in you than a thousand others. What binds the King to you?' He laughed. 'Not your mind, to be sure. Your gift is the one given to every Maiden.'

She knew what he meant. It must be so – for it was undeniably true that there were women who had the power to enchant any man they pleased. She had never before thought of it as a gift from the Great One.

'To what purpose?' she asked.

He had seemed evasive. 'Time will bring forth its fruits,' he had said finally. And then – 'Did you know? – once there was a King in England who believed as we do. May one not come again?'

That was yesterday. Now Hermengild was telling her that Henry was with his Queen. He would come here soon. Joy suddenly flooded her, washing away the worry and the doubt.

He came three days later with a whole train of young knights and their squires. Ethelwig, she was thankful to see, was not among them.

They spent the day together in the little house, outwardly a happy, peaceful day, while the young men sought their own pleasures. Henry's delight in the child was unbounded for already his fresh growth of downy hair gave promise of being as red as Henry's own.

'Did I not tell you he would be a prince?' cried his father, throwing the babe aloft and catching him again in a manner which brought Hikenai's heart to her mouth. 'And he is large. Larger far than the princess, my daughter.'

Hikenai did not look at him. 'She is well?' she forced herself to say.

'Aye, strong, and like to become stronger.' He hesitated a moment. 'God took back my heir three months ago.' He laid the babe back in the crib without looking at him again and took her hand. 'It was a heavy loss to bear.'

In spite of herself, Hikenai felt a strong surge of an emotion that was almost pleasure. She dropped her eyes quickly but when she raised them to Henry again he was looking beyond her.

'I did not deserve that,' he said, and it was almost a question.

'You have another son,' she said in a clumsy attempt at

207

comfort, and then, half under her breath, 'besides mine'.

He sighed. 'Yes, I have another son – and after all, am likely to have more.'

She thought, He thinks I have no more feeling than an ox, and for a second hated him.

Then he said, 'We shall have many more sons, Hikenai,' and she persuaded herself she had mistaken his meaning.

Whatever her feelings were, Henry found himself calmed and refreshed by Hikenai's undemanding company. With her he was at peace; she had never asked for more than his presence and to him, who knew exactly what he wanted and always took the shortest path, such quietness of heart was doubly attractive.

If only Eleanor. . . . At the thought of his wife, an unfamiliar feeling rose in him and he realised with sudden shock that it came close to dislike. She was as unlike Hikenai as it was possible for a woman to be. . . . But nonetheless, he must to Aquitaine with her and leave Hikenai once again. He did not know how to tell her and so, being Henry, he postponed the evil moment. Yet he had one thing to tell her that would surely make her happy.

He laid his finger on her lips for she was talking of some trivial conceit she had concerning the child.

'We shall call him Geoffrey' – he said, and at her blank look – 'for my father'.

She made no comment, only continuing with what she had been saying before he interrupted.

'Does that not please you?' he said sharply.

'It is a fair name.'

Henry was nettled. How could she be thus insensible of the honour he had done her child?

Then she slipped her hand in his. 'Henry is fairer,' she whispered in his ear. He laughed and forgave her.

'No, Geoffrey is better as my father was a better man than I. Geoffrey he shall be. Is it well?'

'Very well,' she said.

When he took his leave of her, late in the evening, he kissed her tenderly, then rose abruptly and stood looking down at her.

'I have arranged to send you back next month,' he said, 'to England.'

It seemed her heart stopped beating.

'I am for Aquitaine,' he continued, 'with the Queen. There I cannot take you – it is her Duchy. So I shall send you all home in charge of my Chancellor.'

'No' – she whispered, 'no –'

His eyebrows went up. 'Yes,' he said briskly, 'I have resolved upon it –it is all arranged. It will not seem too long before I come to you again in London. Fare you well now.'

When he had gone, she wept, and slowly the tears of misery turned to tears of bitterness. She had been sent here to Normandy like a chattel eight months ago and she could count the number of his visits on the fingers of one hand. Now she was to be returned to England in the care of a man she feared and disliked.

'It is true,' she groaned. 'He thinks I have no more feeling than an animal.'

In that she did Henry an injustice. He was not so much insensitive as unable to dissemble, and he was used to give his orders as befitted one who had been reared as a commander of men rather than a statesman. When he saw her tears he regretted the brusque manner with which he had informed her of the necessity for her return to England – and yet, what else could he have done? Thomas must go back, partly because his presence was required at the Exchequer at Michaelmas and partly because old Theobald had fallen ill; he, at any rate, realised the King's difficulties and had no foolish notions of being slighted. It was convenient to Henry's purposes that they should travel on the same ship – she should accept his wishes without question. So he shook off the faint prick of disquiet he felt. She loved him and all would be well.

But, contrary to his belief, all was not well. The more she dwelt upon his treatment of her, the more Hikenai's resentment grew, and the more bitter for being inarticulate. Now she recalled what she had tried to forget, that Ethelwig had given her the names of some London citizens, folk with whom she should get in touch if she were able; in short, names of those who believed and practised the old religion.

Why should she not? If Henry had cared for her, he would not have packed her off to England so summarily. Yet still she hesitated. She did not truly know what she believed but the road to a Christian Heaven was hard and that heaven itself seemed cold and comfortless to her material mind. The practice of the old religion offered fleshly joys here and now – at that thought she remembered Henry's body and wept. She did not consciously marshal facts and come to a decision, yet decision grew in her nonetheless. Henry's action had cut at something deeper than wounded pride and she must assuage her pain in the only way she knew.

These were the feelings in her heart all through the long day they took to cross the Channel. The ship laboured along but Hikenai was unconscious of the passage of time, sitting withdrawn upon the deck with hands clasped loosely in her lap and her eyes fixed on the far horizon.

Thomas watched her sitting there. His own spleen almost equalled hers for he had been stung to the quick by Henry's bald announcement of his arrangements for the transporting of his minion and her entourage. He had not exchanged a word with her, contenting himself with a mere nod when their paths unavoidably crossed. But he had been surprised when he first saw her. She was comely, to be sure – he had remembered that much of her – but there was nothing of the harlot in her face. Irritatingly enough, she seemed as prepared to ignore him as he her. So now he watched her, standing where she could not see him in the shadow of the mast. Above his head the square sail flapped and cracked as the fitful breeze took it and the helmsman shouted and swore, but neither the girl nor the man who watched her heard them.

She had none of the voluptuousness he had expected; she was too calm, too colourless, too like the cold image of a saint before the gilding and enamel is applied. As soon as the simile came unbidden to his mind, he was amazed at the incongruity of it. Yet he saw in her an undesigning simplicity that staggered him. She was like a little child, too young to know that sin exists, as unconscious of good or evil, of modesty or shame as Eve before the Fall. The pull of that primal innocence was strong but Thomas recognised its source. The wiles of the Adversary are many and various, appealing to reason or the love of beauty by turns, and this lure of the old pagan world was more tempting than most for it begged an end to man's struggle with his baser nature.

Live as the beasts, was what it said, they take no thought for the morrow and are content; do as they do and follow the instincts God gave you. It did not deceive Thomas for a moment. Thus would Christ have died in vain.

What had begun as disapproval had turned to fear and distrust and could as easily become hatred. Thomas saw that, too.

She half turned then, and saw him, and made a little gesture. A surprising anger flooded him. Abruptly, he walked away.

Thomas parted from his protégées before they reached London, sending them ahead with a sufficient escort while he took the road to Canterbury to visit the Archbishop. His annoyance had had time to subside and he bade the King's minion farewell with due politeness, thinking only as he did so – she has eyes like a fox, too yellow and too wide apart – he felt the hair rise slightly on the back of his head as he touched her fingers. He wiped his hand furtively on the back of his gown as she turned away from him.

The Dame's thankfulness at coming safely once more into her own city was marred only by the discovery that Alfled had fled with much of her property; but even this was no more than an irritant. Hikenai was listless, it was true, and the babe snotting badly at the nose, but the bags of silver pennies which the King had presented to her (and which had made the journey securely fastened about her waist beneath the undergown) made up for all. Even if he came no more to Hikenai's side, the child was a sure means of revenue, she assured herself. She had not wasted her time. And there were still half a dozen girls in her house near Westminster – she should soon pick up with the old clientèle again.

So the winter passed quietly for all of them, and if Hikenai and Ediva demanded – and gained – more freedom for excursions into the fields and villages round about, Hermengild thought little of it. The times when they were abroad -- All Souls and Candlemas and monthly at full moon – meant nothing to her. Nor did she connect their behaviour with that curious experience at Rouen.

She had been badly frightened by what she had seen there; so badly, indeed, that she never willingly remembered her own participation, or the dreadful sight of Hikenai in the Devil's arms. She had, of course, known that Satan walked the earth, seeking whom he might devour, but. . . . That was as far as her thoughts ever went because her thighs began to tremble at that point and her belly turn to water.

But because of what she had seen she feared Hikenai now and, in one sense, they had exchanged roles. It was now her turn to walk warily and to agree with smiles to anything the girl suggested. She had made Confession and gained Absolution before they left Rouen. She did not know whether Hikenai and Ediva had done the same thing and nothing would have made her ask.

Henry was content enough that Christmas in Bordeaux with Eleanor. There were no other women who attracted him sufficiently to tempt him from his wife's bed so relations between them were cordial, and he had had good news of his rebellious brother a few weeks earlier – the citizens of Nantes had deposed their lord and offered the Dukedom of Brittany to Geoffrey.

This fortunate turn of events would mean that his continual invasions of Henry's lands would cease, or at least, become intermittent. Also, Henry hoped, his own influence would be strengthened all over northern France. If he might only extend his power in southern France, he might squeeze Louis even more tightly into his small domain around Paris. . . .

Nothing put Henry into a better humour than the chance of acquiring yet more lands and power. It was, of course, foolish of the Bretons not to have invited him to take possession of their Duchy – but he was still their overlord. Could he but gain Toulouse, though. . . .

He humped over in the great bed and put his hand on Eleanor's thigh. 'Did not your ancestors have a claim to Toulouse?' he said.

Eleanor had been drifting peacefully into slumber. Relaxed with love, she leaned towards him. 'What is it?' she murmured.

He repeated the question, alert and up on his elbow.

She sighed. 'What times you choose,' she said, 'for such a subject. Aye, they claimed it. So did Louis once through me.' Her eyelids drooped again.

'Well?'

She sighed again with mounting irritation. 'Nothing came of it. Go to sleep, Henry.' The ropes of the bed creaked as she turned her back firmly.

In the dim, half light he grinned to himself. A known claim, at least, was something. It would be well to bear in mind for the future. So he schemed and dreamed of ways to advance his own sovereignty, recalling that he now had a daughter with a pleasure that was more than half self-interest, for daughters are useful pawns in the game of power politics. That turned his mind to his need for more sons, since William's death, and he said a hasty prayer that Eleanor might fall pregnant again from this night's work and bear another boy. He thought sleepily that he would hear two Masses tomorrow for that intention if he could spare the time.

Whether it was, in fact, that night's work or some other, Eleanor knew by Candlemas that she would lie-in once more in the early autumn. She, too, longed for another son. Let him be like William, she prayed, but without much hope. It seemed to her that when God answered prayer, He did so in a devious, labyrinthine way so that the attainment of heart's desire carried with it some inevitable penalty. She feared this hoped-for child would mean exile from her beloved Aquitaine and separation from Henry through the weary months of pregnancy.

So it proved. But they would not be too long parted for he was to follow her across the Channel soon after Easter, and if his anticipation were centred upon a well-known bawdy house and reunion with his Chancellor, she did not suspect it. Indeed, she was convinced that his affair with the English whore had died a natural death so that when the blow fell, it was the more shattering.

VIII

Easter-Whitsuntide 1157

I<small>T WAS THE DAY</small> after Low Sunday and a dark day of sad, drizzling rain, but within the Queen's audience chamber all was cheerful. The great fire roared and crackled valiantly for Eleanor held that fires were a necessity until June in England.

She had received Master Becket, the Chancellor, and had conversed long and amiably with him; now many of his young knights and gentlemen had come in and were talking together at the end of the hall. A fair number of them carried lutes and Eleanor saw the longing, sideways glances of her younger unmarried ladies in their direction. She laughed and clapped her hands.

'Come, we shall have music and verses! Each of the knights must sing a stanza to the lady of his choice and she must cap the last line. Shall we so?'

The young men surged forward and Eleanor ran a considering eye over them. Some of them, she was flattered to see, were gazing at her rather than at the maids. One of them caught her eye immediately, a dark, very beautiful young man, head and shoulders taller than the rest. She hoped he would sing a poem to her.

All went very gaily for a time with the knights singing light-hearted, slightly ribald doggerel and the maids capping them with wit and vivacity. The handsome young man watched the Queen with an unblinking stare that she began to find disconcerting. She turned her head and noticed a small group gossiping with their heads close. All at once the laughter died away in one of those unaccountable pauses that come on a crowded gathering and in the hush, close beside her, Eleanor overheard a snatch of their talk.

'– how he could with such low blood!'

'Sent her and her bastard child home with the Chancellor?'

'Aye, from Normandy where he had her—'

A lusty baritone burst forth and Eleanor jerked her head round and met again the dark, intense stare. A cold chill ran down her upper arms. She was instantly, intuitively certain that it was the King's misbehaviour they were discussing but the worst shock was the mention of the Chancellor's name in such a context. If he had, in fact, escorted one of Henry's lights o' love – and a bastard child!

She felt a deep flush rise in her cheeks and was glad of the heat and noise and merriment where it would pass unnoticed. She felt certain that it was the same one – the English whore. She forced herself to smile, feeling she must look like a gargoyle. Why would the dark young knight not look elsewhere!

She remembered when she had first heard of that – creature – and the words the Empress had spoken then. Easy for her – she had always disliked her husband and the only pain she had suffered had been the injury to her dignity. So be it, she would learn to hate Henry. . . .

That was not difficult in his absence but she knew well that his presence would awaken physical desire. That, strangely enough, appeared to her a better reason for hating him.

Although Eleanor had not noticed him, Reynold Fitzurse stood beside Hugh de Morville in her audience chamber. It was the first time he had seen the Queen except at a distance.

He had not known women like her existed; he was dazzled by her beauty, fascinated by her grace and, above all, by her speech which was quick, soft and curiously accented, the harsh Norman French softened by her native langue d'Oc.

As he stood, mouth agape, Huge whispered, grinning, 'Are you struck by the dart of love, Fitzurse? Will you, too, join the group that sports her favour, and embrace the principle of Courtly Love that asks for nothing but a smile?' But Reynold only looked at him in a bemused sort of way.

After that, Reynold thought much of her in the few quiet moments he had but he was careful not to allow Hugh to notice his pre-occupation. Nor was he ever quite so pleased with Beatrice thereafter; he rode less often to Barham where she had been settled now for more than half a year, and when he did she did not seem so pretty nor so fine as once she had. Beatrice was sharp enough to see it although she did not care much. At present, it was sufficient for her to be the mistress of a fine household with none to say her nay.

Throughout the long, lonely winter months while Henry remained in France with his Queen, Hikenai was receiving full initiation into the service of her God. In Rouen she had for the first time experienced ecstasy; as she penetrated more deeply into the performance of esoteric rites, self-transcendence followed in full measure. The elementary sexuality of her first communion with the beings of the Other World was the gateway to an awareness of those Others, to an escape from her own imprisoning identity.

In the beginning, intoxicants and natural drugs were needed to liberate the self, but in Hikenai the small group of devotees had found a natural mystic, a Maiden worthy of the power that flowed through her to them. With rhythmic movement and the beating of the drums, the Dark Gods would come among them, freeing them all from a dreary present and a bloodstained past. That those Dark Gods took possession of human bodies whose true owners were well known to them mattered not at all; when the human personality is absent or sleeping, all that remains is Godhead.

Sexuality still remained on the lowest level of the rites and to the rank and file that was sufficient satisfaction. For the women there was no fear of conception for the member of the God was but a cunningly contrived contraption of horn and leather, put away after the ceremonies with the animal masks.

Yet for the initiated, there was more. When the God inhabited the body of a man, whose seed will pass in a natural coupling: God's or man's? Hikenai knew with a Maiden's knowledge that should she choose to bear a child, it would have no earthly father.

She never questioned the identity of these dark spirits. True daughter of nature that she was, the thin veneer of Christianity overlying pagan belief cracked and crumbled away. Nor did any qualm of conscience disturb her who was possessed of an inner certainty to equal the faith of any Christian saint. No longer inadequate, that strange Otherness was immanent in her, inherent and all pervading.

Occasionally, she thought of Henry, but with a difference. All the grievance she had felt towards him had dissolved. This new consciousness of power had convinced her that he was in thrall to her, that the Great One had chosen her to be his instrument to mould the King to his own great purposes, and she accepted her lot with the unquestioning meekness that was second nature to her.

Easter came and the air was full of the joyous shouting of bells announcing the Resurrection but neither Hikenai nor Ediva stirred out of the house to hear Mass or eat God's Body, and Dame Hermengild kept silence. She wished now, above everything, that she had never laid eyes upon them. If she might only be free of their terrifying presence. It was her kind heart that had led her to this pass. So she fretted on and on, not knowing that worse was to come.

Between Easter and Whitsuntide came Roodmas, the last day of April; a great feast for those who held to the old ways. On that day Hikenai and Ediva left the house just before sunset while the great bell of St Martin-le-Grand still tolled its last warning of the imminent closure of the gates of London. They walked along the strand beside the river in the gentle evening light, to all intents the young wife of some burgess and her servant, late returning home from the City.

As they approached Westminster, bowered in its orchards, a group of folk on horseback rode clear of the shadows of the trees with a jingling of harness and greeted them.

Hikenai let herself be lifted up pillion behind the biggest man among them. She did not know his name though she suspected him to be a man of consequence, nor did she speak to him, but a long, lit look passed between them because of what they both anticipated. He was the God-man whose body the Great One would inhabit and tonight would be the culmination of religious ecstasy for her. Tonight she would conceive the child of God.

The sun was down now and he put the horse to the gallop along the dusty road for they had miles to go. Already she was half in trance, the thundering hoof beats echoing the strong thudding of her heart. As they rode she remembered their first meeting. He had not accepted her immediately, even with Ethelwig's commendation. He had asked her many questions, and though he had spoken in English, she thought it was not his native tongue. Later, she became certain he was Norman and probably a cleric because of his manner of speech and range of knowledge. She wondered not a little at that, seeing he was so hot against the Christians.

'Are you a follower of the Christ?' he had asked her, 'or will you cast Him out and follow me?'

So she was driven again to a direct choice. Again she wished that they would not force the issue, but force it they did and she had assented. In time, though, her reservation died away, and now she rode to the ceremonies of Walpurgis Night as a bride to her wedding. How it had come about that she had agreed to bear a child she did not consider, any more than she had considered the consequences.

When they arrived at the meeting place, which was deep in the forest of Middlesex towards Enfield, the air was sharpening with the frost which would whiten all before dawn and the clear sky was sown thick with stars. It was not yet moonrise.

Already the fires were burning and scores of people were waiting, drinking and singing; many more than Hikenai had ever seen before. Silently they went by into the Sacred Grove, leaving those lesser votaries to begin the ritual of the dance.

As the rites progressed the air became more and more charged with excitement and the skin-prickling expectation that comes before battle or a violent storm. There was a feeling here tonight of forces about to be unleashed that could overtopple reason.

She moved uneasily beside the God-man. Soon the worshippers would come to pay their homage, she could hear the wild chanting as the procession drew nearer. He turned and looked at her and she recognised nothing human in what stared out through the holes in the animal mask. He was now wholly Another.

He seemed to grow enormous, towering above her; she grew to match him and somehow, they were One Person, huge as the Tree, and the sky was splashed with blinding colours. . . .

Below them the worshippers were like ants. She stretched her hands out over them and lightnings played from her finger tips. She felt the Power begin to flow and gave herself to it.

This time the metamorphosis was complete. They were One, she and the God, and the veil of every mystery was torn away. She understood the inner meaning of things of whose very existence she had been ignorant. Every awareness was sharpened to a pitch that fast became intolerable, beauty beyond belief, glory beyond bearing.

It seemed to her that time stretched immeasurably while her spirit and that Other ranged the crystalline spheres that surrounded the world like the layers of an onion, and all the while, in that small part of herself that was anchored to the earth, she was experiencing, too, a connection with him in the flesh. Gradually the body took precedence and in the gasping, jerking moment of orgasm the visions died away, the music of the spheres became the shrill wild chanting of the watchers, the heavenly scents the reek of animal hide and the sharp stink of sweat.

The God-man drew away from her; naked, hairy and terrible, he reared across her, lifting his head and howling at the sky. Behind him stood another figure, horned and masked, dark against the moon. Without understanding what she beheld, she saw something flash across the God-man's straining throat, a dark line followed it and a great gushing curtain of something dark and sticky poured down, splashing and raining upon her.

He gave one hideous gurgling groan before his body crashed beside her, spattering her face with his life's blood.

The crowded watchers gave a long, wavering moan and then, screaming and howling, ran forward to dabble themselves with the magic fluid, smearing their own and their companions' faces, laughing and weeping, rubbing Hikenai's blood-stained flesh with bits of rag which later they would treasure as amulets.

She lay stiff and terrified, shocked out of her drug-induced chimera. Now she remembered that the God-man must be sacrificed for the well-being of his people. Here, at the very root of her religion, lay the reason for her recurrent terror. But at that moment, she was more than merely human, and with acceptance understanding came.

All must one day die, and to die from choice and for others is the best death of all. From death springs life, the eternal cycle. The Great One had left his seed in her womb; there would be a new life, a new person to worship him. This child she would dedicate to his service. The power rose in her once more and the world grew misty and faded. She was at one with Them again and her fears were dead forever. Only bliss remained.

Henry did not notice Eleanor's coldness towards him when he returned to England; he was too overjoyed at meeting Thomas again. He was young enough to feel that seven months was a long separation and he was delighted and amazed at the ease with which they fell into the old happy relationship. All the little awkwardnesses between them had vanished and their intimacy was as close as it had ever been. Neither of them mentioned Hikenai; Henry because he had temporarily forgotten her in the joys of male companionship and Thomas because he hoped that Henry would soon do so entirely.

Thomas had to remind Henry of something else he had forgotten. They had dined together in the Chancellor's own chamber and now, having talked themselves out, they sat in quiet content while the May twilight settled into dusk.

Thomas said suddenly, 'You have not forgotten the case of Battle Abbey?'

Henry pursed his lips. 'Forgot it? – No, I had thought it settled. Did you not release the charter to the Abbot with the Great Seal upon it?'

Thomas said rather too airily, 'Bishop Hilary has received a letter from the Holy Father. It orders the Abbot to submit to him.'

Henry's head jerked up. He eyed Thomas a moment, frowning.

'What says the Abbot?'

'He refused.'

Henry nodded grimly. 'John of Salisbury is in Rome,' he said.

Thomas said nothing. He knew well enough what was meant. John, the Pope's close friend, worked for Theobald who upheld the Bishop. And Henry did not like John.

His own position, Thomas felt, was a delicate one. He owed much to Theobald and even more to Henry; in an overt clash between them, one of them must think him ungrateful, even treacherous. If he held with Henry and the Abbot, as he must, Theobald would accuse him of self-seeking. He felt even more uncomfortable as he remembered his visit to the sick old Archbishop last autumn and the love which had showed so plainly on the old man's face. And, worst of all, in the very deepest levels of his conscience, he knew that Theobald was right. This was the age-old battle between the secular and the spiritual.

But Henry would not understand if he changed sides. He wondered, just for a moment, if here, in private. . . . No, he could not – even now Henry was marshalling the evidence and laying plans to defeat Hilary. If one of them must think ill of him, let it be Theobald.

In those few seconds, almost unaware, Thomas made his irremediable choice between the pleasures of this world and the things of the spirit, and so swiftly was it done, it scarcely seemed an act of will at all. Yet the memory of it lay hidden at the bottom of his mind for many years thereafter as a splinter may lurk deep in the flesh, festering slowly and insidiously until it must out or corrupt all.

But now his mind was made up and his thoughts leapt forward eagerly to the arguments that lay ahead. Henry should have no cause to complain of half-heartedness in

223

him. They began to discuss in earnest how Hilary and the Archbishop (and the Pope) might be bested.

The trial began on the Friday before Whitsuntide. Henry wore his crown and was supported by the greatest magnates in the realm. That Bishop Hilary was very nervous was obvious. He fidgeted continually and clasped his hands together tightly (that their trembling might not show, thought Thomas scornfully); he crossed and uncrossed his legs and sent quick flickering glances from one to another.

Richard de Luci presented his brother the Abbot's case and Hilary sat with downcast eyes as each successive charter from the first William's down to Henry's own was read out. Thomas decided that in law there could be no doubt of the correctness of the Abbot's claim. Every charter, including the one that Thomas had so recently released to the Abbot, stated clearly that the Bishop had no jurisdiction over the Abbey. Thomas himself questioned the Abbot in evidence and got from him an angry denial that he had ever professed obedience to Bishop Hilary. Richard's summing up of the case was quickly over. The evidence spoke for itself, he said, and the Church must not try to set itself above the law. There was no doubt of Henry's pleasure but he confined himself merely to the judicious remark that he was inclined in favour of the Abbey. The next session, to hear the Bishop's side of the matter, would be after Whitsun, he announced.

Thomas, looking across at Hilary, smiled faintly, then frowned, for Hilary did not now look at all nervous. He only looked abstracted and, somehow, almost complacent.

When the Court met again, Thomas thought he saw the reason for that complacency, for upon Hilary's side of the table were ranged the Bishops of London, Lincoln and Exeter and two Abbots, as well as Archbishop Theobald and Archbishop Roger of York, Thomas' old enemy. He saw that Henry had noticed him too, and a look passed between them; Thomas put his hand over the lower half of his face that he might smile in secret. He wished that pompous, mitred fool knew how the King laughed at him. However, Roger continued to look pompous and disdainful and Thomas leaned nearer the King and whispered to him, keeping his eyes on Roger the while; it was only a comment on the heavy ecclesiastical representation but he hoped Roger had noted the look and would think they were talking about him.

Hilary stood up to state his case. He began well for he was a good speaker but he had taken the Abbot of Battle's attitude as a personal affront and his emotions got the better of him; again and again he brought up points that had no bearing on the case and soon became lost in a welter of prolixity.

At length Theobald who sat on his right hand, whispered to him with some vehemence. Hilary nodded once or twice, and then began to address the assembled company in different vein. This time his mode of speech was so abrupt and unpolished that it verged on the offensive; he announced baldly that it was the Pope's opinion that all spiritual power had been given by St Peter to bishops, not to kings, and therefore the King was not competent to judge upon the matter.

Beside him, Thomas saw Henry stiffen. Hilary is digging his own grave, he thought. He needs no assistance from me.

When Henry spoke his voice was hard and cold. 'This is a strange thing, my lord Bishop, that the charters given by my ancestors with no arguments from the clerics of that time, should be pronounced irregular by you.'

Thomas could not resist the opportunity to deliver his own thrust. 'You are disloyal to the King to whom you owe allegiance,' he said with heavy deliberation.

He saw Hilary's eyes flicker towards the Archbishops but neither made any move to help him. Theobald lowered his head as though in despair and Roger hunched his shoulders and pursed his lips, as one who will consider fairly every aspect, even to his own detriment. Seeing that he stood alone, Hilary began to bluster.

He insisted on his loyalty too loudly and too often; he complained long and bitterly of the obstinacy of the Abbot, though even here he became sidetracked by his own eloquence so that at one point it appeared that he was grumbling rather at the richness of the Abbey's copes in comparison with those of the Bishopric – then with another sudden switch that left them all bewildered for an instant – 'and the Abbot has well deserved of excommunication for his defiance of the Pope who says the jurisdiction is mine, seeing that the Abbey is in my diocese, despite his charters.' He fell silent abruptly, realising too late that he had compounded his earlier error.

'Yet am I loyal to the King,' he said, breathing hard, 'for all that royal grant cannot overrule –'

He stopped again and ground his teeth together, rocking upon his heels a moment. Then in the face of Walter's denial, he swore with the greatest solemnity that he had submitted to him, not once but many times, and proceeded to pronounce the Abbot excommunicate.

Henry sat through this tirade with impassive face but when Hilary had finally run down, more for want of breath than anything else, he raised his hand.

'We shall withdraw to consider,' he said.

Thomas was chosen to answer Hilary's accusations. Abbot Walter affirmed his denial once again and Thomas, at least, believed him for his mulish obstinacy was not in dispute.

The Chancellor's power with words was well known, and unlike the Bishop's, his speech was trenchant and concise. He made his points one by one: what the bishop described as stubbornness in the Abbot might as truly be called unswerving devotion to principle and the listeners must decide for themselves whether they preferred to believe the

226

Bishop or the Abbot on the matter of ecclesiastical submission. The Bishop might affirm his loyalty to the King as loud as he chose, but he stood condemned out of his own mouth. Worst of all, the Bishop had appealed to the Pope without the King's permission.

Hilary's mouth popped open as he realised his position. Sheer panic prompted his reply.

'It's a lie!' he cried. 'I have made no unauthorised appeal –'

He stopped dead as Abbot Walter lifted his hand. In it was the letter from the Pope.

Hilary went first fiery red, then yellow as clay. He sat down abruptly.

'I fear I am unwell,' he murmured, but he was not to escape so easily.

Theobald's face was as pale as his Bishop's, but grim. He signalled to the King. 'I will withdraw my support from the Bishop,' he said into the silence that had fallen.

'No,' said Henry harshly, 'it is too late for that. Your precious Bishop is a perjurer – twice over, more than like. This matter shall not be decided by you.'

Leicester, who was next to de Luci, looked round him to catch Thomas' eye but Thomas was watching Theobald who, confused and shamed, sat with lowered head. Thomas' face did not easily show his feelings but there was something in his expression that made Leicester change his mind about congratulating him at this particular moment.

Hilary did not suffer for his perjury except in his pride for he was forced to give Abbot Walter the kiss of peace and to communicate with him as though his excommunication was not worth the breath with which it was uttered. Henry was never revengeful without reason and a discredited Bishop posed no threat to him.

The creed he was to follow all his life was taking form; he would have his way at all times with all men. To that end, cold calculation lay behind his every action. He had learnt early that his notorious rage inspired fear and used it as a weapon; he had also found that condign punishment of offenders acts as a deterrent to others, and because he believed himself incapable of true malignity, he had a very fine conceit of his own wiliness. He did not yet know that we become what we pretend to be, and when he did, it would be altogether too late.

July 1157

Through the wearisome course of her pregnancy this summer, while Henry unsuccessfully attacked the Welsh among their rainshrouded mountains, Eleanor fed her animosity towards him with bitter memories.

It sharpened her tongue and pulled down the corners of her mouth until Rohesia, not understanding the reason for her mistress' shortness of temper, took her to task. She gained nothing by it but an unaccustomed coldness between them which lasted more than a month. It was ended by news from Wales which pulled Eleanor up short and showed her that her fondness for her husband was far from dead.

A messenger from Chester arrived with a garbled tale of ambush, of desperate fighting in the forest before Basingwerk and of the fall of the English Standard. What the outcome was, or where the King, no man knew, but the battle was lost. The handful of stragglers who had escaped the rout were panic-stricken at the rumours of the King's death and had sent word into England without more ado.

Eleanor was struck dumb with terror.

The moment she was alone, she fell upon her knees. '*Miserere mei*,' she wept, 'Sweet Jesu, Holy Mother' – and there she stopped, for if ever she put this hard, cold lump of terror in her breast into words, it might become reality. She pressed her shaking hands together. He must not be dead – not Henry – she had never wished him dead.

All at once, her control broke and she began to cry

hysterically, until Rohesia burst in and warned of an imminent miscarriage, soothing her, and then roundly cursing all rumour mongers so that Eleanor was startled into the realisation that it was indeed only rumour.

And this was indeed the case, though the Welsh had truly managed to ambush half Henry's army. In the mêlée, Henry of Essex had dropped the Standard but Roger of Clare had eventually raised it again, and they had somehow fought their way out. The King himself had been hard pressed and their losses heavy.

It had shocked Henry, this sudden demonstration that knights too could die in battle. The Welsh appeared to know nothing of chivalry; they fought on foot like savages and took no prisoners for ransom. It was a valuable lesson.

Eleanor too had learnt a lesson. Unfaithful and uncouth he might be but she was bound to him by ties stronger than she had imagined. She decided to make the best of it, and faced the coming ordeal of childbirth with more cheerfulness than she would have believed possible a few months earlier.

August – Christmas 1157
Hugh de Morville had come at last to Yorkshire to marry Helwis de Stuteville. He had procrastinated as long as he could, though he would have been hard put to it to explain his own reluctance. He did not question his own attitude and if any other had asked him why he did not immediately snap up so rich an heiress, he would have answered contemptuously that he would marry when he was ready. He was hardly aware that it was because of his mother that he held a grudge against women. He had been still in the care of females and free of her chamber when he had entered one day, unseen and unannounced. She was not alone and what he had watched there had, at the time, aroused in him no other emotion than curiosity. He went away and tattled about what he had seen of his mother and her Keeper of

229

Horse. For that he had been thrashed as never before in his young life, and though the weals upon his back soon healed and he forgot both the beating and the cause of it, there was always at the back of his mind the feeling that he had an account to settle with womankind.

He never consciously blamed his mother – indeed, he admired her for her beauty and her wit – and as he grew older, laughed with her at his father who was easily fooled. His last vestige of respect for old Sir Hugh died when he saw him one day weeping at his mother's feet; he never knew the reason nor did he care to know; it was sufficient that she appeared to him the repository of all power.

By the time he was ten he knew her name was a byword in the surrounding countryside and was perversely proud of it; because she was his mother and therefore different from other women, she might do as she pleased.

It was about this time that Lithulf, the Englishman, became their steward, and soon attracted the attention of Lady de Morville. Hugh watched them with a cynicism that sat oddly on a child and looked sneeringly upon his father who, doting on her still, saw nothing. But things were not going according to plan, for as the weeks went by, she grew more and more snappish and gazed at the steward with an expression that changed gradually to malevolence.

One evening when the hall was full of guests, Hugh came late from his lessons, slipping past the High Table to his seat lower down. The meal was nearly over, and his mother and a group of her ladies seemed to be playing some sort of game with Lithulf who stood behind and to the left of his lord.

Hugh watched them. His mother had put her hand provocatively on the hilt of Lithulf's short sword and Hugh saw him gently but firmly remove it. He saw his mother's face, and paused with a piece of meat impaled on his knife halfway to his mouth. She said something to the steward which Hugh could not hear and Lithulf put his own hand on the hilt of the sword and, smiling politely, half with-drew it as though about to show the chasing on the blade.

With that she flung herself sideways, away from her husband, and screamed shrilly and clearly in English, 'Beware, make haste, de Morville! Lithulf has drawn his sword!'

Sir Hugh sprang round, staring, to see the steward who stood transfixed behind him with his sword halfway out of the scabbard. He leapt to his feet, drawing his own great sword in one easy, practised swing. Hugh saw the light of the torches flash on the blade as it swung up and then down, shearing through the steward's shoulder and into the side of his neck. Lithulf's face expressed pure unbelief as he crashed to the floor.

Hugh saw it all; saw the dark pool of piss appear and spread, mingling with the blood. He was flooded with an emotion he did not recognise, at once nauseated and gloat-ing, breathless with horror or wild delight, he could not tell which. Avidly he watched as Lithulf choked to death on his own blood. All at once, his stomach heaved, and as he turned to vomit, his eyes fell on his mother's face and the small, tight, exulting smile thereon.

He was never to forget it; women and treachery were indissolubly linked in his mind thereafter.

But a man who is his father's only son must marry and he unconsciously comforted himself with the thought of his bride's extreme youth and innocence. It was the more shock to him, therefore, when he saw her for the first time in the chapel at Knaresborough Castle, resplendent in her red bridal gown and gold stitched veil.

She was as tall as he within an inch or so; of Viking proportions with masses of long, fair hair. All his absurd fantasies of a dove-like innocent who would be his to mould disappeared in that instant. And her father – he had heard rumours, of course, but he had not expected anything like the slack heap of mindless senility that faced him. It was obvious that Knaresborough had been run for years by the kinsmen who stood by, granite-faced, to watch his reactions.

At the wedding feast it was even worse than he had feared. Helwis was not shy, she had a loud voice and an even louder laugh, and when she thumped his back in joyful camaraderie, he was nearly hurled to the floor. She had a habit of doing this – as though she were used to spend all her time with grooms, ostlers and such low fellows, he thought disgustedly – and at length, in self-defence rather than from romantic inclination, he took her hand in his. It was large, square and capable, calloused from riding ungloved, and the arm which she pressed fondly against him was hard with muscle. With an arm like that, she could fell an ox, he thought.

The men who had ridden north with him scarcely lifted their heads from their food, yet the very set of their shoulders betrayed their avid interest. He writhed inwardly imagining their sniggering comments. God be praised that he had allowed none of his peers from the Chancellor's Household to accompany him! She should suffer later.

Nor, he discovered when they were bedded, had she any maidenly shrinking. He was not gentle with her. If the business must be implemented, he would take her like any whore and let her make the best of it. Yet she seemed satisfied – the Saints only knew what the folk in this wild valley had led her to expect. No more than the coupling of cattle, apparently. He made one or two suggestions to her which, after her initial surprise, she accepted readily enough. That angered him further. He could find little pleasure in a willing partner.

As the weeks went by, he found he had no power to wound her. And she was saucy. She spoke to him as to any low churl in her service and persisted in her impertinence in the face of remarks that would have quelled a more susceptible or a more intelligent young woman. She would gaze at him blankly for a moment, then throw that ham-like arm about his neck and nuzzle his cheek with a playfulness that he bore with gritted teeth. Only once did he attempt physical violence upon her and it rebounded upon him.

Driven almost beyond endurance by her silliness, he had fetched her a buffet to the head which sent her sprawling to the strawing where, to his astonishment, she rolled about laughing, and then, so fast that he was taken completely by surprise, she sprang up and crooking her arm about his throat, forced his head forward with her other arm and locked her fingers together at the side of his neck. Shake and twist his body as he might, he could not free himself, and between pain and indignity he was purple in the face. When she finally released him, he could do no more than sit in the strawing himself in order to regain his breath, and it was in that position that he met the baleful stare of a serving man armed with a cudgel.

Helwis was still laughing, and the fellow sent her a questioning look.

'May my dear lord and I not romp together? We did not know he knew aught of wrestling, did we? – and surely, he does not know much! So easy did I get him in that hold! You shall teach him, Wulfstan, that he may defend himself against our Yorkshiremen.'

Hugh's eyes met Wulfstan's and what he saw there made him very disinclined to meet that fellow unless he had his sword in hand.

'Well, go,' said Helwis, 'and do not stare so at my lord. It was only love play.'

When the man had gone, she pulled him to his feet and tried to put her arms around him. He flung aside from her.

'Madam!' he hissed. 'Cease mauling me and listen. I am neither your pet nor your servant! I am your husband and would have you treat me with respect. Those who brought you up have much to answer for. I will tell you this – had I known you before, I never would have married you!'

233

She stared at him with mouth agape, then answered petulantly, 'It is overlate to tell me that! You could have met me many times, but never came.' She shrugged. 'I am well enough satisfied with you, I shall abide my bargain – and as for you, you have gained Knaresborough. When you ride again to your duties, I will remain here.'

Though that was the very thing that Hugh had resolved upon, he was enraged by this calm statement of her intentions.

His voice was dangerous. 'I shall decide what you will do and where you will go.'

'Aye, surely. But I supposed that was what you would wish. I mean to tell you I shall not mind. I have no wish to go to Court.'

That almost determined Hugh to take her, but since she was obviously of that humour that can make the best of whatever occurs, and as he wished never to lay eyes on her again, he nodded.

'You are right. That is my decision.'

As he walked away, she came up alongside him and slipped her arm through his. He shook free of her and turned his head to look at her contemptuously.

Surprisingly, she laughed. 'You are my husband,' she said, and with an intolerable smugness, patted her belly. 'I wonder if I have a gift for you in here?'

He thought, compressing his lips, Where may I find a weapon that will pierce the armour of such obtuseness?

Later, though, when he rode away, he smiled a faint, triumphant smile and wondered if they would ever find Wulfstan's corpse down where the Nidd flowed swift and dark a hundred feet below the castle walls.

So it was that Hugh returned alone, angry and disillusioned with his experience of marriage, to his duties as one of the Chancellor's knights, only to find Reynold Fitzurse irritatingly self-congratulatory with his wife pregnant and his manhood proved, to his own satisfaction at least.

That his prowess had gone to his head was evident by his open boasting and the clumsily oblique shafts he aimed at all the childless men, including Hugh himself. Hugh said very little in reply and answered Reynold's probing questions about his bride not at all, but his black eyes were cold and his expression would have given warning to a more perceptive man.

The last months of the year wore away and when Beatrice's time to lie-in drew near, Reynold promised Hugh, with the air of one granting a favour, that he should be the first to see his son, after Reynold himself. Hugh smilingly accepted. He had never seen Beatrice but the germ of a plan was growing in his mind.

A full fortnight before they expected news, word came from Barham that the lady of Fitzurse was delivered of a female child. Both were well and like to live.

A little smile played about Hugh's lips as he watched Reynold's face. But Reynold bore his disappointment well and hid his punctured vanity as best he could. He called for wine for everyone and told them all that his own father had sired two daughters before ever he had a son.

'It takes a man to make a maid,' he said, voicing the old saw of disappointed husbands.

'Since I was invited to see your son,' murmured Hugh, 'does the invitation still stand?'

Reynold looked at him sharply. 'Oh yes,' he said, 'certainly. Truly I'm glad it is a maid that I may name her for my mother – Maud.' He would not meet the mockery in Hugh's eyes. 'Maud,' he said firmly. 'It is a good name.'

'For a girl,' said Hugh, 'it is.'

Yet when Reynold saw his daughter, his mortification vanished like hoar frost beneath a summer sun. She was so small, so perfect in every particular and so incredibly like himself. To him, at any rate, that was her chief virtue.

235

Hugh privately thought she was as ugly a babe as he had ever seen, with her low forehead and the dark hair lying flat upon it almost to the line of the non-existent eyebrows. It was the more surprising when he met her mother. Here in the flesh was the gentle little bride he had visualised, with her soft, fluttering hands and timid, lowered gaze. His envy of Reynold hardened his half formed resolve.

What he felt for Beatrice in that moment of their first meeting was what he felt for any woman who attracted him physically – desire to take, to possess, to wound. What looked naked out of his eyes as she raised hers to him was lust, but she did not recognise it and Reynold did not see it, being still occupied with admiring his child.

Beatrice saw only the most beautiful human being she had ever met. She was taken completely unawares and had lost her shallow little heart and soul before ever she knew she possessed them. He bent and took her hand and his lips lingered on it until she felt she would faint with rapture, and when he leaned forward and pressed his mouth to hers in the kiss of greeting, she thought her heart would stop.

He smiled then, knowing she was his for the taking, and decided he was in no hurry. Every last ounce of pleasure should be drawn from this affair, and Reynold should pay the penalty for his complacency and self-satisfaction. Yes, he would put horns on Reynold and, somehow, everyone (including his own detested wife) would know of it.

But for Beatrice that smile was part of the bright dream; a smile for her alone, to seal a secret love which would be pure, romantic and in the latest fashion. This comely man would be her knight, honourable and true, and their love would be deathless and unsullied. Beatrice knew very little of herself.

It had not taken Beatrice long to make up her mind that she had married a fool and even less time to decide that certain advantages might accrue from the situation, but

236

the possibilities did not assume any real significance until she fell in love with Hugh de Morville. From that first meeting he occupied her thoughts to the exclusion of everyone else, even her bosom friend, Jehane. She longed for Reynold to bring him again.

Yet when he did, she was ill prepared for it and the sight of the longed-for visitor brought the colour to her face in a way that caused Hugh some inward amusement. However, she kissed her husband very prettily and kept her eyes demurely downcast when his friend saluted her.

Reynold's first enquiries were for his daughter. Beatrice was obliged to admit that she had procured a wet-nurse and left the child largely to her care; her discomposure was as evident as Reynold's annoyance and it was left to Hugh to smooth the father's ruffled feathers. This he achieved with such consummate tact that Reynold gained the impression that the whole idea had been his own.

The visit was a short one but it served to pile further fuel on the fire of Beatrice's longing. She could not help but notice Hugh's intent gaze fixed upon her every time she glanced in his direction, the alacrity with which he would help her to anything she might require so that (dare she believe it?) their hands might touch.

Very soon it was accepted by them all that Hugh was in a privileged position in the Fitzurse Household. Others of Reynold's friends came often, Will de Tracy and the de Broc brothers being the most frequent guests, but however large or small the group, Hugh was always one of them.

Beatrice longed to be alone with him and did her best to contrive it, but privacy was seldom possible, and Hugh was aware that secret conversations were best conducted in a crowded, noisy gathering. He bided his time, and his chance came sooner than he had expected.

Reynold brought a dozen of his cronies to Barham one day to show off his lands, his child and his wife, and as usual in the evening drank heavily and grew steadily noisier and more unobservant. Hugh, while appearing to keep pace with the others, drank hardly at all. He sat in his now accustomed seat at the silent Beatrice's right hand at the High Table, staring straight ahead while around them hanaps clashed, men laughed and shouted and dogs snapped and snarled over bones carelessly dropped on the strawed floor. In the middle of the hall the great fire crackled and spat, sending smoke and sparks flying through the vent.

He slid his hand beneath the board, interlacing his fingers with hers. Seeing the blood colour her throat, he glanced at Reynold whose back was turned as he jested with his neighbour. Only Will de Tracy looked their way and grinned secretly.

'Are you not content, sweet mistress?' Hugh murmured, and saw her blue eyes linger on him with unabashed desire before she dropped them in confusion. He pressed his palm to hers and felt her quiver.

Yet Beatrice still did not understand what was happening to her. Her young mind had been fed on the romantic songs of jongleurs and tales of Courtly Love; she saw no connection between Reynold's unwelcome attentions to her and the love of a pure knight for his fair lady.

Hugh, failing to recognise the extent of her naïveté, was encouraged by her coyness towards him; he started to whisper gently to her, praising her hair, her eyes, her dress.

'Have you not marked the colour I am wearing?' he asked her softly, and in answer to her puzzled look at his white, pearl-sewn tunic – 'It is the shade worn by suitors who know not whether they will be smiled upon or sent hence. Yellow is the hue I long to wear.'

But Beatrice was too young to dare admit to ignorance, especially on so important a subject; she merely smiled with what she hoped was an air of mystery and resolved to question her few friends later. Jehane would know; she was amazingly well informed for a steward's wife.

As Jehane brushed her hair that night, Beatrice asked if she knew the significance of yellow garments.

The tall girl tittered. 'Why, as I heard it, it is worn when the citadel is stormed and won,' she said. 'As the priests will sing Te Deum for victory in battle, so the successful lover wears his yellow for victory in the lists of love.'

Beatrice shook her head in faint reproof. 'Go to!' she said. 'You have a lewd mind. That cannot be so – unless. . . Oh, I see – it is worn when the lady has accepted him as her true knight.'

Jehane's voice was smooth as cream. 'You have it! And will you take him for your knight? Indeed, I must not tease you for I know you love him well.'

She dropped her voice as she heard Reynold's heavy step.

'Sweet dreams, fair mistress. Dream of him who's your heart's desire. If I can help you to him, know I will.'

As she closed the door, she heard Reynold's growled remark – 'I mislike that sly wench. You are a fool to trust her.'

Jehane's eyes narrowed, then she shrugged. Let that great bullock think what he would! He thought he was master here, and he was wrong on that count too.

IX

February 1158

Hikenai was brought to bed on the Eve of Candlemas, on a still day muffled in white mist when every frailest twig bore an inch thick burden of crystal hoar frost, and the warm breath of men and horses fumed in smoking clouds before them.

Towards midday, when she was at the height of her agony, the sky lightened and a pallid, shrunken sun showed itself once or twice; Dame Hermengild, who stood staring out of the window, found she could look upon it with only the smallest squinting of the eyes, all its usual glorious dazzle was absent. Soon the miserable orb vanished altogether and the heavy mist pressed closer, yet it was with the utmost reluctance that she turned back into the room.

Not for Hikenai this time the services of an experienced and expensive midwife; only Ediva and the Dame were present with a girl to fetch and carry. This was a task that must be carried through with unparalleled secrecy. Dame Hermengild had lived in terror ever since Hikenai's condition became known to her and only a wild hope that the King might never uncover the truth and prevented her from turning the girl adrift. She had threatened it, indeed, and Hikenai had turned her head towards her very slowly and shot her a long, measuring look; under that gaze the

Dame's angry expostulations had died away, she had found herself stuttering and tongue-tied with an inexplicable unease. Furtively, she had crossed herself, and since then she had prayed frequently that Hikenai might die in childbirth. That would solve all her problems.

But when she turned from closing the small, horn window pane, she saw her hopes were vain. Hikenai screamed too lustily to be near death and the moment of birth was imminent.

She watched from where she stood while the child was born and after she had marked that he was a stout little knave, she left the chamber.

Later, when she had done all that was necessary for his mother, Ediva washed the babe and swaddled him. Hikenai lay flat on her back, her eyes closed and her face slack with exhaustion. When the tight little bundle was laid beside her, her eyes opened and met Ediva's in a question; then she looked down and gently moved the wrappings away from the child's face.

He looked like any other child. Whatever she had expected, she had not expected that.

March 1158
Sir Richard Fitzurse saw that it was past the ninth hour after dawn when he skirted the demesne field on his way home from Dunster because the villeins had all left to go and work on their own yardlands for the rest of the daylight. The spring ploughing was well along but he reminded himself to speak to the bailiff concerning the cottars who must put in their one day a week at this time. When he came across the bridge, though, he forgot it in the excitement which he found.

Half the village, it appeared, was in his courtyard and he drew rein suddenly, startled at the noise, so that his horse reared and rolled its eyes, backing and neighing. He saw his son, Robert, through the crowd and called to him to help him dismount, asking what was happening. Robert came forward through the people who made a way for him, and grasping his father's stirrup, said, 'We have had a hue and cry this day after Osbeorn. He has slain Viel and injured his wife but we have him fast. He is even now locked in the tower.'

'What happened?'

One of the villeins, Azo by name, pushed forward. He was a lean, gangling fellow, peering through a shock of dust-coloured hair which overhung his eyes.

'I was there, lord,' he cried. 'They were quarrelling all day at the ploughing!' He hesitated a moment and someone at the back called out, 'Viel had robbed him of two foot of his yardland – the strip third from the end – the fertile one.'

Some one else cried, 'Fie! that he did not! Carpenter measured the strip and it was right.'

A babble of indignant, contesting voices broke out and the baron waved his hand furiously for silence. When it subsided to muttering, Azo continued. 'They bickered all day. Viel was lead man with the oxen and Osbeorn had the plough. Viel cursed Osbeorn for that the furrow was crooked.'

'What happened to them? How did he kill him? – and who saw it?'

'It was after we had finished in the manor field. Viel did not go straight to his yardland, he said he had finished his ale and he was thirsty so he would go home for more. Osbeorn went behind him and I came after, but some way behind for, as you know, lord, my strips lie that way. Then Osbeorn catches up Viel – I was too far behind to hear what they say but I see they are still wrangling and pretty soon they begin to shout and then Osbeorn thumps Viel on the side of the head.'

'It was the stone he hit him with – the same that turned the plough aside and made the furrow crooked. He had it in his hand – I see him pick it up and carry it away!' yelled a different voice.

'Blood of God!' shouted the baron. 'Get to the point!' He turned to his son. 'Was he dead of this blow? How did his wife come to be injured?'

'No, no,' interrupted Azo, 'it was when they went within the house.'

'Whose house?'

'Why, Viel's house. Does it not now lie flat? The whoreson cut the posts! And the house fell down, posts, walls, thatch and all, on top of them! Eadgyth was like to suffocate until we got her out and her foot be chopped off.'

'Viel's wife,' said Robert, seeing the exasperation on his father's face. 'Osbeorn ran out even as the house was falling down and this fellow raised the hue and cry.'

'Did Viel die in the collapse of the house?'

'No.' Robert's voice was grim. 'He was topped with his own axe. He kept it sharp, poor fellow. Osbeorn must have run berserk in there – it's like the ruins of a slaughterhouse. Eadgyth will likely die for loss of blood – her fingers are severed, too, on one hand.'

'Jesu!' whispered the baron. 'He shall die for this, the dog!'

A torrent of voices screamed approval, and with a kind of impatient disgust, he turned away to his own house.

There it stood before him, strong and foursquare, and he had a sudden picture in his mind of how it would be if it were destroyed as that villein's house had been. It seemed absurd that their pitiful huts should be dignified by the same title as his own stout dwelling, little better than the lairs of beasts as they were. And not so snug as some, he thought to himself, remembering the nest of beavers they had dug out when their dam had blocked the upper stream. They had been dry and warm in the worst weather. He scowled because of the sense of guilt that was nibbling the edges of his mind and told himself that they deserved no better who acted like beasts.

All the same, he asked after Eadgyth and was told that Lambert the Butcher had amputated what was left of foot and fingers neatly at the joints, helped by Sir Priest who thought that God would take her, anyway. 'Had they children?' he asked gruffly, and was answered, 'None.'

Later, after he had seen the malefactor, he called in the bailiff and unlocked the great chest which was the seat of his chair, and took out the Manor Rolls.

'Come, now, read me these,' he said. 'Osbeorn I shall surely hang, being my own serf, but I would refresh my mind on who is mine and who is free. Also, I would know what each owes me, both for rents and week work.'

So they unrolled the long, awkwardly shaped sheepskins, some still with little tufts of wool on the reverse and some rubbed so thin with erasing that they were almost transparent, and Herluin read the records to his master. He did not appear to listen, but every now and then he asked a question that proved his attention had not wandered far. Underneath, though, he was considering the question why God, who had died alike for all men, had set some into the world to be great lords and others to be serfs, and all the while the bailiff droned on.

'– and the full villeins shall work three days a week up to the Feast of St Peter in August, and thence up to Michaelmas every day by custom, and the half villeins in accordance with their tenures. And the cottars one day a week and two in August. . . .'

'Have you checked that the cottars work their day at this time?' Herluin's look was reproachful. 'All work as they should – or, at least, they spend the time here that they should —'

The baron gestured with his hand. 'Let be. Read on.'

'Walter the Weaver pays twelve pence for his toft and Leofric pays two shillings for a half yardland –'

244

At last the lists were done and since it was apparent that Osbeorn was indeed the baron's serf, and that he had been apprehended by his own tithing (that small group of his peers which was responsible for his behaviour), it was plain enough that his fellows would have their wish: an opportunity to see him hang. For Sir Richard held his lands 'with sake and soke, toll and team and infangenetheof' which meant he had the right, along with de Mohun and all the other great barons of the realm, of hanging his own malefactors without recourse to any other authority.

'And it will be just requital,' gloated Herluin, 'seeing he has deprived you of property – to wit, the work and services of Viel and his wife.'

The baron's lips tightened a little.

'How is it that they quarrel still over the length of the yardland? You have been remiss somewhere.'

'No!' The relish on Herluin's face faded. 'No, lord, I had Carpenter take his rod to prove the distance. It is they who are at fault – they say his is a false rod though he had it from his father, and he from his.'

The baron frowned. 'They are entitled to be satisfied. Can we not prove the rod?'

'Sixteen feet is the length of the rod, but you know that most carpenters will choose short men with small feet to prove their rods, so saving on the length and thus upon the timber they use when building.'

'Select sixteen men of assorted sizes from the villeins, none too big and none too small. We shall place them in single file, their feet toe to heel, and to that length I will have a new rod made. I will keep it in my hall and any who have doubts shall have the right to measure by it.'

He rose and turned away so that he did not see Herluin pull down his mouth at the corners and raise his eyes to Heaven as one who will say – such fuss and cosseting of the lower orders! Herluin had an intense contempt for villeins, being so lately sprung from that class himself.

But as though suddenly recalling something, the baron turned back at the door so that Herluin was hard put to it to compose his face fast enough; he dropped his eyes in some confusion and rattled about uneasily among the quills and sheepskins.

'In all this to-do,' said Sir Richard, 'I had forgot the news I had at Dunster. The priest at Watchet has cursed for his tithes and half the folk lie excommunicate. I will not have it happen here.'

'Indeed!' cried Herluin, all agog. 'He is not loth to curse, that fellow, and he no better born than those –' He stopped abruptly, fearing he had shown his rancour too plain. 'Our tithes are full paid,' he said. 'The Great Tithe to him and the lesser to Sir Priest here.'

'And have the villeins paid the lesser tithe?'

'That's between them and Sir Priest,' grumbled Herluin under his breath, but not so low that the baron did not hear it. 'It is their own souls that lie at stake.'

The baron levelled his staff and poked Herluin none too gently in the chest with it. 'Not so ,' he said. 'Their souls are our concern, too. Do you remember it, and if any come to you with tales that they cannot pay, you shall look into it fairly. And for a beginning, we shall pay Viel's mortuary to the priest at Watchet.'

Robert had come in and heard the exchange; he smiled faintly and held open the door while the rolls were locked away again, then he passed out with his father.

Once outside, he said, 'I had not realised how much he grudges that he has not the priesthood.'

'Aye,' said the baron, 'but he is the sort that were he priest would grudge he were not bishop, and if bishop would grudge he were not Pope. Too many like him are priests already. God's work is their last care.'

'Our priest is not of that stamp.'

'No, he is not. He cares for God. But working his glebe to feed his wife and brood, his time is all used up. When

246

he dies, I will have an unmarried priest and I will have him live within my hall.'

'Yes,' said Robert. 'That will be best.'

He was not really thinking about the priest, though, but of his father's clear summing up of the bailiff, and it occurred to him that such a keen understanding might also see the jealousy he bore Reynold – a soreness that partook nothing of envy of Reynold's wife and possessions but only of his lot and standing as the legitimate heir. He had become very sensitive about his bastardy since Beatrice had first pricked him into recognition of it, and because he bitterly blamed his father, the animosity he felt towards him almost outweighed the affection.

To divert his mind from such thoughts, he said abruptly, 'Had they any news of the King at Dunster?'

'Yes. De Mohun is summoned to Worcester at Easter for the Crown-wearing. I have excused myself on account of my leg. It seems I am become what the King pleases to call an agrarian knight.'

'And I,' said Robert, not looking at his father.

The baron ignored his interpolation. '– And there is a new issue of coinage, of greater purity of silver than any we have had hitherto. De Mohun showed me a penny – it has a short cross on the obverse. There is a rumour, too, that the Chancellor goes soon to France – to make a match, de Mohun says, between Prince Henry and a French princess, lately born.'

'Will Reynold go, think you?'

'So I would suppose. I look to receive word from him—'

At that moment, the horn blew for dinner and Robert did not listen to the rest, being too full of chagrin to give consideration to anything but his own feelings.

April–May 1158

Beatrice Fitzurse sat at her embroidery frame at Bulwick; she had just pricked her finger and was squeezing it with concentration. As soon as a bright bead of blood appeared, she sucked it and squeezed again. Kneeling on her haunches beside her, Jehane sorted tangled skeins of yarn.

'Let be,' she advised, 'it will stop bleeding if you will let it scab.' She lifted her head suddenly. 'Here's your lover coming, mistress.'

Her smile was knowing as she scrambled awkwardly to her feet; her pregnancy was not yet obvious but the weasel suppleness of her movements was gone already. She put her hand against Beatrice's cheek. 'You are pink as eglantine,' she whispered, 'and as fair. He loves you – never doubt it.'

Beatrice kept her eyes modestly lowered as Hugh entered and Jehane slipped out. Even so lately as last week he would have knelt before her when he came and presented her with a flower or some such absurdity as token of his thraldom.

Now – how was it now? He did not kneel this time. He stretched out his hands and pulled her up against his breast and kissed her, hard, insistent kisses that forced her lips apart, that turned her bones to water. . . .

She gave a little moan and twisted her head aside to evade him.

'Not now – not here,' she whispered, 'it is not safe.'

She leaned on him, breathing hard, and opened her eyes slowly to gaze into his face. He held her by the shoulders a little away from him, and having discovered all he wished to know, murmured, 'Nay, love, nay – am I not fine for you?'

She saw, then, the brilliant saffron of his tunic. So it was true, what Jehane had said. But it did not matter now he had come again. After these last days of fearing that she had forever lost him, her guard was down completely.

For she had railed at him like any tavern-wife, calling him adulterer and seducer, laying all the blame for what had happened on his shoulders. And he had laughed. She had

248

thought that unforgivable, and for a whole day would listen to no defence of him from Jehane.

'Be fair to him, at least,' the steward's wife had urged, 'for that you did tempt him there is no denying, and a rampant cock knows nothing of conscience.'

'Why should you plead for him?' Beatrice had cried, and Jehane had said she would not for the world see lovers sorrowing apart, there was no sight more doleful, at which Beatrice had burst into another flood of self-pitying tears.

'Think of his remorse,' Jehane said then, 'in that he has betrayed his closest friend.' She patted Beatrice's heaving shoulders. 'Spare him some pity, too.'

And slowly Beatrice had seen that much of the fault was her own; one small favour after another granted until the refusal of the last intimacy was too much to be borne. And he had begged her to refuse him – forcing her down across the couch, crushing her with his weight, muttering as though in frenzy, 'Say no to me! Say no!' – yet all the time compelling her by brute strength while she struggled and wept.

Even after that violation she had loved him still.

And now – now, he was vowing that never again. . . . She put her hand over his mouth.

'It is done,' she said, 'and cannot be undone. Nor would I have it so.'

He looked beyond her, and she saw that his eyes were truly black as night, without the slightest trace of brown. Or were they the darkest imaginable blue? She thought she saw the struggle in his face and loved him more for putting her honour before his own desire.

Hugh, who understood very well the tenor of her thoughts, considered how to play his hand. That she was ready to fall into his arms once more was obvious. He had evidently over-estimated her sophistication in the oldest game of all. Because of it, he had discovered the exquisite intoxication of rape, of giving free rein to the lust and cruelty that lurked so close beneath his polished exterior. The last thing

249

he wanted from her now was consent. Some means must be devised whereby the pleasure could be repeated.

'The blame was mine alone,' he said. 'Can you think I would imperil your immortal soul? No – nor could I ever honour you again should you accede to – to such gross demands.'

'Oh. . .' said Beatrice faintly.

'Nor may we be here alone,' continued Hugh, putting her away from him and walking to the window. 'See how the sun shines this fine day! Shall we walk in your pleas-aunce?'

She stared at him and could not believe this was the man who had – done those things. She pushed away the memory and told herself she had been right in the beginning to think him a true and noble knight, yet underneath she could not quite repress a pang of bitter disappointment.

He went before her down the outer stair and turning at the bottom, swung her down the last few steps. When she looked into his eyes, she felt a tremor, though whether it were love or fear she could not tell.

Reynold had brought his Household to his manor of Bulwick in Nottinghamshire soon after Easter because he was attending upon the Chancellor who was acting as justice in the area and it was a good opportunity to eat up the harvests there. Very soon now, the Chancellor would go to France, and Hugh and Reynold with him. Beatrice did not know whether to be glad or sorry they were going.

She was bewildered and frightened by what was happening between herself and Hugh. There were times when he treated her as a goddess, presenting her with gifts, begging the favour of a kiss, paying her extravagant compliments: they were the happy times. There were other occasions when Reynold was away about his duties when he would come in different guise and force his way into her bower and fall upon her like an animal. Jehane confessed herself terrified of him yet Beatrice had seen them together more than once, talking and laughing. She suspected that he had bought Jehane's compliance but she was too afraid of discovery to attempt to keep him out by other means.

A dreadful fear was forming in her mind: that he had infected her with some demon of the Pit who possessed him. He had mentioned her immortal soul and she knew now that was mockery. It was not possible he should mock her – no, it was not, she knew he loved her well. Therefore, it was a demon who spoke – but either possibility was terrifying.

And now a worse thing had befallen. She was with child; she knew it with certainty though the monthly cycle was but a few days out of joint. Her breasts were swollen and painful and her thighs heavy. Whose child it was she did not know.

Jehane tried to comfort her. 'None will ever know, mistress,' she said. Beatrice flew out at her, crying that it was very well for her who knew her unborn babe to be her husband's – at which Jehane's eyes slid away and looked everywhere but at her mistress. Afterwards she wondered at that look but at the time she was too upset to make much of it.

She prayed the child was Reynold's while wishing it was Hugh's. If only children came bearing some mark upon them, that their mother, at least, might be certain of their paternity.

In the end, she told both putative fathers of their expectations. Hugh only smiled, but his heavy-lidded eyes swam over her in such a way that she was assailed by a pang of almost physical weakness.

This time, as on that first occasion, she struggled in earnest until he wound his hand in her long, ash fair hair, pulling her head back until she felt it tearing at the roots. She bit him, then, and tasted blood, and the black tide of his desire engulfed her in a roaring madness of pain and delight.

That was the best and worst time. She told Reynold she had tripped and fallen on the stairs to explain the bruise

251

on her cheek and her painful scalp, and she took care to shroud her nakedness from his sight. Only Jehane saw the marks on her body, and gasped – 'Holy Mother – why?' Beatrice saw her horror, and when slow tears gathered in her eyes and rolled down her cheeks, she could do nothing but hold her hands in silence.

She soon wished she had not told Reynold that she was expecting another child. He questioned her again and again as to any differences in her feelings or symptoms from her last pregnancy, seeking evidence that this time she would bear a boy.

'Lie always on your right side,' he said, 'or no – is it the left? Eat no eggs for the first three months. What is that trick they do with barley? Oh yes, I remember – put wheat and barley in a cloth bag and piss upon it daily. If the wheat germinates, it will be a boy; if the barley, a girl.'

'And if both, what then?' snapped Beatrice. 'Or neither?'

Reynold patted her arm. 'If both, it must be twins,' he pronounced, 'if neither – no, none of that – it will come to nothing.'

'Oh, hush your prating!' said Beatrice, 'one would think you were a midwife, not a man. I'll not piss on any corn!'

He only patted her arm again. His affability was unendurable.

June 1158

The King heard Mass in York Minster in no very pious frame of mind for his thoughts were more occupied with the naughty dealings of the clergy in that area than with the Holy Sacrifice itself. He watched the scurrying of the acolytes with a jaundiced eye, wondering how many of them were good and holy men and how many fit only to be haled before his courts like that rural dean who would appear before him presently. Small wonder the citizenry of York had cheered themselves hoarse when he rode under Micklegate Bar, bringing the royal justice to a people oppressed and wrongfully used by those who should have been their loving shepherds.

Later, when the erring dean was brought before him, he thought no differently. He was a hulking, beefy fellow, accused of falsely charging the respectable wife of a burgess of Scarborough with adultery, and blackmailing her husband on that account. Bile rose in the King's throat at the sight of him. To such a pass was the clergy come in his realm. Half of those who were priested had not Latin enough to understand the Mass, and half again of those who were literate lacked honour and truthful dealing. And here in the North the people were too poor to bear the extra burden of leeches like these upon their backs.

This country had never recovered from the devastation wrought by William the Bastard, just as it may have been. Generations would pass before the land would smile again, though trading ships were beginning to ply the waters of the Ouse once more between the louring shadows of William's two wooden castles, high upon their mottes. Aye, William had pressed these northern men hard but he had had both the right and the necessity while these criminous clerks. . . .

With a start, Henry became aware that the Archbishop of York was informing him in a low voice that the defendant had no proof to offer for his slander.

'Ah,' said Henry, for his anger at the shortcomings of the clergy was beginning to encompass even the higher dignitaries of the Church. 'It seems to me that Archdeacons and Deans, by unjust means, exact more money from the people than I may collect in revenue. What punishment shall be inflicted on this one?' He glared, first at the Archbishop, and then at his Treasurer, John of Canterbury.

This John, who knew Thomas the Chancellor well and fancied that he knew something of the King by hearsay, decided to be bold in the face of his flashing eye.

'He should be sentenced to return the rewards of his extortion,' he said, 'and placed in the Archbishop's mercy'.

Richard de Luci, aware that that meant the fine would be payable to the Archbishop's Treasury, raised his head.

'And what will you grant to our lord the King, whose laws this man has broken?'

Henry leaned back with a satisfied nod and waited for the Treasurer to capitulate but John, like every other clerk, clung to the Church's immunities as a rock in a sea of uncertainty.

'Nothing!' he answered roundly, 'because he is a clerk!'

Richard stood up and looked at the King, his cheeks red with anger, but Henry made no move. 'I will not sustain that sentence,' he said furiously and stalked towards the door.

Henry did not recall him but bent a look of menace upon the two other Bishops on the bench. They looked for guidance towards the Archbishop and he, though with a gentle dew upon his upper lip, supported the sentence in a surprisingly firm voice. Thankfully, they added their voices to his.

The King stood up then. 'I shall not accept it,' he said. 'It shall be appealed to Archbishop Theobald.' He looked pointedly at Roger de Pont l'Evêque, remembering that he had been his dear Tom's enemy.

'York is still subject to Canterbury,' he added, and left without kissing the Archbishop's ring.

July 1158

Hikenai was in the garden, suckling the child. When she heard the approaching footsteps on the stony path she thought it was one of the serving men so that she did not at once look up but continued to sit with downbent head, lost in loving contemplation of the babe at her breast.

Henry stopped dead at the picture presented to him, and at the sudden silence, she slowly looked up. The start she gave and the swift, involuntary movement as she jerked the babe from the nipple caused it to cry out sharply.

The silence seemed to stretch interminably. When he spoke, his voice was roughened by shock.

'Did you not tell me that child was Ediva's?'

When she did not reply, he swung round and stared at her as at a stranger but she would look no higher than his boots, which were old, sagging around the ankles, the leather pocked and scarred except where the stirrup had chafed the instep shiny.

'You have lied to me,' he said, 'That child is yours. Or' – his voice was heavy with irony – 'we have a miracle here that you can give suck to another woman's child.'

At her continued silence, his voice rose. 'Who?' he shouted, 'Who got it on you? Why? Did I leave you too long? Could you not—?' He broke off and put his hand across his mouth; his lips were drawn back and flattened, white with pressure, as one who has received a mortal wound.

'Lord' – her voice was small – 'Lord, it is a child of God.'

'What is that to me?' he returned, thinking she meant the child was an imbecile.

'Well, then,' he said. 'I must find you a husband now that all is done between us,' but even as he said it, the pain of her betrayal took him by the throat so that a groan burst from him.

She saw his suffering with a kind of terror. It had never occurred to her that she had the power to hurt him thus – he had hurt her many times, of course, but she was a woman. That a man, too, could feel the pain of love was so improbable that she could hardly accept it. She knelt by his feet, weeping.

'It is not as you think,' she sobbed at last. 'It was no man, I swear to you. It was the God—'

Incredulity warred with comprehension in Henry's face.

'Are you telling me—? God's Nails, what kind of fool are you? Those old rites. . . .' Horror was plain on his face.

255

'Do you not know it for heresy? You ninny!' he yelled and pushed out against her with his foot so that she would have fallen had she not caught his leg.

He bent, then, and grabbed her by the shoulders, pulling her to her feet and shaking her back and forth as though he were settling grain in a sack.

'Dolt! Simpleton!' he shouted, and other fouler expressions, while beside them on the bench where Hikenai had unceremoniously dumped him, the babe screamed long and piercingly. 'How can you credit such mummery? Aaah. . .' and he flung her down with such savagery that she lay as one dead.

'Silence your brat or I will,' he said, and moaning and sobbing, she scrambled somehow to her feet and picked up the child.

'Do not leave me,' she wept, 'Harry – please. . .' But he would not look at her; he stared down the path as though he almost hoped some stranger would come that he might vent his anger on him.

She stood beside him, her face swollen, her hair wild. All her confidence had gone; this was reality and Henry was rejecting her. Had she been deceiving herself these last months, her powers non-existent, the transcendental joys she had known mere imaginings?

'Make ready my son,' he said. 'Him I shall take. I had come to fetch you, too, to go with me into Normandy once more but that shall not be, now. Make him ready, I say!'

Less than an hour later, having spoken no further word to her, he rode away carrying the small boy, Geoffrey, in front of him upon the saddle, but for all the child's merry prattle and excitement, he felt himself to be more wretched and empty than a famished beggar.

When he had given the boy, with no explanation, into the care of the women, he dismissed his followers and sat alone in a small dark chamber that looked towards the river. Soon, he would send the child to join the Queen's children; he should be brought up with them as he had promised long ago in happier days.

Had he expected too much? She was, after all, a villein lass and filled with senseless superstition like all her kind – that she should have kept faith with him was too much to expect. Yet revulsion rose in him again as he imagined the rites in which she had partaken.

'God!' he muttered, 'God! – Child of God!' He was sickened, and rose up, biting his lips and striding the length of the small chamber. Then he began to weep, beating his hands upon the wooden board. What he had lost he did not know, but just now he thought it worth the whole of his dominions.

Henry sailed for France in August to conclude the treaty which Thomas, whom he had not seen for three months, had made with Louis. Just before he left, he had word of the death of his brother Geoffrey, Duke of Brittany for so short a time, and his anxiety over the succession there helped to drive his more personal troubles from his mind.

He thought he had rooted out all remembrance of Hikenai, but the nagging ache persisted. In the unguarded moments when he awakened from sleep, the sense of loss would overcome him before he had time to school himself once more.

He met Thomas in Rouen and here old sores were re-opened when he rode past the little house where she had lodged and where their son had been born. He wondered what his Queen's reception of the boy had been. Well, let her say but a word in protest – he would know how to deal with her, at all events.

Thomas noticed a difference in him. He was even more easily aroused to anger than usual and his ready laughter was notable by its absence. He would sit, too, at times deep in thought, biting his nails until they bled.

When it became obvious that Henry was not going to confide in him, unasked, Thomas decided to approach him delicately. Henry was touched by his Chancellor's concern.

'It is nothing,' he said, 'nothing that need worry you, Tom.'

'Anything that worries you must worry me.'

'Not this,' returned Henry, somewhat grimly. 'It is an affair of the heart.'

'I cannot advise you upon that, I fear.'

'It would even please you.' Henry's tone was bitter.

'How can anything which disturbs you please me?'

Henry looked at him, and suddenly making up his mind said, 'It is Hikenai. Do you remember when first we found her in the forest? And that – that image—' His face twitched. 'That clay figure – to do with the old beliefs?'

'Yes,' said Thomas with a guarded voice.

'She has been seduced into the practice of such mischief. The little dizzard has got herself a child out of it.'

Thomas flinched, abhorrence evident in his expression. He hesitated, looking away from the naked misery on Henry's face, unable at first to repress the gratification that his own opinion had been so thoroughly vindicated. Because he was instantly ashamed of the feeling, his tone sounded sterner than he intended when he said, 'It is well you have uncovered it now. The Church should speak out openly against such conduct. In days of old, she was gentle with the pagans to wean them gradually from their foul practices.'

Loudly Henry said, 'Preach not to me! I do not need lessons in theology. I said it would please you that – that it is over.'

'I take no pleasure in your grief, at least. For that I am truly sorry.'

'I do not know why I should suffer so. But she was the only one who ever touched my heart. No other woman' – he roused himself with an effort— 'Well, I have told you that which none other shall ever know – now it shall be forgotten. But I shall swear you to silence, Tom, upon this matter – and not least to me.'

'Yes,' said Thomas, 'Yes, I swear.'

Inwardly, Thomas felt only relief. Now he must forget her, he thought, and began to speak of what was of more consuming interest to himself: the treaty with Louis concerning the betrothal of Young Henry and the baby princess of France.

It had been his personal triumph, the gaining of Louis' consent to the betrothal. He had gone to France in the early summer with a great train of followers, a greater retinue than many a king. No expense had been spared to impress the French; they had indeed marvelled at the magnificence of the English Chancellor and wondered with stupefaction how far superior his King might be.

Two hundred members of Thomas' own Houschold had accompanied him, besides those the King had sent. The memory of that great, colourful procession still caused him to glow with pride not only for himself but, he imagined, for Henry, too.

Two hundred and fifty footmen and boys, dressed in green, had headed that tremendous cavalcade. Singing songs in English they had danced along, twirling branches of greenery and sprays of wild flowers they had plucked in passing. So happy a picture that the French had clapped their hands and laughed – and then drawn breath and stepped back on to the feet of those behind as the huge, slavering mastiffs came into view, all muzzled and leashed for safety but a sight to strike fear, nonetheless.

Then the slender, sinuous greyhounds loped by and here the watchers had hallooed and shouted, hoping that one of them would take fright and bolt, dragging his helpless attendant along on the end of the halter, for all knew the amazing strength in those skinny bodies and whipcord muscles.

A great roaring and rumbling had followed as the eight, iron-tyred baggage wagons lumbered past, each drawn by five matched horses. Two of those wagons had been laden only with English ale – and how that fine drink had astonished the French, used as they were only to wine. Sweet, clear and the colour of honey, they had exclaimed over it as a miracle of delight.

But the twelve pack horses had excited the most eager comment, every one with a blue-clad groom kneeling on its haunches and – *mirabile dictu* – a monkey chattering and squealing on its neck. The crowd had cried with one voice at such a spectacle, those at the rear leaping up in vain efforts to see more and those with a good view calling out to tell them all they were missing.

Then, not quite so interesting to the rabble, the squires had walked, leading their masters' chargers. But fine horseflesh will always evoke admiration among the more prosperous, and if the eyes of the womenfolk lingered rather on fair, curly heads and broad shoulders, their husbands neither knew nor cared in the general excitement. As for the gaily dressed knights and the black-garbed officials who followed two by two – they called forth many a rustic quip while their mounts pranced and curvetted, fretful at being held to so slow a pace.

It was Thomas himself and the group of his closest associates who silenced the onlookers and left them open mouthed, so sumptuously attired were they, so richly caparisoned their horses. He overheard one innocent who supposed him to be an Emperor, at least, and smiled to think of the churl's amazement could he see within the baggage wagon the twenty-four changes of silk clothing he had brought, and the furs, tapestries and carpets for his bedchamber.

It was June and the fairest summer weather when they neared Paris. All through one burning, golden afternoon they rode, eager for the first glimpse of their destination, but it was nearly sunset before they sighted the stockade, and outside it, the great building with the banner aloft, stirring only lazily in the sweet evening air but enough to show its stark black and white, so that they could be sure it was indeed Beauséant, and this the Temple, and the end of their long journey. Here, Thomas and his officials had stayed, but even this rambling stone warren could not house all his meinie, and it was dusk before all the marquees and tents were erected in the Grève nearby.

There was good reason for his choice of hosts. Henry wanted the three castles of the Vexin and their lands as the princess' dower, but the dower would not be paid until the marriage took place and that might be in the distant future. In the meantime, the territory must be held by neutral hands and the friendly hands of the Templars, still warm with English silver, would serve admirably. If any quarrel should arise, the Templars would surrender the castles to Henry, and the Pope, an Englishman himself, would never censure them. So Thomas had planned and he had found, as he expected, that the Templars were as shrewd in bargaining, as worldly wise and as discreet as befitted men who served an Order as powerful as theirs.

Before he left Paris Thomas had given away everything he had brought with him, even the horses, even his own gorgeous clothes. Everyone at the French Court received a gift and the English students at the University found all their debts paid for them. Thomas had enjoyed meeting these young compatriots of his, remembering days long past when he had been of their number, as poor if not quite as shiftless as they.

One of the students made a particular impression on him with his excellent latinity and sharp, satiric wit. He was a young man, not above twenty years of age, yet already a considerable scholar. Thomas liked him at first sight, attracted by his snapping dark eyes and jaunty air; after weeks of haggling with old men, he found Walter Map an entertainment much to his liking.

But he swiftly discovered that Walter could prick the bubble of worldly conceit even more devastatingly than John of Salisbury. Yet his was a lighter, more mischievous touch that left Thomas with no resentment but only a delighted appreciation of his impish wit; after the pious gloom of Louis' Court, even his irreverence was refreshing.

He was at the back of Thomas' mind now as he described everything to Henry; in the end he found himself telling the King about him.

Henry looked up then. 'Map? I know that name.'

'He is from Hereford, I understand. Of Welsh descent.'

Henry nodded. 'I know of his parents – I assume them to be his parents. He is around twenty, you say?'

Thomas spoke eagerly. 'He will return to England in a year or so. I had thought – I told him to apply to me when—'

'Not so fast, good Tom. My need for clerks is as great as yours. If he is indeed son of the Maps I remember – or is kin to them – I shall offer him preferment.'

'Well,' said Thomas with a satisfied look, 'he will be honoured by the Royal interest, and, as I am a judge of men, he will be worthy of it. He told me of a conversation between King Louis and an Englishman – I cannot recall who it was just now but it does not matter . . . It was illuminating, I think.'

He glanced at Henry and saw his interest.

'Walter said they spoke of the riches of kings – of the gems, lions, leopards and elephants of the King of the Indies. And King Louis said that the Emperor of Byzantium has gold and silken raiment but no men fit for arms for in that matter they are fools. Then this other whose name I have forgotten said that conversely the Emperor of the Germans has warriors and war horses, yet no luxury, and so is all made equal. "Ah, but the King of the English" – thus King Louis – "lacks nothing; he possesses gold, silk and precious stones, men and horses, wild beasts, fruits and all else. We in France have nothing but bread, wine and joy." '

'Hmph!' said Henry. 'He protests his poverty too loud.'

'Aye, maybe,' answered Thomas, and considered what else he could say that might console him.

'I have no great opinion of him,' he added. 'He lacks your strength of purpose.'

And mine, he might have said, seeing that he had had no great trouble in bending the none too eager Louis to his own master's desires. He said instead, 'I cannot think that he has either the means or the will to interfere if you decide to move against Toulouse.'

Henry's face brightened a little at that. 'God's Teeth! I think you know more of my secret intentions than I do myself! So you had your ears about Louis' Court on my behalf? I thank you for it but there's time enough to think of that when I have the Princess Margaret in my custody.'

Thomas accepted that, but he set himself in many subtle and devious ways to influence the King towards the enterprise in Toulouse, for the embassy to Paris had done more than merely win a bride for Henry's heir — it had fired Thomas himself with ambitions to ride again with a great host, and not in peace but in war.

He had found that he had a taste for fighting in the campaigning with Henry against his brother two years ago; latterly, the company of his knights with their talk of past skirmishes had revived his old desires. They were pleased to teach him the finer hints of sword play, proud of a lord who was not only a great Chancellor but a born swordsman. Thomas was content in their company, happily unaware of the existence of the small clique who for reasons of their own disliked and resented him.

So Henry went off to Gisors to meet the King of France, where he was successful not only in obtaining Louis' consent to his over-lordship of Brittany but also in arranging to take custody of the baby princess in a few weeks. Here, too, he received the news that his Queen had borne another son. Two boys in one year! He decided to name this one Geoffrey after his dead brother.

Yet somehow, none of his triumph had the savour it should, and when Conan of Brittany, cowed by the sight of Henry's army of mercenaries gathering at Avranches, came to surrender his claims, Henry accepted his homage and installed him as Duke with singularly little of his usual self-congratulation.

For Henry, as the last months of 1158 passed, time dragged its heels. He took his mercenary host and laid siege to the reputedly impregnable castle of Thouars, whose lord had offended him. It fell within a mere three days. Lacking further enemies, he bit his nails to the quick, slept with washerwomen and trulls and drank himself insensible on occasions. Still the misery would not lift. At Christmas he would meet Eleanor in Cherbourg and, for the first time, he could not care whether he got a child on her or not.

Yet for her sake or his own, he was prepared to make an effort when they met again. He did not know that she was not.

After the dreadful shock she had experienced in the summer of 1157 when Henry was ambushed in Wales, Eleanor had become reconciled to her lot, but after the birth of the child Richard in September that year, she became a new woman. Henry marked the change in her and thought once more that childbearing was good for the strange humours of women.

He could not know that Eleanor had seen in the babe the reappearance of her first-born son. At birth the likeness had been strong enough to awaken that outpouring of maternal love that poor Matilda had so signally failed to arouse, and little William's memory haunted her no longer. As Richard grew the resemblance diminished, but the pattern was set and to the end of his life he remained her favourite child and the prime object of her affection.

And as her love for him increased, her preoccupation with his father lessened. She no longer listened to the whispers about the Court but cocooned herself in a bland indifference to Henry's amours. She had managed to accept his casual traffic with harlots when they were unavoidably separated –now she believed she did not care about his long-standing association with his English whore, either.

So mild and sweet had been her temper that she accepted everything he suggested without argument, including that idea of the Chancellor's (or so she thought) that her son, Henry, should be betrothed to the daughter of her ex-husband, Louis of France.

Yes, she accepted everything – but this last she would never accept.

She had been in the castle of Cherbourg some hours when he returned from his hawking. He came, as always, with neither ceremony nor warning, as though he expected that she should always be waiting graciously to receive him. He waved his companions back at the doorway and entered alone; then he stood there, looking round consideringly, his booted legs wide apart, idly slapping his thigh with a hawk-shredded glove.

He looks as if he has come straight from the stable, she thought contemptuously, and smells like it, too. And yet he imagines he is acceptable in a lady's bower.

Eleanor had had an unpleasant Channel crossing; she was tired and not yet finally unpacked and settled. She motioned to her ladies to go, and putting down the mirror she had been holding while Rohesia brushed her hair she held out her hand. He took it between his own rough, wind-reddened hands but did not kiss it; he fondled it absently, not looking at her but watching the other women with sly, measuring glances as they gathered up the articles of toilet. She pulled her hand away.

When they had gone he sat down on the furs at her feet and began immediately to talk about Louis and the treaty for the betrothal of their son. She did not hear the half he said because her mind was running on what she would say to him, but at length his close proximity and the strong aroma of horse which clung to his clothes annoyed her enough to interrupt him.

She made an impatient movement. 'My Lord!'

He pulled his lip and looked at her for the first time.

'You have not once mentioned our new son.'

'Well?' he said shortly. 'He thrives, I trust?'

She breathed hard. 'He has been baptised Geoffrey in accordance with your instructions. Why I know not, seeing you have already one son – baseborn' – her lip turned down – 'of that name'. Two red spots of colour rose into her cheeks. 'And have forced him into the household of my children!'

'You may chafe all you will,' he said indifferently, 'but so I'll have it'.

She shouted at him 'Whose brat is he? Son of some strumpet among my children!'

He watched her, brows drawn down, a little line between his eyes.

'I know whose child he is,' she shrilled. 'Child of that English whore! Do you know what they say of her?'

Abruptly he stood up and his hand on her arm was like iron.

'Be still!' he said. 'Your jealousies pour out like pus from an infected wound. Keep your tongue from her in my presence! You – to call another woman whore! You know too much of the ancient game for one whose only other husband was a poor tool like Louis! Where did you learn your arts? Eh? Eh?'

He had thrust his face close to hers and to her fury, she could not hold his gaze. She felt herself flinch away from his impassioned glare and then her own rage came to her rescue.

'You have foisted her bastard upon me who am your Queen,' she hissed 'and you shall rue it!'

'I?' he yelled, 'I? Rue it? By the Teeth of God, you go too far!' His glare was murderous; lips drawn back he raised his clenched fist over her but she was too quick for him; she sprang aside, back to the wall, and faced him there, eye to eye.

Cornered, her warrior's blood came to the fore; she would fight him to the death with any weapon she might use.

'Take care! Do violence on me and I will see that all men know it! I am a Duchess in my own right and the lords of Aquitaine have never loved you. You shall see such rivers of blood as you have never dreamt on!'

He stopped dead. She had lighted unerringly on the one thing that would give him pause, the spectre of revolt, a threat to his power over his wide-flung dominions.

She could not leave it there.

'Did you think I did not know of your low-born minion? I have known all along! But why should I be jealous of such? She is below my notice and you have lowered your-self to her level. The truth is that you may feel at ease only with the meanest and most vile – there is a coarseness in you that must seek out its own kind. Why do the common people flock around you when you ride abroad? – to admire your kingly dress and manners?' She laughed shrilly. 'See now how you present yourself to your Queen!' and she pointed at the front of his tunic. Involuntarily he looked down and saw the old food and wine stains upon it, and his boots muddied to the calf.

She saw his head jerk and heard him grind his teeth together and waited for the storm of rage to break again; at least, she thought with satisfaction, he has heard the truth for once.

When he spoke, however, his voice was quiet though he sounded as if he were strangling. 'Be assured, madam, that

267

I shall not inflict my uncouth presence on you again, either here or in your bedchamber. And you shall never bear another child of mine. If I could deny you those you have already, I would do it. Yet since they are my children, too, it may be that your filed tongue will cut the cord that binds them to you. As for that villein blood you scorn, I have found finer feelings there than ever I did in you.'

He flung across the apartment and as he reached the door, his spur caught in a fold of the long tapestry that clothed the wall and trailed an inch or two upon the floor. It was a tapestry of Tristan and Isolde, new-made and hung but an hour since. It was Eleanor's dearest possession. He ripped at it with an oath and it tore along the length.

She leapt up. 'Boor!' she shouted after him.

He slammed the door with such force that the heavy oak sprang and shuddered and the iron sneck rattled upon the catch.

She sat down again but when her hands ceased to tremble, a feeling of desolation overcame her. She had thought to punish him with the threat of withholding her wifely duties; that he might forswear her in favour of his harlot had never occurred to her. Yet when she remembered his bastard in the Household of her children, anger stiffened her again. Titles and high honours might be granted to such but to treat a natural child as the equal of legitimate issue was unforgivable.

Oh, Jesu!, she thought, why – once free of Louis – did I thrust my neck again into the yoke of marriage? But she knew well enough that a woman, even a Duchess, must have some protector, either a husband or the garb of religion. Better Henry with all his infuriating infidelities than a moon calf like Louis, always running off to hear some fiery new preacher threatening damnation or urging a Crusade.

She recalled Henry's reference to Louis and his suspicions of herself with suddenly burning cheeks, yet in that

268

disquieting subject lay a grain of comfort. It had never been duty that brought Henry to her bed. He had hungered for her as much as she for him. He would not find it possible to reject her. And when next he came to her bedchamber, she would make him suffer before she granted him her favours.

All was silence in the outer chamber, her waiting women presumably doubtful of their reception should they disturb her. She picked up the mirror again, unseeing; then, with a sharp breath, looked more closely. There was a tracery of fine wrinkles round her eyes and her cheeks, once so smooth and plump, had a drawn and delicate look. She frowned and deep lines scored across her forehead.

I look old, she thought in sudden panic. How old was she? Thirty-five or six, she could not be sure, and Henry was but five and twenty. Why had she thought he would still find her desirable? But it was his fault she showed her age – five children in six years was too many.

Try as she might, her innate honesty would not allow all the blame to be laid at Henry's door. The cool self-know-ledge that was allied to a body of more than usual sen-suality recognised that the flesh must pay the price for its own pleasures.

And were those pleasures now to be forgone because she had told him the truth? For if she could not have Henry she could have no other man. She was not wanton, what-ever men might say.

She looked in the mirror again and took heart. She was only three months past childbed and not at her best. Her women should prepare lotions and unguents for her com-plexion, and riding and hawking would improve her thickened figure. She placed a little stiffened cap upon her head and picking up a strip of cloth one of her ladies was embroidering for a girdle, she drew it firmly underneath her chin, pulling the ends up to tuck them into the head-dress. Pleased with the effect, she netted her long brown hair

269

into a gold crespin and turned her head from side to side. Definitely, she looked younger.

After a while she began to sing softly under her breath the old song that the jongleurs had dedicated to her when first she was Henry's Queen.

> If all the lands were mine
> From sea's edge to the Rhine,
> I'd gladly lose them all
> To have the Queen of England
> Lying in my arms.

Suddenly, she began to weep.

Boiling with rage, Henry strode away. Here, then, was the truth from the wife whom he had thought to be loving and faithful to his interests, whose opinions he had respected and whose advice he had valued – and had taken, more than once. But never again! Now he knew self-interest alone had moved that sharp-witted, interfering bitch. Because he had married her, she thought she owned him – but she would soon learn differently for henceforth she should have no part in him, neither of mind nor body.

When Henry entered the hall a sudden quiet fell and the servants who were setting up trestles skipped nimbly to a safe distance so that a wide space opened before him. Henry went through like a blast of cold air, shouting for de Mandeville to attend upon him – to be ready to ride at a moment's notice – to this one to get down to the quay to warn the Captain of the King's Ship to make ready to sail upon the tide – to that one that silver must be forthcoming – to another to summon a scribe.

De Mandeville, who had been changing his clothes in readiness for the evening meal, came running. He took note of Henry's bloodshot eye and kept his own eyes steadfastly on the rushes.

'You return to England on the first tide,' announced

Henry, without ceremony. 'Ride with all speed for London – to the house near Westminster – you remember it? – and the wench you took thither?'

On his averted face, one of Geoffrey's eyebrows rose the merest trifle. He did indeed remember – it was that day's work, he was certain, that had regained for him his father's old Earldom of Essex six months later. So the old flame still burned – and after three years.

The King was still speaking. 'If she has no scribe nor clerk, you will read the letter to her. And you will bring her here with you – alone. None other.'

'Here?' said de Mandeville blankly.

'To Normandy. And in haste! Get you gone!'

De Mandeville was gone on winged feet to give his own orders to his lieutenants, and they in turn to rout out their men from ale houses, from warm firesides and the beds of whores, and let them mutter and groan as they liked at the prospect of another winter sea crossing.

Something had awakened the King from his apathy and the whole Court was on its toes once more.

In her apartments, the Queen wept still.

X

February 1159

BEATRICE FITZURSE WAS NEAR her time to lie-in. She sat in her small chamber screened off from the hall at Barham whither the Household had returned at harvest time. The room was very warm for a great fire burned against the wall although the weather was unseasonably mild for February. Christmas had been green and damp; it seemed there would be no real winter. Already there were fat shoots breaking through the earth, and in the woods the wild pansies showed their purple.

But in Beatrice's heart it was cold winter. Jehane was four months dead and on her grave the grass was springing green. Her grave and her babe's. It had never been born.

Nothing that anyone at Barham could do would release that child from its fleshy prison. How she had screamed! Those cries of agony rang still in Beatrice's head. Three days she had suffered, and Beatrice with her, holding her hands, bathing her brow, watching her die with an appalling helplessness.

When Beatrice's time came, the birth was easy but the child, a boy, was born yellow as an autumn leaf and as frail; he lived only two days. She could see no likeness to anyone in him; it seemed the worst thing of all that she would never know whose son he was. She buried her dread and her repining with him and resolved that she would, henceforth, be a true and loyal wife. She would find some means of letting Reynold know that Hugh was dangerous, that he must not come here, and God of His grace permitting, she would forget him and her sin.

September 1159

Hugh de Morville lay on the pallet in the dim obscurity of his tent while his page prepared a draught from an infusion of willow bark for his aching head. Outside, the midday sun glared down upon an array of brilliantly coloured pavilions and marquees pitched half a league from the white walls of a city. The armies of the King of the English were laying siege to Toulouse.

Now and then a party would sally forth from the gates but they never came as far as the encampment; a few of the English knights would ride to meet them and there would be a short, sharp exchange of blows – 'like a joust' thought Hugh – and then they would retire within the walls and back to the tents. No one had been seriously hurt in these encounters and it appeared they would sit out the rest of the summer here in boredom. Unless we get dysentery or fever, and in this heat it is more than likely, his thoughts ran on, and he began to wonder if he were already sickening and this appalling headache the first sign.

'Come, lad, be quick about it,' he said to the page, and winced again at the flash of pain through his left temple as he moved. More likely, though, it was the furious heat of this southern sun striking on his helmet that had caused the migraine.

At last, the boy brought him the cup and Hugh drained the sour, unpleasant liquid, sighing with relief, and closed his eyes. The noises of the camp came to him faintly, the creak of guy ropes and the soft flapping of canvas in the warm breeze, the far off whinny of a horse and the gruff voices of men, and that sound which is apprehended by the teeth rather than the ears as someone nearby began to sharpen a sword. He dozed gently and then came wide awake as the tent flap was lifted, letting in a flood of blinding daylight. He opened one eye cautiously, and saw that it was Reynold Fitzurse.

'Are you feeling better, Hugh?' he whispered hoarsely. 'Do I disturb you? I've news.'

De Morville opened the other eye. 'News?' he said.

'Yes. They say the King of France rode into Toulouse last evening.'

Hugh raised himself. 'With an army?'

'A few troops, but he has sent for reinforcements, they say.'

Hugh's smile was like a wolf's. 'Shall we see action, then?'

'I doubt the opposition, but we shall if our master has his way.' Reynold meant Thomas the Chancellor whose knights they were. 'He would rather fight than sit around a council table. Who would have thought it, Hugh? Could we have been wrong about him? It was he who planned this whole campaign.'

Hugh's voice was soft. 'And, clerk though he is, did squeeze the scutage from the Church as well as the lay barons . . .'

Reynold, as usual, missed the point. 'Aye! Shield money! That's an outlet for old women. And because of it my father sits at home on his manor nursing his bad leg.'

Hugh smiled faintly. His migraine was passing off though whether the relief was due to some magical property of the willow or to the rest in the darkened tent, he did not know. He did know that Reynold hated his father, though, and it pleased something deep inside him. He set himself to kindle Reynold a little further.

'There is your bastard brother, too,' he said. 'Does he hold him in such esteem that he would rather pay a pound of silver than let him cross the sea?'

Reynold shrugged. 'Robert has little taste for a knight's

274

life,' he said, 'but the cost for a knight was two marks as I heard it. And, by'r Lady, if they choose to sit at home like mice – let them – there's booty here in this rich land for those who're men enough to take it!'

'And the King of France, who's overlord to our King, in Toulouse itself?'

'Him!' said Reynold with the greatest contempt. 'He'll creep away again. He'll not fight, I tell you. He has a liver to match his badge.'

'Then why has he come? I'll tell you what he can't stomach and it may drive him to fight – you recall that our Queen was once his wife?'

'Aye.'

'And brought him but two daughters in sixteen years? King Henry has got already four boys upon her while he has only another girl from his present wife. It must gnaw at him like a maggot! Not only that but our King's lands are double his and more. Shall he let him take Toulouse and not lift a hand?'

So they managed to persuade themselves that a battle was imminent and consequently were in a cheerful frame of mind when they were summoned with some others to a meeting in the King's pavilion.

It started quietly enough with discussion of the difficulties of the long supply lines, and since the Chancellor had proved his worth as a commander when Cahors was taken, he was put in charge of strategy. It was his innocent suggestion that provoked the trouble.

'Once we are within Toulouse,' he said, 'our supply troubles will be over. And that is what I suggest, my lord – that we attack now before reinforcements come up. We took Cahors by storm; we may do the same here.' His tone was vehement, his face alight with enthusiasm.

There was a little silence at the long trestle for Henry did not at once answer. Although they were in the pavilion to escape the merciless sun, it was no cooler here, the air was

275

still and heavy with the odour of stale sweat and hot metal. The King flapped his hand before his face as they all waited, then he said, 'No, we shall forbear.'

Some of the barons nodded as though satisfied, others looked blank, but Thomas' face showed stupefaction.

'Forbear!' he exclaimed. 'You cannot mean it, sire. This is our best chance.'

Henry did not look at him. 'I cannot attack one to whom I have paid homage,' he said.

Thomas said slowly, 'You cannot be serious.'

Although only those nearest caught the remark, there was an abrupt mounting of tension. Henry swung his head round and looked at Thomas sideways; there was a curious expression on his face.

'He is my overlord.'

Thomas stuttered. 'But – but that was the reason we came here – to fight for Toulouse. Your claim is just, through the Queen, your wife. I do not understand—'

'You are right, you do not understand. To fight against the Count of Toulouse is one thing, to fight against my overlord another.'

Thomas' temper was rising. 'This is casuistry,' he said sharply. 'You have fought him before.'

'Only for my own.'

'But this is your own – or so you would have us believe.'

Their voices had risen so that everyone could overhear. Hugh nudged Reynold and they craned forward.

The King said heavily, 'If you cannot see the difference, you cannot. But I will not raise my hand against him. Nor, I think, will any other here who has given homage. What example would that set our own vassals?'

'But he has sided with your enemies against you! This talk of homage is nothing but foolish superstition.'

The pavilion fell so quiet that each could hear the breathing of his neighbour and a heightened breathing it was, in

276

many cases. A low muttering broke out here and there – 'He's but a commoner, after all' – 'How should such as he comprehend the knightly code?' and much more in the same vein. Hugh whispered to Reynold, 'Much our homage meant to him!'

Thomas had never felt more alone. No one would meet his eyes; it was as if he had just developed some hideous deformity. The scarcely veiled contempt of those who remained silent was harder to bear than were the disparaging remarks he could overhear concerning his origin. The youngest page was more at home here than he was. He had fancied himself one of them because he enjoyed fighting and generalship – now he saw the chasm that yawned between noble and commoner. It was a bitter moment.

The King did not look at him – he simply announced that the armies would withdraw northward on the morrow, back to Cahors. But when Thomas rose to leave he suddenly shouted at him that he, who owed the King of France no fealty, might stay and give him battle if he wished. A babble of conversation broke out.

The Earl of Cornwall plucked pensively at his beard and surreptitiously watched the King who sat now with his chin sunk on his chest; his expression boded ill for any who might interrupt his thoughts. Under cover of the hubbub Cornwall addressed himself to young Gloucester, though in a sidewise manner, speaking out of the corner of his mouth and not turning towards him – 'What do you think of that little exchange, nephew?'

Gloucester shrugged his indifference. 'His attitude is what one might expect. The sooner the King sees him in his true colours the better. I like not these upstarts who sit now at the very Council Table and put forth their froward suggestions as of right.'

Unexpectedly, Cornwall sighed. 'I am afraid young Henry is not the warrior his mother was – we have not fought a true battle alongside him once. Oh, yes, bring up the armies, lay siege to the cities, fight a few skirmishes even—'

'Time he was brought low,' said Gloucester, and Cornwall saw his tight, secret smile; he knew then that his nephew, along with so many of the other nobles, hated the Chancellor. He sighed again because he could not help but like the man and felt there was truth in what he said: that Henry was using his fealty to the King of France as an excuse to avoid the battle. Perhaps it was just as well that Gloucester had not noticed (or had ignored) his own remarks about the King's lack of taste for open warfare.

Outside Hugh de Morville, Reynold Fitzurse and a few of their close companions watched Thomas walk back to his own pavilion. He went, as always, tall and unhurried, and looking, in fine tunic of Lincoln red, a great deal nobler than most of the chivalry of England or of France. The bands of embroidery around hem and sleeves were sewn with innumerable small jewels; they flashed and glittered in the sun. The thin murrey mantle, pushed back from his shoulders because of the heat, was knotted through an ornate ring of heavy gold at the side of the neck, and his beard was dressed forked in the latest fashion.

Hugh's eyes were narrowed against the glare from the brazen sky and he said between his teeth, 'Fine as a popinjay bird he walks', – and indeed, with the Chancellor's characteristic walk with his head poked forward and his fine, large Norman nose now red with sunburn, they were irresistibly reminded of some immense, important bird.

Reynold said slowly, 'Did we do well to take him for our lord? What if he fall from power?'

'Well . . .' said Hugh. 'The cloak of his disgrace will not stretch so far as to cover us – nor do I really fear he'll be disgraced. Whatever else he may be, he's a good campaigner. We'll stay here if we must and fight with him – aye, and win! Then he'll be back in favour.'

Reynold nodded, but doubtfully. 'It was my father's mind

to place me with him,' he said. 'I had rather be the King's man.'

'Or the Queen's perhaps,' Hugh twitted him; but Reynold turned a deaf ear to that.

Thomas had not looked at the group of young knights as he passed them yet he sensed their relish at his discomfiture. John of Salisbury had long ago cautioned him to prudence and in his vanity he had discounted the warning. Not for the first time, Thomas began to wonder if the eminence he had gained were worth the worry it brought him.

Yet pride upheld him. The King had said he might fight on and he would do so. He would show them all that he could be as great a commander as an administrator. Mentally, he girded himself and thrust away the memory of his recent humiliation. Soon the King and his barons with their odd notions would be gone and he could prosecute the war as he thought best.

But with the King's going, he saw that it was impossible to subdue Toulouse itself, so donning helmet and hauberk, he led his troops in forays about the whole province. Fire and sword were taken to village and town alike until the entire region of the Quercy was blackened and laid waste and then, satisfied that Toulouse must starve this coming winter, he chased the terrified remnants of the population across the Garonne.

Now, in the company of men whose tastes coincided with his own, who also knew the fierce answering beat of the heart to the tap of drums and galloping hoofs, who also thrilled to the fluttering pennants and the clash of steel on steel, whose blood, too, coursed faster and hotter in the lust of battle, Thomas discovered the truth about himself.

For years he had moulded his impetuous, warlike spirit into meek conformance to a cleric's life; by prayer and fasting he had confined the latent Viking and concealed him under a mantle of humility until even he believed the grace of God had changed his very nature. But all his mildness and resignation was but a thin, outer rind, stripped away in the twinkling of an eye at the first challenge. He was like a man released into free air after years chained in a dungeon. He had lived in the world for forty years, blind to his essential self, but now, finally, he recognised it, and recognising, gloried in it.

How good was God who had given every man a nature best fitted to His own inscrutable purposes! The plan and pattern of his life was at last emerging, for how else but through Holy Church should such as Thomas of London have risen to be a great warrior? His whole soul went out in gratitude to his Maker.

Only one memory flawed what he later thought of as the happiest period of his career. His army had assaulted a small town and somehow, in the heat and excitement of the battle, he had outridden Henry of Essex, the Constable, and the handful of senior knights who always accompanied him.

As darkness fell he found himself alone in a mean alley with the noise of fighting ever receding into the distance. He drew rein to listen – all was quiet here – and worried at the lame gait of his horse on the cobbles, he dismounted. It had cast a shoe. He stood a second, undecided, hand on the hilt of his sword, then leading the horse, he moved off down the alley on foot to investigate. It was too dark to see much for the walls sagged drunkenly towards each other overhead.

He went cautiously, prodding ahead of him with the sword, in search of a route back to broader thoroughfares. Something yielding at his feet almost tripped him and he narrowed his eyes in an effort to see. He thought for a moment it was a sleeping beggar – one of those anonymous bundles of rags that infested the corners of every town he knew. Then he saw that this sleep was one from which the churl would not wake. The back of his head was smashed like an eggshell; through blood and shattered bone a greyish mass protruded. A mace or morning star had dealt that blow.

He stood still, gradually becoming aware of a horrid sound nearby, a snorting, gulping, gasping noise that set his teeth on edge. He forced himself towards it, head half averted for fear of some ghastly sight. But it was only a starving cur, tugging at some refuse it had found.

It snarled at him, unwilling to relinquish its prize and unable to drag it further, then, as his eyes became accustomed to the gloom, he saw more. A dead child lay against the wall, half disembowelled by a pike thrust, and the dog – the dog . . . was finishing the task . . .

Thomas jerked upright, sweat bursting out on his face. He swung up his sword, two-handed, and cleft the animal in two.

He could not breathe. He leaned on the wall over the mutilated corpse, retching and panting, while icy tremors chased themselves up and down his back. 'Oh, God,' he said, over and over again, 'Oh, God, oh, God.'

Those accursed mercenaries! They had run berserk, killing everything that moved. This was not a battlefield, it was a shambles. Blood was everywhere in pools on the path and splashed on the walls. His hand, running along the rough stone, encountered it; it was sticky and still warm.

Up ahead was noise and the crackling of flames; as he rounded a corner towards the centre of the town the ruddy glare leapt out at him. They were burning some wattle and plaster houses and there were women running and screaming. As they ran, the men-at-arms tripped them with their pikes.

Thomas found his strength again.

'Enough!' he roared, and came at them with as much speed as he could in the heavy, mailed surcoat.

They turned in amazement to see who dared try to stay them and he saw that they were mercenaries. These were the men who killed for silver and took their pleasure later

281

in looting and raping. That was what they were about now – he realised they were not killing the women but driving them out of the houses where they had hidden and herding them in a group.

Their heavy, brutish faces glowered at him; one raised a pike but another, evidently recognising authority, knocked down his arm and spoke low under his breath.

'What are you at?' shouted Thomas. 'Release those women!'

The man who had recognised his right to command said sulkily, 'These be only the town whores, m'lord. It's part of the agreement with them as hires us that we takes our pickings from any town that's invested.'

Thomas stared at the women. Certainly they looked like whores. He began to feel foolish. The mercenaries were growling amongst themselves and one said loudly, 'That a'n't the Constable. Who's he to tell us what we can do?'

One of the women came forward. She had no teeth and her breath reeked of wine; Thomas could see the ingrained dirt in the creases of her face and neck even in the dim, smoky light of the fire behind him.

'Thanks to ye, master, for saving us,' she said hoarsely. 'But if ye see that they pay in good silver, we'll see they has their pleasuring' – she caught at his arm as he turned away –'Ye'll be saving more innocent women from them,' she said.

Reluctantly he turned back and looked at her and then looked again at the mercenaries' hard, sullen faces.

'Do what you must,' he muttered in a voice he scarcely knew for his own. 'Keep them here with you the rest of this night and I will see you are rewarded on the morrow. But do not let them down into the town again. Know you who I am?'

'Aye,' she said, and at that moment a fresh burst of shouting broke out nearby and then the sound of horses' hoofs on the cobbles and a ringing voice proclaiming, 'Hath any here seen the lord Thomas the Chancellor – lord Thomas the Chancellor?'

Thomas felt an enormous sense of relief. Here were his knights out searching for him.

'Hola!' he shouted, 'Here I am!' and then they were all round him, and the women and the mercenaries melted away into the darkness.

Nonetheless, the knowledge of the effect of war upon the common people did not deter Thomas for long. He placed the blame squarely upon the mercenaries and then forgot it.

As the fighting in the south waned, Louis and his allies began to harry the Norman marches, and Thomas marched north with his army, back to Henry who greeted him as though they had never had a difference of opinion on the conduct of the campaign.

Thomas distinguished himself again in the border raiding, leading his troops in person and rallying them with calls on a long, slender, silver bugle. This instrument, which became known as the 'Chancellor's Horn', gave rise to many a bawdy jest. He had learnt more than military tactics from his knights over the last few months, however, and accepted it all in a philosophical if somewhat pained silence. He knew that his companions thought his chastity odd but as long as he had the love and respect of his intimates, he could endure these small digs at his manhood.

And he felt himself acquitted when, in single combat, he unhorsed the finest of the French knights, Engelram de Trie, and brought back his charger as a prize. Henry's delight was unbounded – his clerkly Chancellor had proved himself a better horseman than the flower of French chivalry. He ordered a great feast in Thomas' honour.

The huge hall was so full that many of the younger, less important knights must sit in the rushes and manage as best they could; that would have been no hardship in Thomas' hall where his insistence on cleanliness caused the herbage to be changed every day but here it was a different matter. Old food, dogs' excrement and bones were scattered in the strawing of the floor; Thomas frowned as he looked around and caught the eye of Hugh de Morville who sat in the litter with apparent unconcern.

Hugh lifted his cup to his master and Thomas nodded and looked hard at him, remembering that he had been one of the search party who had found him in the burning town. He wondered again what went on behind that black, bland gaze.

'To your health, sire, and greater glory,' said Hugh, and drank.

Thomas motioned him nearer. At least he was one of his own, sworn to be his man and here, among these great barons who had witnessed the rift between the King and himself, he felt the need of support. He had forgotten that Hugh, too, had looked upon him with disdain.

Almost without knowing it, he set himself to charm the younger man. He had never found it difficult to make men love him and his vanity was pricked by Hugh's cool assumption of equality – this was no empty-headed dolt to be discounted but a man of wit and intelligence; a man, in short, fit to serve one such as Thomas conceived himself to be.

'I never thanked you for your help in seeking me that night when I became separated from the Constable,' he said in a low voice. 'It was an unpleasant experience to find myself alone among mercenaries. Not' he hastened to add, 'that I had any difficulty in controlling them. But the result of their butchery was not pretty.'

'Ah' – said Hugh. 'It was a sight new to you then, being a commander? I have seen it many times,' and he smiled idly, shifting about in the foul rushes and not looking at the Chancellor.

'Their conduct was bestial.'

284

Hugh lifted an eyebrow. 'Bestial? Surely not?'

Thomas nodded. 'They had killed without mercy. Ordinary folk – children – women, too, after they had had their way with them.'

'I fear you do the beasts an injustice. It seems they behaved like men. And blood-lust leaves but little room for pity.'

Thomas stopped with the hanap halfway to his lips.

'You blame them, Chancellor? But you employ them, and what they do for payment, knights are bred up to as duty. To deal out death is their function, also – and their pleasure. It is mine – and yours, too, I think.'

Thomas stared at him, thunderstruck.

'You mistake me,' he said stiffly. 'It is an honour to fight for the King but no pleasure to kill. I did not kill Engelram de Trie.'

'Why, no. He was a knight. But were those others in the Quercy any less men because they were not clad in mail? I have ridden behind you, sword in hand, a dozen times' – his voice was sweet as honey – 'and because I rode in your wake, I have seen the carnage you have wrought – and given the *coup de grâce* to many a one left by you to die of wounds and thirst.'

For the first time Thomas saw behind Hugh's smiling mask. Hatred enough to freeze the blood was there though even now he could not believe such virulence was directed against himself. But beneath that – worse by far – lay a suave, uncaring ruthlessness and a relish for bloodshed surpassing anything he had seen among the mercenaries.

His hand shook as he raised the hanap again to his lips. How had he ever thought that such a one might love him? He had placed him, Thomas of London, on the same level as those brutes . . .

And then, as though Satan himself had jogged his elbow; the vivid recollection of the moments before the charge, unforgotten and unforgettable, flashed upon his mind. Despite himself, he knew again that shivering delight, the thigh-prickling, palm-sweating eagerness, the long, deep breaths jerkily exhaled. He saw it plain. Blood-lust.

Thomas had not always succeeded in turning away his eyes from what he did not wish to see. He knew the face of lust. Lust of the flesh and blood-lust were different sides of the same coin, then; the one as much sin as the other.

Thomas found himself in deep waters, and as he turned away from Hugh he saw that the other knew how deeply his thrust had gone home. Strangely enough, it did not seem to matter. Hugh's impression of him was immaterial, something of much more importance was here at stake: his own good opinion of himself. The very foundations of his self-esteem were cracking.

Afterwards he scarcely remembered the feast; he smiled and accepted the toasts and congratulations but was not sensible of them. He was beset by an anxiety he had not known since childhood, a fear of some deficiency in himself. Had he deceived himself from the beginning? If the high-principled integrity he had arrogated to himself were a delusion, he was utterly unworthy of the admiration he had enjoyed.

That could not be, and because it was not possible, he began mentally to rehearse what he had thought of as his virtues. When he came to valour his mind seized upon it with thankfulness. It was not that he would excuse himself of the charge of blood-lust – no indeed, he accepted it, but with the qualification that it was a necessary part of a warrior's fearlessness. It was a pity that the innocent should suffer but every Prince was responsible to God for his own people and if Princes deal unjustly . . .

Having thus exculpated himself and censured Raymond of Toulouse for indirectly causing the deaths of his subjects, he turned his thoughts to Hugh de Morville, who was of all men blameworthy for his ingratitude to his liege. He remembered his own condescending affability towards him with

an inward writing. Hugh had disparaged him and somehow duped him into accepting his imputation as the truth.
Without ferocity, a fighting man was ineffectual and the
proof lay in his victory over Engelram de Trie. He had
ridden him down with the same force and fury he had used
against the Toulousains; Engelram had not expected that,
any more than would Henry, he realised, for it was all of a
piece with his quibble over attacking Louis. These contests
with the French knights were a kind of game, as unlike
the howling, shrieking bedlam of true battle as were the
jousts in Provence for ladies' favours.

The deduction came to him quite suddenly so that he
jerked his head and stared, causing old Cornwall, whose
turn it was to share his dish this night, to relinquish with
some guilt a particularly choice morsel.

He, Thomas, fought only to win while knights would
abide by a code he would never understand. It occurred to
him to wonder whether he would be thus honoured and
feasted had he killed Engelram instead of merely unhorsing
him. Hammering out the matter to such a conclusion, he
felt easier. And the knowledge that no outworn code but
only God's laws bound him, glowed still and small but
warmly comforting in his heart.

Later that evening he sat in private with Henry and a few
others including the King's minion. He watched her covertly,
marvelling at the transparent beauty of her face – that
face which by some trick of Satan himself came always to
his inner eye when he prayed to God's Mother. Why had
Henry received her back into his favour? After what he had
finally brought himself to tell of the matter, Thomas found
it inconceivable that he should wish ever to see her again.
That he had quarrelled bitterly with his Queen, Thomas
knew – but the way of man with woman was a closed book
to him and he thanked God for it.

Withdrawn still into his own musings, he heard only

snatches of the talk that flowed around him until Henry's voice, suddenly loud, broke through his reverie, declaiming that Boulogne should not revert to Louis if he could help it – and others answering that Louis was overlord and Earl Warenne had left no heir. Thomas pricked up his ears. He had heard of the death of William of Warenne, Count of Boulogne, on the withdrawal from Toulouse. William had been the last surviving son of King Stephen.

Henry laughed. 'Yes, but Earl Warenne has left an heir – not of his body, true, but is not the Abbess of Romsey his sister?'

There was a silence and into it the King triumphantly announced that it was his intention to marry her to Matthew of Flanders – 'for, do you see', he said intently, 'thus shall I bind Flanders also more closely to England. She is sole heiress to Boulogne and through her, Matthew will become Count.'

Thomas stiffened.

Cornwall's voice was dubious. 'What if she is unwilling to leave religion for marriage?'

'A dispensation may be obtained –'

'Pope Adrian has lately died – do you think the new Pope—?'

Someone said, 'Which new Pope?' and a shocked voice interposed, 'An Abbess! –'

Henry looked at Thomas. 'Have you nothing to say?'

Thomas thought swiftly. Dare he again directly oppose the King – and before these same noblemen? But somehow, now, his spine was firmer. 'I could not agree without a dispensation,' he said. Nor with one, he thought inwardly.

Henry gave a short bark of laughter. 'I care not who agrees,' he said, but pleasantly enough. 'You're acquainted with the matter now and we'll think on it later. This night's not for policy making. Come, drink up!' and he fell to fondling his minion again.

'After Christmas the Queen returns to England,' he in-

288

formed Thomas, 'to be Regent, for I would have you here with me. Aye, and this moppet also. I shall not part with her again – nor with you, neither, Tom,' and he reached out and patted Thomas' arm.

Thomas saw some of the nobles look askance at one another, though whether it were in disapprobation of the King's fondness for himself or for his paramour, he could not tell. And foreseeing another head-on collision with Henry, he felt a prick of fear lest he be disowned of all. Then he told himself that God and the right were the surest buckler a man might have and knowing he had them, was himself once more.

When Henry told Thomas a week or two later that the deed was done, the ex-Abbess of Romsey fast married to Matthew of Flanders, they quarrelled violently. Henry had never before been the butt of Thomas' icy anger; he was at first dumbfounded and hurt, and later, angry in his turn. He refused absolutely to listen to any of Thomas' reasons for disliking the match, preferring to believe that the Chancellor found his action offensive on religious grounds alone. In that he was indubitably right, but Thomas annoyed him further by pointing out that Matthew was easily influenced and as Count of Boulogne could not help but absorb much of that Court's traditional hostility to the House of Anjou. His smouldering anger was fanned into flame when he discovered that Thomas had written to the new Pope Alexander, urging him not to dispense the Abbess from her vows.

'Much good will that do!' he shouted. 'Can the Pope restore her maidenhead? That's a miracle I never heard of!'

This reminder of a *fait-accompli* was more than Thomas could bear; he said, tight lipped, 'You may sneer as you please at woman's most prized possession—'

'Ha! Prized! What do you know of such matters? I tell you most women cannot wait to be rid of it—'

'Some have died rather than lose it—'

289

'Well, Mary de Warenne did not, Abbess or no. As for those Roman virgins reputed to have done so, they were nothing like the women of this time!'

'Nay, for today Christianity is no more than lip deep with many, and with some few not even that—'

Thomas stopped short at the blaze of fury on Henry's face, recollecting too late that false, un-Christian wanton whose defection and subsequent reinstatement he had never dared mention. Bitterly regretting his careless choice of words, he tried helplessly to resolve the misunderstanding, but without mentioning that which he had been forbidden to do, the case was hopeless.

Because Henry was truly angry, and with Thomas who was like his other self, he did not fly into a passion as he usually did; he sat quite still, clenching and unclenching his hands and breathing heavily. There was a white line around his lips.

'Take care,' he said. 'Take care, my lord Chancellor. You, like any other, may presume too much.' He crooked his hands into claws and stared into Thomas' eyes. 'No man is indispensable to me,' he said.

If Thomas saw his downfall in the King's face, he did not flinch but merely bowed his head in acknowledgement; only when he left the chamber his face was paler than usual.

But the habitual round did not alter except for the silences between them when official business was over; in the end, it irked Henry more than Thomas and he visited his constant irritation on the heads of those nearest him. Thomas knew that the courtiers saw themselves as his whipping boys and it was this, as much as anything, that made him sue the King for pardon.

Henry, appealed to, could always show himself magnanimous; it pleased his vanity and, in this case, his inclinations. He had meant to frighten Thomas but Thomas had not been frightened, or so Henry thought. In the end, Henry had frightened only himself because the loss of his dear friend's love, which had before seemed impossible, had suddenly assumed reality. But Henry who was a King and had never learnt to ask, had known no way out of the impasse.

So when Thomas knelt before him he was ready to go more than halfway to meet him, and pulled him up and kissed his cheek before the plea for pardon was half said. They were alone. Since theirs had been a private quarrel, the reconciliation was private, too. None other should see his friend humble himself. Perhaps it was as well there were no other eyes, less loving than the King's, to notice that his Chancellor was not so very humble anyway. They might have thought the humility was more on the King's side.

Henry's tone was gentler than many would have believed possible when he said, 'I cannot let you rule me, Tom. Friends we must be for the love that is between us, but we are still master and man.' He paused as though to choose his words with care. 'Have I not listened with patience to your homilies? But that other whom I love – try not to make me choose between you.'

Thomas kept his eyes down lest the King see the spark that sprang in them. 'You misunderstand, Harry, I swear it. I did not think of her—'

Henry's look was noncommittal. 'I have seen you look at her. But you must accept it, Tom. Your dislikes are your own concern –but hide them from me.'

'Not dislike. Distrust, maybe. Her influence upon you worries me.'

'Your lack of trust in my judgment is hardly flattering. And you are wrong – she has never tried to influence me, neither is that possible. What is between us is a personal matter and essential to my happiness.'

'Harry – believe it is only my concern for you that allows me to mention it but – will you give me leave to ask one question?'

Henry bit his lip but finally nodded.

'Has she renounced her' – Thomas had been about to say practices but substituted 'associations?'

'Yes.' And then, 'I know not. But now I keep her by me always. I left her too long before. There can be no opportunity.'

'She is with you always?' Thomas was amazed. 'In camp?'

Henry shrugged. 'There are always women in the camp. Her appurtenances are listed along with theirs. 'Item – sheets for Belle-belle's bed, 4d." The clerks will think it is some casual whore.'

He looked up and saw Thomas' expression. 'I know what you think,' he muttered, 'how inflexible your scruples. But I have begotten legitimate heirs for my kingdom and the days of youth are soon over. You are lucky that you have lived into the ripeness of your years but no man knows the numbering of his days and I am already nearly twenty-seven. I may have ten more years or twenty – or I may be food for worms before another year is past. I would have something for myself before I die.'

Thomas stared at him. This was a very different Henry he was seeing.

'—if you must judge, let it be with compassion.' Henry threw out his hands and at the open entreaty, Thomas clasped his arm with answering emotion.

'God forbid that I should judge you!' he said as he had said once before.

'Then is all well again between us?'

Thomas grasped him by both shoulders and looked into his eyes. 'God grant it!' he said fervently and then, seeing the shine of unshed tears in Henry's eyes, he shook his head ruefully back and forth at him. Henry leaned his head for a second on Thomas' arm.

'Oh Tom,' he said, 'If she is my heart, you are my soul.'

Subsequently Thomas marvelled not a little at the strength of the love the King bore him. He, too, loved Henry in his way but an inner core of self-containment was never touched.

None but God would ever touch it. And it was because of this, he realised – because God had possession of his heart – that he had misgivings about the King's concubine. She and her like were traitors in the camp of Christendom, more dangerous than the Jews who were plainly recognised as enemies of Christ. Misbeliever as she was, she might steal Henry's soul from God, destroy his faith which was none too hardy at best. For Thomas was very well aware of his dear friend's scepticism and he knew, too, that Henry was himself unconscious of it. Should she, in subtle ways, undermine his confidence in Christ. . . . The worry continued to gnaw at him.

That the King's rationalist attitude might also extend to Hikenai's own beliefs did not occur to him, any more than did the fact that the matter over which they had quarrelled was still unresolved. He had clean forgotten the Abbess of Romsey. It made no difference, anyway, for the new Pope, who had his own troubles and doubtless his own reasons, granted the dispensation for her marriage on the first asking.

Christmas 1159
For the whole of the week before Christmas the land had been gripped by an iron frost; now, on the afternoon of Christmas Eve, a few light sprinklings of snow fell at intervals; where it lay fine and thin on the paving in the bailey of Falaise Castle, it looked as though the cooks had floured the stones for pastry.

Within the hall, though, all was light and colour but an unusual hush lay over all. That was because Ethelwig the minstrel was singing, his golden voice mourning some long-forgotten tragedy. When the last haunting notes died away the women sat in dreaming silence for a few moments, still caught by the magic, until one sighed deeply in purest pleasure and they all looked at one another and smiled, sharing that delightful, unreal sorrow that comes at second hand.

293

Old Rohesia wiped a furtive tear from her crumpled cheek and bent lower over her embroidery, completing the half-made stitch on which her hands had fallen idle when Ethelwig began to sing. The Queen gazed into some far distance with soft eyes and parted lips; she thought, for no reason, of woods in autumn. Then she remembered.

Beauty and enchantment were in that recollection and in spite of herself her unquiet heart yearned again for her lost beloved. It was a little while before she realised grief had died. Pain, too, had vanished – only the tender memory of youth and love remained. She opened wide the closed door in her mind and tried to see once more that face which had been all her sunrising. For one flashing instant he was there, ruddy and laughing, his hair wind-blown, then the mental picture faded and was gone.

With sudden shock she knew the trick that time had played on her. Her will had done its work too well; in refusing to suffer for his loss, she had lost him utterly. And alas! – it did not matter. So much for deathless love, she told herself, and the sweet nothings of which Ethelwig sings. The passing years betray us all alike.

Henry's voice upraised at the other end of the hall broke abruptly into her reverie. He was in a bad temper today and any small irritation would bring on one of his screaming rages.

Even since word had come concerning that indefensible scene during the Conclave of Cardinals to elect a new Pope (for Adrian the Englishman had died last September), when a hand to hand struggle for the white cope of the Papacy had developed between the Princes of the Church, the question of Pope or Anti-Pope had taxed men's minds, and Henry's temper.

He was determined to choose for himself but the conflicting advice he received from every quarter was trying his patience to the limit. His own inclination was towards Pope Alexander but he also wished to preserve good relations with Emperor Frederick Barbarossa whose creature the rival Pope Victor was known to be. Unlike Louis of France Henry was not at all worried by the schism itself, only by its political repercussions. He felt that if he might only withhold his allegiance to either long enough, some advantage could be got from it. Even his beloved Tom had urged him to temporise for a time until events showed which of the two had the blessing of Almighty God.

Eleanor remembered Henry's anger at the presumption of Bishop Arnulf of Lisieux who had zealously urged him to recognise Alexander immediately – that, in itself, was almost sufficient to push him in the opposite direction. Now, even she, cut off by the rift between them, had heard of the letter he had received, ostensibly from Theobald of Canterbury but penned by John of Salisbury, advising him to the same course. And Henry had not yet forgiven John for his outspoken condemnation of the tax on Church lands which had helped finance the abortive Toulouse campaign.

'Nor does it befit your majesty', John had written, 'to place at the head of the Church in your kingdom, without consulting it, a man who was not elected and is commonly said not to have the grace of God. He dares to seize this position only because of the favour and decrees of the Emperor, for the Roman Church is almost entirely in favour of Alexander.'

Henry had nearly choked with rage when it was read to him. 'Without consulting it!' he had howled. 'Without consulting whom? The bishops? Who rules the English – they or I?' and he had worked himself into such a fury that the physicians had feared he would have a seizure. Eleanor, who did not fear his rages, had shrugged. She did not care about the schism either but she suspected the Chancellor did. When he became convinced of the soundness of the claim of one of them, he would urge Henry to recognise him with more fervour than anyone. She had a great deal more sympathy with Henry's own attitude, but none at all with his displays of temper.

So now she tightened her lips at the sound of her husband's angry voice and her glance fell upon Ethelwig who, dissatisfied with the note of one of the strings, was tuning his lute. She watched him, glad to be diverted from her thoughts, while he hummed softly to himself, handling the instrument with loving care.

He was young, in his early twenties perhaps, with a broad, almost fat face and a body softening already with the good living he got in her service. She thought him quite unhandsome, yet when he sang nothing else mattered. Her younger ladies squabbled endlessly as to who should sit next to him. She knew nothing of his private life except that he was unmarried; he was always there when required and that, of course, was often lately since Henry had ceased to seek her company. She had been invited here today only in honour of the festival. She had heard her maidens murmur that the minstrel was indifferent to women and she wondered with the discomfort of the normal whether he was of that company who prefer the love of their own sex.

He met her eyes and she looked away abruptly. There was that in him that set her teeth on edge so that she rarely exchanged words with him and felt uncomfortable under his sly, sliding glances – yet she would be loth to part with him, that tender, lulling voice paid for all.

She heard the King's tones rising shrill again and looked towards him anxiously. He was striding up and down, shouting at his companions, and she made a sign to Ethelwig to be silent for a space. But he did not see; having tuned the lute to his satisfaction, he began to sing again.

Henry turned and stared; he spat one sharp expletive through his teeth, then came down the hall with his quick, jerky stride while Ethelwig sang on unheeding, his eyes half closed. Behind the King came his flurried nobles, Cornwall, slow and lumbering as ever, bringing up the rear.

Henry's movement was so swift that Eleanor scarcely realised what was happening. The cessation of the song, the sharp sound of breaking wood, a sudden involuntary cry from one of her women – a bulky knight was blocking Eleanor's view so that she, too, cried out and pushed at him, and as he moved, she saw the minstrel crouched in the rushes, pawing at his broken lute while the King stood over him with lowering face.

Ethelwig screamed something in his own barbarous tongue; whether the King understood it or whether he took exception to the tone Eleanor did not know, but he caught the minstrel by the throat in the crook of his elbow and bore him struggling backwards across his knee. Eleanor heard the short swords hiss from the scabbards as the group of men closed around them; she cried out wildly and thrust between them. She saw Ethelwig's face purpling from the cruel pressure on his throat and her eyes met Henry's across his slack body.

'My lord,' she gasped, 'I pray you – do not kill my minstrel. He will choke if you hold him thus!'

'He shouted at me!' said Henry between his teeth. '*Your* minstrel shouted at me! Is this the way you train your servants?'

'Dear God!' she cried, pulling vainly at his arm. 'Will you kill him here before my eyes? Please – please!'

Henry flung the minstrel to the floor so that she cannoned off into one of the onlookers. It was the Chancellor. Gently he held her upright and made as if to escort her back to her seat but she put his hand aside and stood looking down at Ethelwig.

'Well, madam,' said Henry, and his voice was deadly. 'Your Household is one minstrel less.'

'He cannot be dead,' she whispered.

'Not yet,' said Henry with a look that turned her blood to ice. She thought, it is because of me he will do this, and knowing she could not plead again before them all, felt

297

her chin begin to shake. So even Ethelwig's singing was to be taken from her.

He started to groan and gurgle then and someone pulled him into a sitting position. She saw the Chancellor regarding him with what she thought was pity and a wild hope seized her. The Chancellor would not let Henry do this thing! She would send him a note asking him to intervene for Christian pity at this holy season. When she looked back at Henry his face did not move at all, only his eyes flickered a little sideways and she knew he was wondering what his dearest Tom would say.

She sent a note to the Chancellor that evening and though she received a prompt answer assuring her of his best endeavours at all times, she heard no more. Ethelwig was imprisoned somewhere over the whole Twelve Days of Christmas and in mid-January she was to sail for England.

It was a day of bitter cold when they took ship; though the great frost had abated, a terrible knife-like wind had arisen. Even Eleanor, good sailor as she was, looked at the turbulent sea with misgiving. Huddled in her fur-lined mantle, she came upon the heaving deck to be met by Rohesia who had gone aboard before with the ladies to prepare her cabin. The lady-in-waiting's face was alight with joy.

'Your Grace!' she cried. 'He is below! Your minstrel! The King has sent him back to you!'

Eleanor stopped short and a great wave of relief washed over her. Not, as she realised instantly, because of Ethelwig. No, because of Henry. He must have some softness towards her still; even the Chancellor could not have persuaded him unless he had.

'Oh, let us below out of this wind. Is his throat recovered? Come, you shall tell me all when we are comfortable.'

But it was not until they were back in England after as swift a winter crossing as any Eleanor could remember that Rohesia did tell all. She brought the Queen her nightly posset and being ordered to remain and talk, warmed her hands at the brazier. The Queen, her hair unbound, lay on the great couch, luxuriating in the stability of dry land. Contentment out of all proportion to her pleasure in Ethelwig's deliverance filled her.

'In my heart, I knew he would pardon him,' she said softly. 'We all know he can refuse the Chancellor nothing – but I am grateful, nonetheless.'

Rohesia kept her face averted. 'Nay,' she muttered. 'I will tell you lest some other should. . . . It was she who craved his life – that other – the King's wanton – and he granted it her.'

Eleanor's head jerked on the pillow. 'Why should she?' She sat up abruptly. 'He is English, like her. What connection is between them?' She pressed her hands together. 'God's Wounds! Can they be akin? How much else must I bear?'

'I know not why she asked it.'

All of Eleanor's old repugnance for the minstrel came to the surface. 'I'll not stand this. I'll turn him off!'

Slowly the old woman turned and eyed her mistress, then she came over and took Eleanor's tensed hands between her own plump, wrinkled ones. 'He's but a singing man – no true jongleur. His pretty voice is all he has.'

Eleanor shook her head from side to side. 'Oh, Rohesia,' she said, low and feverish, 'I shall not rest easy till she be dead.'

'Nay – nay, say it not. You could not—'

Eleanor stared and then began to laugh hysterically. '*Di meliora!* Who would perform such an act for me? Old fool – can you think that of me? But I fear nothing will go right between the King and me till she is no more in the world. A whole year now and he does not come near me. And now I am dismissed – back here to England.'

'You are to be Regent,' said Rohesia with a faint attempt at comfort.

'A bone to a dog whose hunting days are done. But if I could come upon her' – she tried to laugh again and failing, set her teeth together hard – 'did I that very thing, I should not know her. I do not know her likeness.' Her voice sharpened. 'Have you seen her?'

'I? No, but I've spoken with those who have. Some say she is fair, some say not. Beauty is in the eye of the beholder.'

'And the King's eye sees beauty. Well, so be it. Yet the minstrel shall go – let her have him who saved his life.'

There was a silence then between them while Rohesia laid away the Queen's garments. Eleanor watched her through her lashes while she put away the under tunic, but when she started to shake out the silken fouriaux that had encased the Queen's plaits, she bade her hurry quite curtly. Rohesia did not seem to move any faster but she knew her mistress wished for solitude, and when she had placed the half-bend of yellow gold beside the veil, she went towards the door.

'I'll sleep without,' she said. Eleanor nodded. She knew, and Rohesia knew, she had so ordered it, but by making the statement herself Rohesia's touchy, old woman's pride was saved.

When she was at last alone, Eleanor flung over in her lonely bed. Old fool! she thought again, She took me seriously. Had I but the power, though—

XI

April–May 1160

Ⅰɴ Somerset spring was late, and when it came summer
trod hard upon its heels, so that the silvery hazel catkins
and golden powder-puffs of sallow were swiftly overtaken
by the white froth of pear and the blush of crab apple.

To six-year-old Cicely this abrupt burgeoning came as a
revelation. She viewed the world with wonder and delight
for every day brought something new to see, carpets of
primroses and wood anemones, and a little later, lakes of
glistening pale gold by the ditch and along the brook where
celandines and kingcups grew.

At this time of year the mill was not working full time
and her father was cultivating the yardland; it was a job
he did not like and one which he felt his wife should under-
take, so when he speared his foot on a rusty quarrel turned
up by the plough, no one was surprised at his complaints
of a stiff leg and an inability to carry on. Beta's sympathy
was running short by the time he began to grumble about
jaw-ache; she told him his teeth had been rotten for years
and pretty soon they were at it hammer and tongs. Cicely
slunk quietly away.

She came back very late for dinner, for the sun was
nearly at the zenith, and as she skipped merrily along the
path by the brook, her shadow skipped too, close around

her feet. She hurried then, and more so when she heard a confused noise of shouting, but when she rounded the bend in the path and saw the boiling mass of neighbours by the door of the mill, she stopped dead. At length, she crept up closer and hovered at the edge of the crowd and then began to push and cry, 'Let me pass! What ails you all?' but the women tried to hold her back and keep her with them, saying, 'Do not let her see! Sweet Mother, hear him howl!' and others said more quietly, but still within her hearing, 'He is possessed!'

She became frantic with fear and began to weep, and at last finding a way through the press, forced a way in and up the stairs. She stood in the doorway and watched the miller who was writhing on the floor, and even as she watched, his body arched itself into a great bow, straining, with all the muscles rigid. Her mother held his head and two strong men dragged at his feet but it was useless, they could not straighten him. His face was contorted and the sounds that burst from him made her cover her ears with her hands. The priest stood in the corner, showering holy water in all directions and shouting to assault the very gates of Heaven but all to no avail; still Warin's body arched in spasms.

Then she heard the baron's voice, for someone had fetched him, and she ran to him like a terrified animal and pushed her head into his long, blood-red mantle, trying to blot out the sounds. It smelt pleasantly of his horse and dogs, and a little of himself, too, and so was comforting. She loved the baron for he came constantly to the mill and made much of her. He picked her up, swiftly and tenderly, and saying briefly, 'It is hopeless; he will die. Priest, have a care for his soul. Say the prayers for the dying and shrive him that God may know His own,' he carried her down the stair, waving away the staring villeins, and handed her up to his son, Sir Robert, who sat outside on his horse.

'Take her to your wife,' he said. 'I will stay till all is over. I have seen this thing before and it is very sure it is the end of the miller. God send that it be quick! Ride now, while I get rid of these fools.'

Sir Robert said not a word but pricked his horse, and they were away down the stony track at a speed that made the pebbles the horse kicked up fly into the stream with sharp little plops.

When Cicely had been put to bed upon a pallet in the corner of the room where Robert and Ysabel slept and had cried herself to sleep because of the manner of Warin's death, the baron came to look at her. She lay upon her back with an arm thrown up, her flushed cheeks still damp and a straggle of fair hair plastered across one of them. He bent over her, shielding the rushlight with one hand for it was dark in the little chamber, although outside the setting sun still shone. He could hear the rattle and squeak of trestles as the boards were dragged out for supper, and the low murmur of servants' voices as they went about their tasks.

She should not go back to the mill where the miller lay stiff and cold upon a plank while a coffin was prepared; no, she should stay here in her rightful place henceforward and soon her mother should come, too. And if my lady misliked it, she might do as she would. And his whey-faced daughter-in-law, as well. She had as yet produced no children to carry on his name; she had no voice here.

He put the rushlight down upon a press and sat upon a little stool. He had thought on this matter a long time and now his mind was made up, or rather, the miller's death had made it up for him. He wondered, with a faint self-contempt, why he had ever thought it necessary for Beta to marry at all. He had long forgotten his old fear of causing pain to others for now all the passion and tenderness of his nature was concentrated on the little girl he watched. Other men kept their bastard children – aye, and forced their wives to bring them up along with their own. There was good precedent – the King, too, had a base-begotten son among the Queen's children, if gossip were true. It had completely slipped his mind that he had done it once already.

He smiled and gently kissed the child's soft cheek, and taking up the rushlight again with care, went back into the hall. They were all around the board waiting for him, Lady Maud with tight-set mouth and Robert with the air of a man who listens intently to an inner voice.

'Now, my lord,' began his wife when he was hardly seated. 'Why is that villein child within the house? Is there no cottar in the vill who can shelter her?'

'Later we shall speak of her and of my intentions,' said the baron briefly. Lady Maud bridled but bent her head, and all ate in silence.

When the meal was over, Sir Richard said abruptly, 'Tomorrow the miller shall be buried and afterwards, his widow comes to this house to be with her child.'

There was a long silence, and Ysabel's eyes travelled from one to another and came to rest upon her husband, who would not look at her.

Lady Maud said in a choking voice, 'Not while I live shall that woman serve me!'

'No,' said the baron pleasantly, 'She shall not serve you, wife. But come she shall tomorrow, and there's an end on it.'

Lady Maud stood up so suddenly that she banged against the table and all the dishes leapt. 'Shall you treat me so?' she cried.

Sir Richard merely stared at her with narrowed eyes, and at last hers fell. 'It had been well had I beaten you in the early days of our marriage,' he said. 'A kind husband makes a saucy wife,' and he turned his head and looked at Ysabel so that she flushed darkly.

Though she could not hide the working of her lips, Lady Maud held up her head; then with a slow deliberate tread she went across the hall. She paused by the door a moment, lifting her heavy skirt away from a sniffing dog, and there

304

was dignity in every line of her squat, dumpy figure. She passed without, and they heard her go up the outer stair to the tower chamber which had lately been converted into her bower. The baron let her go.

Later that evening when the baron had retired, Ysabel spoke to Robert. 'Husband, will you not speak to your father?'

'No,' said Robert, quick and sharp.

'This is a sore, sad thing he will do to your – to his wife.'

He toyed with his mug and looked at her hard. 'I had thought my lady was not so high in your esteem,' he said.

'It is not a matter of my feeling. Will you not speak?'

'You have seen how he is with that Cicely – his life goes round and round about her. She is the sun in his sky.'

Slyly she said, 'And perhaps will put you out of some inheritance if she is here to twine around him further.'

He frowned at that. 'Nay,' he said slowly. 'My father will marry her as high as he is able, that is all. Say no more, wife, it is useless.'

'Oh, you men!' she cried. 'What you will have, you will have, and that which you will do, we poor women must endure!' and she sprang up and went weeping, hippity-hop, behind the screen.

Robert sat on, drinking with a grim face, and all the calm beauty of the twilight, seen through the open door, did nothing to soothe his spirit. As ever these days, his thoughts flew to a pair of flashing black eyes and a slow smile that promised long delight. He shifted about on the bench, knowing that he was in thrall, and that underneath like a subterranean stream, his love for Ysabel flowed unchecked, but quiet and slow, unlike the prick and fret of this new desire. But it was little comfort to him to know he still loved his wife – indeed, he would almost have preferred not to, what with the goading of his conscience and the silent reproach of her glances when he stayed long and unaccountably away.

The fact was that since Ysabel had had her front teeth

pulled by the monks' Infirmarian, after a great pain and swelling of her face, her smile had made him quail – and she had ceased to smile now, having once seen his eyes swiftly averted. He knew his coolness caused her pain, and that annoyed him, so that he began to look for other defects in her whom he had once thought incomparable. And now, her awkward, rolling gait that had before roused him to a fury of love and pity, made him angry, though whether with himself or her, he could not tell.

He began to dwell again upon that Agnes, who had been the Carter's girl and now was wife to Carpenter, and any man's bawd as he knew, until at last, in helpless rage, he banged down the horn mug on the board, making the wine within splash out all over his hand. Then he swore a violent oath and getting up, he flung off into the dusk, down to the cottars' huts, to seek her.

Three weeks went slowly by, and Cicely and Beta settled into the baron's household, though not without some back-biting and squabbling on the part of a number of the servants, who resented seeing those whom they considered bone of their bone set up above them. Beta answered not at all and warned Cicely to silence.

Lady Maud remained up in the tower chamber and only Mold went up to serve her. She clung to her mistress and never acknowledged Beta by so much as a look for she knew she was better far than the baron's leman. And not a one of my children was a bastard, she told herself. She betrayed my lady from the beginning – what else can be expected from one whose forebears were slaves before the Normans came? Sometimes I am minded to wonder just who did father that child. But when she ventured to say as much to Adam, he laughed her to scorn, pointing out that none could see the child and the baron together without knowing them related by the strongest ties of blood. The knowledge that it was true only increased her resentment, particularly as her husband went on to say that Cicely was far more like the baron than any of Lady Maud's children.

So an uneasy feeling hung over the house at Williton, and only Robert felt that he did not know where he stood, being torn between loyalty to his father and a kind of impatient pity for Lady Maud.

Then came a day when the baron, whose leg was troubling him enough to confine him to his chair and also to make him wish to vent some of his asperity on others, sent for Robert.

'What is this I hear of you and Carpenter's wife?' he began sharply, staring at his son and thinking that he looked less and less a Fitzurse with every year that passed. He was the spit and image of his mother's kin and what trouble might that not lead to? Saints be praised that he had no desire to be at Court!

Robert scowled and wished he dare say, the same as of you and Miller's widow. He did not, though, partly because he did not think it was the same; between Agnes and himself was none of the gentleness he had often witnessed between his father and Beta; partly he simply dared not because the baron's stick lay close to hand and he feared he would feel it across his shoulders. So he stood in surly silence.

'Answer me!' said Sir Richard testily. 'Is what I hear the truth?'

Robert muttered, 'I know not what you have heard.' Then he thought, Am I a green boy that he should speak so to me? and he lifted his head and said, 'I have whiled away some time with her as others have done' – he laughed shortly – 'aye, many others before me!'

The baron bit his thumb. 'What if she should bear your child?'

Robert laughed again at that. 'She has been wed these five and more years and only God knows how many men have had her, yet is she childless. Likely she is barren.' He thought,

That is all he cares about. He fears I may take it as precedent that he has brought his own bastards here. He said aloud, 'Who told you of it?'

Sir Richard shrugged. 'There is talk. One overhears it. If you are sure. . . .'

'Only God is sure,' said Robert, and then – 'Sir, I cannot help myself.'

The baron looked at him and sighed. 'Such women are a curse on men,' he said, but his tone was pleasanter. After a bit, he added, 'Your wife has no child, neither. I had thought. . . .' He leaned forward and jabbed at the sulky fire with his staff, sending up a shower of sparks.

Robert waited, watching him. When he sat back, he began again. 'It was to you I looked for an heir to Williton – but – no child in five years of wedlock! Reynold has at least his girl.'

'And a dead boy.'

'The fault lies not with him. He gets them on her – that's his part.' His mouth turned down. He looked hard at Robert. 'Does the fault lie with you? – or with your wife? Have you ever sired a child?'

Robert felt his cheeks redden. 'No. But this is the only other woman—' He frowned slightly. 'How may I inherit Williton? When last I was in Taunton, I spoke with the King's justices and they say he will have the law of primogeniture in England, that large estates may remain intact. The eldest son shall inherit all his father's honours, they said, and the younger ones make shift as best they can. Of bastards they spoke not at all.'

As always, when he thought of the irregularity of his birth, he felt an inner shrinking, made up of ignorance of his maternal antecedents and of old heart-burnings left too long unaired, so that when he spoke his voice came out loud and bitter. 'I am but your bastard son and as such, have no rights. Nor may I inherit anything which is yours.'

'Reynold shall not have Williton,' said the baron flatly,

308

'despite the laws, old or new. He has his manor in Kent and lands in Northampton besides that which his wife brought him. He must content himself with those.'

Secretly, he was thinking that he would send a man to my lord of Leicester as soon as he came back into England; if any could arrange the matter, it was the Chief Justiciar. The time was past when a baron might assert his will against his prince by force of arms. Now guile must take its place. Yet it went sore against his grain to beg as a favour what he felt was his incontestable right, to dispose of his own as he would.

Robert only shrugged, thinking that a dead man's writ does not run far. Once Reynold knew that their father was cold, he would invoke the due processes of law and pay the relief for his inheritance, and he, the bastard usurper, would be dispossessed. All the old anger against his fate rose up in him, and he said harshly, 'Truly it says in Holy Writ that the sins of the fathers shall be visited upon the children! I am no less your son than Reynold, yet so the King will have it.'

The baron's mood had softened or he felt some guilt for he made no reply to Robert's outburst for several seconds. Then he said quite gently, 'Do you feel your bastardy a stigma, then? I never knew.' He sighed. 'Yet the blood that runs in your veins is higher far than any here.'

Robert lifted his head and looked at him. 'Higher than Reynold's?'

The baron laughed at that, a curt and caustic laugh. 'Higher far. Your mother was a most noble lady – of a great Norman house whose name would be familiar to you – nay' – he lifted his hand in denial – 'I shall not tell you, nor will you ever persuade me. Let the past bury its dead. Yet never feel shame that my wife is not your mother for you outrank us all in blood.'

'And am a landless man.'

'I will not leave you landless. I shall enfeoff you on the

309

land at Orchard. All else will fall to you – trust me, my son.'

Robert wondered how closely he resembled this unknown woman who had been his mother – this daughter of an illustrious house who had been prepared to follow his father into England and bear him an illegitimate child. She must have loved him. He knew his father too well to suppose that he had coerced her in any way.

'Am I like her?' he said, daring because of the warmth that had developed between them.

The baron smiled faintly. 'Aye, very like.'

'Did you love her?'

'I was – fond of her.'

In that hesitant answer, Robert felt, lay the clue to their relationship. She had pursued his father, then – how relentlessly even he could not guess.

'How did she die?'

'In the wars. When I came again, she was dead – whose doing it was I never discovered. They were evil times – every man's hand was against his neighbour. It may even have been a mistake – a kind of madness came upon men then, laying waste and slaughtering—' He fell silent, staring at the tip of his staff as he pushed it idly among the rushes. 'Why do we talk of those old days?' he said.

But Robert's mind had drawn a parallel between his mother's pursuit of the baron and his own blind determination to have Ysabel – aye, even to the point of abducting her had it been necessary. He had thought of it, at any rate. When had passion died? When he had realised she was incapable of it?

'I find it strange that love breeds love so seldom,' he observed. 'That is a kind of madness, too.'

The baron's tone was dry. 'What – have you repented of your bargain? What complaint have you, then? Your wife loves you.'

'No.' said Robert slowly, 'No. She does not love me –

not *me*. She would have loved any husband who was kind to her.'

'Think yourself lucky, then,' said Sir Richard grimly. 'Better to be unloved than stifled in love you do not want.'

He meant Lady Maud, but Robert thought he was again referring to his mother, and all the sympathy he had been feeling for his father evaporated. He made an impatient movement and the baron frowned.

'Get yourself an heir,' he said.

'Aye,' said Robert, 'easier said than done, it seems. But at least, I know now what I am—'

'That blood must go on,' said his father. 'The finest blood in Normandy. Try again on your wife.' He looked sharply at his son, remembering his own young manhood. 'All cats are grey in the dusk,' he said, not without pity.

Upstairs in the tower chamber Mold watched her mistress. Lady Maud sat crouched forward on a stool warming her hands at a brazier for the May day was so chill that the bright sunshine seemed like treachery. A bitter wind had scoured the sky of cloud and left it a pale and shining blue. She muttered to herself as she sat, and every now and then her voice rose louder so that Mold could make out the long catalogue of complaint.

The Captain's wife thought of the words she had spoken a week ago. 'It is very sure he means to do away with me,' she had whispered vehemently. 'I have known for long that they all wish me dead. . . . All but Reynold, and he comes not. Even the servants – I have been watching them these many weeks. You are the only one that I may trust. You will help me, Mold?' – her voice rose wildly. 'I cannot go below to dine for fear they will put poison in my dish.'

Now she did not seem to be aware that she was not alone. Mold moved gently about gathering up the dishes from the last meal, keeping her eyes upon her mistress the whole time, even when she must peer awkwardly back over her own shoulder to do so. She backed out through the door when she had finished, through as narrow a space as she could, lest the blast of cold air disturb the withdrawn woman in the middle of the room. When she had closed it cautiously behind her, she stood a moment at the top of the stair looking down into the yard below, but at last, as if she had made up her mind to something, she started down the steps with an air at once nervous and determined.

After she had taken the dishes to the kitchens and exchanged a word or two with the cook, she went into the hall to seek the baron. When she had told him what she had to tell, she stood twisting her hands in the front of her old, drab gown.

'And she refuses to come below again to dine?' he said, rubbing his chin.

'Lord, she is certain sure that some are venturing to poison her,' Mold told him, 'though who she thinks 'they' are, I know not, nor I think does she, for she will say only 'they' – 'they' will do this or do that. When I asked her who 'they' were, she answered not but only repeated the tale of how she had watched them and seen them whisper behind her back—'

'You have not swallowed such a farrago of nonsense?'

'Nay – I have done all I may to persuade her it is false but so she will have it' – she hesitated a moment, then went on – 'Lord, that which my lady has eaten for the past week has come straight from the kitchens – the same meals as your own – but to quiet her mind, I did tell her I had prepared it myself. Had she known, she had refused it. She talks of naught else.'

The baron moved irritably. He knew the pain in his leg made his temper short but he would not be ruled by it; if his wife hoped to goad him by this perversity, she would be unsuccessful. He said, 'She hopes to gain attention by this means. . . . Do not go up again. Leave her alone a bit.'

As Mold went she murmured under her breath, 'Alone! She've been alone all this past week for I do think she knew not I was there. Aye, and afore that – there be none in this place that care for her, poor lady, not a one!'

After a bit, the baron picked up the little hand bell beside him and rang it with a grim look. When a servant hurried in, he said, 'Send for the chaplain to come to me.' Then he sat gazing abstractedly into a fire which seemed to throw out no heat, so dully did the sappy wood burn. A fat, white slug clung to the topmost log; as the warmth penetrated, it crept slowly along until coming to the end, it fell suddenly into the red heart of the embers beneath. Sir Richard watched it with unmoving face as it hissed and bubbled in the fire, then he heard the soft footsteps of the chaplain coming across the hall and turned to face him.

Master Ralph was not really a young man but somehow his neatly combed fair hair and soft plump cheeks gave him a spurious look of agelessness. He had an eager, ingratiating way of rubbing his hands together while he approached his face closely to whoever he was addressing; it was because his sight was poor but the baron did not know that and it irritated him. Now he leaned well back in his chair as the chaplain bent obsequiously over him and spoke more sharply than he had intended.

'Have you noticed any oddness in my lady's behaviour of late?'

The priest breathed heavily and opened his eyes very wide as one who is prepared to speak with the utmost frankness. Nonetheless, he brought his lips into close proximity with the baron's ear and spoke in little more than a whisper. 'Full glad am I that you have mentioned this, my lord, for there are matters I have had a mind to speak on – but that I scarcely—' He stopped and began again. 'Since you have

313

mentioned it to me, I feel that I may speak—' Then he was silent, chewing at his lip.

'Speak, then.'

'My lady comes not to Mass in the chapel and so I have carried the Sacrament to her – not that I mean to complain, though she is sound in body—'

'Speak closer to the point,' interrupted the Baron testily.

'It is thus, my lord,' said Master Ralph, all in a rush. 'I know that she has confessed to sins she cannot have committed. I feel that I must consult with the Bishop—'

Sir Richard raised his hand. 'Did you give her Absolution for these imaginary sins?'

'At first I asked for times and places – nay, more I cannot tell you, but that when I tried to reason with her, knowing them for false, she wept and swore on all that she held holy – aye, even upon this holy relic' – he held out his hand with a ring upon the finger in which was inserted a hair of St Lawrence – 'even upon this she swore, so that I came to know that it was not she who spoke but a devil who has possessed her and who would try to trick her soul down to Hell.' He drew a deep breath. 'I saw the devil look out of her eye at me,' he whispered, and Sir Richard saw that he was trembling.

The baron gave a sharp, involuntary movement and the sudden excruciating pain in his leg made the sweat start out on his forehead. 'Sit ye down, Master Ralph,' he said, waving his hand towards a stool. The moments while the chaplain seated himself and arranged his gown around him gave him time to collect himself, besides placing the priest's face farther from his own.

'What did you then?' he asked while Master Ralph kneaded his shaking hands together.

'I said "Fie on you for a naughty lady!" – though truly I knew it was not she—'

'So you have said,' returned the baron drily. 'It is an

314

extreme view that will hold my lady possessed. I cannot say that I have ever found her over scrupulous with the truth.'

Master Ralph's mouth popped open. 'Upon the holy relic—' he began.

'St Lawrence may have been more heavily maned than the lion in the King's menagerie – indeed, he must have been if every reputed hair of his is a true relic – but I beg leave to doubt it. Perhaps my lady doubts it, too.'

The chaplain looked sulky.

'What is your remedy?' said the baron, at last.

'If the Bishop will license me to perform an exorcism—'

'You shall not see the Bishop on this matter,' said Sir Richard with finality.

'We might beat her with rods to drive the devil out—'

'As well beat me.' The baron's face was grim as he stared past the priest at nothing. Then he looked at him and his expression was inscrutable. 'If anyone has devils, it is I. Will you scourge me, Sir Priest, in her presence and drive the devils out of both of us?'

The little priest gazed at him, open mouthed.

The baron inclined his head. 'I take your silence for assent. Bring your nine-tongued scourge, and Master Ralph, think not to tickle me. Lay on with a will, or by the Mass, I swear I'll wrap it round your own plump shoulders in a way you'll not forget!'

When Master Ralph had crept away, he thought, It will, at least, make me forget the pain in my leg for an hour.

The scourging took place two days later. Everyone was there to watch at the baron's order, Robert, Ysabel, two visiting knights with their squires and serving men – all except Cicely and Beta. Even the servants were clustered at the door, roused out of their usual stolidity by so unexpected an event.

When they explained to Lady Maud why she was to come below she came without demur. Throughout the scourging she sat with calm, untroubled face (and it was a true scourging; Master Ralph laid on with such good heart that the baron felt a belated admiration for him) – only when it was over she fetched a long, deep sigh and hung her head.

Someone helped Sir Richard to his chair and two pages gently smoothed goose grease over the bloody weals on his shoulders. He did not even wince but looked at her and said, 'Is your heart now at peace, wife?' She rose and came towards him, smiling for the first time since he had brought his leman back to the house.

At that moment, the door in the screen banged open and Cicely ran in. She stopped dead at the sight of the assembled company, and then she saw the baron, bare shouldered, with the chaplain nearby and the scourge still hanging from his hand.

The servants slunk aside to make a way for her but their eager, expectant glances fell before her puzzled face. Slowly she came on while Lady Maud stood as if turned to stone with the smile frozen on her lips. Then she sprang forward, moving so suddenly that all were taken by surprise. She was upon the child before any one could lift a finger, and the long, sharp carving knife that had lain upon the board was in her hand and raised aloft. Someone screamed shrilly.

Then the men were around her, pinioning her arms, while the baron with a face near demented bent over Cicely who lay amid the rushes. But it was Ysabel's bright blood that dripped beside her as she swayed, greenish-pale, above the little girl. Quicker than the rest and nearer, the knife had slashed across her arm when she had grabbed the child.

The baron raised a grey face. 'She is unhurt,' he whispered, and then, '*Deo gratias!*' He saw Ysabel and his face changed.

'Fetch cloths!' he shouted, 'Quickly!' but Robert and the servants were already around the fainting girl.

'Keep hold on her,' he said to the panting men who

316

struggled to subdue his wife. Wild eyed, she strained and gasped while dribbles of saliva ran down her chin.

'Yet does the devil live!' she ground out. 'All in vain the scourging. The succubus is yet amongst us!'

'Truly she is run mad,' he muttered. *'Deus misereatur!'* His face hardened. 'Take her above,' he bade them, 'and fetch chains. I will not risk her amongst us again. When she is locked away, bring me the keys.'

He cradled the crying child in his arms. 'All is over now, sweetheart,' he murmured. 'None shall hurt you. Do not weep so. See, here is your mother. Go now to her,' and he passed Cicely to Beta who stood trembling at his elbow.

When they had gone, he turned to Ysabel who lay back in his great chair and smiled at him feebly. 'You are a warrior and will bear the proof of it upon your body henceforth,' he said, and knelt and kissed her other hand. 'I owe you more than life.' His voice was hushed and hoarse.

She had never seen a man humble himself before a woman, and the sight embarrassed her so that she made light of her action and told him that, truly, the thing was done without conscious thought, by instinct, as it were.

He nodded, grave faced. 'That is my point. Blood tells. There have been times' – he hesitated, then continued. 'I should have known ere this—' He flushed, seeing her suddenly quizzical look. 'I am a poor judge. But you will forgive me?'

She nodded silently, for the hall was beginning to sway round her again and dissolve into grey mist.

'I am a fool as well. She has lost much blood,' the baron said in a louder voice, but there were only Robert and the chaplain to hear him for the servants were all gone and the knights and pages withdrawn to the other end of the hall where they were whispering excitedly together.

'You shall not find me ungrateful towards your wife,' he added formally to Robert. 'Henceforward she is mistress here and shall carry the Household Keys at her girdle.'

He shivered, realising that his shoulders were yet bare from the scourging. 'Fetch me a fresh gown,' he ordered, and the chaplain hurried off to see to it. 'Watch your wife,' he continued to Robert, 'as I will watch mine—'

He paced up and down before the fire until his man ran up and helped him into a fresh gown, and then he knocked upon his breast and Robert thought he heard him mutter, '*Peccavi!*'

Afterwards he went up the outer stair in the windy darkness, accompanied by Master Ralph who carried a flaring pine knot. He had forgotten his bad leg until halfway up he must stop and rest, though the stair was not so high. He leaned against the wall and heard the whine of the wind round the corner and the fluttering of the new leaves on the barren pear tree close beside him, and thought of Lady Maud: This is the last time that I shall look upon her face. Everyone knew that the mad must be locked away lest, like the excommunicate, they contaminate others.

But when he had negotiated the rest of the stair and went within and faced her, he was not so sure. She was sitting on a pallet and a chain was fixed to a band of iron about her ankle, and also to a great staple screwed into the wall, but her face was tranquil. She rose when he came in and the chaplain behind him stepped aside quickly so that the flame of the torch wavered and jumped. The room was very cold for the brazier had gone out.

She said, 'My lord, you must not believe the lies they report of me!'

'Lies?' he said. 'What lies?'

'You know,' she said.

'Nay, I do not. None have acquainted me with anything concerning you.'

'Did they not report that I had devised to poison you? Why else did they take the Household Keys from me?'

He stared at her, puzzled at this change of tack. 'On my orders, madame. This night murder was nearly done—'

'Murder!' Her voice rose. 'More lies! Nay, nay, my lord.' An expression almost artful crossed her face. 'It is murder only where Norman blood is spilt.' She stopped abruptly.

The baron nodded coldly. 'That was true in time gone by. I see your wits have not entirely left you. Is that your defence?'

She shook her head blindly and tried to kneel before him but the chain incommoded her so that she half fell beside the pallet. 'There was a devil there,' she whispered harshly. 'Did you not see it? Oh, my lord, it was only of my love for you—'

Master Ralph's eyes met the baron's and they both drew back.

'Go to your rest, lady,' said the baron heavily.

Once they were outside on the stair again, the little priest said, 'You believe now a devil is within her. Yet if you will treat her body to hardship, he may leave her, for devils will not stay where they may feel suffering.'

'Well, if you mean that I should starve her and freeze her, I cannot do it,' returned the baron sharply. 'She shall have fires and she shall have food—'

But not the sight of me, his inward thought ran on. Nevermore the sight of me.

That night he could not sleep. His conscience was clear but slumber would not come. Scurrying like mice about the corners of his mind, his thoughts ran on and on. Is it my fault I cannot love her, nor never could? The guilt is my father's, who would marry me to her against my will – and yet, God knows, I pity her for I know she loves me.

He dwelt for a time upon that pitiful circumstance until the idea struck him that that very painful, helpless loving was the weapon she had always held at his breast. I am still trapped, then, he thought, held fast by what I am and what she is. It were kinder in God to take her to Himself, now

319

that she has come to this. Why should I fear the blame is mine? He turned uneasily upon the couch as though to escape from something. But still, she has the better part – she had always the certainty of rectitude. And then – Were I another manner man. . . . He sighed upon the futility of such a thought and fell asleep.

A week went by and Lady Maud remained in the upper room of the tower with no change in her condition; at intervals she could be heard shouting wildly and then none would approach her, but latterly all had been quiet and Mold reported that she did not speak at all.

All the same, the thought of her was never very far from the baron's mind. He would be thinking of something else entirely – his granary which was lower than it was this time last year, the rumour he had heard that the Queen was back in England acting as Regent, the new kindness between his daughter-in-law and himself – and he would suddenly become conscious of an underlying discomfort fretting him as though his hose were wrinkled in his boot; then he would remember her up there alone.

Because of this he was more silent than usual when Ned, his man, came to give him his weekly shave. Ned had a club foot and the baron had taken him early from parents who worked him too hard so that Ned loved him devotedly, being convinced that his master was endowed with Christ's own compassion. Only the baron knew that was not true; it was done for his own peace of mind. And it was long ago, whether he would do it now was another matter.

While Ned laid out the shaving things he thought again of Maud's plight; yet, knowing most certainly that there were devils everywhere waiting their chance to creep into the mouth of man or woman and bring a soul to destruction, he still could not believe she was possessed. She was still too much the Maud he knew, foolish, illogical, obstinate. She had managed to persuade herself that witchcraft was afoot in her house and somehow it had come back upon her so that she must suffer the consequences.

It had all gone wrong for her as it always did, and once again, the eternal question 'why?' arose. She was no less worthy, no less comely than many another wife whose life had taken pleasanter paths, whose husband doted upon her and whose children were her devoted slaves. Yet he bore with her as with a crippling burden, not one of their children had shed a tear when marriage parted them from her and she was ill served by everyone except Mold who was of that same deadly stamp herself. He had never been able to feel any fondness for her, only a sinking of the heart when she was near and a terrible pity that he knew would enrage her did she suspect it. And she was a good Christian; there was no taint of heresy in Maud such as he sometimes surmised in himself; that made it more unjust.

He sighed heavily as Ned wrapped him in his gown and the man looked at him with the eyes of a devoted hound. 'Do you love me, Ned?' he said.

'I'd cut off my right arm for you,' said Ned with sincerity.

The baron shook his head in wonder. 'Why?'

'Why?' Ned stared. 'I'm your man and you are my lord.'

'That's no true reason.'

Ned shrugged and draped the linen cloth around the baron's neck. 'I'll love a man who loves the poor and weak for Christ His sake,' he said. 'There's none so many.'

The baron lifted his chin as Ned bent over him with a soapy badger's foot in his hand; he thought the man had told the truth as he saw it but he knew, deep in himself, that we are as likely to be loved for no reason as for false ones; the winds of love blow where they will with neither list nor cause.

XII

May 1160

Since a truce had been agreed with Louis of France, many of the English knights returned home – 'better they eat the produce of their own manors than live out of my pocket', the King had remarked to Thomas.

Hugh refused Reynold's offers of the hospitality of Barham. Beatrice was relieved. She had not wanted to talk about the death of her child, more than a year ago, before Hugh; she feared that Reynold, obtuse as she knew him to be, would sense the undercurrents between them. As it was, she could weep freely without the creeping discomfort of his sardonic gaze.

But Reynold was kind. He spoke of it quietly and did not blame her, saying only that they had many years before them to breed fine sons. She did not answer and he did not press her.

Later, when they sat together, he asked her in an airy way, but watching her closely the while, how things had gone upon the manor. How had she managed with no man but Steward? – had she called for assistance to any neighbour? – had any young knights ridden hither? Guessing the reason for his questions, she told him she had fared very well without male help; Steward was capable enough. As for any young knights riding hither, she had not laid her eyes on any man but her own servants, as little Maud, now two years old and full of childish prattle, could tell him.

He seemed easy in his mind and started telling her about the Chancellor.

'And you, sire? Were not the French ladies fair?' She did not really wish to know anything about his amours but she thought she might discover something of Hugh's behaviour through him.

'Oh, fair enough,' he said, grinning.

'And your companions?' she asked, 'Sieur de Tracy and Sieur de Morville? Did they find a lady whose favour they might sport?'

'We saw little enough of damsels,' he said, 'but that'd not fret Hugh.'

Warmth glowed in her.

'Not while there's a pretty lad about,' he finished.

It seemed a sharp blade pierced her vitals. Her cheeks were stiff; she felt her face would shatter if she tried to speak. He did not see her stillness but talked on.

'That page of his – he's an obliging, pretty boy. That's what Hugh likes – someone who'll oblige him. They all fall deep in love with him, women and boys alike.'

He pulled at his lower lip, distorting it, and she thought, you are so ugly, and hated him.

'I thought *you* had a fondness for him once,' he said.

She stood up suddenly and fearing she would faint, held fast the table while the room moved sickeningly.

'But then, I warrant you saw he'd as lief a boy as a woman,' he continued, and then, 'Jesu, but I'm dry! Where's the wine?' He beat upon the table impatiently. 'Time the master came home! If this is how you're served—'

Steward came then with wine and little honey wafers and she sat down.

'Not I,' she said, 'but you. Always you hung after him. Why did you bring him here?' To her surprise, her voice was normal.

'Me?' said Reynold and shouted jarringly with laughter. He caught her expression and stopped suddenly, looking puzzled. 'Nay – and yet – there's none like him.'

She said, 'I think he has sold his soul to the devil.'

'Aye?' said her husband, 'Marry! if he did, Satan had the worst of the bargain! I could tell you tales of him—'

Then he recounted to her the story he had been burning to impart ever since he came home.

Beatrice kept her head down. 'He did not tell you – or the others – who this woman was?'

'No, only that she was the wife of some baron. He duped her most befitting – we had many a laugh about it. Thinking him a noble knight! and there he was, screwing her tiring woman, too.' There was reluctant admiration in his voice. 'He's a very prince of whoremongers! And a fitting match for faithless wives!'

He leaned towards her; the wine was going to his head and his cheeks were flushed. 'I'll tell you what I think – his wife's some great North country mare he don't fancy. He'll let none of us see her, will he?'

He began to stroke her arm and she closed her eyes.

'Time for bed,' he said. He thought he would essay a few of the tricks Hugh had spoken of.

July 1160

In spite of Henry's keeping Hikenai close by him now, her life was lonelier than before. He was not uxorious; his passions slaked, he could forget her until the needs of his body reasserted themselves, nor did he ever wonder how she who had not been bred to read or embroider could occupy the empty days.

Much of his time was spent with Thomas hearing lawsuits for since he was the fount of justice, the cases with their prosecutors and defendants must come where he was. His old dream of legal reform had come to nothing yet but it remained in the background of his mind as a cherished aim. He knew he would face difficulties; he had sworn to uphold the established order at his coronation and his English, more than any other of his peoples, clung to the principle that their old laws were as immutable as God Himself. 'The old order changes' was an idea they would fight to the last drop of their blood. So far he was popular with them because he had used the royal justice to safeguard and punish evil-doers; that the system of fines he had instituted had proved profitable to the Crown was a pleasant accident. Henry knew, though, there were loop-holes in the law by which the innocent could be oppressed and his strong sense of abstract justice was offended. He *would* promote reforms despite the resentment of his English barons.

He had taken one tentative step in that direction last Christmas at Falaise when he had issued a decree that 'no dean shall bring an accusation against any person without the testimony of such individuals in the neighbourhood as are of good life and reputation'. That had been the outcome of his brooding on the case of the blackmailing Dean at York eighteen months ago, when Theobald upheld what Henry considered far too light a sentence.

But first this business of Pope and Anti-Pope must be settled. The whole matter made him irritable. He could, he felt, spend time more profitably than in listening to tales such as that repeated by the Bishop of Lisieux: that Pope Victor had surrendered the Fisherman's Ring to the Emperor of the Germans, receiving it back again as a sign that he was invested with the Holy See by Frederick Barbarossa. While each of the two Popes hurled anathemas and excommunications at the adherents of the other, he, the King of the English, must cool his heels like any commoner awaiting the outcome of a battle.

However, more and more men of influence in western Europe were rallying behind Pope Alexander. In England, it appeared, Victor's only follower of any importance was the Bishop of Winchester, Henry of Blois (he who was brother to the late King), and that presumably was because the Anti-Pope claimed some distant kinship with him. It was, at last, enough for Henry to make his decision. England should follow Alexander.

In June he received a very circumspect letter from Theobald (or John of Salisbury, it was all the same) informing him that the English clergy advised the same course, and he immediately ordered the Norman bishops to meet him at Neufmarché to offer their counsel. At nearby Beauvais, across the border, Louis of France was conferring with his bishops on the same problem.

All the bishops had known for some time what was expected of them. Indeed, Rotrou of Rouen had already issued the order to recognise Alexander to his suffragan bishops through his nephew, Archdeacon Giles, and it was Giles' eagerness to attest his Archbishop's willing acceptance of the King's will that caused the pother.

His smile was smug. 'The orders are already gone out, sire,' he lisped.

'What orders?'

'Why – the orders to recognise Pope Alexander.'

'Ah . . .' Henry's eyes glittered. 'You knew in advance of the rest of us what the decision of this Council would be? You deal with necromancers, perhaps?'

Thomas closed his eyes and looked away from the agonised wrigglings of the unfortunate Archdeacon.

All of Henry's pent up acerbity burst forth. He called upon his Maker to witness the disobedience – nay, the impertinence of subjects who put themselves above their Prince. He cried upon Him to strike down this miserable worm who had dared to – at this point, he smote the table with such force that for several seconds he merely gibbered, rocking back and forth nursing his bruised hand, and finally he swore so long and horribly that Thomas drew a sharp breath of protestation.

When the tears of pain and outrage in his eyes had dried,

326

the King leaned back and snapped his fingers for the Captain of the Guard. He pointed to the quaking Archdeacon.

'Know you his dwelling? The small house next the Archbishop's? It shall be torn down, stone by stone. Those are my orders! Let him be as his Master – that hath not where to lay His head!'

Thomas looked up abruptly, his expression of dismay almost comical. 'My lord – my lord King!' he exclaimed. 'It is true the house you have ordered demolished belongs to Archdeacon Giles but – but it is my lodging!'

Henry scowled, but he was feeling a great deal better after his outburst and the Archdeacon was weeping in a most gratifying way. He watched him for a moment.

'Well,' he said, 'you hear, Archdeacon? You have my most noble Chancellor to thank for the saving of your house. For, mark me, if he had not required it—'

Archdeacon Giles fell upon his knees before the King and Thomas. Henry grinned suddenly, his old irrepressible boyish grin. He had, all at once and for no reason, thought of Hikenai. She should come to him tonight. He slapped Thomas on the shoulder, ignoring the bishops. 'Come, Tom,' he said, and then with a cursory glance round, 'We'll meet again tomorrow and I'll hear from those of you who have not spoken yet.'

But Hikenai did not come to the King that night. He received a message that she was sick and feared to come lest she infect him. Henry considered sending for one of the town whores and then dismissed the idea. It would not be the same. He hoped, with some impatience, she would soon be better. It was annoying that on the night he required her she must feel unwell. He spent a restless night.

He met with the bishops again the following day and, once more, trouble ensued. This time the culprit was the Bishop of Le Mans, who had been foolish enough to obey Archbishop Rotrou's orders and promise obedience to Alexander's legates who were in the district awaiting the result of the synod. Henry's anger at this presumption was not to be so easily assuaged today. He signed orders for all the Bishop's houses to be razed and none of Thomas' pleading could make him change his mind. He was their lord and they should know his power. If the Chancellor had been silent then, Henry might have forgotten their recent differences of opinon, but Thomas' concern for the Bishop outweighed his customary caution when dealing with his choleric King and Henry was reminded that this was not the first time his friend had tried to usurp his authority. His upper lip lifted like a snarling dog's as she shouted, 'No! and no! and no!' and Thomas sank back, startled.

That night he hatched a little plan, and next day gave secret orders to the messengers to ride as slowly as possible to Le Mans, hoping that in the meantime Henry's anger would cool and he would have time to head them off before they reached their destination.

But within two days, Henry's thoughts were as far removed from the Bishop of Le Mans and his threatened property as they could possibly be. He had had a garbled message from de Mandeville, who had it from one of his captains, who in his turn had had it through who knew how many — a message delivered by a drab who knew not whom she wanted nor of whom she spoke. The lord's whore lay gravely ill — aye, let the lord know his whore lay near to death. Which lord? — how could she know? — the lord who dwelt within, no doubt. Here was the place to which she had consented to bring word and it looked as though she would not get a penny for her pains although she had lost good silver by coming. Her sullen muttering and wild looks had not inclined the gate keeper to place much credence in her information — he had but mentioned it to his superior in order to complain of the wretched manner of folk who dwelt hereabouts, and he had not thought it important enough to postpone his supper for. One way and another, it was two nights and a day before the King heard anything.

He heard it with disquiet. There was always fever in the town in summer and he had heard of a few deaths – not enough to cause concern in the ordinary way, but now. . . . He sent de Mandeville post haste to her lodgings.

De Mandeville, who had grown much in goods and confidence since the day he had escorted that wench to London, was pricked in his pride; he felt himself worthy of better tasks than to play the pander. He did not dare to disobey, but sent his squire to hammer on the door of the house next the smithy while he sat his horse with an air of high-nosed arrogance that went oddly in such surroundings.

'Go in,' he told his man, 'see for yourself how sick she is.' When the squire returned, he spoke sharply, 'Well? Does she lie near death?'

The young man signed himself. 'Sick enough, my lord, to be out of her wits. She surely has a fever.'

'Who cares for her?'

'Only the goodwife. She it was who sent the message. There was none other she could send and she said she dared not leave the King's love while she lay so sick.'

De Mandeville clicked his tongue against his teeth. 'We must inform his grace,' he said, 'and that with speed. If she should die before he comes. . . .'

In the little room where Hikenai lay ill, it was dark and very hot, for in spite of the summer weather a huge fire burned in the middle of it. The smoke made its way up through a hole in the roof above but when the door was opened, it swirled around the room, acrid and pungent from the herbs the smith's wife cast upon it at intervals. De Mandeville's squire had not come in; he had stood in the doorway, peering through the gloom at her. She was not conscious he was there.

This intermittent fever had first come upon her nearly a year ago when she was in Toulouse with the ragtag of Henry's army, but until now it had never interfered with her associations with the King. The attacks would begin with a violent headache, sometimes with vomiting, and she would crawl away to her couch and wait for it to pass. She suffered it like an animal, alone. Nor did she ever speak of it except to those who saw her while she lay stricken, and she accepted all their various remedies without discrimination, vile as most of them were.

It was this peasant submissiveness that had enabled her to leave the babe Peter to the care of the monks at Merton. Henry had ordered it and there was nothing else to do. He would be bred up a Christian monk and never know his divine heritage but that, too, must be part of the God's design. And Geoffrey – her child and Henry's – would never know her, either. She did not ask for reasons. She knew that human life was ruled by forces too remote and implacable for human understanding. Compassion and benignity were far beyond her comprehension. The God gave power and passion and pleasure; he did not know of love.

There had been times after she came again to Normandy when she had wept with despondency. Henry's presence could not compensate her now for a greater loss, though she was blind to its identity – until she once more heard the whispered gossip of doings at full moon, gossip that ceased abruptly with finger on lip and sidelong glance at strangers.

Gradually she had been accepted and had danced again around the Sacred Tree, though always on the fringe of the rites as a guest. Never more would she sit among the Great Ones. But at least she was a votary; she was not shut off eternally from that supernal ravishment.

And she had made friends with one of the old crones who dealt in magical potions. From her, she had procured the receipt for the flying ointment – henbane, monkshood and deadly nightshade, mixed, the old woman had confided, with the fat of a pig which had been slaughtered at the dark of the moon. She had sold Hikenai a precious potful and

330

she kept it hidden away among her most treasured possessions – an elfshot she had found as a child, a chain of yellow
gold the King had given her, its fair colour dulled with
encrusted dirt, a piece of silken stuff she had begged from
Dame Hermengild because its bright, deep blue sheen filled
her with inexplicable yearning, an oddly shaped root that
resembled her talisman of long ago and a vial of dark green
glass containing a syrupy fluid. It was all that remained of
the enchanted elixir used by the adepts to bring the God
among them at the height of the ritual observance. She
also had a thumb ring (the stone was a ruby), which Henry
had given her after Geoffrey's birth; she thought it pretty
but did not value it overmuch.

Now she lay tossing and muttering on the pallet in the
dark, foetid room as the glaring July day softened into sunset. The watching goodwife heard the jingling of harness and
the gentle blowing sounds of horses outside but she was
unprepared for the sight of the Duke himself. (So she thought
of him, being a Norman.) Another gentleman was with him.
Henry had persuaded Thomas to accompany him, not
without some difficulty until he had brought forward the
Church's injunction to visit the sick. Then Thomas had
agreed.

The goodwife was in something of a fluster because she
had taken the opportunity to seethe some puddings on the
fire for which the Duke was paying, but to her relief, he
ignored her presence altogether and went quickly over to the
pallet in the corner. He turned away from it abruptly, not
saying anything, but she saw how his face had dropped and
the lost, helpless look on it.

'Where's the physician?' he muttered, and at that moment
another man came in, cowled so she could not see his face.
He knelt by the sick woman, laying his hand upon her
sweating brow and lifting up her heavy eyelids, then with a
questioning look at the Duke, pushed back the coverlet and
laid his ear to her breast. He examined her neck and the

331

insides of both arms and finally sat back on his haunches and appeared to be thinking. All the while, the Duke watched him as a child will watch his mentor, caught between faith and fear. He spoke then to both the Duke and the Chancellor, as though it concerned them equally; it was medical lore and the goodwife did not understand a word of it.

The Chancellor turned towards her. 'What have you given her?' he said.

'Hot ale to make her sweat', she told him, 'and the root of elecampane.'

'Nothing else?'

She hesitated, then told him of the paste of mouldy bread and lees from the brewing which a neighbour had provided.

'No use – no use at all,' pronounced the physician. 'That will not drive this demon out. I will make up a draught.' He began to murmur under his breath to his assistant who had crept in behind him – 'Honey and child's faeces well blended, fly droppings and human urine—'

She did not strain her ears to hear the rest but bent to stir her puddings. She had rather have the wise woman's remedies than such stuff as doctors dealt in. However, when the medicine arrived, she dosed Hikenai with it and because or in spite of it, her senses returned to her a few hours later, and she slept peacefully through the night.

Henry came again next day, alone this time, kicking aside the squawking chickens that pecked around the threshold. When he saw she knew him his face brightened but her pallor and listlessness soon brought back the troubled look. He told her anxiously that the doctor had forbidden her being moved and that he could not stay long now – 'but I will send the Chancellor to ask after you, my love. He will bring a priest to you later – it was he who thought of it, to my shame. "There's no finer cure than the Sacrament for any ill," Tom says.'

'No,' she said.

Holding her hand, he stared at her.

'No,' she said more vehemently, 'no priest – I want no priest.'

It was the first time she had gainsaid him.

'But you are sorely sick – but yesterday we feared sick unto death. . . .'

'Shall I die, then?' she muttered, and her whiteness suddenly terrified him. 'I did not look to die so soon.'

'No!' he said, 'you shall not die! I'll not—'

'Give me your word,' she whispered. 'If I should die – swear you will tell your son and mine of his brother. Swear it, Henry, that I may die in peace.' Her voice grew more feeble. 'Both are my sons. Geoffrey has you but Peter has no one. It is an ill thing to be without kin.'

'You shall not die. Have I not said it?'

She made the faintest attempt at a smile. 'King of the English, does your power run so far? Pledge me your word.'

He closed his eyes. She will not really die, he thought, and feeling the insistent pressure of her fingers, said, 'I swear.'

He felt her hand relax in his. When she seemed to sleep, he called the goodwife to watch over her. 'I shall return later,' he informed her, 'and will leave a man to carry messages.'

She nodded and watched him ride away. When she returned Hikenai opened her eyes and said with an effort, 'Give me the leathern purse from out the coffer.'

The woman's eyes were bright and curious as she laid the purse upon the couch. 'He's much concerned for you,' she said, prepared to remain and gossip.

Hand upon her purse, Hikenai waited. 'I will rest now,' she said.

The goodwife stood a moment, uncertain. She was aware she had been repulsed but since she found it difficult to place this girl in the tight hierarchy of the lower orders, she did not know whether to be offended or not.

333

Left alone, Hikenai drowsed. An inexpressible longing possessed her, a yearning that went too deep for words. If she might once more know that glorious communion with Him. . . . Ah, not the hot and hairy revels, no, it was the bright mystery which beckoned, the sweet seduction, entrancing, enticing past all earthly love. Once she had walked in that sublime sphere beyond the world and been at one with Him. . . .

She moved and felt the purse beneath her hand. With fumbling fingers she untied the thongs and laid her possessions out in front of her. Here was the pot of flying ointment and the vial of precious liquid; the rest she pushed aside. These two small objects would, she believed, call the Great One from the Other World – call Him here to this room. Would He come to her alone with no other supplicants to offer worship? And take her with Him past that shining threshold?

Carefully she untied the string and removed the piece of pig's bladder from the top of the pot; she applied her nose to it and her wan face twitched. Then she scooped her fingers in, and pushing her hand beneath the coverlet, began to massage the greasy stuff into her belly and loins. The effort made her sweat again.

After a while she unstoppered the vial; she smelt that, too, and hesitated a moment. Her heart was beginning to beat erratically and she felt dizzy. She put the vial to her lips – how much? She could not remember. It seemed she was swinging up and down between Heaven and earth – how amazed would the smith's wife be should she fly clean away! Abruptly she swallowed the contents of the vial at a single gulp.

Because of his anxiety for Hikenai, Henry summarily disposed of his Norman bishops by an unexpectedly early announcement that their arguments had swayed him in favour of Pope Alexander and that henceforth all his subjects would owe allegiance to that Pontiff. Diplomacy alone had obliged him to listen to what was euphemistically termed advice, but even courtesy to the Church could not be allowed to interfere with his personal concerns. Having wound up the Council with a lack of ceremony that made the bishops look down their noses, he arranged to return immediately to the sickbed of his love.

He had just mounted his horse when he saw the tall figure of his Chancellor approaching, and pulled hard on the reins.

Thomas was breathless. 'The priest I sent has this moment returned,' he said. 'She – she has refused his ministrations.' He shot the King a swift glance under his eyelids but Henry made no answer.

Sir Eudes repeated her words to me – 'let me die after my own way,' she said, "I will not eat your Christian God." He was in much perturbation for he thought her nigh unto death.'

'Blood of God!' said Henry. 'She was better – much better.' His face was distraught. 'I must go!' and he spurred his horse forward so that Thomas must leap sideways. 'Bring the physician!' he shouted over his shoulder. Thomas' lips tightened a little. The greatest friendships may be presumed upon and he was beginning to wish he had never been brought into this affair.

The trembling goodwife met Henry on the doorsill and beating her hands together cried that it was none of her doing, she had done no more than give what the doctor sent – Henry's arm brushed her aside as though she were no more than a persistently buzzing fly.

He heard the slow, uneven snoring as soon as he entered and it came to him as a shock that he feared to approach, feared to look close. He turned to call and realised he was alone; in his haste, he had given no orders for the escort to follow.

'*Miserere mei, Domine*,' he muttered hoarsely and suddenly saw the priest sitting in the corner, who sprang up

335

at the sight of the King and started to repeat what Thomas had already told him. 'It is a strong demon that possesses her,' he said, 'and yet – and yet when I sprinkled her, she did not flinch. I thought no demon could abide the touch of holy water.'

'Let be, let be,' said the King harshly, and then in a voice that struck the priest as piteous, 'She must not die!'

He merely crossed himself and stood aside, being certain from experience of many deathbeds that she was past all help.

Henry's eye had fallen on the strange assortment of objects on the counterpane; the ring and chain he recognised and he sat down, dully fingering the rest. Thus Thomas, following with the doctor, found him.

When the physician slowly shook his head and spread his hands in indication of his impotence, it was Thomas who nodded permission for him to leave. Henry continued to sit with downbent head, making no move to wipe away the tears that dripped steadily from his chin. Sick with pity, Thomas looked away. As with every helpless onlooker at unbearable grief, the longing to escape was paramount. Quietly he edged away but Henry's hand shot out, staying him.

The hours they sat in silence save for the murmur of the priest reciting the Prayers for the Dying were eternity to Thomas. He saw the oddly shaped root on the pallet and its likeness to that other thing the dying girl had owned was clear. That, and her refusal of the Sacrament, meant only one thing. A qualm that was almost fear assailed him. She was of the faery folk – her small stature should have given him the clue. Well, she could harm none now, if the harm were not already done. As to her destination after death, he need not dwell on that. Yet what could he say to the King, whom she had enchanted and whose love for her had been sincere, if unhallowed? He prayed for guidance.

The stertorous breathing slowed and paused, began again

336

with a gasping effort and quieted. Henry leaned nearer as she gave one last long rattling sigh and died.

Thomas put his hand on the King's shoulder and felt it begin to shake. Henry made no sound; he just stared dumbly at the dead clay on the bed. He had wept all his tears. Only silence meets the case when the world ends.

When he knew that there would be no mercy and he must keep on living, he spoke in the direction of the priest and his voice sounded unnatural, even to himself. 'You will mention her refusal of the Sacrament to no one. It was not she who spoke but the – the sickness which killed her. She is with God' – he looked at his Chancellor as though daring him to interrupt and any inclination Thomas may have had deserted him in that instant – 'and it is my will that she be laid to rest in Rouen Cathedral. See to it. Wait for me without, Tom.'

Thomas and Sir Eudes did not exchange a word, nor did they allow their eyes to meet as they left the smith's house. Thomas sat on the bench outside and bit his knuckles after the priest had ridden away; he did not even notice the handful of loiterers, who, scenting news, had gathered a little way off.

When he was alone Henry sat on the stool beside Hikenai's body, elbows on knees and his head in his hands. The ashes of the fire sighed and settled on the hearth, and he raised his head and stared about the room. He spoke aloud then in a wild, lost voice, 'How could You do this to me?'

After a while he began to whisper to himself, or perhaps to anything of her that lingered still. 'You were ever gentle, love. Gentle and meek as I found no other. How shall I fare without you?' He rocked to and fro, remembering how he had ever waited indulgently on her slow answering. Now he might wait throughout eternity.

And in eternity how should he come upon her? What place for her in any Christian Heaven? He had taken a

337

perverse pleasure in her link with the dark, archaic mysteries that surrounded the legend of his faery ancestress, yet his own beliefs, however tenuous and mingled with remnants of pagan superstition, were Christian and he could not reconcile one with the other.

Theological doubts were new to Henry. None but madmen would question the truth of Christianity. Had she truly said, 'I will not eat your Christian God'? Surely they had mistaken her meaning – but even the violence of his desire to do so could not make him believe that. No, it was as he had told them, the sickness working in her mind.

Yet a kind of revulsion was rising in him against any and all beliefs. How had he deserved to suffer so? In his mind, the first seeds of dubiety were sown; a doubt that God truly cared for Henry FitzEmpress, and many layers beneath it, the concomitant response: that neither should Henry FitzEmpress care for God. From those seeds a bitter crop would come to harvest in the future.

When Hikenai's body had been taken to the nuns, the King rejoined Thomas. They rode together in a silence that Henry did not notice and Thomas found unendurable. He broke it by murmuring condolences so vague and general that the King merely shook his head.

Thomas was in a quandary. He knew this was a bad time to mention the matter but if he could not persuade the King otherwise before nightfall, the Bishop of Le Mans would lose his houses. Unless he sent messengers tonight they could not intercept the original force. Somehow he found the words to frame the plea.

The King slowly turned his head to stare at him. Something in his expression made Thomas think of the way he had looked at him when they had quarrelled outside Toulouse, and he was puzzled.

He said gently, 'Do you not recall that you gave orders to destroy the Bishop's houses?'

338

'I remember,' the King replied, still staring at him in that odd way. 'Well, have your way, then. It does not matter now. Nothing matters now.'

Thomas frowned slightly. Henry was taking the death of his minion very ill, yet words of comfort were hard to find. It was even more difficult than he had anticipated to pretend sympathy for what he felt was the best thing for everyone.

'You will not always hold that view,' he ventured at last. 'And though sorrow overwhelms at first, grace may come of it. Remember that pain willingly accepted will gain its reward. God will never be outdone in generosity.'

But the King gazed at something only he could see. He was thinking that God might grant him the world, but that on his side no gratitude would be owing. He was out of God's debt for ever.

August – November 1160

Eleanor the Queen sat in her privy chamber in the Palace of Westminster; a courier had come this day with letters from Normandy and among them was one she would not open until she was alone. She fingered it now, wondering. The lady who had written was the wife of one who had accompanied Henry, and her faithful friend. If she had written, there was news of moment, over and above the usual gossip of the King's doings.

With the official missives which she had read earlier was one from Henry ordering her to Normandy next month, accompanied by the royal children so that Young Henry, now five years of age, might do homage to Louis of France for Normandy. It seemed to her that he was over young for such a ceremony and she was struck by a sudden premonition that Henry might be ailing. Certainly, it was unlike him to delegate any of his honours. If he truly intended to invest their son with the Duchy. . . . With sudden decision she broke the seals of the letter.

It was very short, no more than a few lines and evidently

339

penned with difficulty by the lady herself. After she had read it twice Eleanor sat with a faraway look, her hands smoothing the parchment on her knee. Then she stood up, walked to the window and read it again. Rohesia, at her eternal embroidery, raised her head and watched her with some interest.

'The English whore is dead,' said the Queen and offered her the letter.

Rohesia did not take it. Her eyes widened a little and then fell; she did not know where to look but she would not look at the Queen. There was silence between them.

Eleanor laughed harshly and addressed Rohesia's averted head. 'Prayer is sometimes granted then,' she said, 'for he has sent for me again.'

Rohesia looked up then, and accusation and censure were plain in her expression.

Eleanor drew a sharp breath. So Rohesia imputed to her not only the wish but the deed – and all for hasty words spoken in a moment of stress. Yet something in her – pride, or honesty, perhaps – would not allow her to exculpate herself. For she would have arranged the deed had it been within her power, and knowing it, could not deny it. Aye, Rohesia knew her capable of such an act, and so there was no more to be said.

No more to be said, but something to be done. Rohesia should be pensioned off. She was growing old – too old for the incessant, weary journeys of Court life. Eleanor made up her mind that when she travelled again to France, Rohesia should be offered a haven in some Norman convent. Why, if she were still here, and that other child in her Household, the bastard Geoffrey, should sicken and die of some childish ailment, she would see the Queen's hand in it. Eleanor knew she could not live with that silent condemnation. Mabille, who had proved herself a true friend, should be offered Rohesia's position.

Yet the necessity for the action galled her. To cast off

Rohesia was like cutting off her arm. It was just one more item to be added to the list of injuries that whore had done her. . . . But the savage joy that she was dead!

When Eleanor saw Henry again, she was shocked at the change in him. He looked much older; indeed, he had more grey hairs than she had herself and his face was pale and drawn. The pity that she felt for him surprised her. If he would but turn to her in his unhappiness, she would forgive him gladly.

But he was polite to her, no more, seemingly dependent on his Chancellor for entertainment and company. Surely he would recover in time – and receive her back into favour. She was his wife; her very availability must help towards a reconciliation.

Young Henry did homage to King Louis for Normandy at the end of September and although Eleanor was not present, she heard how well he comported himself and how everyone remarked on the manly bearing of a child so young. She wondered what Louis' reaction was at seeing the son he had never managed to get on her, and in a moment of unaccustomed generosity towards him, hoped that his imminently expected heir would be a boy.

But it was only another girl, his fourth, and hard upon the heels of that news, word came of the death of his Queen. That caused a stir and there was much speculation which became excited comment when hurried arrangements were made for another wedding. Louis was to marry Adela of Blois, sister of the two Counts who were betrothed to his daughters by Eleanor.

Henry sent for his Queen. Thomas the Chancellor was with him, looking very well pleased with himself, and Eleanor, though taken aback at what was evidently an official audience, greeted him with a graciousness designed to gratify both him and her husband.

Henry cut into the greetings with impatience. 'Tom

341

here,' he said, 'has got the permission of the Papal Legates for Young Henry and little Margaret to marry!'

'To marry? Those babes?'

'Aye.' He was grinning, more like his old self. 'For, see you, if they marry, I'll gain the Vexin now. It is all arranged. This sly fox' – he smote the Chancellor on the arm with what Eleanor considered a quite unnecessary familiarity – 'has arranged long ago for the Templars to hand over the castles when they marry, and now the Pope will do nothing about it for fear we'll go over to the other side and recognise Victor.'

'But why the haste?'

'Louis may have a son. If he does, think you I shall ever get the Vexin as Margaret's dower?'

Eleanor smiled slowly. She saw now how foolish her good wishes towards Louis had been. 'My frontier will be advanced to the Epte,' Henry was saying, and she sank back and listened. This was like old times and even Henry's incessant 'me' and 'mine' when he should have said 'us' and 'ours' no longer irritated her. In any case, it was a step forward that he was consulting her about the wedding. She surmised that that, too, had been the Chancellor's doing and felt warmly towards him again.

When it became obvious later that Henry expected her to leave him and the Chancellor alone together, she felt a pang of disappointment she could not quite suppress, but took her leave of them with more hope for the future than she had had for a long time. True, Henry had not once looked at her with the old desire but he had been friendly. She would be content with that for the present.

The marriage was fixed for the second day in November. Eleanor sat beside her husband and watched the two small children joined in Holy Matrimony and, almost instinctively, her hand stole out and touched Henry's as it lay upon his knee. He turned his head and looked at her and she

342

bit her lip. She heard him sigh, and then he took her hand in his and thus they stayed all through the ceremony.

Afterwards, not understanding anything of what had been done to them, the bride and groom were returned to the nurseries, fractious and half asleep. The king smiled wryly. 'If the first words spoken after the wedding are anything to go by, their marriage will be as fruitful of quarrels as any,' he observed.

Eleanor glanced at him quickly but there seemed only resignation in his face. 'Quarrels are inevitable, I fancy,' she ventured, 'and the true worth of a marriage is to be seen in the reconciliations.'

He raised his eyes slowly from his winecup and bent a long look upon her. Although they were in the midst of a crowded, noisy gathering, it seemed to her that they were more alone than they had been since he had courted her while she was still the wife of Louis. Her heart began to beat a little faster. She knew she was looking fair, it was reflected in his eyes. Now was her chance to win him back, she realised, while his mood was soft.

'The worth of a marriage is in its fruit,' he said. 'That may be the result of reconciliation, I grant you.'

She straightened her shoulders to give him the benefit of her fine bosom outlined by the tight green gown and saw his eyes slide over her. Confidence was returning to her by the minute but – gently, she told herself, he does not like a woman to be in command of a situation – and – watch him, he must drink enough and not too much. For a moment she felt she was playing the whore herself, then rejected the half formed thought. Was he not her husband?

When it was time for her to leave the feast and retire with her ladies he was talking to the Chancellor, but as though her thoughts had called him, he turned his head in her direction. She looked down quickly but was conscious of his eyes on her as she withdrew.

Henry watched her go. He knew what she wanted and he

343

wanted it too, and was angry with himself. All the same, he knew he would visit her tonight because he had been too long without a woman. That was the only reason; he had not forgiven her her thrusts when they had quarrelled, nor would he ever do so; she had come too near truth for that. But he was not going to allow that to inconvenience him, and Hikenai's death had spoilt him for the hunt. For the time being his wife could fill the gap in his life and much good might it do her.

Little was said between them when he came to her bed; too little for either to feel it was a new beginning. Henry left with a bad taste in his mouth and a sourer temper, and as for Eleanor – after the flood tide of passion and satisfaction, she could not sleep. Why – now that she had gained her heart's desire and her body's satiety – why did something in her wince at the memory? What more could she wish for?

Nothing, she told herself, nothing, and blamed the elusiveness of slumber on the rich meats of the feast.

Bibliography

Appleby, John T.: *Henry II, G.* Bell & Sons 1962.

Arnold, Ralph: *Social History of England*, Longman 1967.

Bagley, J. J.: *Life in Mediaeval England*, Batsford 1960.

Barber, Richard: *Henry Plantagenet*, Barrie & Rockliff 1964.

Barlow, Frank: *Feudal Kingdom of England*, Longman 1955.

Barrow, G. W. S.: *Feudal Britain*, Arnold 1956.

Brooke, Christopher: *From Alfred to Henry III*, Nelson 1961.

Brooke, Iris: *English Costume of the Early Middle Ages*, Black 1936.

Chamberlin, E.: *Life in Mediaeval France*, Batsford, 1967.

Coulton, C. G.: *Social Life in Britain: Conquest to Reformation*, Cambridge University Press 1918, revised edition 1956.

Duggan, Alfred: *Thomas Becket of Canterbury*, Faber 1967.

Eades, Geo. E.: *Historic London*, Queen Anne 1966.

Hughes, Pennethorne; *Witchcraft*, Longman 1952.

Hutton, William Hoden: *Thomas Becket*, Cambridge University Press 1926.

Lyte, Sir Henry C. Maxwell, KCB., FSA., FBA.: *Fitzurse*, Somerset Archaeological and Natural History Society. Proceedings: 1922. Vol. LXVIII, pp. 93–104.

Murray, Margaret: *Witch Cult in Western Europe*, Oxford University Press, 1st ed. reprinted 1963.

Murray, Margaret: *God of the Witches*, Oxford University Press, 1933, Tiranti, 1962.

Quennell, Marjorie & C. H. B.: *History of Everyday Things in England: 1066–1499*, Batsford, 4th ed. 1957.

Round, J. H.: *Geoffrey de Mandeville*, Longman 1892.
Stenton, Doris Mary: *English Society in the Early Middle Ages*, Pelican History of England, III, 1951.
Stuart, D. M.: *London Through the Ages*, Methuen 1956.
Tomkeieff, Olive: *Life in Norman England*, Batsford 1966.
Winston, Richard: *Becket*, Constable & Co. 1967.